R0202256897

D0284617

2021

ON AN OUTGOING TIDE

ON AN
OUTGOING TIDE

Caro Ramsay

**SEVERN
HOUSE**

First world edition published in Great Britain and the USA in 2021
by Severn House, an imprint of Canongate Books Ltd,
14 High Street, Edinburgh EH1 1TE.

Trade paperback edition first published in Great Britain and the USA in 2021
by Severn House, an imprint of Canongate Books Ltd.

severnhouse.com

British Library Cataloguing-in-Publication Data
A CIP catalogue record for this title is available from the British Library.

ISBN-13: 978-0-7278-9075-7 (cased)
ISBN-13: 978-1-78029-763-7 (trade paper)
ISBN-13: 978-1-4483-0501-8 (e-book)

All Severn House titles are printed on acid-free paper.

Typeset by Palimpsest Book Production Ltd.,
Falkirk, Stirlingshire, Scotland.
Printed and bound in Great Britain by
TJ Books Limited, Padstow, Cornwall.

For Big John and Wee Moira

PROLOGUE

The quiet purr of the cooling fan filled the room, wafting still air, highlighting the dust motes drifting in the brilliant beam. On the screen, a young fair-haired man, a square-shouldered Adonis, braced himself against the cold waves of the beach. He was laughing, pretending that the sea was warm. He dipped his hand in the water, flicking a few cold drops at the cine camera, which wobbled a little, and took a step back. The view panned to the outcrop of rocks being sprayed white by the breaking waves. There's a young child on top, naked apart from her sunhat, her arms stretching out towards the man, commanding rescue from her rocky island. He waded over, long, muscular legs moving easily through the surging, foaming waves. Reaching out his strong arms, he plucked her from the rock, holding her high before swinging her round, as if she was a weightless doll. She giggled in delight, floating through the air, rolling round his neck to settle on the arc of his hip. He controlled her movement with the grace of a dancer, the precision of a gymnast. The updraft of the sea breeze caught the sunhat and plucked it from her dark hair, but the man was faster, and he nipped the hat mid-air, catching it between thumb and finger. One hand had the child, the other had the hat. He placed the small cap on his own head, where it sat precariously, and he threw a cheeky grin at the camera, kissed the laughing child on her forehead, a quick peck, then he slipped down, bobbing backwards into deeper water, taking her further from the rock, further from the shore.

ONE

Her body had been found at two o'clock in the morning, lifelessly drifting on the outgoing tide, pushed by the undertow. Her arms swayed below her, legs apart, then together, then apart, one red shoe on, the other foot bare. Her spanned fingers moved to and fro with the ebb and flow of the river, waving the coast goodbye, carried by the black waters of the Firth of Clyde.

It was the bright-red dress they had spotted in the searchlight, her cousin's red dress, which she had borrowed to celebrate the reopening of the nightclub.

The boat neared her, light beams rolling over the dark infinity of water, the glistening rise and fall that flashed and died on the surface, until they hit crimson and flesh. The outboard was cut, the rigid inflatable boat moving forward slowly, the bow nodding in the waves as they approached her, side on, carefully. For a moment, it looked as though she had recovered some vitality and was independent of her watery grave. Long tendrils of ebony hair fanned out like Medusa, the serpents writhing with her in a slow, sinuous dance. Dipping under the surface, the waves closed over her like oil, claiming her, and she fell, sinking.

The pilot throttled back, wary of bumping into her, causing her more injury as if she were still sensitive to pain, or as if she were capable of knowing fear and that she might escape, diving to the depths. Or simply drift out of reach.

Once the pilot was close enough, he leaned over the gunnel with his boathook at the full reach of his arm, steadying himself before placing the curve of the hook on the small of her back, just a gentle pressure to steady her. He braced himself against the powerful surge and push of the waves, holding her as still as possible while the cradle was dropped with a silent splash.

The casket sank on its ropes, then dropped underneath her.

Her hair seemed to sense the trap – it twisted and fanned, winding round the side of the cage in an ebony convolvulus. The boat, the girl and the cradle were steady, all three moving at one with the water.

The boat circled once before heading for Greenock. She was going home now, wrapped in her plastic shroud in the bottom of the RIB, rolling with the swell. The pilot could see the welcoming beams of the headlights at the landing slip each time they crested a wave. He radioed ahead: they were on their way back.

When they pulled up to the mooring, the private ambulance reversed down the jetty. Two detectives, huddled in their warm anoraks, waited until she had been raised from the boat on to terra firma before they started the short walk to greet her. The search had taken twenty-eight hours and now she lay in front of them, looking comfortable but cold in her plastic cocoon, her upper body and face covered in fronds of hair, like italic script. Silently, the forensic scientist, somebody the detectives didn't know, opened the cradle tap and ran the water that surrounded her off into a sterile container. Then he stepped back, letting the two senior officers have their first look.

'It's her.'

'It certainly is.'

'There're not many women with hair down to their waist,' said DCI Colin Anderson sadly. His hopes for a different outcome had vanished with the tide.

'The dress is an exact match.' DI Costello pulled up a picture of Aasha Ariti at the nightclub, sitting with her arm round her best pal, toasting the occasion, celebrating. She showed it to her boss. He glanced at it and nodded. It was sodden and the lace at the neck had been ripped, but it was the same dress.

'Jesus, twenty-three years old and this. Five years at university, a glittering career ahead of her, her first night out post-lockdown and this. She never even made it home.' DCI Colin Anderson knelt down beside Aasha and looked into her face; her dark eyes staring and ghostly, her nose and cheeks cut and bruised where they had been bumped and scraped. Her fingertips were wrinkled; she had lost a couple of bright crimson nails, painted to match her dress.

Anderson lifted a pen from his anorak pocket and delicately moved a few of the long tendrils of ebony hair from the side of her face, before placing them down to lie over her forehead. Anderson took another look. For a long moment, he saw his own daughter, Claire: the cheekbones, the wayward strands of hair that ran in a fine cord from her ear to the corner of her mouth. Aasha looked as if she might have the same habit of chewing her hair when being asked a question that she did not want to answer. The question of the moment: *So what happened to you, Aasha?*

He had said it out loud.

But this face was battered, eyes looking over his shoulder at the grey clouds of a dark summer night.

Costello looked at her watch and stepped forward, reading his disquiet accurately. 'Colin, do you want me to take this from here?' She stuck her hands deep inside her jacket pockets, hunching her shoulders a little. It was June, but the breeze off the water carried a deadly chill. 'It's gone two in the morning. We've been here for three hours and you have a big day tomorrow, with the girls going away. Moses isn't well, the dog's not well. You can't leave Brenda to deal with all that. You need to prepare to interview Poole. Especially now we have found her.'

'Yes. Yes, I should,' he said, glad to be going, feeling guilty about leaving Aasha, but Claire was driving to Tyndrum that day, his daughter's first long drive since she had passed her test. What were Aasha's parents thinking now? What were they thinking when they sent her back on the train to Glasgow to finish her studies? What was her aunt thinking when she said goodbye as Aasha left the house on Saturday night? You never believe, not for one minute, that they are not going to come back. 'Are you OK to inform the aunt? She might want to tell the parents. Or she might want you to.' Anderson stood up and ran his hands through his short fair hair, staring out across the waves, looking every inch a Viking god of the sea. 'I promised them the minute we found anything we'd . . . The aunt has a nice neighbour, Pamela somebody . . . you could get her . . . and make sure Florence at Family Liaison gets the call before you go.'

Costello glanced at her watch. 'Yes, of course.' She took one final look at the cold, churning water before turning round. 'I'll catch up with you tomorrow.'

Costello walking along a beach, accompanied by a cat she did not own. Strolling along the water's edge, letting the oncoming waves run over her feet, thinking that her toes were not getting wet. The sand was dry because this was only a dream. This was her world. She wasn't going to get pulled into the deep by a student in a red dress who was called Aasha and who wanted to apologize for keeping her up most of the night. A boy called Anthony was combing the beach, searching, calling out Aasha's name, but he couldn't see her, even though she was floating in the waves only a few yards from shore.

In her dream, she looked over her shoulder and Aasha was gone. Anthony was still on the beach. The waves were now rattling and banging on the sand as a voice told her that time for sleep was over and she should really answer the door.

She said goodbye to Anthony, to the beach, and woke up. As she sat up, she had to steady herself on the arm of the sofa, waiting for the dizziness to subside before padding her way down the hall in her socks, seeing the swaying shadow behind the glass panel of the door of her flat.

Apart from it being daylight, Costello had no idea what time it was. She placed her hand on the door handle, slipping the chain on just in case, before opening the door wide enough to see the concerned face of her downstairs neighbour, Mrs Allan. It looked more important than the usual running out of sugar. She closed the door again, sliding the chain off.

'Can you come, dear? Can you come over? I can't get Vera to answer and her door's open. It shouldn't be open, should it?'

Costello wiped the sleep from her eyes; the name did not mean anything. 'Vera?'

'Mrs Craig.'

'Of course.'

Her elderly neighbour had her hair neatly curled and was smartly dressed in beige slacks and a brown jumper. The long fawn cardigan slung over her shoulders was a response to the morning chill of the landing. Mrs Allan stood to the side so

Costello could see that the door of the flat across the landing was indeed slightly open, revealing what it always did: the side view of the hall table with her ivory-and-ebony Viking longship in its glass case; above it, silver spoons arranged in an arc on the wall. Everything looked just as it always did.

'Sorry, dear, did I get you up?' Mrs Allan was contrite, concerned, but crabbing towards the door across the landing.

Yes, we pulled the dead body of a young woman out of the river this morning. 'We had to work a night shift. It happens. Don't worry about it.'

'Oh, I am sorry.'

'No trouble. Let's have a wee look here,' said Costello, suddenly aware of her haystack hair, dog breath and crumpled clothes as she stepped outside on to the carpet, trying to clear her head of lack of sleep. 'You knocked and she hasn't come to the door?'

'She won't be out. She knew I was coming up at nine.' Mrs Allan stood and looked at her, obviously wanting Costello to do something.

'I saw her yesterday,' said Costello as she walked towards the clean glass pane, its fine lace curtain and the gleaming nameplate underneath. She placed her hand on the door. It had been sitting slightly open and it edged further under the slightest pressure from her finger.

And then she smelled it.

Blood. Recent blood.

Professional instinct kicked in. She turned to her companion and told her to stay there for the moment, reaching for her mobile before realizing it was probably still in her jacket pocket from the previous night. Had the door been closed when she arrived home in the small hours of the morning? She would have noticed. Or would she? She had been getting the groceries of both neighbours through the twelve weeks of lockdown, but now that it was over, she had barely given Mrs Craig's door a second glance. She had been tired and emotionally drained after talking to Aasha's family.

She walked down the short hall, the mirror image of her own flat, but carpeted in dark brown and beige, big patterns on the walls that made her eyes ache. She paused when she noticed a few spots of blood on the cream skirting board. Well, she had entered in good faith – no point in turning back.

'Mrs Craig?' Costello had never called her by her first name, and she had never been invited to. Opening the kitchen door, peering in, checking that everything was neat and respectably clean, everything in its place. How many times had Costello dumped a two-pint carton of milk there, a big bag of potatoes and a wee bottle of the Edinburgh Gin Company Rhubarb and Ginger during the last twelve weeks?

'Is everything OK, dear?' Mrs Allan called from the landing, her voice less confident now.

'So far so good.' Costello jumped across the hall to the bedroom door. Again, it was slightly open. The bed was neatly made, the smooth pink-and-white duvet cover, two decorated pillows. A large china doll, wearing a matching pink flowery dress, leaned against the top pillow, watching with her steady painted eyes, her pursed ruby lips disapproving. In the living room, the pale-brown curtains were still pulled across the big window, giving a sepia quality to the light, but Costello could easily see the small smattering of blood that curved behind the three-seater sofa.

Behind the settee was a pair of brown shoes.

And there she was: Vera, lying on her side, fully dressed in a smart blouse and skirt, a trickle of blood on the back of her wrist, a matching stain on the carpet under her head.

'Shit, shit,' said Costello to herself, leaning forward, touching the wrinkled, still warm skin of the neck where she felt a faint pulse. She looked around. How many times had she been in this flat and never noticed where the telephone was?

On the far side of the sofa, hidden by a soft cushion, was a side table with a couple of photographs and the upright handset of the phone. She pressed 999 for the emergency services, requesting an ambulance and the police, adding that she was both a neighbour and a serving police officer – a detective, in fact – and the scene looked suspicious. She had no real idea why she said this, but then she realized that she was looking straight at the door handle, covered in dark-red smears that evidenced somebody had tried to wipe the blood away.

She ended the brief conversation once she had confirmed the

address, not wanting to be talked through the procedure by somebody young enough to be her daughter. Mrs Allan was still standing at the end of the hall, wringing her hands, her face full of concern. She had overheard the phone call.

'Can you put a coat on, Mrs Allan, and wait downstairs – maybe up on the road so you can make sure the ambulance gets the right block of flats?'

It was the best way to deal with shock: give them something to do. She went back to Vera and made sure her airway was clear; her breathing was laboured but still rhythmic. They were close to both the Queen Elizabeth Hospital and the old Royal Infirmary. It was past the morning rush hour. The weather was good, visibility was fine. The worst of the virus was over. Hopefully, ambulances were available.

She looked at her neighbour, a frail figure curled like a child. Her cream blouse had come loose from the thin belt fastened round her waist. Costello resisted the temptation to tuck it back in. Vera's nostrils were flaring, the blood still oozing from a cut on the back of her head. She had got dressed and done her hair, but hadn't got as far as putting on her face powder. Costello noticed that her neighbour was in the habit of painting her eyebrows on; it wasn't just blood loss that was giving her this pallor.

She heard the door behind her open further, a thin reedy voice that she could hardly hear. 'Oh, my dear goodness, oh my God.'

'Can you wait downstairs, please? For the ambulance?' asked Costello again. 'Get your coat first. It's cold out there.'

When Colin Anderson came downstairs, he was showered, dressed, iPad in hand, ready for his breakfast and a quick walk with the dog before work. Then he noticed that Nesbit the Staffie did not get out of his basket; his favourite dry food lay untouched in a bowl. The dog's ears and eyes tracked Anderson's movement, but the contents of the food bowl remained uneaten. Anderson poured some water into his cupped hand and knelt down beside the dog bed, proffering him some fluid. Nesbit didn't even raise his head.

And that was when he knew.

He debated whether to stay or to sneak out to work and leave Brenda to deal with this, use Aasha Ariti as his excuse, but the thought was gone before it took traction. He called the incident room and asked Patterson to brief the team on the discovery of Aasha Ariti's body. He'd already submitted a brief report in the early hours. The evidence was pointing increasingly to Anthony Poole being the man who had killed her. There was a public appeal for any dashcam footage around the Robertson Street/ Broomielaw junction in Glasgow recorded between one and two o'clock on Sunday morning, looking for the taxi that Poole claimed Aasha had got into. That was a job he could leave to Costello.

He got off his mobile, hoping that Nesbit had eaten something, but he was still in his basket, ears twitching occasionally at the frantic footsteps high above him. The girls were leaving for Tyndrum this morning, though from the excitement it might have been Las Vegas. When Anderson offered the dog more water, the brown eyes barely responded.

He didn't want Claire's holiday spoiled, or her concentration to be affected because of the death of the much-loved family dog. Driving with tear-filled eyes was no good for anybody. Equally, he didn't want Nesbit's last minutes on earth being stressed by two over-excited teenagers running around trying to find their mobile phone chargers. He had lived the nightmare of the packing drama every day since Claire and her friend had decided to do a charity challenge in Malawi, which lockdown had transformed into a cabin in Tyndrum.

Anderson felt it was good for them to get away after twelve weeks of forced togetherness: Peter gaming, Claire painting, Paige constantly dyeing her hair, Brenda trying to do the garden, and everybody taking a turn with Moses. He was only too happy for them to take over the holiday let. Paige had even got a job in the Real Food Café which was doing takeaways; Claire was working in the Green Welly and doing some painting.

He listened to the chaos above as he stroked the velvet head of his dog. His dog. Always his. He was the one who had brought Nesbit back from the police station – what, ten, twelve years ago? It was supposed to be just an overnight until he could be taken to the rescue centre. Of course, as soon as the kids saw him, that had been it: wee Nesbit had his paws well and truly under the table. He was going nowhere. He had been a great family dog, never a minute's trouble. Mischief here and there, but his high spirits were naughty, never malicious. He had looked after the children, protected Brenda, but he had always been Colin's dog. Always his wee pal, always three inches away from his master's heel.

There was loud footfall on the stairs. Moses, his biological grandson, now adopted son, started screaming, and then Brenda said, not unkindly, 'Oh, for God's sake, you two, be quiet. You've woken up Moses,' and then Peter's voice shouted from behind his bedroom door, 'And you've woken me up as well.'

Then Claire was screaming back that it was only zoomers who were asleep at this time of the morning, and Peter screamed back that . . . Anderson had had enough and picked the dog up, wrapped his blanket around him and carried him out to the car.

The vet's surgery was only a five-minute drive from the house, but it was the longest five minutes of his life, aware that Nesbit was already slipping away from him. He was a very old dog, who started life as bait for dog fighting, but what a grand wee pet he had turned out to be.

And the vet, a bearded young man whom Anderson had not met before, made all the right noises. 'He has lived a long and happy life. Look how he ended up!' Then he had caressed Nesbit's velveteen ears and muttered the terrible words. 'It's the best thing you can do for him now.'

The conversation made Anderson want to bolt for the door, but he had to stay there and cuddle Nesbit as the vet prepared the needle. He nuzzled the dog's head, saying his name over and over, hoping that there was enough awareness in there to know that he wasn't alone, that they were still together. The vet was talking again, now saying that there was no real neurological response and he was going to pass away either later today or tomorrow. It was kinder to put him to sleep right now.

He hoped, really hoped, Nesbit knew that he had not left him to die in the arms of a stranger. The ears that turned more in response to the noise of a gingernut being snapped than they ever responded to his name gave a little flicker. The dark-brown eyes had opened, rolled up to look at him; he was saying thank you. It took very little time for his friend to be gone.

TWO

The door of the ambulance slammed closed, shutting Vera and Mrs Allan from Costello's sight.

There was more than one head wound. The old woman had been groaning but was otherwise unresponsive as the paramedics wired her up to a heart monitor and gave her oxygen before transferring her to a stretcher. Costello handed Mrs Allan a bag full of medication and asked who Vera's next of kin was. To Costello's surprise, her neighbour knew vaguely of a daughter who lived in London, but she couldn't recall a name. Then the cheery paramedic had persuaded Mrs Allan to go in the ambulance with Vera. She had been reluctant, but the paramedic was seamlessly manipulative in the way that those who deal with shock need to be. And Mrs Allan might genuinely be in shock; she may have spoken to her old friend for the last time. Before she went down in the lift, she tearfully took a long look at Vera's front door. 'Joan?' she said. 'I think the daughter's name was Jane or June? Something like that.'

'It might come to you when you aren't thinking about it, so here's my card. Call me if you need picking up later. I'm not sure what areas of the hospital are open yet.'

With that, the lift doors closed over, silencing the voice of the paramedic waxing wistfully about a nice cup of tea.

Jane? June? Costello had never heard her neighbour mention a daughter. But then she'd never mentioned her mother to Mrs Craig. She never mentioned her mother to anybody. She stood in the flat for a few minutes, taking in the situation, trying to address the conflict of tiredness and adrenaline. She pulled back the curtains a little to reveal a view similar to her own: a wide ribbon of slate-grey river over to the clam shell of the Science

Museum, and further down to the *Glenlee*, the three masts of the tall ship just visible.

Costello suspected Aasha had gone into the Clyde somewhere in the city before she started her thirty-mile drift downriver. She needed to get back to the incident room. A quick look at her watch told her it wasn't yet ten o'clock, but she couldn't leave this flat until the scene was handed over. She walked around, taking care not to touch anything but noting that items of value were still present. A jewellery box was untouched, the spoon collection looked complete, and Vera's beloved Viking longship was resplendent in its glass case. She looked up at a knock at the door: two uniformed officers, one standing at Vera's door, the other knocking at Costello's.

'I live there,' she said, knowing she had already mentioned this to everybody she had spoken to.

'PC Howie and PC Follet. We need to take a statement about the incident with your neighbour.'

'Yes, I know. Can we get hold of her next of kin first, just in case it all goes tits up? Scene-of-crime is going to take ages, but Vera is old and suffered a nasty head wound or two. All I have for the daughter is the name Joan, maybe June.' Costello was already turning to go back into the flat.

'Stop.' Howie looked at her, at her hair, her crushed T-shirt, her dirty socks. It could have been a look of complete disdain if he had put in a little more effort. 'I don't think so.'

'Look. Mrs Vera Craig? The victim? She has a daughter I've never spoken to, so can I stick something over my shoes and have a look about for a phone number? Can you radio in and see if they can trace her?'

'Nope. Did you find the body?'

'Yes. She's not a body yet, but in case she becomes one in the near future, I'm keen to get hold of Joan.'

'In good time. We have to secure it. This could be a crime scene.'

'Yes, I just said so.'

Howie was pulling his notebook from his pocket as slowly as possible. She waited for him to lick the end of his pen and bend his knees like Dixon of Dock Green. 'Can you run through what happened here?'

'Happily, once I've got hold of her daughter. It's possible she was attacked.'

'What makes you say that?'

'The marks on the floor, the fact that somebody tried to clean up the blood, the fact that—'

'Sorry, who are you?' PC Howie waved his pen roughly in her direction.

Costello spiralled her finger back at him. 'That's just what I was going to ask you.'

Costello was sitting in her own flat, with her door open, listening to the two uniforms out on the landing, talking rather carelessly, in her professional opinion.

Some neighbours had drifted through the landing to see what all the bother was about, most of them concerned for their old neighbour, but they were quickly moved on by Howie, a cop who had undergone some surgical procedure to remove all trace of humanity.

Costello ruminated on the case. She couldn't see any forced entry, and she couldn't see Mrs Craig letting a stranger into her flat. Her injuries appeared recent. She had got up that morning and got dressed, and then something had happened. These were expensive riverside flats; the residents tended to be older – those who had already downsized but liked the large rooms and the big picture windows. These were people who checked the ID of any visitor, and there was zero tolerance of loud music, children and bingo.

There was a hiatus now. She had offered, as a DI, to make a start, write it up, then report when somebody else was assigned. Her offer was politely refused.

Maybe they were wary. She could have attacked the old dear herself for all they knew, so she slumped back into her own flat, leaving the door open, saying that she was going to have a shower. Howie asked her not to, not until she had been interviewed, in case they needed to take evidence from her. He then added the words 'for exclusion'.

Costello nodded and retreated to pick up cushions and lie back down on the settee, pulling her favourite fluffy one across her chest, wrapping her arms round it. She phoned work and found out that Anderson had also called to say he'd be in later. He had not yet started the interview with Poole to inform him that they had recovered the body. Costello didn't like Anthony Poole – just a bias she had against entitled arseholes. The boy admitted he was the one walking with Aasha away from the Debut nightclub. Before they reached the Squiggly Bridge, he went up an alley to have a pee, and while they were apart, she vanished. Poole believed she got in a taxi, but they were having trouble tracing that vehicle. The working hypothesis was that he had become outraged when she refused his advances. Had she walked away from him? Had they struggled and she had ended up in the river? Then DC Wyngate, a born computer nerd, had checked Poole's social media and there was now the racist question on the table. Nightmare. While she was on the phone, Costello reported Vera Craig's incident number so they could keep track of it if they wanted, but they couldn't put her on Vera's case because she knew the victim.

Costello rubbed her eyes. The enforced stillness had allowed her tiredness to catch up with her. She liked her workload to be framed and focused so she could help trace the mysterious Joan. She had DC Wyngate and DS Mulholland on tap as they had just returned to normal duties after spending the last few weeks training people for the post-lockdown viral policy, Test and Protect. They'd find her in five minutes.

Her mobile beeped: Anderson texting to say that Nesbit had been 'PTS' – put to sleep, she guessed. She texted back that she was sorry to hear it, but it was the best thing. She'd have to keep an eye on her boss – his daughter away, the wee Down's son being ill and the stress of that so much more due to the virus. And, of course, Brenda being caught up in this situation with Rodger the conman meant that gossip followed Anderson round the station like a smirking shadow.

She lay for a while, realizing that she was hungry. If Howie and Follet had been nicer, she would have offered them a cuppa, but they looked a right pair of little shits. Just as she was thinking about putting the kettle on, she heard the approach of the lift, the doors open and somebody getting out.

The landing stayed quiet.

She crept into the hall and heard Howie say something she

didn't catch, but the tone was derogatory. So not CID, she thought, not a fellow police officer. She wondered who it was; the greeting had been familiar in its venom. She slid along the wall to her front door as silent as an assassin.

'What the fuck did they send you for? Was nobody decent about?' Howie's sarcasm.

'I do as I am told. So what's happened here?' A businesslike but nervous response. A voice she recognized.

But she was not familiar with the slight tremor it held now. Fear?

'Some old dear got her head bashed in. There's a witness over there, in that flat.'

'So it's suspicious?'

'That's a decision for your pay grade,' Howie sniffed. 'So you'd better interview her and be careful. She was first on the scene, she called it in. So you'd better not mess up, PC Big Ears – sorry, DC Big Ears.'

The Detective Constable turned round, his face going pale when he saw Costello standing in her doorway. His eyes drifted slowly from her to Howie, then back again. 'I thought the address meant something to me.'

'Meant something to me, *ma'am*,' corrected Costello, asking for the salutation she despised. Wyngate knew it, and his face relaxed into mischievous contrition.

'I apologize. So you were first on the scene, ma'am.'

'Yes, Detective Constable Wyngate,' she said in mock politeness. 'Please come in and you can take my statement while I make you a cup of tea. Your colleagues here can look after the crime scene. You are partial to a Hobnob, aren't you, DC Wyngate?'

'Yes, ma'am, I am indeed,' he played along beautifully.

Costello held her forefinger up, 'But first, do you have any shoe covers with you? I'd like to get the contact details for the victim's daughter – Joan or something. She might be married, so not sure of the surname and . . .' As they were talking, Gordon Wyngate was already digging out some fresh shoe covers from his pockets, and a couple of pairs of nitrile gloves, handing them over before they entered Vera Craig's flat together, forcing Howie to stand to the side. 'Make a note on your entry log that we are going in. It's ten thirty-eight.'

In the hall, she pointed out the drops of blood on the cream woodwork, the smear round the handle of the door. 'I think somebody tried to clean that away. Wyngate, I know your mum passed away recently. Where did you find her important papers? Passports. Wills. All that kind of thing.' Costello had picked up the telephone and was looking at the contacts list. Vera might know her daughter's landline number off by heart, but those of a certain age struggled with the eleven digits of a mobile.

Wyngate looked around the living room, the photographs on the table. 'There are no photographs of a daughter's wedding, no school pictures of her.'

'Families are families. Vera might regain consciousness and tell us, but just in case. I think she has a Doro phone somewhere.'

'This will be a piece of piss after the tracing we were doing for the virus. My mum had a Doro but kept the numbers on a bit of paper in the phone case. The other stuff she kept in the sideboard. Or under the bed. Or in the freezer.'

'Yes, Vera's the sort who would have the numbers on a wee card, in neat squiggly writing. I think I remember my own number going on there. And she'd carry that about with her, wouldn't she?'

Wyngate pointed to a handbag at the side of the easy chair that had the best view of the television. He picked it up in his purple-gloved hand and started to rifle through bottles of hand sanitizer, tissues, throat pastilles and face masks, unzipping a side pocket and pulling out a well-folded bit of paper, bordered by four pink roses and flamingos. The last name on the list was 'Joanna', with a landline scored out and a new one written in, and then a mobile number written in a much firmer hand next to that.

Costello pulled out her own mobile and keyed the number in. 'What did I hear those two out there call you when you walked out of the lift? They didn't exactly bring you up to speed efficiently, did they?'

'Nope.' He turned away.

'And?'

'We were at Tulliallan together. They called me Big Ears.'

'They do have a point there,' agreed Costello. 'That would make them PC Plod and Knobby.'

'Noddy,' corrected Wyngate.

'I know what I said,' said Costello, swiping her phone closed with some venom.

It was a sunny afternoon but by three o'clock the wind was blowing a bit of a hooley off the water. Dennis MacMillan pulled his sunglasses down, his collar up and tucked the scarf round his neck a little more tightly. It was supposed to have hit twenty degrees at noon, but at Invernock, on the Firth of Clyde, the wind still blew with a bitter bite. He carried two shopping bags, had the *Guardian* folded up under his arm, the local paper stuffed down the side of one bag and Lambert McSween's funeral order of service in an envelope safe in his breast pocket. The bags swung from his hands as he strolled up the hill, not in any hurry. He had rolls, six eggs and two packets of potato scones that he had bought on a BOGOF deal. His wife was away, and with lockdown easing, he had started to have a cup of tea with Mr Pearcey, and maybe today, with him being a bit late, he might suggest that they have a wee snack together, maybe a chat about the Bible. The death of a close friend often concentrated the mind on mortality. And how old was Mr Pearcey? Nearly eighty?

Walking up the path to the bungalow on the hill, he said hello to Donald at number five, moving into the road to keep his distance as the man wrestled with his electric hedge trimmer on the pavement. Elsie Fortune at number seven was also out in her garden but didn't appear to have done much gardening; her white flowery jacket was spotless, her hands clean. She threw him a friendly comment about the sunshine being deceiving and then asked, 'Everybody keeping well? How's Maria?'

'Still down south. The wee one is growing every day,' he answered but kept walking, recognizing this as an opening to a conversation he'd find difficult to close. Elsie – or Radio Fortune, as Mr Pearcey called her – was a right chatterbox, so he preferred to keep moving. This had been his route for the better part of three months, since the earliest pandemic advice about the elderly staying inside. A note had gone round the church about those in need, and he'd offered to do Jimmy Pearcey's shopping, a man he had never actually set eyes on, which was strange given the tiny population of the village.

That first day, he'd had to stop at the steepest part of the path and take a minute to admire the fabulous view across the Clyde just to get his breath.

Now he was fitter and able to admire it without gasping, but why would an elderly man live up a hill as steep as this?

MacMillan had got into the habit, as he had come to know Mr Pearcey better, of taking a daily photograph of the view on his phone and showing it to the old guy, sitting in the garden as they waited for the kettle to boil, while Norma the dog ran around the back lawn chasing magpies. Dennis was supposed to be doing a 'pop the shopping at the front door and run' type of delivery, but within a few days he was glad of the company, and Jimmy Pearcey was not as weird or eccentric as Radio Fortune had implied.

The old man just liked his own company, he liked the quiet spot where the house was located, and he liked the view from behind his hedge. Dennis's wife Maria was caught down south when the lockdown happened, looking after the new grandchild. With his daughter and son-in-law being key workers, it made sense for Maria to stay put. Coming up to see Mr Pearcey had given Dennis some routine to an otherwise anchorless day. He sidestepped round the overgrown twigs of hedge, thinking that he'd bring his own loppers up in the car later if the weather stayed good and get that seen to. Mr Pearcey had a lot of time on his hands, but none of it was directed towards his garden. He wouldn't let Dennis cut the hedge down, though; he liked his high wall of foliage. The wee path to the front door was almost hidden by the thick growth of laurel that swarmed the rusting black gate, growing over the sign that said *Beware of the Dog*. Dennis joked that it couldn't possibly refer to Norma, the small wiry mongrel who'd lick you to death in an instant. Mr Pearcey had nodded and said that appearances can be deceiving, and just to remember it was best to keep the gate shut. Maybe it was more that Mr Pearcey was not fit to chase after Norma if she made a run for it.

Dennis didn't really like dogs, but he'd grown fond of Norma. He loved the way Jimmy talked to her, and how she reacted. As he approached the front door, he moved the Snackeroos from the bag to his pocket, out of the reach of her ever-sniffing nose. He rang the bell, immediately hearing her panting and scraping behind the front door.

He waited, pulling the sterile gloves from their pack, then his mask up over his face, their wee routine until they got settled. Norma was bouncing around in the hall, visible through the glass panel, but there was no shout from Mr Pearcey telling her to behave.

Dennis was keen to get out of the wind and have a cup of tea and a roll, sitting at opposite ends of the living room. They had it all worked out. Their friendship was twelve weeks old and had a well-established routine. Mr Pearcey would open the door, then retreat to the kitchen as Dennis entered the hall, leaving the shopping on the floor before taking a seat in the living room with the biscuits. Viennese Whirls, as it was Tuesday. Mr Pearcey was very fit but he was old. Things were easing, but they still had to be careful.

He waited, listening to the whimpering getting louder. The dark shadow of the dog was now prancing frantically from side to side. Did Mr Pearcey have his hearing aid in? Was he in the loo?

Dennis took out his mobile and dialled the landline number, waiting until he heard the ringing echoing inside the bungalow. He frowned, aware of a lack of shifting shadows behind the laced glass panel. He listened carefully to the sound of persistent ringing before he set off round the house. First, he walked backwards down the drive, looking at the front of the bungalow. The curtains were open, but the dormer window had its curtains closed as usual. Taking care not to fall as he stepped on to the weed-filled flowerbeds, he looked in at the bathroom window. He knocked on the glass. No response.

'Is everything OK?' It was Elsie Fortune from number seven.

'Oh, hello. I'm not sure, to tell you the truth. There's no answer at the door. Have you seen Mr Pearcey? Norma is in.'

'He only ever goes out with that dog. Do you have a spare key?'

'No, I don't, but he told me there was one in the garden somewhere. I'd asked him what would happen if he got ill. I wish I could remember what he said.'

'Well, we just need to look around.' Elsie was bustling with efficiency. 'Under one of these old planters – maybe one of the smaller ones so he could lift it? These were left by the Gibsons who lived here before. That wasn't yesterday.' Elsie strutted around, Dennis hurrying to keep up. The fourth planter revealed a rusty old key underneath, which Dennis cleaned on his anorak sleeve. It didn't fit the front door, so they went round to the rear, Norma getting to the back door before he did. After a little persuasion and rattling of the door, it finally opened. Norma barrelled past them, nearly knocking Elsie over, desperate to get to the garden where she immediately squatted and emptied her bladder. There was no aroma of freshly brewed coffee, the one smell that Dennis associated with Mr Pearcey. Dennis felt panic twist his stomach. Mr Pearcey had been well the previous morning, no sign of the virus. But he was elderly. And the virus could hit very quickly.

'I'll stay out here with the dog. You go in,' Elsie said quietly, her face rather paler than it had been a few moments before.

Dennis nodded and walked into the very clean if old-fashioned kitchen. The sink gleamed, and a white-and-navy tea towel was folded over the handle of the oven. The dining chair was pulled neatly under the table for two, and on the table was a mat, a knife and fork, salt and pepper, yesterday's *Guardian* folded over at the crossword page. He usually filled that in with his black fountain pen. Mr Pearcey was a man of routine.

Dennis looked in the bedroom, which was just as tidy – nobody lying on the floor, no sign of disruption – and he was pleased to see the Bible on the bedside table. The hall looked as though the carpet had just been vacuumed – just a few foot-marks and a couple of rectangular dents where something had rested. It was a small two-bedroomed bungalow – a good look round took one minute, with an extra peek in the spare room. It had the same characterless neatness. Some ironing folded on the bed, ready to be put away, and the wardrobe doors closed, mirrors free of smudges and smears. A black suit hung on a hanger on the handle of the wardrobe door. Mr Pearcey had been thinking about going to his friend's funeral and then something had changed his mind.

He checked that the pictures on the wall were level – mostly Scottish landscapes with bleak mountains and bleaker skies.

There were no signs that they had been knocked during a disturbance. There was no evidence of any disorder at all, except . . . except one picture was missing from the hall, the empty hook hanging like a question mark. That was unusual. He tried to think what was missing, then he found the framed photograph lying face down on the occasional table in the living room, between the Doulton figurines. Turning it over, he recognized it as the family group: Jimmy as a young man, two other men – his brothers maybe – a dark-haired woman and five children, ranging from two to ten or so, all perched on a rock, clinging to each other, laughing as they were about to fall off. Dennis had asked Mr Pearcey who they were, but he didn't think he got an answer.

Dennis stood still and looked out of the window. The hedge cutter from number five fell silent, and the only noise now was the chatter of a couple of magpies. He felt Norma totter into the back of his leg, curious to see what was going on.

'Do you think he has gone somewhere?' asked Elsie from the door.

'Nowhere to go. But he's not here,' answered Dennis.

'Hospital? Maybe they kept him in?'

'Did you see an ambulance? A taxi? His medicines are in there.' He nodded at the roll-top desk.

She looked at the dosette box. 'Would he go away without this? He'd take this with him, wouldn't he?' She checked the date. 'I don't think he had his medication this morning. Or last night.'

'Something's not right,' said Dennis.

'Could he have wandered off, got lost?'

'His brain is sharper than mine.' Dennis shook his head. 'Mrs Fortune, could you ask Donald if he's seen Mr Pearcey this morning? He looks as if he's been working in his garden all day.'

'He's been making that noise since breakfast. I'll take the dog with me,' said Elsie. 'Give her some fresh air.' She bent to clip a lead on the collar, but Norma growled viciously. Elsie retreated, muttering she'd put the wee sod back in the garden.

Dennis stood looking around. Even the magpies held a truce, but it was still not quiet. The silence was accompanied by a continuous hum, quieter but more invasive and persistent than the white noise from the fridge. He walked out to the hall, where the sound was marginally louder, then put his head back into the living room to check. It was definitely louder in the hall, as if somebody had left the heating or an extractor fan on. It seemed to be coming from above him.

He looked up and saw the loft hatch in the ceiling. Could it be coming from there? Mr Pearcey could never manage to get up. Then he looked again at the indentations in the pile of the carpet. The feet of a ladder? Dennis had never seen one in this house. He glanced around him, at the walls and at the light switches, noticing one that was oblong, not square. It was white, new, where the rest had turned slightly cream with age. He flicked the switch, the hatch above his head slid open with the purr of an electric motor, a ladder unfolded itself towards him, two handrails arising from the side panels. It extended into place, the feet resting exactly in the dents in the carpet.

As he started climbing, a roll of heat unfurled over him. Then came the smell. By the time he had registered the third thing, he was already falling down the ladder.

THREE

Colin Anderson looked into the takeaway coffee cup. It was down to the bitter grains, a bit like his life. Well, God giveth and God taketh away.

He had lasted half an hour in the house, devoid of the girls, his elder son and the dog, and he decided to get out to the drive-through and have a coffee. Desperate times.

The house was far too quiet, too empty.

He checked the blister on his hand, a nasty bubble of red fluid on the web of skin between finger and thumb. It had taken him a long time to dig the hole in the far corner of the garden, near the wall, underneath the Japanese maple, where he wrapped Nesbit in his favourite blanket and laid him to rest, deep enough so the foxes would not disturb him. Anderson had gone back into the kitchen, put the kettle on and sat down at the table for about five minutes before the emptiness got to him. So many things that he had to do, but he needed some space in his head to think. In the end, he bundled Moses into his car seat and went for a drive-through coffee – a very simple but pointless post-lockdown pleasure.

Anderson wanted to prepare for the interview with Anthony Poole. He wanted to wipe that smug smirk from his face.

He planned to listen carefully to the recording of Anthony's statement on his iPad as he sipped his coffee, refreshing his mind as to what exactly the young dental student had said. The story never varied, but there was something about him that wasn't . . . trustworthy? 'Likeable' was maybe a better word. Anderson was vaguely aware of it, but while Costello had taken an instant dislike to Poole in accordance with her prejudices, there was nothing that Anderson could put his finger on. A sense of inbred superiority? Poole was polite but dismissive. His career trajectory was to get his degree and then move into cosmetic work, because that was 'where the money is'. Anthony Poole, aged twenty-two, had said that and looked right at Anderson's mouth as if he was going to suggest some corrective appliance. There was bravado in his every gesture, maybe a little too forceful to be genuine; he had been out to impress. Anderson attached the headphones to the tablet, put one earbud in and made sure Moses was still snoring gently before he swiped play and listened.

The voice was clear, the syntax as precise as the story. He and Aasha had known each other from uni. They were not on the same course but they had occasionally been part of the same study group. He hadn't recognized her immediately when they met in the Debut nightclub. As it was the first Saturday night that the venue had been opened, it was ticketed at half capacity and was not busy. He had been out for a cigarette and was on his way back in when he met Aasha on the stairs. She wanted some fresh air and he went back out with her, as witnessed by the internal security cameras. The bouncers on the door had remembered both him and the girl with the black hair down to her waist. It made Aasha an unusual victim, so very easy to recognize. He had seen the camera footage of the meeting on the stairs taken at 1.07 a.m. They appeared to be genuinely pleased to see each other. She had taken a step back as if to show him her new dress. They had moved as if to hug each other and then, being medics, they joked about touching elbows instead. Then there was lots of animated chatter, catching up on news as they went back down the stairs to the street because Aasha 'wasn't feeling well and wanted some fresh air'. She had left her leather jacket with her friends inside, so she had intended to go back in once she felt better.

So what had happened?

Anderson checked on Moses again as he waited for the next bit of the tape. Poole's voice continued; he'd had a mouthful of something – coffee, perhaps – in the interval. He and Aasha had gone outside, and as they walked, he realized she was more drunk than he had thought. They walked along the north bank of the Clyde towards the casino, then turned round and walked back again, past Debut and on towards the Squiggly Bridge. It was a warm night, and they were strolling slowly, out for maybe twenty minutes. At that point Anthony had wanted to relieve himself from the non-alcoholic beer that was gathering in his bladder, so he nipped up a side alley. When he came back, Aasha was gone. Poole said that he saw a taxi heading along the expressway and made a connection, so he went back to the nightclub and rejoined his friends. Anderson made a note to have the friends re-interviewed. Initially, they had said there was no sign of stress or injury; Poole's white linen shirt and black jeans were immaculate.

But that had been a casual chat when Aasha was merely missing. Now she had turned up dead, their stories might be different.

Anderson suspected that a flirtation might have gone wrong. Aasha had been at home in Romford during lockdown and had just flown back up. They had not planned to meet at Debut, and they were with different groups of friends, but it was the 'go to' place for young professionals, so maybe it was not such a coincidence. Unless Anthony had learned in advance that she would be there.

Was that stalking? The last few weeks had been a strain on everybody; odd was the new normal. Anderson stopped the recording. No message from Brenda. He checked the traffic on his phone. The road up the loch side was a solid red line; he hoped Claire behaved herself. Peter might have claimed his mother's attention for a look around the Apple Store or PC World, and they were now in a social-distancing queue somewhere. Anderson didn't grudge them a bit of mother-and-son time. Peter was quiet and often overlooked because of the two screaming divas who lived at the top of the house. And now there was wee Moses, a lovable, rotund snot machine but another thief of attention that was rightly Peter's. Peter was usually so engrossed in *Call of Duty* that he appeared to neither notice nor care. The last time Anderson had played a computer game with his son, he had been totally baffled by Sonic the Hedgehog.

His family was remarkable. Odd but remarkable.

There were times in his life when he had stayed out late and not told Brenda the 'whole truth'. There were many nights he had been held up at work – it went with the territory of the job. But there had been the affair with Helena, his late boss's wife, who had then passed away, leaving him, and by default his family, her not inconsiderable fortune: the house, the paintings, the art gallery. Then Rodger the conman had nearly relieved them of all that. The Andersons' marriage had been ripped apart by that affair, but when Helena died, he and Brenda had become friends again. The big house had lent itself to comfortable house sharing, with the kids all under one roof. Then last year Brenda had got involved with the seemingly boring accountant who had charmed her, charmed them all, with the purpose of hoovering out their bank accounts. That had destroyed Brenda's confidence but somehow brought the family closer together.

Now there was a trail of victims being unearthed. Some wanted revenge, some wanted to forget they had ever met him.

It was another complication in a life that was already complex. Anderson had thought long and hard about how easily Brenda – all of them – had been taken in by Rodger. All except Claire's friend, Paige, whose bullshit meter was on constant high alert. Rodger was skilled in deceit, insinuating himself into the family by looking after baby Moses, driving the girls home from parties at three in the morning, playing the part of the prospective stepfather to the Anderson children to perfection, while setting up his own access to their assets. Rodger had even mentioned marriage to Brenda, and Brenda had then mentioned divorce to Colin. There was a logical discussion that centred on little Moses. The best plan was for Brenda to keep the big house and Anderson to move out. How ironic was that? The wife living in the house that had been left to her husband by his lover. But Helena would have wanted what was best for the children. And no doubt there would have been a new will drawn up, and then divorce would follow. Rodger played a very long game.

Moses, the innocent with the extra chromosome, deserved the very best of everything. Rodger had threatened that. Anderson drained his coffee and crushed the cup to sate his anger. He looked at his watch, then at his phone, where the line of traffic was still red and solid. There was a snuffle from the back of the car, and he twisted in the driver's seat to check on his son. The boy's chest wasn't quite as resilient as it could be, and they were keeping a close eye on him.

If Anderson hadn't been snowed up in a Scottish glen, he might have spotted evidence of Rodger's consistent drain of their financial resources, his gradual control over Brenda. The gentle drift into the red became an unstoppable tsunami the moment Rodger beetled off down the M6 in the middle of the night.

Thank God for Paige who had clocked Rodger for exactly what he was, on the basis that it took one 'manipulative devious shit' to spot another. Seeing signs of Rodger's secret departure, Paige had sought out an ally in Peter and the two of them had fouled the escape of a professional conman.

And so the Andersons had become witnesses for the Met's Operation Felix. There was a team of detectives, a battery of forensic accountants all grateful to Paige for setting the trap. Two women, emotionally and financially stripped after a relationship with Rodger, had committed suicide.

Rodger, whose real name may or may not be Simon Russell, was fearless. He had tackled Colin Anderson, a DCI, and his wife Brenda, a chartered accountant – not exactly the easiest of targets. Lee Galbraith, working with Operation Felix, had asked awkward questions. How did Rodger worm his way in? Did Anderson want to give evidence? How embarrassing was all this going to be? Had he thought of that?

Colin Anderson knew exactly how humiliating it all was. Only too acutely. He knew that every time he walked into work.

He had met Galbraith the day before, and the forensic accountant had been chatting about the money trail, then produced an envelope and pulled out photographs of the women who had been scammed. A young widow stood up at the altar. Another had a son with a brain tumour; Rodger had worked tirelessly to raise funds for specialized treatment in the US, then disappeared with the money. The boy had died, just two years older than Moses. The detective said that Rodger – Simon Russell – targeted single women, traumatized women, offering to help.

And looking back, Brenda was an ideal victim. Intelligent but isolated by Anderson's work and by looking after Moses. And rich.

Anderson pushed that thought from his mind, dialled the station and asked to speak to Costello, only to be told she had phoned in to say her neighbour had been injured so she was dealing with that. He was put through to DS Patterson and asked if anything had come up on the dashcam footage or the further interviews with the nightclub staff.

He heard his usually chatty colleague go very quiet on the other end of the phone.

'What's up?'

'Are you still the SIO on this case? Aasha Ariti?' Patterson asked in a way that suggested he might not be.

'I was at three a.m. this morning,' he joked, then realized that Patterson was deadly serious.

'I think that you have been redeployed – reassigned, as they say – to something at Invernock. Nobody told you?'

'Nope. Why? Did somebody complain?'

'Not that we have heard. We were just told – email came in about eleven.'

'Who made that decision?'

'Detective Chief Superintendent "Toastie" Warburton. He sent the email. I only got it because I have to report an update to Tony Bannon at half three today.'

Anderson swore very loudly. 'Tony Bannon? From Complaints?'

'The very same.'

'Nice bloke, but when did he last head up a murder squad?'

'I don't think he ever has, but there's something in the wind.'

'And Costello? Is she still on the team?'

'Well, as she didn't come in, I'm not aware that she knows one way or the other. If she's staying with the Aasha case or if she has been shifted.'

'Did you say shifted or shafted?'

'Same thing, isn't it?'

PCs Donnelly and Nicholson drove slowly, keeping close to the gutter of the wide street, Donnelly peering through the side window of the police car as he tried to spot number nine and a panicking woman in a white anorak with flowers on it.

Then Nicholson tapped him. A tall broad figure stepped out into the road, emerging from what had appeared to be a solid high hedge, a woman moving like a flower-bedecked galleon sailing round a headland. She was waving at them, her hand flapping in panic, the floral jacket flapping in unison. This would be Elsie Fortune who had phoned about an issue with a neighbour. She stopped running as the car rolled gently towards her.

'. . . wasn't opening the door, so we found a key and now he's unconscious . . .' She was gabbling as the two cops got out of the car, following her, trying to make sense of her incoherent ramblings. Nicholson was pretty sure what they would find. An eighty-one-year-old was registered at this address; both police officers were familiar with the phenomenon of an older person being fit one day and found in respiratory distress the next. The virus took its toll and it took those alone, those on the fringes of society where there was nobody to call 111 when the first symptom appeared, nobody monitoring them or pushing them to get help. When they were discovered, having slept away with lungs full of oedema, the friends, the relatives and the carers all suddenly felt terrible, their offers of help just too late.

Just like Elsie Fortune in her flowery anorak. Too late.

The two officers crossed the pavement and went through a narrow gap in the unruly hedge, with its American-style letterbox, and they were back in the 1950s. The concealed bungalow was covered in peeling white paint, the grass at the front was waist-high, the path crumbling, and inside, in the middle of the hall floor, at the bottom of a loft ladder, lay an unconscious man.

The woman knelt beside him, her hand cradling his shoulder.

'You did call an ambulance?' confirmed Nicholson, as the woman nodded. Donnelly shouted that the ambulance had just pulled up. The man lying on the carpet was middle-aged, slim, fit-looking. There weren't any obvious sign of injury, but his colour was ghastly. Mrs Fortune wasn't doing too well herself – she was pale, swaying slightly, even though she was kneeling on the floor.

'He has a pulse,' she said. 'I checked that he still had a pulse. I was only gone for a couple of minutes. I've taken Norma to the neighbours.'

'His wife?' asked Donnelly.

'Dog,' corrected Mrs Fortune.

PC Donnelly immediately took charge, taking her out to the garden as the two paramedics examined the man lying on the carpet. The cop sat beside her on the step and started gentle questioning, trying to ascertain what had gone on here beyond the obvious. The neighbour had fallen from his loft. She had already said that she couldn't gain access to the house and then she found her neighbour on the floor, having fallen on his head from the look of it. Donnelly had been told that number nine was solely occupied by James Pearcey, who would be eighty-two on his next birthday. The man at the bottom of the loft ladder looked terrible, but he was not in his eighties.

'Any ID on him?' he asked the senior paramedic as the other carried in a stretcher.

'MacMillan, Dennis MacMillan. I think he lives in one of those houses down the path.'

'So what is he doing here?'

Elsie was keen to correct the confusion. Dennis MacMillan had been visiting Jimmy Pearcey, but Jimmy didn't open the door. She had joined Dennis to find a key and had been out in the garden with the dog when MacMillan had actually fallen. She then remembered that when they had walked through the hall a few moments before, the loft ladder had not been down, and she was totally at a loss when she found MacMillan on the floor. She then formed the opinion that the ladder had come down and hit him on the head.

Donnelly was mulling over the plausibility of that as MacMillan was carried past them on a stretcher.

The bungalow was spotless, not a thing out of place. He walked into the front room, which would have looked on to the street had the view not been totally blocked by the height of the hedge. It didn't feel right – there wasn't the smell, the slight chaos of victims of the virus, the scent of sweat and decay, glasses and cups lying around. More than once, he had seen a duvet on the sofa, slippers, an open box of paracetamol. But not here. 'It's like the *Mary Celeste*,' muttered Nicholson to himself, trying to break the tension, thinking it through. There's no sign of forced entry, no sign of anything untoward. He walked back to the front door. 'So we are missing Mr Pearcey? Are you sure he didn't mention going away?'

'I've never spoken to the man, but he wasn't the type to go away. And the dog was still here. The neighbour down the road has it now – number five.'

'OK.' Nicholson turned and looked at the steps up to the loft, a very solid arrangement. 'So what do we have up here?' He climbed the steps, admiring the carpentry on the way up, easy steps, his gloves gripping the strong handrails. He slowed as he got to the top. The rails went higher than the hatch, making it easier to walk up without an undignified scrabble at the top.

The first thing he saw was the screen, the image of the toddler sitting on a rock, surrounded by waves, her hat pulled down over her face, her dark eyes blackened by the shadow of a summer sun.

Then he turned round.

FOUR

Anderson got out of his car at Hill Road, Invernock, and stepped into the circus of tape, lights and the twitching of the neighbours' curtains, spectators on the morbid.

He hoped it didn't show that he had no real handle on what was going on. The term 'going in blind' didn't quite cut it. It happened in the police as it did in any other large organization. Messages didn't get passed on, cases moved faster than the paperwork, and incidents happened in the order they happened; they didn't wait their turn. But at some point, the buck stopped, and Colin Anderson had a feeling this was going to be at his door. For now, though, he was totally in the dark. All he could think was that Aasha's case was close to resolution and he could run the two investigations for a while. Patterson had got hold of the wrong end of the stick. At least he hoped that was the case.

He wasn't sure that he had the energy to give this new case everything it deserved, but felt slightly better when he spied Costello's Fiat bumped up on the pavement. If he was in the shit, she was in it too.

He walked up the cracked pavement to the front of the bungalow, picking his warrant card from his pocket, noticing an elderly woman sitting in one of the police cars, a uniform sitting with her. The woman's pose was familiar and spoke volumes; her head down, she was shaking. Either a relative or the one who had found the body. Then he realized what had caught his eye initially were the pricked ears and head of her dog, front paws up on the dashboard, panting, watching the comings and goings in and out of the house.

The uniform at the door signed him in. Anderson noted Costello's loopy signature four signatures above. After picking up a couple of shoe covers, he entered the house, seeing the loft ladder immediately, the gaggle of cops round the bottom, sensing that something horrible had happened. It was quiet, no wisecracks.

'Do you want to go up and look?' asked the young cop who introduced himself as PC Nicholson. He offered a wan smile; his relief that others were coming to take charge was obvious.

'Yes, who's that outside in the car? The woman with the dog?'

'That's the neighbour, Elsie Fortune. Lives at number seven. PC Donnelly's just explaining to her what's going on. She nearly fainted. We didn't think she'd be able to walk to her own house. The guy at number five made her a cup of tea.'

'Did she find the body?'

'We think a man called Dennis MacMillan found the body and promptly fell down the loft ladder, knocked himself out. I nearly did the same thing myself.'

'You OK now?' Anderson asked.

'Yes, thanks.'

'So who is MacMillan?'

'He's been visiting Mr James Pearcey, the eighty-one-year-old deceased, during lockdown and came round today to deliver his shopping. He couldn't get in, so he called on Mrs Fortune and they gained access together. They still couldn't find Mr Pearcey until Mr MacMillan looked in the loft. The ladder wasn't down when they first entered the premises – it was MacMillan who opened the hatch.'

'Why did he do that?'

'It's a bit odd, sir.'

'Obvious cause of death?' Anderson asked.

'You'd better look for yourself.'

'That bad? And the bloke who's still unconscious – a paid carer?'

'More a neighbour. He attends the local church and—' Nicholson was interrupted by a 'Hey!' from the loft hatch.

Costello's head appeared, her blonde hair up in a net. 'Anderson, you need to get up here. Nicholson, can you give the hospital a ring and see if MacMillan's regained consciousness.'

'Yes, ma'am.'

Her head retreated, loudly quoting the Jane Tennison line about her not being the bloody Queen.

Nicholson pulled up his Airwave as Anderson put one foot on the loft ladder.

'Did MacMillan go up here?'

'Nobody witnessed it, but he fell from somewhere.'

James Pearcey was sitting in a chair, a comfortable chair with wooden arms and thick cushions, head rolled backwards, eyes open, staring at the image on the screen of the young girl in her sunhat. Blood ran from the side of his mouth, down his light-blue shirt to a cascade on his lap.

Anderson looked in horror at the garrotte round the victim's neck which had caused the eyes to stare and the purple lips to swell, the dark engorgement of the skin. The thin band of dark blue may have been his own tie. A black marbled fountain pen was caught in the back, twisted tight. This death had not been peaceful or quiet. He recoiled when he saw the small grey circles on the back of the swollen wrists, the head of the nails hammered through the joints, pinning his hands to the wooden arms of the chair. And then the dark congealed bloody mess, the crimson apron that seeped from his groin over his lap, the chair, spilling on to the carpet underneath.

He acknowledged the revulsion that twisted his stomach and ran through the scenario. The home cine film, the image of the naked young girl, maybe two or three years old. His heart sank further: the covert nature of the little cinema in a roof space – these images would be for private viewing, private pleasure. And Pearcey had been up here and joined by somebody for whom he had not provided a chair. Pearcey himself was calm, now the business of his agonizing death was over, content to look at the girl for his eternity.

In an incongruous nod to domesticity, a small table sat beside the chair, with a cup and saucer, a plate and two ginger biscuits. It was the only furniture in the room, apart from a small book-case tucked under the eaves, full of metal film cassettes. Behind the chair was a huge projector, most of the film on the second reel. It had been paused, stuck for ever. Pearcey sat in his room, devoid of any furniture, any natural light, and watched his cine films.

Anderson looked round to view the image on the screen properly. The naked child sitting on the rock, waving at the camera, palm of her hand out, her hat falling over her forehead, throwing the shadow over her face.

Costello stepped forward, her eyes also drawn to the screen. 'Well, there's your answer, Colin. They just can't leave it alone, can they?' She looked back at the body on the chair.

'Who had been forced to watch what, I wonder.' Anderson wanted to close his eyes, turn off the cine film, but he let his gaze linger on the purple face for a while. This looked very close and personal. This had taken time.

Had Pearcey felt comfortable enough to take somebody upstairs to this private viewing room? Or had he been forced?

Costello was pointing at a pair of binoculars sitting on top of the bookcase of film reels, so Anderson walked to the Velux window and lifted the blind a little. Now he had a direct line of sight to the play park across the road. The hedge, the dog, the American-style letterbox at the end of the path. Nobody came near Pearcey's house until lockdown had demanded it. What had the Good Samaritan, MacMillan, found out?

He looked closely at the film cans, each sitting in a small groove in the wood of the shelf. Numbers were handwritten on peeling white labels. They looked like dates. 24 06 59. A long time ago. Pearcey was in his eighties. The kids on here would be filmed live in those days. As a crime, it was as old as death itself.

Taking a final look around, the white screen hanging from the rafters, the kid in the sunhat, the conversion of the small loft to this secretive room, the special stairway, he had the sensation that a cold dead hand had just stroked the back of his neck.

'Costello, can you get these films logged and transported back to base as soon as possible? And dig up a projector.'

'Or take this one. If we get forensics to prioritize it?' she offered.

'Good idea.'

Costello joined her boss at the side of the body. 'Is this Pearcey?'

'That's my working hypothesis . . .'

'Not an easy man to get any background information on, on a first pass, but I will get the boys on to it.'

'Not easy as in "kept a low profile"?'

'From the look of it. No wonder. James Pearcey? Mean anything?'

'Nope, not at all.' Anderson shook his head.

She looked around. 'This looks like a pervert's paradise – isolated from the house, sitting there nibbling his ginger biscuits while looking at naked children in his own wanking castle. It's disgusting.'

'Can we keep an open mind, Costello?' he said with no real conviction.

'You are ignoring the obvious. If you hear hooves, think horse not zebra and all that shit. If you get a brown envelope from the taxman, think bill not rebate. There're laws in the universe.' It was Costello's turn to look at her watch. 'Can I go and see MacMillan now, get his story. It's gone five and, remember, I got the short straw to go to Jim Bryant's retiral barbecue tonight.'

'Sorry about that. You'd think food poisoning and a global pandemic might have put him off. Yes, you go,' Anderson said. 'One of us should. I've not been told who else is working this.'

'I was told to attend, that's all. You know MacMillan is a Christian?'

'Yes, Nicholson said.' Anderson frowned at the non sequitur. 'Is that against the law now?'

'A Christian finds the body of a paedophile who has been tortured to death. Might be something there?'

'Oh. Those Christians. They go around doing this to defenceless old men, do they?'

'They might if they are a fire-and-brimstone, burn-in-hell-all-ye-who-don't-put-the-toilet-seat-down type rather than the scones-in-the-vestry type. They do sing a lot. I'll interview him. Just a bit curious about this finding the key and getting the neighbour as a witness. It's a bit too neat.' She shouted down through the hatch, 'Is MacMillan able to talk?'

'He will be by the time you get there. What are we doing with Norma?'

'Who?'

'The dog? It's Pearcey's dog. But Elsie's man is allergic, as she's told Donnelly a hundred times.'

Costello rippled her fingers, asking for Anderson's car keys. 'I'll get to the hospital and take a statement, get hold of his clothes. Where does he live exactly?'

'No idea. Nicholson will know,' Anderson said, handing over his car keys without really thinking; he was busy looking around the room, taking it in so he had a reference until the crime scene pictures were ready. 'I wonder who the girl in the film is. Was it left deliberately on that frame? We could get that face enhanced, even with the shadow. Do you think aging software can do that, from two years old to what? Sixty? Fifty? The date will be on the can.'

'It'll be crap if she likes Botox. So who did it? A female perp? Somebody smaller and weaker than him? Even with him being an old man, they had to nail his hands to the arm of the chair to take their time over killing him.'

Anderson looked and swore. He then said very quietly, 'Costello, Tony Bannon has been put in charge of the Aasha Ariti case.'

'Yes, I know. I said I'd rather be reassigned to this with you.'

'Did you?' He was touched by her loyalty.

'Yes, I'd have to train him; it's taken me years to get you under control.' Costello's tone was light, recognizing that her boss was struggling with something. 'The Aasha case is going to be a poisoned chalice, Colin. You are being given a get-out-of-jail-free card. Bannon's being thrown to the wolves. He's been out of CID so long that he doesn't recognize the scent of them circling. Give it a week and he'll request a post back to Complaints – they're used to being unpopular.'

'What do you mean?'

They both looked down at the sound of somebody important arriving – lots of 'Sirs' and 'Hellos'.

'Paedophilia. Racism. The media are going to be all over these two cases, no matter what we do. Zeitgeist and all that.'

'Do you think Aasha was a race issue?'

'She had dark skin – of course it will be a race issue. Even though she's a Catholic born in Romford, the bampots on both sides will turn it into one.' She looked round. 'And then there's this – all this here. And Pearcey sitting there, enjoying it at his age.'

'Maybe we should wait until we see what's on the rest of the films.'

'Well, you can watch them. I'll sit that one out, thanks. I'm away to talk to MacMillan.' She knelt down to clamber through the hatch, leaving him to his own thoughts. No doubt her boss was back looking at Pearcey and trying not to imagine the pain.

Anderson waited until Nicholson's head appeared through the hatch and asked him to fill in the blanks. 'So what happened here exactly? The deceased didn't trust MacMillan enough to give him a key? Is that right?'

'The friendship was a very recent thing, sir. But Mrs Fortune said MacMillan was very concerned to gain access – understandable, good community spirit, post-virus in a small village like this. The loft ladder was up and the hatch closed when they first came in. She goes out with the dog for, quote, "a couple of minutes". And came back in to this. She claims to have no prior knowledge of the attic space.'

'Despite the Velux window?'

'The blinds were never open, so she presumed that Pearcey was too old to get up there. When she comes back in, MacMillan's unconscious and the loft hatch is open. She called an ambulance.'

'Why?'

'Why what?'

'Why did MacMillan decide to suddenly open somebody else's loft hatch? What was he looking for?'

'No idea.'

'I'll come down now before I feel any more nauseous.' Anderson climbed down into the hall which was now crowded with crime scene techs. 'That ladder's an impressive bit of kit.'

'I think it's more substantial than usual due to his age,' Nicholson said. 'The ladder lifts into the hatch by this electric motor – there's a switch on the wall. The handrail folds up inside it. It's light but very strong.'

Anderson had noticed the two handrails, enough to help an elderly man who might be struggling with his balance to gain access to the loft, frequently and safely. 'Does Pearcey have children? There are reels and reels of film up there.'

'If these are family films, why not keep them in the spare room? There are some photographs – there's one on the table next to his chair. Same people – family?'

'Well, offenders don't go round with the words "I am a sex monster" on their forehead. If he's kept under the radar, he did that for a reason. Did somebody know and take revenge? Was the killer a victim?' Anderson walked into the front room, reminding the crime scene tech that they'd like the films, the cans and the projector back at the incident room as soon as possible. How long had it taken Dennis MacMillan to gain Pearcey's trust? Not enough trust to give him a spare key.

Anderson looked at the photograph on the table: the one thing in the room that wasn't in its rightful place. It was still in its large frame, and the old string on the back showed that it had been hanging until recently. A family picture – three men, one of whom might have been the deceased aged about forty. One woman, three boys, two girls – the kids ranging from young teens to toddlers. Could be something or nothing. There was nothing else lying around, no half-done jigsaw, half-read book. He told the crime scene tech to dust the picture for prints in case it had been handled. And who were these people? He took a photo of it on his phone before he looked out of the window into the back of the hedge, then lowered himself, hearing his knees squeak, to the level of Pearcey's chair, the slightly odd angle it sat at. Now he could see through the gap in the hedge, the play park neatly framed by the cut of the laurel.

He hoped MacMillan was talking. Was he involved in some kind of ring? Had he come here to destroy the evidence? 'Has anybody found a computer?' he shouted as he walked into the hall and bumped into Jessica Gibson and Mathilda McQueen. 'Pathology and forensics, joined at the hip?'

'May as well be,' said Gibson. 'There's not many bosses I can ask this, but is it safe up there? You know?' She patted the growing bump on her stomach.

He nodded. 'Yes, I would think so,' he reassured her. 'It's horrific and bloody, but there's no sign of drug abuse or needles – just take care going up the ladder. When is it due?'

'Another eight weeks yet,' she said, looking warily at the loft ladder.

'Well, enjoy the sleep while you can. Mathilda, the deceased may be a paedophile, so we need to secure any electronic devices.'

'I'll get the tech boys on to that. What's going to happen to that dog?' asked McQueen. 'It's sitting in your car, Colin, as if it's desperate for a shit.'

'Bloody Costello. I'll see you two later,' he said, leaving them to their jobs.

He knew the drill, but there was something bothering him.

Not the fact that Costello had left the dog in his car. While he'd feel guilty taking another dog home, he'd feel worse if this wee dog was dragged off to the rescue centre. There was something else. What was it? The timeline was wrong. It was about half past three when the body was discovered at number nine. He had responded quickly. What time had Patterson said he'd got the call from Detective Chief Super Toastie Warburton to 'redeploy' him? About eleven? That meant either there was a gap in the space–time continuum or Warburton knew in advance that this was going to happen. Interesting.

He signed out of the crime scene, the uniform at the door gave him his keys back and asked him if he was going to the retiral barbecue, adding that it was going to be quite an event – rumoured there was going to be a free bar. Anderson lied that he was sorry that he couldn't make it but he had a sick two-year-old in the house and he needed some sleep. Those were the words spoken, but the words running through his mind were that he'd rather poke his eyeballs out with a stick. His wee dog had just passed away; he really wasn't in the mood for good humour. He asked for MacMillan's address to see where he lived in relation to the deceased's bungalow. The sky was clearing and it was getting colder. And that recalled to mind the wee mongrel who might be having a dump in his car. He hurried back to where he had parked the old BMW to find Norma rolled up in the front seat, a wee scrappy, spikey dog, shaking like a leaf in her sleep. Hearing him, she woke up and jumped, front paws padding on the window, her tail wagging like a metronome.

Norma. She'd go to the police kennel where she'd be outside all night, whereas in his house there was a warm bed under a radiator. Yes, it was his own dog's bed, but Nesbit was a generous spirit and he had no use for it now. Anderson turned, pulled up the zip on his jacket, opened the door, got the dog out and bent to make sure her lead was secure. But as he placed his hand on her collar, she cowered and retracted her top lip, showing a set of very fine canines.

He removed his hand before she removed his fingers, and apologized to her. She wagged her tail in forgiveness, then they started down the path towards MacMillan's house. His phone told him that the road was the long way round and the path that crossed the grass was much quicker. MacMillan had good reason to be present at the house. He wondered if the good Christian had a daughter. He definitely had a wife who was conveniently away at the moment. A man of faith might well be infuriated by child abuse, but it would take a father to be provoked to violence, or a victim not strong enough to fight back. It was finding the key so conveniently that troubled Anderson, a thought he tumbled over in his head as Norma trotted alongside him. Had MacMillan fetched Elsie Fortune for corroboration purposes? MacMillan being unconscious meant they had not spoken, so Anderson would soon know if their stories did not tally, but the neighbour had secured a witness to that fact that he had discovered the body, even if they had not been together at that precise moment. The dog was a good way to get Mrs Fortune out of the house, while . . . While what? While MacMillan went upstairs to perform that degree of injury to James Pearcey and nobody heard a thing? That was rubbish, not plausible even to his own ears. It didn't mean that he hadn't been over earlier to kill him and then made sure he had a witness when he found the body. That fitted better. It was convenient. It was all just a little too convenient.

FIVE

Costello arrived at the hospital. Still quiet, a sense of tired panic reigned. She was quick to find that her patient was in Accident and Emergency, waiting to be moved to a ward.

'How is Mr MacMillan? Is he talking sense?' she asked the nurse, who was scribbling on a patient chart fixed to a clipboard.

'He'll be fine. Can you put a mask on? There's a box behind you.' She nodded at the worktop. 'I can see no reason why you can't interview him, but I'm not going as far as to say that his recollection of events will be clear enough to be repeated in court as a reliable account. It was quite a knock on the head.'

'You've been on this horse before, haven't you?' smiled Costello.

'Many a time. This is Greenock. He must have slid on the ladder steps as he didn't hit the ground with much force – more like banged his head on the way down. No bleeding in the brain – only signs of minor concussion. We're keeping him in for twenty-four hours' observation as he'd be on his own at home. He's fit, healthy for a fifty-year-old, but he has a head injury and rules are rules. He's tested negative for Covid. He's in the second door on the right. Clothes, personal effects including his phone are in our office in a bag marked "Hazard". He hasn't asked for them yet, which might be shock or it might be that he knows we have already spoken to his wife and he has nobody else to speak to.'

'Is that all the family he has?'

She glanced at the form. 'Yes, the wife, down south with the daughter and the grandchild. She's been there since before lockdown. They'll call back later to check up on him.'

'You didn't sense any issues within the family?'

'Not at all, they seemed very nice.'

'Thanks,' said Costello, noting the nurse's name for the record.

'Dennis MacMillan, but I'm guessing that you know that.'

'DI Costello, Partickhill, seconded to MIT.' The man with the white dressing on his head looked confused. 'We deal with the big stuff. Don't bother shaking my hand.'

MacMillan nodded gently. 'Has Mr Pearcey passed away, then?'

'Yes, he has, sadly.' She pulled over a chair, protecting her hands with a paper towel, and made herself comfortable while staying distant. 'Is there anything I can get for you? Are you allowed a tea or a coffee?'

'A drink of water would be nice, thank you very much. That's very kind.' His smile lit up his small pointy face; creases around his clear blue eyes spoke of a kind heart and a life of smiling. He was very slightly built, going a little bald and grey round the temples.

She got up and ran the tap, filling a plastic tumbler. As she handed it over, her hand wrapped in a tissue, she noted how much MacMillan's hand was shaking. 'Do you know what happened?'

'Did you say you were an inspector? Is that not quite high up?'

'Short-staffed and multi-tasking. I'm really here to collect your clothes, and ask if we could have a look through your mobile.'

MacMillan looked rather shocked.

'It's all routine – there's nothing to worry about. We have to tick boxes like everybody else, but I'm sure you can understand that a murder investigation is a big machine – we just go through the process. You were the person who discovered that body. I'd be talking to the person who did that, no matter who it was.'

'Murder?' MacMillan looked into the far distance, remembering. 'I'm not sure what I can do to help. All I remember is falling through a hole, then I woke up in here. He was a very nice man, Mr Pearcey – a lovely man. Is Norma OK?'

'Norma?' asked Costello. 'Oh, the dog. Yes, she's being well looked after, don't worry about her.'

'Poor Mr Pearcey.' MacMillan looked down. His small, feminine hands smoothed the top of his duvet, plucking at nothing, searching for something to do.

'Can I ask what made you go up into the loft?'

'I think I heard a noise.'

'What kind of noise? Like a scream or a clatter? Somebody moving about?'

'No, it was quiet, like a hum. I thought somebody had left a fan on or something. I've been in the hall many times and not been aware of that noise before.'

'So that made you open the loft hatch?'

MacMillan gave a little shrug. 'There were marks on the carpet, and I thought he might be up there – maybe fallen down, got stuck – so I went up . . .'

'Was Mr Pearcey a close friend of yours?'

The question confused him. He shrugged, then explained about the church and the call to help out the vulnerable in the village during lockdown. 'I volunteered to look after Mr Pearcey as I live close to him, along the path. Do you know Invernock, Miss Costello?'

'I think I visited the outdoor swimming pool with the school when I was a kid, but as an adult? No.'

'Oh, well, it's a strange wee place, but very friendly. Mr Pearcey kept himself to himself. I can't even tell you how long he had lived in that house.'

'But you got on with him?'

'Yes, he was very nice, very clever, interesting to talk to. I think he was lonely, with the lockdown thing. Weird, as he never really spoke to anybody – he should've been good at isolation. Poor man. I'd be in one corner of the room, him in his chair. All distanced and correct. He was very polite – a bit posh.'

'It's interesting how you see a side of people you don't normally see,' said Costello, thinking that chatty was the way to get MacMillan talking. 'I'd been looking in on a neighbour while it was all going on – she has family but nobody local, and we all need to do our bit. Do you know if Mr Pearcey had any children or family? Did he ever mention anybody?'

'He never mentioned anyone, except a friend who had died recently, but I got the impression they hadn't seen each other for ages. He spoke to Betty who runs the village shop, of course. I think he asked the guy at number five to stop using his power tools so early in the morning . . .' He shook his head, not able to think of anything else.

Costello leaned forward with her notebook. 'So in your own time, Mr MacMillan, just talk me through what happened after you left your house to visit Mr Pearcey . . .'

Half an hour later, she went back into the office to collect MacMillan's personal effects and took them through to him. He watched as she took out his wallet, his phone, his house keys, an A5 white envelope, a train ticket, two masks and a bottle of sanitizer. MacMillan was happy for her to flick through his wallet, confirming that the contents were all present, then he unlocked his phone with the code 2003 – the year he had become a Christian – before scrolling through the texts, showing her the ones from Jimmy Pearcey, requests for shopping, kind comments about the grandchild. The phone rang. It was his wife, so Costello said her goodbyes and left him to it.

Anderson had stood under a hot shower for a very long time and was now sitting in his kitchen, tired, his energy spent. He started making a coffee, then gave up and poured a glass of red wine, ignoring the wiry innocent face of Norma looking at him from the comfort of Nesbit's bed – a snappy wee dog instead of his lovely Staffie. He was trying hard to like her, but couldn't. She was the wrong dog. He and Brenda were keeping Norma and Moses separate in case the dog snapped again. Moses was too young to understand, and he'd try to cuddle her the way he'd cuddled Nesbit. Norma looked angelic now, but she'd tried to bite Anderson again when he stopped her jumping out of the car.

The pain from the blister on his hand, gained by digging Nesbit's grave, reinforced the fact that Nesbit had gone. Was that only this morning? Well, this terrible day would soon be over; he was home, it was ten past nine, the wheels of the murder investigation were in motion, and he had a nice Merlot for company. The world outside was darkening, despite it being so close to the longest day. Dark and quiet, as was the house. Claire and Paige had now arrived at Tyndrum. The madness of the last few days – running around the house, losing shoes, finding sunscreen, washing dirty jeans at the last minute – was over. They had driven Brenda insane and now, in this peaceful hiatus, she was lying on the sofa in the living room, snoring in front of the TV, tired out by the day. Peter was in his bedroom, playing on his computer.

Even Moses had gone to sleep after two chapters of *Tartan Witch*, Anderson using the book's rich phonetics to encourage his son to formulate some kind of word. But the small lips had remained steadfastly closed.

The house was far too quiet.

Nesbit was cold in his grave.

Little Norma was watching him with small beady eyes. What would happen to her now? She'd not be an easy dog to rehome – too quick with her teeth. No addresses or numbers of any

immediate family had leapt forward when Nicholson searched
number nine. Anderson had a pang of guilt. How would he feel
if it had been Nesbit, and nobody tried to help? He got up and
knelt down beside her, stroking her ears. Norma closed her eyes
slightly, finding comfort in the touch of his hand, then he moved
his fingers along to the ruff of her neck. Her head whipped
round, mouth open, teeth bared. But she didn't snap.

He got out his mobile and put the torch on. After a minute
of careful poking and prodding, he found the bloodied scabs,
in a neat line round her neck, red and pink, swollen and sore,
one still weeping a clear fluid that crusted her wiry hair. Had
her collar been tightened and screwed round her neck, like a
garrotte? Was she used as leverage on James Pearcey?

He left her to rest and went into his study, carrying his bottle
of red with him and leaving the door open so he'd hear when
Brenda woke up.

He powered up his laptop. The last time he checked, there
had been little movement in the Aasha case. But he was out of
the loop. As far as he knew, he was still SIO and should stay
that way until he was told officially to back off.

His bosses had known where he was all day and there had
been no contact, so he was pissed off when he opened the file
in his laptop and the icon immediately appeared. He had an
email to his work address. A couple of hours ago, there had
been nothing, so whatever it was it had been important enough
to email him at eight o'clock at night but not to call him during
the day and speak to him directly. He opened it, and his heart
fell. There it was: a request from the Detective Chief Super for
him to report in at nine a.m. the following morning. His brain
ran with his argument to his superior. He had already prepared
his interview with Anthony Poole, all the evidence was gathered,
and his team was closing in on a motive. They were ready to
go. He had been there when they pulled the girl's body out of
the water, yet, as he read the second paragraph of the email, it
was clear the case was being given to Tony Bannon over at
Partick Central. It was official. Patterson had been right.
Anderson read that paragraph again, paranoia creeping in. Was
this at the request of the parents? Had Costello done something
to upset them? Or the aunt? He knew he should have attended

himself to inform the family about the passing of their daughter, but it was two in the morning. Was he not allowed a night off? He'd been working on the interview with Anthony Poole from the moment he had come forward as the man on the stairs in the nightclub.

Tony Bannon was an OK cop, but he had been working in Complaints for – what? – five years or more. The fox was back in the hen house – his team would resent that. The story of the way Bannon's boss had treated the widow of a young police officer during the Haggerty case was well known. Nobody wanted to touch Diane Mathieson and, by association, Bannon. He'd find it tough to get the guys to work well under him, and the people who would suffer were Mr and Mrs Ariti. What the hell was Warburton thinking? But he was new to the post and Bannon was only just back to normal investigative work – maybe there was a connection. Give Bannon something already 'solved' to ease himself back into the job. Or it might be, as Costello had suspected, a poisoned chalice. In the present climate, anything with the merest suggestion of a racial element had to be ultra-transparent. Was Anderson being moved sideways for his own good?

He'd go into the meeting tomorrow, demand to see the case through, kick up a huge fuss. It would make him feel better but achieve nothing. Or he could play the bigger man and hand over what he had. He'd offer to explain it to Aasha's parents, introduce Bannon, and say that now she had been found, the investigation was moving on to a new phase that Tony Bannon was more expert in. It couldn't be further from the truth, but it might ease their minds a little. It was looking like a slam-dunk conviction for Anthony Poole anyway, once they found a motive – if they needed one beyond a young man and a beautiful woman both drunk by a river in the small hours of the morning. There might be more evidence to come from the post-mortem or camera footage. Wyngate and Mulholland were on the case; they had done good work under his leadership, so he was at a loss as to why they were removing him from the case.

Well, he'd find out tomorrow.

He minimized that email and opened up another from Lee Galbraith, the Met civilian working on Operation Felix. There were two victims of Rodger the conman coming to the fore, elderly this time. In a lock-up near Tilbury Docks, the police involved in Operation Felix had found a stash of everything that Rodger had purloined in his long and successful career. Galbraith explained that most conmen – by that he meant thieves like Simon Russell – made the mistake of trying to offload stolen goods too quickly, whereas Russell had worked on a ten- to fifteen-year delay. By then, any stolen items of value had slipped under the radar and could easily be passed off as a Russell family heirloom. Russell himself would have changed appearance, address and name multiple times by then, and be gone.

Russell was being charming and cooperative, saying that he was given lovely items by his lady friends, for doing good deeds or because he was in a relationship with them. This was a clever tactic, and it became a point of law. Would any victim admit to being so stupid as to have been taken in by him? Russell was offering to give the presents back if they really wanted them, if they had changed their mind. And in Brenda's case, he was saying that she had allowed him access to her bank accounts and that he was in the process of reinvesting the money for their future together and for little Moses. It was only when her husband, the cop, found out that she changed her story. And, Rodger had pointed out, Brenda Anderson was an accountant married to a detective, so if anybody was security-conscious, she should have been, and therefore she must have given him the numbers of their bank accounts willingly. The money had not been spent – it had been invested. Would Brenda be able or willing to testify that this was not so?

It was a mess.

But the son of one of the older victims, an Ian Prentice, was not for backing down. He had emailed the police after recognizing Russell's picture and subsequently provided a list of valuables that had walked out of his mum's door with Russell, including his mother's engagement ring and his grandmother's tea service, a Clarice Cliff. Russell had held on to that for fourteen years, knowing its value but keeping to his long game, planning to retire at fifty. The estimated value of the goods in the shed ran into a million plus. Anderson had to read that again. It would take a long time to return the property to its rightful owners, although they were often accompanied by a signed document as proof of change of ownership with an almost convincing signature. And that didn't include the funds secreted in various bank accounts in different names, which Russell had explained was a bit naughty, but each name was a different account of a different friend whose funds he was looking after. He was careful not to get them mixed up, he said. Galbraith was positive he would get to the bottom of it all – he was a terrier after a rabbit, following Russell down every single loophole of the law until he caught him.

Anderson took a sip of his wine. The five hours he and Brenda had spent with Galbraith, going through every step of Rodger's deceit, had been harrowing. By the end of it, Brenda was sobbing her heart out and Anderson was quietly furious. Galbraith had been upbeat: Russell was a worthy adversary and could have been a very successful accountant with his knowledge of tax avoidance. Most of the goods were being held as evidence. The Crown Prosecution Service in England and the Procurator Fiscal's Office in Scotland just needed to know who was willing to give evidence. Anderson was leaving that decision up to Brenda, as his own judgement would be prejudiced by the embarrassment of a DCI's wife being conned so completely. Anderson was very protective of his family and had been warned by the press office what would happen if they went ahead. The Anderson family had everything that the tabloids adored. The husband, the wife and Simon Russell. It sounded like a sordid threesome sex scandal. And, of course, Paige's background and Claire's dalliance with cocaine. None of that would be in the best interest of Moses, the two-year-old son with Down's syndrome. And his back story? Nobody should have that blasted over the newspapers. It was a stick with two shitty ends; he had to take hold of one of them.

And Russell would be betting on that.

Brenda's confidence had been broken by Russell. She had changed. At the end of the day, Anderson wasn't absolutely sure which way the tide was going in his marriage, but this was not going to help.

Things were changing: the girls were growing up, Moses had

appeared in their lives, Peter had come out of his room, Nesbit had gone and it looked as if Norma, another abused orphan, had arrived. Brenda had always been the hard, logical one. They had split up, got back together, not as a married couple, but they did share a house and he liked that. He didn't like to think of power in any relationship, but he could sense a subtle but definitive change in the house.

He poured himself another glass of Merlot and heard a tap at the open door. He said, 'Come in', thinking that it was Brenda not wanting to disturb him. Then he felt a small warm body push past him at knee height: Norma, coming in to see what he was up to.

Costello was wondering why her life had sunk as low as this. She had spent the last hour running a very tired and distressed Mrs Allan home from the hospital, her passenger's nervous rabbiting about Vera, Vera's daughter, the anarchy in the country, all feeding her headache. Wyngate had traced the daughter, Joanna, to Ealing, and she was flying up, so at least Costello should be able to absolve herself of that drama. Now, at half past eight, hungry and teetering into a bad mood, she was slinking around the periphery of the guests at a barbecue, trying to find one person who she actually wanted to talk to. She didn't want any of the half-cooked food, she didn't enjoy being attacked by midges. The occasion was the retiral of a colleague who was at best unpopular, at worst a bully. The guests were in attendance out of duty, sitting in his large back garden, all decking and gazebos, drinking, distancing as much as possible, but they had come united to get it over with and finally knock the nail in Jim Bryant's career coffin. Costello continued to nod and skirt round socially distancing drunk folk, looking as if she was heading to join her own group of friends elsewhere, avoiding people the same way that she would avoid them if she ever spotted them in Tesco.

Like her, many of them had drawn straws with others in the office and had lost. In their little group, it was between her and Anderson – Mulholland's leg was bad, and Wyngate had claimed, not without logic, that his wife had been in lockdown with three small kids for twelve weeks, so he felt that he really should be home when he was supposed to be home and not out enjoying himself at a fantastic barbie with a free bar.

He was being sarcastic, of course.

So here she was, sneaking around, looking for a friendly face to talk to, among the drunken banter and chatter. *Mambo No. 5* was belting out from a small electronic device inside a gazebo. There were three barbecues burning, while everywhere people were keeping some distance until Pissed Up Paul from IT support appeared and tried to get everyone together for a group hug. He was smartly rejected. When he persisted, he was told to piss off. Then Costello saw an arm wave. It was Myra McMuir, a constable she knew only vaguely but who was always good for a gossip. Costello sat down beside her on a chair placed about three feet away.

'What have you got?' she asked, looking at a red mush on Myra's paper plate. 'It looks like something that Prof. O'Hare might keep in his bottom drawer in the hope that he might be able to resurrect it.'

'Don't know, but there were no flies crawling over it. It tastes disgusting.'

'So disgusting that not even the flies would touch it. What are you doing here? Making sure the wee bugger is actually going?'

'Yes, and you need to get a plate of something in front of you or Jim's missus will come over and drag you to the buffet, enticing you with botulism burgers and a side order of dysentery.' Myra took a huge gulp of red wine, contorting her face in agony as it burned her oesophagus on the way down. 'The red wine is like vinegar, but Joe here thinks the alcohol-free beer is tasteless, which might be a mercy.'

'That will be a no then, but thanks anyway,' said Costello, glad she had her own bottle of water with her.

'How is the totally gorgeous but mysteriously unavailable Vik Mulholland? I haven't seen him for ages. Is he still attached?'

'I presume so. His girlfriend's never here. His leg is hanging off. Nothing much changes.'

'Have you heard what Anderson is doing about all that money he lost to the scammer?' asked Myra, revealing the reason why she called Costello over in the first place.

'Nope.'

Joe from traffic mumbled with a mouthful of burger. 'Well, it's Buddhist, isn't it? I mean, he inherited all that by shagging someone else's missus, so it's kind of poetic that some bloke comes along, shags his missus, then takes off . . .' Joe clocked the chill in Costello's stare and fell quiet, a sentiment that spread among the five colleagues, then Myra cleared her throat loudly while nodding at the dance decking.

Costello turned in time to see Archie Walker come into the garden.

'There's yer pal the fiscal,' Myra whispered loudly, and Costello had actually lifted her hand to say *Hey, we are over here*. Probably nobody else noticed but she felt embarrassment flush her face as her hand was still in the air when she saw Archie was not alone. Costello, Myra and Joe watched as Walker brought his mystery guest into the garden, guiding her across the decking to the table that functioned as the bar. His small companion was introduced to two of Archie's colleagues from the office, and from the manner in which those introductions were made, rather polite and formal, she was not a work colleague. His hand was behind her back, cradling her waist, helping her in case she lost her way in the distance of about ten feet or so. So somebody he knew well . . .

It was Myra who voiced what everybody else was thinking. 'She's the dead spit of you.'

'But younger,' admitted Costello. 'Much younger.'

'Younger and prettier,' said Joe, safely out of striking distance. 'Much younger and much prettier. So where did he get her from? And wherever that was, he can take her straight back, because one Costello is enough.'

Myra leaned over. 'She really does look very like you. She even dresses like you. I mean, who comes to a barbecue wearing a suit?'

'Well, me obviously, but I've just come from interviewing a concussed man in hospital and playing taxi for a neighbour. Where the hell has she been?'

'So she does the same job you do?'

'Poor guy obviously never learns,' muttered Costello. She turned round in her seat, Archie ignoring her as he said his hellos to the gathering. He blanked her for the next hour, which showed he was feeling more awkward than she was. Or that he was a totally heartless bastard and couldn't be arsed to breathe the same air as her.

Then the final insult. She watched as Tony Bannon, the man who was now in charge of the Aasha case from Partick Central, sneaked up behind Archie's mystery woman, grabbing her by the shoulders and saying something in her ear. It was obvious from his approach that Tony had mistaken Archie's companion for Costello. Archie simply pointed over to where Costello was sitting. He had known she was there all along. Tony made a point of boogying across the decking with a *Who the hell was that?* look plastered over his face.

But the blonde companion, now aware of Costello's presence, was suddenly rather keen to leave.

SIX

Wednesday 17 June

Email
7.30 a.m.
To: DCI Colin Anderson
From: DS Tony Bannon
Hi Colin,

I believe that I am taking over from you as the SIO in the suspicious death of Aasha Ariti. I was talking to Costello at the BBQ last night and she said it was OK to email you for some guidance. Now the body has been recovered, the parents are in Glasgow, in the care of FLO McLeish. From what I see, Aasha was the middle daughter, in her final year of medicine at Glasgow, a good student by all accounts. The interviews say that she said she was feeling a bit queasy in the Debut nightclub (I think the phrase used was 'she was going out for some fresh air'). It was a relatively warm night. Anthony Poole is sticking to his story that he saw her going downstairs, recognized her and went out with her to 'keep her company'. He says they walked off down towards the river. We have now checked all the CCTV images. Anthony and Aasha are seen walking together at 1.29 a.m. He's seen going up a side alley to have a slash. By the time he's seen coming out, Aasha has already walked out of view. CCTV images from the nightclub support his version of events. There are no images of them together from this point on, which backs up his story that he saw a taxi pull away and presumed she was in it. He went back to the club, got drunk with his friends, then left to get the night bus home with an Iain Watson. The security guys at the nightclub agree with these timings. I was going to pin Watson down for a more precise time but he was, by his own account, 'out of his face'.

Two things of note. I think you said Poole had no issues in speaking freely when you first contacted him about Aasha's disappearance. Well, he's tightening up now. And although he claims he was close to the victim, her pals have no knowledge of him. They didn't even know his name.

And, of course, Aasha is a Christian of Indian and Italian ethnicity. I see that some groups are trying to capitalize on this, saying that there's a racial element to her murder. I don't see it – well, not yet – but the press will be all over it. If anything, I suspect a sexual motive. Let me know if you think I am way off base with this.

Tony

Costello was spreading Marmite on her toast, assessing the online coverage, or lack of it, of Pearcey's murder. Only a very small paragraph: a man found dead in suspicious circumstances in the quiet village of Invernock. Somebody had put the brakes on the reporting of his violent death. The coverage of the discovery of Aasha Ariti's body, however, was still in the headlines. Each article mentioned her Indian ancestry, ignoring her Italian father, and that the community was rallying round. It also said that 'police enquiries are ongoing' rather than a 'twenty-two-year-old man is helping police with their enquiries'. Costello sipped her tea as she read, nursing her headache from another night of little sleep, smarting over Archie's behaviour at the barbecue. It wasn't so much his appearance or the carbon-copy girlfriend that had got to her, but the fact he had ignored her. How childish was that? What would happen when their paths crossed again? She had wished he had been on his own, so they could have a chat about nothing, proved to themselves that they were both over it and could move on, but he had deliberately, and so publicly, avoided her. And that rankled. But the expression on the face of his mysterious companion intrigued her.

Busying herself, Costello had a quick glance through her work email. There was one from the office of the new Detective Chief Super Toastie Warburton. She was being asked – well, told – to report to Partickhill Annexe rather than Partick Central, which was like going back to school. There was going to be some reassignment of cases due to the 'ongoing situation'. Which situation this referred to was not clear, but from what Bannon had said last night, she could well be on the Pearcey case now.

That was unfortunate as she felt they were close to arresting Anthony Poole. Anderson had gone home yesterday to prepare for the interview with the main suspect. Up until now, it had been nicey nicey. Poole had been cooperative and had a smart answer for everything. Somebody had said that Poole had a history of being racist on social media. Anderson had tasked DC Gordon Wyngate with tracking that down – so far there had been a mild comment about Asian students being competi-tive, asked as a question, but it was there. If she was allowed, she'd check up on that before the interview today. This would be a chat in the cold stark interview room, and Anderson, or Bannon, would, at some point, when Poole didn't expect it, slide the photographs of the dead girl's body across the table towards him – maybe the close-up of her face, a beautiful young woman with the end of her nose nibbled off by fish. It would be interesting to see what colour he went.

Poole was confident that the police had nothing on him. His dad was vociferous in his defence. Before, they had no true evidence against him. Now they had the body, but Costello wasn't holding her breath for forensics. Aasha had been in the water too long.

If she was still on the case. If.

They could argue that Bannon would not be up to speed.

She scrolled through some nonsense, then read the email from her contact at the river authority, about the tide and the flow of the water from midnight Saturday to midnight Sunday. They had attached charts and diagrams that she couldn't make head or tail of, so she jumped to the end where a simple graphic displayed areas of the river bank where Aasha might have entered the water, the most likely area in bright red, fading to gentle pink with lessening probability. The red area was a short stretch, and Costello thought, her pen tip-tapping on the tabletop, it was also within walking distance of the nightclub. Aasha had high-heeled shoes on – kitten heels to be precise. She would not have walked far. There was a maximum distance that Anthony Poole could have covered if he walked out and back in the time frame when he was absent from the club. Costello logged into the system while her access was still valid and looked for the report of the witness interviews on the door of the Debut nightclub. They had all been reasonably consistent. The CCTV that the team had so far viewed was in concordance with their statements. Anthony Poole had been gone for about forty minutes – they would be able to firm that up once all the CCTV had been viewed and analyzed. She knew exactly where Aasha had last been seen at 1.29 a.m.

Costello had a think, knowing that she should send the information on to the investigation room where it would wait in a pile for a junior officer to input the data. But her headache was getting worse, so she left a message to say that she was going to walk the route, time it, see how easy it was to get down to the river. There were the old docks and new flats, but everywhere had good fencing, too many drunk folk around the city centre for it to be otherwise.

The doorbell rang. She swore and put the toast down, licking the Marmite from her fingers. It would only be the postman. She went to the door, in her old brown woollen jumper that went down to her knees, her hair sticking out like an electrocuted porcupine, and opened it to a woman she didn't know. It took her tired brain a while to catch up; the dark eyes, the Italian complexion, taller and wider than her mother, an imposing figure. Vera's daughter, Joanna Craig, in a well-cut suit, a Gucci holdall and a perfect bob. Costello was suddenly very aware that she hadn't brushed her teeth or washed her face.

'Miss Costello?'

'Hi, you must be Joanna. How is your mum?'

Costello stood back as far as possible, continuing the 'six feet apart or six feet under' rule that they had got so used to during the various stages of lockdown, and the fact that she knew she smelled like a mature gorgonzola.

Joanna frowned. 'She's not regained consciousness yet.'

'Oh, was it that bad?'

'To tell you the truth, I'm not sure. They're going to do some more tests on her today – a scan probably. She's being well looked after and she's in the best place. But what I'd really like is a key to the flat. I came up on the shuttle last night, been at the hospital, and now I really need to get a shower and some sleep. Her own keys are in her flat and the police still have the spare.'

'Oh, hang on.' Costello reached round to the key rack on the wall behind the door and flicked through them until she found the right one, suddenly reluctant to let it go. 'Here.' She handed the key to Joanna. 'Are you going to see her today?'

'Yes. Can you tell me where the nearest supermarket is?'

Costello told her, adding that her mother's freezer was always well stocked as there was no way she was going to starve during any global pandemic.

Joanna Craig did not flinch. There was not a flicker of humour anywhere in her face, and Costello thought that for somebody who had been in the hospital all night, her dark hair was sitting very neatly in its bob. Her neighbour's daughter gave her a piercing look, a glare that went on for a little too long and was a little too fierce, before she slowly took the key, gave a curt nod and crossed the landing to her mother's front door.

Costello closed the door of her own flat, then slumped behind it and threw her the finger. Maybe that's why Vera Craig kept so quiet about her daughter.

She was a monumental pain in the arse.

'Didn't think I'd see you again so soon.' The vet was cheery, wiping down his examination table. 'How were the family – you know, without Nesbit?'

'The girls don't know yet. They're on holiday and we didn't want to spoil it for them. I'm hoping that they'll not ask about him until they get back here. But I wanted you to look at this little lady.' He pointed at the terrier beside him who was simultaneously eyeing the vet suspiciously and wagging her tail. 'She may have been injured in a crime. She's called Norma.'

The vet ducked his head to look past Anderson's leg to the dog now sitting on his shoe. 'So what do we have here?'

'She's not mine, so we've no consent to treat her, but it's not treatment I'm after – it's an opinion. If you could have a look at her. Her owner is deceased and she's in my care temporarily.'

'Has this got to do with your job or mine?' asked the vet, indicating that Anderson should put the dog on the examination table.

'My job, I think. From all accounts, this is a very friendly wee dog.'

'A bit Border Terrier, bit Staffie and goodness knows what else from the look of her,' said the vet, patting Norma on the head.

'Well, she'll bite your hand off if you touch her round the neck. There's an injury there.'

'And you want me to get bitten instead of you?' joked the vet.

'Yes, and a guess at what caused those cuts.'

'I will give you my opinion, but for use in court you really need an expert.'

'But I need a reason to request an expert, because they cost money.'

The vet pulled a face. 'That's a bit arse for elbow.'

'Welcome to Police Scotland.'

The vet started to examine the dog, but not before pulling

one thick glove on to the hand that was nearest the sharp end. Norma wagged her tail happily, then slightly more cautiously as the vet's fingers neared her collar. Then the tail stopped and the upper lip retracted just enough to show her impressively sharp teeth.

'Hmm,' said the vet, finding something confirmatory of a hypothesis he had already formed. 'There's a bald spot here at the side of the neck, and' – he shone a torch with one hand as he separated the hair with the other – 'she has a semi-circular laceration on her neck here, and another here. They look very painful – there's a lot of inflammation around there and it's still quite swollen.'

'What docs that mean?'

'She's in a lot of pain. She's a brave wee lady. I've seen this before. Can I cut this collar off? You will need it as evidence. I can sell you a halter before you leave,' he joked. 'I know exactly what has happened to her.'

Anderson watched as the vet clipped through the leather band with a pair of very sharp surgical scissors. The dog relaxed immediately. Slowly, gradually, the vet massaged Norma with his strong fingers, starting at the top of the tail and working his way towards the shoulders, and then on to the front of the dog's throat, his eyes slightly closed in concentration, feeling for something deep within the tissues. Norma rolled her eyes at him, showing a few teeth but not attempting to snap.

'Someone has attempted to strangle this dog. You can feel the damage here all round the windpipe, and you can hear that she's a bit raspy. There's also a couple of cuts where the collar has been twisted, probably while she was suspended by it. It's nasty. There's still inflammation present, so I presume it happened in the last forty-eight hours or so.'

'What's your best guess? So I can tell our expert and he can agree with you.'

'Well, she could have been lifted up by something that was attached to her lead, or a stick was put through her collar like a garrotte, then she was suspended and the stick twisted. There are reports of folk doing this to be rid of dogs they don't want, stringing them up over the branch of a tree and then spinning the poor wee buggers so the noose gets tighter and tighter. A sad indictment of our society and the cruelty that walks among us. But I am sure that I don't need to tell you that.'

'No,' said Anderson quietly, looking at the pricked ears, the anticipation of a treat, all the previous insults now forgotten. 'Poor wee bugger.'

Costello had checked in to see if there were any further developments on Aasha before she left the flat. Nothing. The family liaison officer was still in situ. So she could be absent for a while.

Her own flat was on the north bank of the river, and she had decided that it might be a good idea to spend twenty minutes walking into the city, and then follow the most probable route that Anthony Poole had taken when he had left the Debut club with Aasha. The air in her flat had become foetid and unhealthy, almost diseased. She had her appointment at the Partickhill Annexe later; once trapped in there, she might never get away.

She wrapped herself up in her jacket and went down the stairs rather than use the lift. As she passed, she cast a glance at the front door of Mrs Craig's flat, which had taken on the personality of a brick wall.

Once she got to the riverfront, she stuck to the walkway, setting off for the Debut nightclub, a dark, run-down stinky place at this time of the day, harsh in the daylight, devoid of the hubbub of youngsters milling around outside and the deep bump of the bass from within.

Although the sun was out, the wind was still bitterly cold. It blasted right up the Clyde, making progress difficult for anybody out for a mind-clearing stroll along the riverside walkway. As she hurried along, Costello tried to get into Aasha's mindset. Her friends had admitted to a bit of recreational drug use but reported that Aasha never did. It was their first night out; they would have been excited. Aasha had been doing some frontline work during the crisis in an Essex hospital. She might have been very glad to be alive. Then a thought struck Costello. She had no doubt that hardcore substance abuse had continued over lockdown, but what if the recreational drug users had been denied their drug of choice for a few weeks and then, all of a sudden, it was there in front of them – a bit of booze, a bit of a dance, a wee snort here and there. Might they have over-indulged? Maybe their tolerance had decreased, and they had gone back to the usual weight of white line with fatal effect.

The post-mortem would tell.

Costello, the daughter of an alcoholic mother, didn't understand drug abuse and never tried too hard to get her head round it. She'd leave that to those who hadn't spent their childhood wiping up shit and vomit while dodging a left hook.

She had read some of the stuff Poole had posted on Facebook and Twitter, the racial angle on the situation gaining more traction with the Black Lives Matter campaign, but his friend Watson said Poole wasn't racist at all. It was just that he had a thing for Aasha. When Poole had posted that stuff, his chance to train as a doctor – a Scottish boy wanting to train at a Scottish university – had been taken away from him by English and foreign students. And no matter the plans he had for his dental career, he wasn't going to be a doctor, which was what his father had wanted. The post was written years ago now, but it was coming back, copied out of context, next to the picture of Aasha's face. The dead girl.

Warburton had made a televised statement asking for the speculation on social media to stop as it was not helpful to an ongoing enquiry. Costello wished him luck with that.

She walked on, getting to the nightclub within thirty minutes. She looked up and down Robertson Street, wondering what might have happened that night. They met on the stairs: Aasha going out, Poole on his way in. It was a warm night. Many people were still wary, and Debut was not crowded. Costello looked around at the amount of CCTV coverage in this street; all had been applied for and scrutinized. She walked on, knowing the route they had taken, and so she set the stopwatch on her phone, the direct route from here to the Squiggly Bridge.

Walking, following a path she could have walked in her sleep, her mind drifted back to Archie, her anger making her walk too fast if she was replicating the journey of a slightly tipsy twenty-something in heels. Was Poole in pursuit and Aasha trying to get away? The hunter and the hunted? Or had they walked quite happily, the post-lockdown chat about mutual friends once they were out of range of the loud music. She passed the West Car Park, the narrow access street where they had parted when Anthony said he needed a pee. Costello set her mind on Aasha saying goodbye to her companion. He said he had offered to run her home. Did she say no, she would get home on her own? But then why set off south, walking away from the city centre, the taxis, the buses – walking away from civilization? Anthony had left his car on the south side, but closer to Portland Street Suspension Bridge, so why walk to a bridge further downriver? He said he had been on Bud Light only, but made a point of getting drunk afterwards. Was there a reason for that? There were no independent witnesses. Costello paused, imagining the time it would take for Anthony to relieve himself and come back. The road was long and straight – surely he would have seen her if she had carried on? Hence his belief that she had hailed a taxi.

What if she had crossed the river?

She walked on, slowing her pace as she walked over the bridge, ignoring the black, undulating water below.

Her mobile went. She looked at the number and her heart fell a little. Well, it was now or later: Valerie Abernethy, Archie's goddaughter. This was going to be humiliating.

'Hi, Costello, how are you doing?'

It was there, that slight gushiness Valerie affected when she was sober, indicative of the fact that she wasn't really sure of her worth as a human being.

'I'm fine, Valerie. At work at the moment. That rush you can hear down the phone is the wind blowing up the Clyde.'

'Are you on the Aasha Ariti case?'

Valerie might be a recovering alcoholic, but she had been a very good lawyer when she was at the top of her game – she was sharp and Costello tended to forget that. She owed her life to that sharpness. Costello wished she could like her, that they could be friends.

'For the moment. I'm timing the route back from the nightclub so I need to—'

'I heard about what happened last night at the party.'

News travelled fast, especially the slightly salacious variety. 'Your godfather was a little odd.'

'I can't believe he'd do something so insensitive.'

'It wasn't insensitive; he had no idea I was going to be there.'

'Oh, he knew – he told me. I was hoping for some kind of reconciliation.'

'Really?' Costello kept her voice neutral. 'Well, that's more odd. And she looked so out of place, so she's not a cop or a lawyer or anything. She appeared quite shocked to see me. Do you know who she is?'

'Nope, but I heard she's very young. I think she's a paralegal,' said Valerie. 'I don't know what he's thinking. Well, I do, but he's not thinking with his brain. Bloody men.' She went off on her usual tangent, about how Costello had been such a good friend. To this day, Costello had no idea how Valerie Abernethy had ever got that impression. Helping lost causes for no good reason was Anderson's thing. Or maybe, in the mess that was Valerie's life, anybody who had not stabbed her in the back, or called her a useless drunken bint, was considered a good friend. Since the case they had worked on together had been solved, Valerie had tried to keep in contact with Costello. She was an unwelcome ghost ship trying to seek solace in any port she could. She was lonely. A soul without anchor. Costello leaned on the wall of the bridge, just saying yes or no every now and again, looking over the oily surface of the water as Valerie twittered on about a new project she was working on through her advocacy service, helping others because she couldn't bear to help herself.

Costello listened as she watched a man throw a ball for a fat Boxer. The dog disappeared from view into the long grass in the gardens of the riverside flats, then returned with the ball. She wondered how Anderson was getting on without Nesbit, if Pearcey's wiry wee dog would end up in that lovely house. She was walking to the corner, having followed the wall to the fence and on to the pavement and towards the gardens. Why would Aasha be here? Where was she going? Ahead, it was mostly warehouses, car showrooms and then the no-man's land to the motorway. If she had come this way, she would go into the complex of riverside apartments surely. Did she know somebody here? A friend? Costello walked round, crossing a small undeveloped plot of grass and fine rubble, still watching the dog, still listening to Valerie. The dog was there one minute, gone the next, and then he was pirouetting in the long grass, bounding out to his master. She watched, thinking about the grass between the flats and the riverside, the tall mature trees, fully in leaf, the windows that were supposed to afford the residents a riverside view. The dog was now rolling on the grass, as the owner was walking back to his flat in the far block, the one covered in scaffolding. She stood and looked. Something was not right. There was a break in the metal barrier between the grass and the drop to the water.

'Valerie, I'll need to call you back. Something has come up.' She cut the call and walked down to the barrier. A section had been removed, the section right on the turn, to allow access to some heavy lorries, judging by the tyre-tread indentations on the grass, some deep enough to cause muddy ruts. Were there also thin tracks? Drag marks?

Costello was sure she was walking the way Aasha had come. She could have come down here and fallen in. Or was she thrown into the water? It was the closest exposed part of the river. There was no fence to climb, and nobody overlooked this stretch. It had been dark that night, clammy with cloud cover. Had Anthony followed her this way to the secluded bit of greenery and planned his seduction? Had she objected?

Costello looked up at the flats – boxy, small windows, the bigger windows facing towards the water – then she looked around her. Anthony had been perfectly sober. It was only after he went back to the club that he had decided to get drunk and leave the car for another day. Or so he said. She cast her eyes along the hedging she had just passed on the other side, from there to the path to the green grass, where the dog had been, and walked closer to it.

Then she saw it: something red lying among the green – not at the edge, but a little way in, as if it had been thrown or kicked in. She knelt down and mentally called up the image of what Aasha had been wearing on that night in the club, before swiping through the pictures on her phone, looking for the picture that showed the victim's feet. There was one, she was sure. She found it: Aasha, her wine glass held out to the phone camera, her arm round her friend, her legs crossed, her left foot fully in view. Costello spread her fingers, zooming in on the red shoe, then looked into the hedge.

SEVEN

'I had wanted you to sort out a little situation for me. It was a bit delicate but now it is somewhat urgent. Events have caught up with us.' Detective Chief Superintendent (Crime Division) Jimmy Warburton, generally known as Toastie, eased his seventeen-stone bulk into his office chair and moved two piles of folders around on his desk in an attempt to see DCI Colin Anderson who was already occupying the opposite seat.

'I'm sure you have a whole department for seeing to delicate situations, sir. Do you want me to put some of that on the floor for you?' Anderson offered.

'Aye, dump it in the corner over there. Bloody paperless office. What a complete load of shite.' Warburton flashed Anderson a smile. It was the same smile that a double-glazing salesman gives those that have big windows and small budgets. Predatory. He was full of big-man bonhomie, but he was nobody's fool.

'I am presuming that you were going to take me off the Aasha Ariti case, but not now, surely. We have found the body, and I believe that Costello has made a breakthrough this morning. She has the forensics unit with her as we speak. We may have found the site where Aasha went into the river,' he added.

'Yes, she found a shoe. It matches the one the girl was wearing at the nightclub.' Warburton looked at his computer screen. 'A red shoe with kitten heels – whatever they are. So thanks to the good work by your team, Bannon now has a locus to investigate forensically. You are still off the case.' He rummaged around in the papers on his desk, barely paying him any attention.

Anderson knew that this was part of an act, an act to disarm and obfuscate. For all his chaotic appearance, Warburton was an extremely astute police officer. 'Why? Was there some complaint?'

'Oh, no suggestion of that. More the opposite – you are too good for the Aasha case, now that we know there is only one way it is going to go. I'll be blunt, Colin. We could be in trouble and we need an officer of your public reputation to front another investigation, especially with the situation with James Pearcey. Thank you for going out to that, by the way – great job.'

'His murder was very violent, very personal.' Anderson resisted the strong urge to place his hands on Warburton's and still them. 'So couldn't Bannon take Pearcey and I can continue with Aasha? It'll be problematic for Bannon to get up to speed so late in the day.'

'I see your train of thought, but we are playing to our strengths here. I've every confidence that Tony Bannon can cope with Aasha. He's taking over from the time the body was recovered. It looks like Anthony Poole did it. He followed the girl when she left the nightclub, they had an argument, and he thumped her and put her in the river – and maybe Costello now has further evidence that supports our working hypothesis. So until we find out anything that is contradictory, that idea will stand. There is nothing that contradicts that, is there?'

'Not yet.'

'And Poole has a racist agenda at times?'

'I've no evidence of such activity with regard to the victim,' said Anderson carefully. 'If anything, I'd say he was a bit fond of the girl. He's certainly not a far-right Britain First type of racist.'

'You have somebody trawling his social media accounts?'

'Of course.'

'Bannon needs to tread carefully.'

'Indeed.'

Warburton glanced up to see if Anderson was being sarcastic. Seeing nothing, he said, 'I'm sure he'll be glad of any advice you can give him and . . .' He was looking to move the conversation on.

'I was going to speak to the parents and—'

'Which would be nice, but I have explained the situation to the Aritis myself on your behalf. You've never met them, have you?'

'Well, no, but—'

'Good, so is Poole sticking to his story about the taxi?'

'He is. The last CCTV image looks as though she's walked away from him, and we've found no footage of him catching up with her, so maybe not so cut and dried.'

'Bannon is following every lead; he'll be fine. I think the PM has been scheduled for later today, or tomorrow if they are pushed.' Warburton took a deep and weary breath. 'However, you do have a reputation as being good in a delicate situation, and Pearcey is the more delicate matter of the two.' He stared Anderson straight in the eyes.

'Really?'

'Yes, it's not something that we want getting into the hands of the press or, God forbid, the mindless electronic witch-hunt that passes for social media. We need to head this off at the pass, so to speak.' He grimaced. 'So make me happy. Could you go and see these two ladies – one and then the other?' He held out a piece of printed A4 paper.

Anderson tried not to reach out and take it. 'I am really busy at the moment.'

'Consider yourself unbusy.'

'But I'm on the Pearcey case, so why am I doing this?'

'I think that there is a very close connection. You're heading down to Invernock again. You will speak to Mrs Lyonns and then Clarissa Fettercairn – yes, I know it's a mouthful. Lyonns is a pain, but Fettercairn is worse. See what she has to say and what she's going to do about it. And if she's going to do something about it, talk her out of doing it. Charm her out of taking any action and let her think it was her idea to do nothing after all.'

'Persuade a woman to change her mind while letting her think that she hasn't changed it?' asked Anderson sarcastically. 'I could cure cancer in my lunch hour before I go, sort out global warming before teatime . . .'

Warburton smiled. 'Look on the bright side: it gets you out of the office. One lady reads the *Daily Mail* and would shoot anybody who is unemployed, and the other is a journalist who hates the police.' Toastie waggled the paper to insist Anderson took it. 'Charm her.'

'Back to Invernock? Where James Pearcey lived?'

Warburton nodded meaningfully. 'Mrs Lyonns lives down near the marina. Call her. She's waiting by the phone. Arrange to meet her, tell her you'll have a Dan Brown book under your arm. She sounds the type who'd be impressed by that.'

Anderson didn't move. He had leaned forward to read the address on the piece of paper that now lay on the desk. He remained in his seat, forcing Warburton to explain.

'It's to do with the death last night. Well, we think it is. Somebody sent a threatening letter, then somebody died. The letter might have gone to the wrong house. It's a mess. You need to find out. I had you pencilled in for it before the murder took place.'

'OK,' Anderson nodded. 'So the murderer got to him first.'

'It would appear so.'

'So did the recipient come straight to us with the letter?'

'Via the press. That's your second visit. What were your first thoughts, Anderson? About Pearcey?'

'I don't like to judge. There are films to be examined. First impressions are that he was involved in paedophilia. I dropped his dog off at forensics to be photographed as she was injured in the assault. Possibly tortured – maybe that's how they gained entry.'

'Do you trust the team you have left at the locus?'

'I do indeed.'

'Good, let them get on with it. I want you, Costello and the other two . . .'

'Wyngate and Mulholland?'

'Yes, at a central point and stay there. Let the intelligence come to you. Now, what are we up against?' Warburton pointed at his computer. 'Well, just look at the news this week. A government minister has resigned because he didn't speak out about a rumour he heard once in 1978. That's the kind of world we live in now. Suspicion can be created where there is none, and this could become one great unholy mess, Anderson. Go and talk this woman down. Find out what the journalist is going to do about it.' He tapped the address with his fat fingertip. 'Then see if you can backtrack, find out who sent that letter, get hold of it for forensics. What does the writer know? Where did the letter come from? Where is the rumour coming from?

Who's spreading the shite? Is there any truth in it at all? Try to get to the source of it. Have a wee drive out to the seaside – the weather is going to be warm later. Have a blether with Mrs Lyonns with two Ns, then speak to Fettercairn. Report back to me with your thoughts, on my mobile, night or day. Give it priority.'

'Seriously?'

'I'm not going to be accused of providing you with prior knowledge that'll force you to fall foul of confirmation bias. You go, see what you come back with, then report to me. These two women have a story to tell you, and I want you to investigate what they say. And assess it in light of what happened at number nine, Hill Road.'

'OK,' said Anderson slowly.

Warburton leaned forward and took his glasses from his face, rubbing the bridge of his nose. 'Somebody is up my arse with a Dyson, Colin. Somebody upstairs wants this done.'

Anderson picked up the address. 'It's just that I am a DCI, usually an SIO, and this is more like babysitting. I'm not objecting, but it's the kind of hand-holding we have community uniform for.'

'Yes.' Warburton leaned back and swung his seat from side to side. He stared at the ceiling, narrowing his eyes at a spider's web that was dangling from the light shade. 'But we need charm for the lovely Mrs Lyonns who will stone anybody not British by four clear generations, and I need somebody with brains because I can't fathom out what's going on here. She'll appreciate a man of your rank – it'll make her feel she's being taken seriously. We are taking the "working together to achieve results" approach. And you will have the undying gratitude of Police Scotland.' He stopped swinging. 'Have a look at the swimming pool, have an ice cream – make a day of it. How's your wee boy doing? I heard he was poorly.'

'He's fine,' said Anderson. 'He's prone to chest infections, that's all.'

'Well. As soon as he's fit, get him down to that outdoor pool – that'll put hairs on his chest. Look what it did for me! Aye, take the day, sort it all out. Like I said, gratitude of Her Majesty's finest.'

'God, that will be a first.'

'Indeed, close the door on your way out.'

And Anderson did, his brain tumbling over the phrase 'look what it did for me'. So Jimmy 'Toastie' Warburton was familiar with the village – very familiar.

Detective Chief Super Warburton closed his eyes. He had endured that discussion twice – once with Bannon, once with Anderson – and neither of them had left his office happy.

When did Police Scotland become a kindergarten where he decided who played in the sandpit? He could sense DI Costello sticking her nose into both investigations already. But all three were experienced officers. They had the teamwork mindset; they'd work together.

He put his head in his hands and felt like weeping. A thirty-year career, spotless. He had suffered stress, as anybody did in the job nowadays, but to be threatened by a newspaper article that morning in that phone call from Fettercairn, and now a meeting he had to attend with media liaison to see what they wanted to do with it . . . He had put his best man on the job. That was all he could do. There was no way this could be kept quiet, and it should not be kept quiet. But why had it come to light now? He cursed under his breath, wondering, not for the first time in his career, exactly where journalists got their professional standards from. The sewers, from the look of it. The phone call may have been disguised as a request for information, but it was a threat. He had needed to pass it down to Data Protection; not to do so could lead to more suspicion later – maybe even accusations of a cover-up.

Colin Anderson was the man to deal with it. He was both charming and astute. And he didn't like journalists. Warburton thought that a woman like Clarissa Fettercairn might just bend a little to a man like Anderson – quiet, dependable, handsome, with a disabled child whom he adored. Anderson had a lot of good cards in his hand and would know how to play them, and as long as the journalist didn't dye her hair red and weep, the DCI would play those cards well.

He checked his emails. The archived files had been located and were being collated ready for delivery. He looked at his watch and then the email date stamp: the files would be on their way. He had requested all of them. Did it look too much? For completeness, he'd said. It would take a Transit van to transport the paperwork – all documentation, cartons of papers, files and evidence boxes and bags. He had been careful in his wording of the request, saying that DCI Anderson might be questioned by the press about this case, so he would appreciate all background material as well as the full files of the case in question, plus any other materials listed in the log, including those pertaining to any previous charges, arrests and convictions of the individual in question – the whole kit and caboodle.

All because, instead of calling the cops like any normal neighbour would do, this woman, a Mrs Doris Lyonns, had decided to call a journalist immediately because 'it's in the public interest and people have the right to know'. He could have rammed the phone down her throat when she said that. Then she bandied a few names around, threatening him with all kinds of exposure. He had scribbled the words *Fuck off* on his notepad, but kept his voice calm before volunteering one of his senior officers to speak to her. That placated her a little, so he pressed home his advantage by insisting that the meeting might be more productive if the detective was allowed to come up to speed with the original case in question as it was such a long time ago. Then maybe she and the detective could both come to it with fresh eyes. She wasn't happy, but she went off the phone saying that she'd hold off until she had spoken to DCI Anderson. The mention of his name and rank seemed to impress on her that they were taking her allegations seriously. Her allegations, which were merely a repeat of somebody else's allegations, more than forty years ago.

Birdie Summer.

It was all going to come back and bite him in the bum.

He leaned back, pulled off his glasses and started to rub his eyes. Why now? Why him?

Costello looked at her watch, fuming. She had carried out some good old-fashioned detective work, only to be rewarded by incarceration. It was one o'clock and she was stuck in the old annexe at Partickhill, slowly being covered in the dust that coated each tattered box of evidentiary material that entered the room. It was an older part of the building, with large rooms and huge windows that turned the place into a greenhouse. The fluorescent lights swung on heavy metal chains, and some of the grey floor tiles were stuck down with gaffa tape. A tall blackboard on wheels and a psychotic maths teacher at the front wouldn't have been out of place. She had already arranged a desk in each corner, a nod to social distancing while they choked on the dust.

At first, she had stood holding the door open for the two uniforms bringing the boxes in, then she got bored and lifted a blue cardboard file from the uppermost box. She pulled the elastic bands apart and saw the contents were handwritten. It looked like a diary. Before she could read it fully, her phone went. She stuck a box against the door to hold it open, and took her phone to the big ledge at the window and tossed the blue file into her handbag. She was hoping the call was a quick update from the guy at forensics, either about the dog collar or about the red shoe, as she really wanted the chance to put that in front of Anthony Poole and watch his face change. Had he thought the river would carry Aasha out to sea? Had he thought he'd get away with it?

But when she looked at her mobile screen, it was a number she didn't recognize. It was Joanna Craig who said that she was back at the hospital and that her mother was still unconscious. The brain scan had shown a minor bleed. She then asked Costello if she thought that anything had been taken from her mother's flat, if there had been anything stolen. Costello replied that she saw no sign of disturbance, and she'd had a quick check and all looked in place. Joanna replied, as quick as a flash, 'Yes, but somebody attacked my mother.' Then she said something else that Costello couldn't catch and was gone before she could ask her to repeat it. Costello stared at her mobile and swore quietly. Joanna's tone had suggested that, in some way, the bleed in the brain was Costello's fault. Maybe it was just Joanna, abrupt and a bit anti-social. She might be shy. At least she had called.

Costello felt rather odd waiting for the Pearcey case to come to her, like a chef waiting for the guests at the dinner party to arrive. Normally, Anderson had some idea what was going on, but she had heard nothing from him except for a swift rant about a wild goose chase. He had been assured, in a roundabout kind of way, that both Pearcey and Mrs Lyonns, whom he was going back to Invernock to meet, were both part of the same case, but he didn't sound convinced. So she called him, impatient to get on.

'So you are saying there was a threatening letter and then he was killed? Did the threat say something about his predilection for little girls?'

'Don't know yet, but Mr James Pearcey has never been convicted of anything that involved a child. Absolutely nothing. But not convicted doesn't mean he didn't do anything. It's not the same thing, Costello.'

'So is it all connected?' She tapped the side of one of the newer-looking boxes. 'The most recent paperwork coming through the door is a review from DCI Arthur Kelly in 2010.'

'Review of what?'

'Operation Pavo?'

'Never heard of it.'

'I've searched the computer archive and I need to call in, so it's hush-hush. Do you smell a Savile situation?'

'Who knows, but that whole murder scene was about something. I'm reporting back to Toastie Warburton after today, and then he'll see how he wants to take it forward.'

'All these boxes are historical, though. I keep thinking about all those Radio One DJs,' muttered Costello. 'They can hardly show any old episodes of *Top of the Pops* . . .'

Anderson's phone went quiet as he drove under a bridge somewhere, then his voice returned. 'So if we take what Pearcey appeared to be watching at its most criminal interpretation, I suspect there have been allegations, reviews, etcetera, and now it will all be coming back to us, especially if the evidence points to him still being active as the other investigations have floated by him, leaving him untouched.'

'Does that sound like a cover-up in a high place? And Warburton suspects it?'

'Oh, please, no.'

'If it is, they'd put a small close unit like ours on it. And it fits the amount of stuff that's coming into this room.'

'I suspect there'll be more by the end of the day. I'll call in once I've some specific questions for Warburton and maybe get a straight answer out of him.'

The silence that followed showed they both knew that was not going to happen. 'Anyway, the background report for Dennis MacMillan will be in your inbox now in case you are bored.' He hung up before he could catch the full range of her swearing.

She sat down at the open window, opened her tablet, still pointing to where she wanted the boxes stacked, while she tried to concentrate on the report. It was much as she thought. Dennis MacMillan was squeaky clean; in fact, he was as clean as a human being could get. He was fifty years old, born in Helensburgh, happily married to Maria for twenty-eight years, with a daughter, Sarah, and a grandchild, Sophie. He had worked in retail, selling furniture for a big department store, the same company for thirty years, before retiring early with a mild heart complaint. Maria also took early retirement as a school cleaner in 2018 when they moved to Invernock, where she had grown up. There were no police reports of any abuse. Their daughter checked out with no issues, no visits to hospital; she had attracted no attention from social services.

Costello wondered if the heart condition would render him incapable of fighting with an eighty-one-year-old man, or whether he would have needed to nail him down first. Nicholson's enquires round the village portrayed a cheery wee man, who cut the grass at the church and did odd jobs around the village – he'd help anybody out in a crisis. And why not? He was retired and his family were four hundred miles away.

It was much as she thought. MacMillan went up the ladder because he was looking for his friend. Costello closed the document and looked around. The cartons and boxes were stacking up like the Berlin Wall. The room was starting to smell. It would take ages to go through these. The door opened further and DC Gordon Wyngate appeared from behind the barricade, almost knocking it over. He nodded a greeting to Costello and threw his jacket into the corner in a fit of temper. 'I've just been to the hospital. I don't think much of that Craig woman. What a cow.'

'Ahh, she's just called me. I think it's all a bit inconvenient for her. How is Vera? A brain bleed, I heard.'

Wyngate shook his head, looking like a puppy that had been left out in the rain. 'No change at all. She looks so tiny lying there, just like my mum before she died. They become diminished somehow, lying in a hospital bed.'

She waited to see if he was going to talk about his mum, recently deceased. She knew nothing about his parents. For all the years she had worked with them, she had known all about Mulholland's bossy Russian mother, but had known only of Wyngate's wife and kids – nothing about his mum except that she had had him late in life and was then widowed. It might explain a lot about his kind nature, the ease with which he dealt with the vulnerable.

'There are a couple of injuries to her head, so she may have been hit with something. But, boss' – he hesitated while he looked for another window to open – 'the daughter, she asked a strange thing. She asked me if I was in that flat on my own?'

'She phoned me to ask if there was anything missing, although how would she know? I don't think she's ever visited her mother there.'

Wyngate's face looked troubled.

'You weren't, were you? You were there with me and then with Plod and Knobby.'

'Then she asked if you were in the flat on your own at any time.'

'Why?'

'I don't know. I said I wasn't there for the entire course of events, so I wouldn't know. Not sure what she was getting at, and not sure if she liked my answer. I mean, Howie and Follet were around, but I'm not sure they followed me in. I know they should have . . .' Wyngate leaned against the desk, then looked at the piles of boxes, as if seeing them for the first time. 'She wants to meet me at the flat to discuss her complaint. But, as you say, how would she know? Her mum hasn't regained consciousness to tell her anything.'

'And Follet and Howie – Plod and Knobby – were on their own, waiting for you to arrive. I don't even want to think about that. Maybe in the past, Vera has been feeding her a line about what was in the flat. Who knows? Anyway, we need to get a start here . . .'

'What is it all? It's a hell of a lot of stuff.'

'It's documentation for something that we don't know about. Some of this goes back to 1973 and before.'

'Isn't this for a cold case unit?' asked Wyngate. 'Or can we not afford one of them since we left the EU?' He peered over a box, wiping dust from the label with his sleeve.

'This evidence refers to a case listed as solved, so it might be up here by mistake. I'm not sure what our remit is. We might be better waiting for Anderson to come back.'

'Where is he?'

'Finding out what is going on, I expect.' More boxes were carried in. These looked as though they had been in deeper storage and were followed by a mushroom cloud of dust and the scent of damp paper. 'So where do you want to work?'

Wyngate was about to answer when one of the uniforms said, 'Some folk will do anything to avoid giving us a hand.' The voice from behind the box stuck a foot out, holding the door for DS Vik Mulholland who was following them in, dressed in a beautiful suit, cut neatly into his shoulders, the male model effect rather spoiled by the stick and the bad limp.

'Is the old war wound still bothering you?' asked Costello.

'It's bloody sore.' He flopped on to the nearest seat, leaning his stick against the stack of stained beige boxes.

'Did that last op not fix it?' Costello, noting the code number on the box and moving it into a corner.

Mulholland rolled his blue eyes. 'Nope. Hence the stick. If anything, I think it's worse.'

'Can your girlfriend not amputate it for you?' She regarded him. In his youth, he had looked like Johnny Depp, and he was aging just as badly.

'She's in Dorset or somewhere. Might get home soon now the hospitals are getting back to normal. So here I am once again, stuck to a desk as your IT man. And don't think for a moment that I am helping you move any of this about.'

'Well, you could help by not getting in the way,' said Costello. 'Sit over there.'

'I'm not good walking around,' said Mulholland.

'Yes, I noticed that a long time before you buggered your leg.' She hushed her voice as more and more boxes came in, stacked three high on trolleys, one of the uniforms muttering that he hadn't signed up to be a porter. Costello told him to think of the service he was doing for the community. 'DC Wyngate here has been out heading up an entire investigation, probably a violent crime that led to grievous bodily, all on his own, and here you are, DS Mulholland, incapable of sitting on a seat without moaning.'

'So we are no longer working with Aasha Ariti?'

'Nope.' She brought him up to speed on the discovery of the shoe while handing him a laptop. 'Can you kneel down and plug that in over there? Oh, you can't, can you?'

EIGHT

Doris Lyonns sat on a bench on a grassy knoll overlooking the marina. The light smattering of sunshine and the windchime ching of the wires on the yachts did nothing to lighten the glower on her face. She was a thin, bony woman who looked as if she never warmed up, her small dark eyes permanently narrowed behind her glasses. The lines on her face were evidence that she rarely smiled. She said she'd be wearing a green coat, but Anderson had pencilled in the grim expression for himself. Her preference to meet at a bench on the seafront was due to her 'not wanting that kind of thing in my home'. Her face said that she was not going to be trifled with. There was something about the downward set of her mouth, the arch of her left eyebrow, the rod-straight back, the feet crossed at the ankle that reminded him of the Queen in a foul mood. On closer inspection, she had a black velvet band in her grey hair, something that made Anderson very suspicious in anyone over four years of age. She wasn't exactly hard to identify. He approached cautiously, introducing himself with his name and rank. She responded with a regal nod of the head. As she almost stood up and performed an undignified shuffle

along the bench, allowing him to sit while maintaining some
distance, he wondered if she had some mental health issues,
teetering from eccentric to something more medical.

'We never knew.' She thrust the envelope towards his face.
'I never knew and I think people should know.' She snapped
her lips closed after the last 'know'. He tried to place the accent
and settled on Welsh or somewhere near the Welsh border. 'So
after I spoke to Williamson, I got straight on to the papers.
There's a campaigning journalist – she said she had already
spoken to the police about this. It's bad enough when it all
comes out after they die, but what about catching them right
here and right now, these child abusers? Too much of this kind
of stuff going on, and too many of your kind are happy to close
their eyes and let it happen. So I am making myself clear: if
this is not acted on by the police, then the papers will go
with it.'

Anderson nodded, trying to keep up. Had she meant
Warburton when she said 'Williamson'? 'Let's just start at the
beginning.' It was always a good line when the witness liked
to get a rant in. 'So, hand-delivered?' he asked, studying the
plain brown envelope unmarked by any address.

'Yes, hand-delivered – and don't tell me that there wasn't
anything in it, because we saw the police cars go up the hill
last night. That' – she pointed at the letter – 'came through the
door sometime Monday night or Tuesday morning. It was lying
on the mat first thing. People have a right to know. There are
children in the street. There's a play park up there where he
lives. It's disgusting.' She pulled a face as if a wasp was trying
to get up her nostril.

'So that was delivered Monday into Tuesday? You must have
got off the mark early to get this in front of a journalist.'

'She's on the internet. ForgottenVictims,' she said, as if that
explained everything. 'I'm not sure the first police officer took
me seriously, but then Williamson called me back, but only
because I had said I was going to the papers . . . that's the
only reason he took me seriously and got you to come out here.'

'So there was a journalist already working on this story and
you got in touch with her before you spoke to anybody?'

'Well' – she tapped the letter – 'she's not the only one.

Somebody else knows, somebody knows . . .' She nodded, nudging her forefinger at the letter again as if flicking a fly from it.

He pulled his hands into gloves and opened the envelope. There was a single A4 sheet, plain white paper. He kept it balanced on his fingertips, steadying it in the cold breeze, wondering how many people had touched it before him.

'"Expect death soon, you paedo bastard, I know where you are,"' he read out, his throat going dry, realizing what Warburton had been getting at. Somebody had indeed got to Pearcey first.

'It's not for us, and not for my daughter. So do you know who it refers to, DI Anderson?'

He didn't answer her.

'I think that journalist does. Exactly. She knows.'

'Mrs Lyonns, we have a whole department that deals with this kind of stuff, and in this case, which I confess I am new to, I suspect the person in question has already been subject to review and nothing was found.'

'So it was a cover-up.'

'It's not likely. It's more likely to be malicious rumour.'

'If it has been investigated, then why are you investigating it again?'

'I'm investigating the source of the rumour. I want the person who sent this to you.'

She opened her mouth, her eyes narrowed in outrage. She looked like a viper.

'The person who sent this' – it was his turn to tap at the letter – 'might be in possession of knowledge that they're not giving us. Or they are just muckraking and upsetting people, including yourself, and wasting police time. It's incredibly dangerous.' *And it may already have proved to be so*, he thought. 'So my first question has to be: Can I send an officer round to take the fingerprints of everybody who has touched this letter? And my second is: Why was this letter put through your door? I need to establish that somebody in your house could not be – incorrectly, of course – targeted by this kind of thing, Mrs Lyonns. You wouldn't want anybody thinking that your family was involved in this.'

'Of course not.'

'And the residents of number nine may feel exactly the same way.'

She snapped at him. 'We live at number nine.'

'Do you now?' He allowed the inflection to invite a response.

'Number nine, Hill Avenue.'

'Not Hill Road.'

'No, that's our house just over there.' She pointed to a large sprawling bungalow that looked sterile. Anderson recognized it – it was very close to where he had walked with Norma. Mrs Lyonns lived within a few houses of Dennis MacMillan.

'We know most people, but nobody knows the man who lives at number nine, Hill Road – that's the odd house on the street, the only other bungalow in the village. That's where the police cars were last night. Nobody lives up there, except that tall man and his stupid wee dog. So we worked out for ourselves that the letter is for him. Why is he walking the streets? Nobody was going to phone me unless we sorted it . . .'

'Mrs Lyonns, despite talking to the Chief Super and getting his assurances that we would do something, you still spoke to the journalist, to Clarissa Fettercairn. Why? Surely you can see how that would inflame a delicate situation.'

'It is my right.'

'The man at number nine may be innocent.'

Mrs Lyonns snorted.

'You've heard about the girl's body we pulled out of the water yesterday, not a couple of miles down the coast from here?'

'The Asian girl? Yes, well, I suppose you will be falling over yourselves with that one.' Her dismissal was palpable. 'It's all over the papers. I've been threatened by a letter and I want something done.'

'It's being done.' Anderson let her enjoy her inhalation of deep disgust while glancing at his watch.

She spluttered to her story again. 'So my husband did some more research on the computer and we found Miss Fettercairn. At least she listened, she got the ball moving. And you are trying to hush it up in case we inflame the situation?'

Anderson looked out to sea, thinking about Aasha Ariti and what she went through in the last few moments of her life. From here, he could see the stretch of water where they had found her in the small hours that dark windy morning. So young, such a promising life snatched away. And he had been dragged off that, for this.

He wanted to smack Doris in the pursed, self-righteous mouth. Instead, he asked her just how well she knew Dennis MacMillan.

Anderson felt as if he needed some fresh air after sitting on the same bench as Doris Lyonns, so he let her march back to her house and waited, watching the yachts nodding in the marina, listening to their tinny chatter. He checked his mobile phone, made a few calls and walked up to Dennis MacMillan's house, two beyond Mrs Lyonns' bungalow. He then carried on the path approaching the Pearcey house, taking the same route that he had walked the afternoon before. Ruskin, the crime scene manager from Greenock, was a competent officer, and Anderson always believed that good people didn't need looking after. Ruskin and McQueen had the scene under control, and the local investigation was being run by DS Robbie Ross, with Nicholson and Donnelly doing most of the leg work. He knew the plan had been to talk about a 'violent incident' and to keep it that way for as long as possible until any next of kin could be informed, but next of kin were proving very difficult to track, which in itself was interesting. Warburton had wanted to be kept in the loop, which suggested to Anderson that there was a connection with the case further back in his career – something, or somebody, Toastie had not quite let go.

He kept his eye on his watch, not wanting to be late for Clarissa Fettercairn. He could see what Warburton was worried about. If they were seen to not play along in any way at all, Fettercairn would suspect they were stalling, part of a cover-up. It was better to be transparent, which was a laugh seeing as Anderson himself was being kept in the dark.

But somebody else knew. Somebody had delivered that note to number nine. Could they have got it wrong? Delivered to one address and then killed in another? The two incidents had happened in a matter of hours. Still, it was difficult to retrieve a letter once it had gone through a letterbox.

The police activity was all inside the house. Outside, there were only a few unmarked cars.

As he walked to number nine, he noticed that Doris Lyonns was correct: there were only two bungalows in the village. He continued up the old tarmac path, through the gate in the high hedge, and guessed that the neighbours knew very little about the comings and goings of Mr Pearcey. Until now.

He felt his heart sink. No wonder Warburton wanted to keep this all quiet. And who the hell had given the green light to a suspected paedophile to live where there was a play area in full view? The lack of information about James Pearcey was starting to suggest that there was an official ring-fence around him. Fettercairn might be on to the truth. At the moment, the play park was closed off by yellow tape. Chains locked the steps of the chute, the climbing frame and the seesaw. It looked sinister, but it was in the line of sight of Pearcey's favourite chair. If Mrs Lyonns and her journalist friend got their way, they could be on the brink of vigilantism, mob violence and ritual castration.

He spoke to Nicholson about the door-to-door. He said he'd send in a report later but there was nothing much – the usual dog walkers, various sightings of a white car that somebody thought belonged to the district nurse, and a dark-blue or black car driving around the lower part of the estate, generally thought to be looking for the way out to the motorway, on or around six p.m. The neighbours didn't see anything, didn't hear anything at the house. The attention was sparked by Dennis MacMillan not being able to gain access. Up until that point, nobody had noticed a thing.

The back garden was very old-fashioned. A back green, as Anderson's mother would have called it – a flat patch of grass with a metal pole in each corner for the washing line. Two garden chairs were still out, exactly two metres apart, waiting. He stood outside: silence and birdsong, a fence, fields, trees, easy access to the property by somebody who was fit.

Returning to the house, he confirmed that the cine film reels had been parcelled up and were on their way to Partickhill. He looked in the spare bedroom and walked over to the desk that appeared to have been searched already. He flicked through the pile of documents and found some old photographs, wrapped in folded paper, waisted by the indentation of an elastic band. They had been bound together until very recently. He looked through the photographs – old, faded, the colour bleeding. Then he asked the crime scene officer to put them in with the evidence, signing for one himself, which he placed in a small evidence bag and slipped into his jacket pocket. He was sure it was Pearcey in his younger days – one of three men in their early twenties, dressed for the dance halls of the early 1960s. He wondered idly if Jimmy Pearcey had been gay. He didn't appear to have been married – no wedding ring, although that was usual in a man of his age, no wedding pictures, a few pictures of a family group, the same three young men with combinations of five children. He couldn't say if any of those kids was the one in the film, the child the film was paused on. He wasn't looking forward to finding out.

He saw a black suit hanging outside the wardrobe, a padded wooden hanger latched into the wardrobe handle. Had Pearcey been getting ready for a funeral? Maybe somebody close had died, but lockdown had meant he couldn't go. It might be useful to find out whose funeral he had planned to attend. He poked around in the main bedroom. A new Bible. He flicked through the thin papery pages, the red ribbon marked Leviticus 18:22 in the cramped text. He read a few words – the bit about not lying down with a man as you do with a woman. Interesting.

Anderson wondered if he might have liked Jimmy Pearcey, or the face that Jimmy Pearcey put out to the world. If he turned out to be an innocent man, which he doubted – but *if* he did – and his secret was being gay, how difficult would that have been? Growing up in the west of Scotland, industrial Clydeside? He thought about the picture of the three men; something about them intrigued him. Brothers? Something else? He had no doubt, way back in the day, that gay people, like any persecuted minority, found each other. They had their own covert way of bonding as people do in a society that rejects them.

Anderson took his seat first on the big easy chair next to the window, confirming that from here Pearcey could easily see the swing park. And the kiddies.

It had been a terrible way to die. The law should be allowed to run its course. What if the law had let somebody down, and that person was now hitting back in the worst possible way? If Jimmy Pearcey had been a monstrous paedophile with the fortune not to be caught, then maybe he just deserved what he got; being old was not exculpatory. Pearcey was keeping under the radar. He was cut off from all family and friends. Anderson needed to track down that funeral – perhaps it was a connection between this life and Pearcey's previous life. Maybe he had become genuinely wary of opening his front door. Then lock-down had forced him to ask for help from the local church. No relatives, just the church.

Anderson's phone rang. It was Costello.

'Yes, I know I said I would be back, but I decided to come up to the house and have a walk around now that it's quiet. What do you want?'

'Just checking the details of the deceased. James Andrew Pearcey, date of birth thirty-first January 1939. Nine Hill Road, Invernock.'

'Yes, I think so. It should be on the documentation that Nicholson sent over last night. Do you not have that?'

'Oh, yes. I have *that*,' she said with the emphasis on the last word. 'The problem is that James Andrew Pearcey does not exist.'

Peggy Jane's was a popular roadside diner just beyond Glasgow, heading east. It had been chosen by Clarissa Fettercairn as a good place to meet. The sun had been in Anderson's eyes for most of the journey, yet there was still a cutting chill in the air that the weak summer sun had failed to warm. He had been driving for an hour, trying to think about the case and why Pearcey was in receipt of a new identity, but his mind kept drifting back to Nesbit and the huge dog-shaped hole in his heart. He hoped Norma was OK, feeling better on her drugs, and that she was being looked after while her wounds were being photographed and measured. Was the killer forensically aware? Or were they appearing to wear a mask and gloves for legitimate reasons? He thought it would be beautiful justice if Norma held the forensic key that solved the case, a trace of material left when they had slipped their gloves off to torture her.

Then, for some reason – maybe because of Aasha and the river, or the dismissive tone of Doris Lyonns – he thought of the wee girl he had tried to save, ten, fifteen years ago. The girl who had been tied on to the ladder in the docks at the Clyde and left to drown with the incoming tide. And yes, there was a connection there: the ladder was a hundred yards or so from where Costello had found the shoe. A lot of water had flowed down the river since then; the banks of the Clyde had undergone huge regeneration in the intervening years. He wondered what Aasha's last moments had been like. He hoped a smack on the head had knocked her out and she had known nothing of the watery grave that awaited her.

He longed to still be the man who would pursue the shit who did that. He wanted to be the man who would chase down the perpetrators of child abuse, no matter how historic, so he needed to listen to this journalist and take on board what she had to say. He needed to rise to that challenge, and it concerned him slightly that he was not up for it, not now. Was he too old, or was it that he suspected everybody had an agenda? Costello had Pearcey marked as a predator. But he had been given a new identity. Had he been a whistle-blower? He had a nice dog. But even Hitler loved his dog, as Costello was fond of telling him.

And here Anderson was, wasting time to sate the appetite of a journalist who would never have her appetite sated. It was the nature of the beast. But she wanted to talk, and he needed to listen. If she had information, he might have a go at her for obstruction. It was all a game of chess.

From her picture, she looked like the sort of woman who didn't like dogs.

Or if she did like dogs, she would keep them in her handbag.

Clarissa Fettercairn turned out to be a broad-shouldered, tall woman with shiny brown hair and a camel-coloured linen jacket that she wore with black trousers and low-heeled court shoes. She looked posh, too clean for most of the journalists he had known. She had the demeanour of a lifestyle editor for a magazine except for the fierceness burning in her eyes.

'DI Anderson?' she asked, sitting down opposite him.

'DCI Anderson, just so you can get your facts right, you being a journalist. What can I do for you?'

'I want to know what you are doing about yet more accusations of paedophile activity around Invernock.'

'Yet *more*? We don't know of *any*. All we have is a threatening letter to an innocent party. People can get hurt by that. Very hurt.'

She leaned forward. 'Innocent? You see, I have something.'

'You should have brought it to the attention of the police, then.'

'I think it rather stems from you lot – the forces of law and order.'

'*Services* of law and order,' he corrected. 'We do not force anything.'

She smiled rather slyly, but her eyes began to twinkle. 'I doubt that if I gave it to you, you'd be allowed to do anything with it.'

Anderson wondered how many men had been sidetracked by that smile. 'Try me,' he challenged.

'Of course, I don't go into battle without a few aces up my sleeve. The Chief Procurator Fiscal of Glasgow has a few options when he decides to move a case forward. And sometimes he may talk out of turn.'

Anderson felt his stomach contract. If this was going back to Costello, they were dead in the water. But he couldn't see it. 'While he is one man, he is actually fronting a whole office.'

'Maybe I misspoke? What if his options are perhaps contrary to the public account?'

'And he confided this in you, did he? Not through the proper media channels.'

'Of course, he should have. Mr Archie Walker knows better, but he was talking off the record – which was a mistake. Then he made a bigger mistake of scorning his friend. So she came to me as she thought that this may be of public interest.'

'Of course. Did you pay her for being so public-spirited?'

Fettercairn ignored him. 'It's a very interesting story about the lack of movement on a historic child abuse case. It's the fiscal's office who decide when and where to proceed with a prosecution, and Archibald Walker has decided not to proceed.'

'Then he doesn't have the evidence or he doesn't think that it's in the public interest to proceed.'

'Is that a quote, Mr Anderson?' That smile again.

'Not until I have all the facts rather than just gossip and hearsay, but that is what I would interpret from what you are saying. You could, of course, ask Mr Walker himself.'

She sighed resentfully. 'The public have had enough of historic child abuse not being chased down. And if the police will do nothing, and I feel it is in the interest of the public, then it leaves me no option but to publish the story. And if this goes as far as I think it goes – i.e. all the way to the top – then I think I will get a book out of it.'

'So who is Deep Throat?'

'I beg your pardon?' She looked genuinely confused, even a little shocked as if he had made some sexual reference.

'Go and watch *All the President's Men*, see how decent investigative journalists do their jobs, instead of just repeating what they are told.'

The easy smile was back. 'Well, I am talking to you. I am trying to establish the facts, but you are not giving me any.'

'There are no facts to give.'

'There's no smoke without fire.'

'To be technical about it, there can be lots of smoke without fire.'

'What happened in Invernock? A letter arrived and then a violent incident?'

He could tell she was fishing. 'I was trying to establish that before I came here.'

'And what are you doing about it?'

'Nothing – I am sitting here talking to you. So we are agreed that this is not the best use of my time?'

'I have a source that says paedophile activity in Invernock is being tolerated.' She gave a creepy little nod. 'Maybe by somebody in the procurator's office.'

So Clarissa knew something. Was that why Toastie was making him take two hours out of his busy life to talk to this woman?

He waited to see if she was going to add anything, but she didn't.

'Do your sources have a professional relationship with Mr Walker?'

Clarissa thought for a moment, playing with her spoon, then nodded slightly. 'Not altogether professional. He is, as you said, perfectly entitled to seek out female company. He's a fiscal, not a monk.'

'Do you not think that Mrs Lyonns was very quick off the mark?'

Again nothing.

'And that there may be a reason why she behaved in the way she did?'

'Are you suggesting that she might be sensitive to this? Do you think she has to be a victim to do her civic duty?' The anger fired the amber flecks in her eyes.

'Do you think of Mrs Lyonns as a victim?' he asked quietly. She had given herself away, and just for a second it crossed his mind that Fettercairn may be a victim too. All that polish was a cover. There was something unresolved, and she was angry, still angry.

'We must all be careful to be neutral in the way we look at things. I have two children, Miss Fettercairn, and I can't let that affect the way that I deal with a case like this.'

'Maybe you would be a more efficient police officer if you did let it affect you.'

'I beg to differ on that one. You should stay away from situations where you have emotional involvement . . . Clarissa.'

That hit home. She leaned forward, chin first, forcing Anderson to lean back. 'I need a quote about the approach of your unit to the allegations of a historical paedophile ring in Invernock.'

'It's under investigation, so I cannot comment on it at this delicate stage.'

'Can we expect an arrest or a statement soon?'

'I am not at liberty to say.'

'So the same wall of silence that went up then is still in place today. How many times has this case been reviewed?'

'I am carrying out a review of all documentation to see if there is any pertinence to current events.'

She reached for her handbag. 'Well, that's exactly what I

thought you were going to say. It's been a bit of a waste of time really.'

That was the first truly honest thing she'd said.

NINE

t was half past six when Colin Anderson walked into the annexe at Partickhill Station, still furious, still swearing. 'She really was an awful piece of work.'

'Who?'

'The lovely Clarissa Fettercairn.' He looked around him at the files and boxes piled high. 'What the hell is all this?'

'I did warn you. It's a biohazard – the dust of those boxes is sticking in my throat. This is the evidentiary material mountain.'

He looked over to see Vik Mulholland sitting, his trousers protected by a black bin liner, wiping the tops of boxes with a mild solution of bleach. 'This is the evidentiary material mountain' – he mocked Costello's accent – 'for a case that, as yet, I can't find the index for. And this is all they could fit in the van.'

'And it was a Boxer van, not a Transit. You should have seen the guys try to get them up the stairs,' said Wyngate from underneath a desk, holding on to two power cables.

Costello was trying to be efficient with a clipboard and failing. 'Some of it's recent. From the labels, there're boxes from three different investigations.' She pointed at a leaning stack of old cardboard boxes full of faded and curling documents. 'Some have electronic back-up – that's the paperwork relating to an Operation Pavo. I found this online.' She turned round her screen: a picture of three men in good suits posing on a dance floor.

'Let me see.' Anderson looked at it carefully. 'Snap. I found this photo of those three guys at number nine.' He pulled the photo from his pocket.

'Where somebody who wasn't called Jimmy Pearcey was

living,' added Costello. 'Ross is sending more evidence from
the scene. Let's get that picture blown up, then make a start on
this Pavo thing. We need to get this all organized in some way
or we're going to spend all our time just looking for stuff.'

'Who is it all about?' asked Anderson, leaning against the
desk, suddenly tired.

Costello held the photograph up. 'These three men. Douglas
McSween, Eddie Dukes and Frankie Scanlon. Are we thinking
that this' – she flicked the photograph with her finger, indicating
the tallest of the three – 'is Jimmy Pearcey, known as Eddie
Dukes? Both have that Michael Heseltine hairline.'

'Eddie Dukes? Dukes? That name means something to me.
Edward Dukes?' Anderson let his mind run around his memory.
'The word that comes to my mind with the name Eddie Dukes
is "murder". Not "paedophile".'

Mulholland coughed and stopped wiping, then said,
'The latter might be because of what you saw yesterday. Your
confirmation bias going into overdrive.'

'We'll wait for confirmation of our bias before we go too
far. If he's on a protection programme, some suit will call us
soon enough with an ID.'

Costello flicked her pen at the labelling on the boxes. 'So
these are all to do with the Dukes case. He killed the wife of
one of his friends – this bloke here actually' – she tapped
at one of the other figures in the picture – 'and did jail time for
it. That was in 1978. All that paperwork is here, but it's solved,
so I don't think we need to look at it. This stuff here' – she
waved her pen again – 'is the 2010 review of some paedophile
accusations that mention Edward Dukes, who we think is James
Pearcey, plus the two other guys. Operation Pavo.'

'The Peacocks?'

'Indeed. We can stack these boxes over there, in the hope
that we never need to open them. Which desk would be easier
for you, Mulholland? Once you get working, you need room
to stick your leg out. We don't want you toppling over and
breaking your neck.'

Anderson started moving boxes around. 'So where are we
with getting a correct ID for Pearcey at that address?'

'I did call the number the trace referred me to. I'm awaiting

a call back. Witness protection? Or general protection or . . .'
She turned to see Toastie Warburton blocking the light as he
stood in the doorway.

Warburton raised an eyebrow. 'So you've got that far already.
You're correct, DI Costello.'

'She normally is,' muttered Mulholland under his breath.

'Eddie Dukes is the man you know as Jimmy Pearcey. He
was jailed for a very regrettable murder – just a spur-of-the-
moment, flash-of-temper, "belt you in the face and goodnight
Vienna" type of murder. Not a stalking, basement, gaffa-tape
and bin-bag-of-body-parts type of thing that they get up to
nowadays because they have seen it on Channel Five.' He moved
into the room and sat down, making himself at home, causing
Anderson and Costello to exchange glances. The seat creaked
under his weight, and the podgy fingers reached out across his
immense stomach, his eyes casting over the photograph of the
Peacocks on the wall. He didn't need to ask who they were.
'Yet the word that came to your mind at the scene was "paedophile", not "murder". What the general populous today regard
as worse than stabbing a kid through the neck.'

'Surely not,' said Anderson.

'You still have remarkable faith after talking to Lyonns and
Fettercairn,' he sighed. 'Some of them surely do. But somebody
out there has conducted a long campaign of hatred towards
Eddie Dukes – you will see from the records how often that
man has been driven from his home. Yesterday, that campaign
came to a dreadful full stop. But I repeat: there is not and never
has been any evidence of inappropriate activity by Eddie Dukes,
or any of the Peacocks, towards any child. Ever.'

Mulholland was staring hard at Warburton, looking for
answers, or maybe trying to think of the right question.

'Could the manner of Dukes' murder be linked to the murder
he committed? I think that some folk might take the violent
death of a loved one a tad personally,' suggested Anderson.

Warburton gave an ironic smile. 'Funnily enough, Anderson,
that did cross my mind. A few of the grey cells are still func-
tioning, but I doubt that's the whole story here. I repeat: there's
no evidence, then or now, that he was ever involved in anything
that involved children. Well, not any evidence that we have ever

found. But that does not stop these dangerous and insidious rumours. That was the reason he got a new identity. And then this Lyonns woman gets a letter, not intended for her, and she maintains it's about the deceased. She'll not let up until she knows what you are going to do about it.'

'So tell her there's nothing in it,' said Costello impatiently.

'She wouldn't believe it. And Dukes was a free man who has the right to live without fear, I suppose,' offered Wyngate.

Anderson said, 'But thinking about it, the best way to whip up righteous anger is to send the letter to the wrong address. I thought the wrong letterbox thing might have been deliberate, but it's interesting that the letter was delivered during the night, and Eddie was probably killed at some point later that night. So either they knew the right address all along or they found it in the hours of darkness.' Anderson looked at Warburton, asking an unspoken question. 'I thought they might have known about the bungalow, posted the letter, and as they drove away, they saw the second bungalow with a very similar address. That might account for it.'

Warburton nodded. 'It's a murder enquiry, and you will conduct it like any other murder enquiry, but the answer will lie in this room somewhere. There's a recording in here of Dukes talking to Artie Kelly in the 2010 Pavo review. You should listen to that.' He raised his eyes to the photograph, and a slight smile pursed his flabby lips. 'They were quite famous in their day, the Peacocks. They made their way round the dance halls of Glasgow. Cumberland Gap, Petite Fleur, Ice Cream, and then they were joined by a girl, a woman, called . . .' He paused for a minute. 'God, I can't recall her real name, but she was known as Birdie Summer or something like that.'

'Birdie Summer? Sounds like a porn star,' said Mulholland.

'Birdie used to join in with them, dancing, doing their thing. She became the girl who all the girls wanted to be. And the girl who all the guys wanted to be with. She was stunning, in the way of the late fifties, early sixties.'

'Dancing? Really?'

'Google the Nicholas Brothers – that will give you an idea. In the Gene Kelly days, before two hundred TV channels, before the sequinned shit of *Strictly*, the dancers were super-fit, athletic

– gymnasts almost. In the days when Glasgow was full of street gangs and slashing, here were these three clean-cut guys, dancing to everybody's delight. They'd draw a crowd if it became known that they were going to be in a certain dance hall on a particular night. Birdie had a relationship with Dougie McSween' – he pointed to the smallest of the three men in the photograph – 'but later married Frankie Scanlon' – again he pointed to the picture – 'and had two wee kids. Frankie Scanlon mean anything?'

'Crime family?'

'Close. A murder squad detective in the old Glasgow City Police,' corrected Warburton. 'He was known as a thief-taker.'

'A man whose friends could prevent an investigation of paedophilia getting anywhere?' asked Costello. 'Back in the good old days.'

Warburton looked through her with eyes that could melt lead. 'Because of these rumours, Artie Kelly did his review. His team found nothing.'

'Some might say that the police just backed up the cover-up of the previous cover-up,' said Anderson. 'It's more or less what Fettercairn said. Am I right to presume that in among all this is an original complaint? About the police? A complaint about child abuse?'

'Yes.'

'So if we are being accused of a cover-up, then you should really have Tony Bannon work this – it's his field,' added Costello. 'His background is in Complaints. He knows how devious police officers can be. You should swap us, and we can stay with Aasha. They both—'

'No. Just listen to the tape, listen to it. Find out who sent that letter and find out who killed the man who was born Eddie Dukes. Just like any other murder enquiry. The answer to those questions lies among all this lot.'

The four detectives looked at him.

The Detective Super sighed. 'What about this MacMillan? Is he looking good for it?'

'He's a good actor if he was involved. He appears to be a good Christian man, but there's no doubt there are some things about it just a little too perfect for my liking.'

'Yes, but maybe not the best use of our limited resources. Mr and Mrs Lyonns?' asked Warburton.

'Squeaky clean, according to the local community cop. They're not that sort of weird. Doris complains about everything, while Hector sits in his shed and listens to the shipping forecast. Their daughter, Belinda, was, quote "a bit of a girl in her day". But none of them capable of that type of horror. They would think it unhygienic,' said Anderson.

Wyngate was already wrestling with a file, prising open a rusted paperclip that held a creased black-and-white photograph. 'So what happened to the Peacocks, sir?'

'They stayed friends,' said Warburton, getting up to leave. 'You'll read about it in here. It was a very hot summer day in June 1978, the same day as a bank job in Barrhead which kept the murder off the front pages. Eddie Dukes stabbed Birdie Summer, his best friend's wife, to death. That murder is solved; the murder of Eddie Dukes is not. So that is what you are investigating.'

'That and nothing else?'

'That and who sent that letter. One and the same is my instinct.' He walked towards the door, his hand on the handle. He turned to look at them. 'I wish you the best of luck. Oh, Wyngate, you have an appointment with Complaints at nine tomorrow morning. About property missing from premises you entered unaccompanied at the Riverview flats.'

'Bloody hell,' said Wyngate, his mouth falling open.

'She's at it, Gordon. Forget it,' said Costello.

'Warburton's very well informed,' commented Mulholland, his eyes still watching the door where Warburton had exited.

'A bit too well informed,' said Anderson and Costello together.

The cine projector and cans of film had been sitting at the back of the room, waiting, nobody really wanting to see their content. Costello and Mulholland said that they would do the initial viewing and make a judgement about what they had in their possession, then call Anderson for a further opinion. Anderson and Wyngate both had young children – their talents could be better employed trying to organize the documents in Wyngate's case and steering the investigation in Anderson's. There was no point all four of them sitting in front of the screen for hours on end. Two of them would assess and call in a specialist unit if needed.

Anderson made excuses to leave and collect Norma. Wyngate was sent out for coffee and told to take as long as he needed, so he could calm down. The summons to the meeting at Complaints had left him physically shaking. He also needed to phone his wife and explain why he was going to be late again.

Costello pinned up the small photograph of the Peacocks with names noted to keep them focused. Eddie Dukes had never married. Frank Scanlon had married Birdie and had two children, Veronica and Ben. That would leave the other girl as Loretta, Dougie McSween's daughter. He had two younger sons, Brian and Andrew, but as yet she could not work out who he was married to at the time. She needed to remind herself she was investigating the murder of Eddie Dukes. Everything else was shifting sand.

No words passed between Costello and Mulholland as they settled down. The air in the room was tense. Mulholland fed the film through the projector and Costello pulled the blinds down, leaving the windows open. She got out her phone and primed the stopwatch, just to mark places in the film that might contain scenes of evidentiary value. They did think to start with the film that Dukes had been watching at the time he had been murdered, but in the end Mulholland had picked the one closest.

The familiar purr of the fan, and the initial few clear frames shot through the projector, small snakes of dark hair or cracks in the film flashing across their eyes.

The film started with a car, an old green Ford, driving into a car park – a sandy area with long grass. The doors opened. A small, slim woman, a scarf round her head, got out the passenger seat and held the door, pulling the seat forward so two kids could bundle out of the back. A very young boy and an older dark-haired girl. Then the driver got out. Frankie Scanlon in motion.

'That's the same kids as in the photograph,' said Costello, the knot in her stomach tightening as the kids ran on to the beach, the camera following them. Then three other kids joined them – an older girl and two younger boys – and the camera moved around, catching them putting a tartan rug on the beach. The woman with the scarf and another woman in a hat started a primus stove and were boiling water. Two men in swimming trunks played football on the flat sand with the children. Then the ball was in the water and the camera view followed it in. The kids ran into the waves, laughing, splashing around, and the man they now knew as Eddie Dukes picked up the smallest boy, swinging him round, a variation of a jive dance move. The boy seemed to love it.

Seemed to.

'It's the same characters all the way through this film except that one woman. The two girls are Loretta and Veronica. The three boys are Brian, Andrew and Ben. The dark-haired woman is Birdie,' Mulholland noted. 'The varying woman is McSween's wife or girlfriend of the moment.'

Mulholland changed the reel and selected another film. The children were all a little older – different fashions, but same people, same content. The two cops found themselves getting involved in the jumping competition, the cheating, the pushing over, the splashing in the river, the ice-cream eating, the laughter – there was a lot of laughter. Two families on holiday. The three men looked like close friends. Kids having larks together on a day out at the beach.

'What do you think, Costello?'

'Looks idyllic. Joyous. I wish I'd had holidays as happy as that when I was that age. Or any age. To me, those kids act perfectly normally in the company of those adults. They are happy to play and run about – there's a bit of rough and tumble, but the kids look genuinely relaxed. The dark girl is a right wee tomboy and the other one is slightly shy. It looks very normal. And see the way the tall guy – is that Eddie? – helps the wee lassie off the rocks when she gets stuck. And he goes back when the wee chap gets scared of the seaweed. He's the one acting like a dad.'

'He's not their dad, though, is he?' said Mulholland. 'That might be the point.' Then he realized how easily Costello had got absorbed – a voyeur watching a family life she had never had. 'They are not related at all. There's a lot of bare flesh.'

Costello ignored him. 'Oh, here we go with the jumping competition again.' It was on every film, spanning six or seven years, the kids jumping across two marks in the sand. The winner got a bar of chocolate. It all got very competitive. Loretta was in the lead.

'That was a good jump – she gets some speed on the run-up,' said Mulholland. 'Oh, here's Veronica.'

They watched the small dark-haired girl run and land, her heels falling a few inches short of her friend's mark. Dougie and Eddie made a point of measuring it, a mock disagreement, prodding each other on the chest, some clown fighting. Eddie ran away with a comedic high-stepping gait, and the kids laughed. The two women shook their heads. Then back to the business of the competition. It was four-year-old Andy's turn. Dougie was pointing to the line he had to beat, and the camera closed in. A foot appeared to land over the winning line. Wee Andy swinging high on Eddie's long arms. At that point, the kids all piled in, the chanting of 'Cheat!' on their smiling lips, and then Eddie allowed himself to be pulled to the ground where he was buried in sand by the gang of children with their buckets and spades.

Costello sighed. 'Every holiday an adventure.'

'They are all there, aren't they, all the actors on the stage. It's the same group as in the photograph Colin said had been sitting on the table beside Pearcey's – Dukes' – chair, the one where they are all piled up on a rock.'

'As if he had been looking at it – or showing it to somebody, more like?'

'Why did they just not walk over to the wall and look at the picture in situ? Did the visitor lift it and shove it up into Dukes' face – "Oh, there we all are, looking so innocent, after everything you did to me"? I hope it comes back with some good fingerprints.'

'It did. Eddie's and only Eddie's. Mathilda will send it for more testing if we request it, but we're hoping for something off the dog collar. They're getting nothing off the house – nothing at all.'

'And Eddie was far too neat to leave a photograph there and not place it back on the wall.'

'Maybe that's why he was watching that film – taking him back to a time before it went wrong. Or is it, though? Two of the Peacocks were married with kids. Eddie was the bachelor uncle from the looks of it. Warburton said they stayed friends. Would you be pals with somebody who murdered your wife?'

Mulholland shrugged. 'Anderson might.'

Costello ignored him. 'I'll get a psychologist to look at the behaviour of the children. Are they behaving naturally or not?'

'Why was that film paused on that frame? The wee girl with the dark hair? Veronica?'

'Maybe no reason at all. Or did somebody hear a rumour and decide to take the law into their own hands – somebody totally unconnected?'

Mulholland dropped his head into his hands. 'I bloody hope so. What if they are innocent, and all this is puff?' He started to cough, deep and retching.

'You feeling OK?' Costello asked.

'Just tired. Was a bit wound up about what we were about to see – got the adrenalin going a bit.'

'I'll call Colin and tell him that it's safe to come back.'

TEN

Wyngate was the first to return, with coffee and sandwiches. Their appetites were back; the films had not been what they had thought. In a bin bag, he had a cassette machine and a fan, borrowed from Partick Central without their permission. Mulholland reopened the blinds, then continued to wipe down boxes. The sun streamed in through the open windows, highlighting the layers of dust that were gathering everywhere.

Anderson had taken the dog home and grabbed a bite to eat. Now he was looking at a reel of film manually, using the light of the low summer sun. 'Are we in danger of missing the bloody obvious, because these films look innocent? Maybe they are a sanitized version of the "other activities" that were not appropriate to store in his house. Was he a paedophile, always was, and probably still would be active if it was possible? Do they ever lose their appetite?' Anderson looked back at the pile of film cans, not knowing if he was frustrated or relieved. 'Are we seeing what we want to see? I have video of my kids at that age – naked, on a beach.'

'That's because you have kids, Colin. But we are not investigating you, are we? We are looking at who killed Eddie. The film is only relevant because of the girl paused on the screen, who I think would be Veronica. First, we need to get the "family", the Peacocks, all traced and interviewed. It looks as if Ross is coming up with nothing from the crime scene.'

Half an hour later, Anderson was sitting looking through a pile of files, dismissing some very quickly, going through other pages in detail. Occasionally, silently, Costello would hand him a dehydrated page from her pile for him to look at. He'd pull his notebook across and start scribbling. 'God, this story reads like the worst soap opera ever.'

'Which part of it? The murder of Birdie Summer or the murder of Eddie Dukes?'

'The whole Peacock thing. We have these three men – educated, handsome, single, talented, so popular that people queued up to see them. In the late fifties, early sixties, they have their entire life in front of them; their charmed existence suddenly goes horribly wrong.'

'I think we might have got that by the manner of Eddie's death, which was a little more than unfortunate. Has anybody seen a white box that ends in 20 AKZ/2338?' asked Costello.

Wyngate, who had settled with his coffee and an egg mayonnaise sandwich, pointed to the top box in a stack in the corner, disguising the fact that he was composing a text to send his wife and mulling the implications of his domestic unpopularity.

Anderson removed his reading glasses and pointed at the photograph. 'The Scanlons were a tragic family. After Birdie dies – is murdered – Frankie takes compassionate leave from the force to look after his kids as best he could. In those days, that would be . . . unusual.'

'Something to be admired,' said Costello dryly.

'What are you getting at?'

'Well, it allowed him easy access to his own kids. Was Birdie killed because she found out and had to be silenced? Did he pull out of the police force to get on with his other activities? Did he surround himself with children? Did any of them accidentally die, suddenly become unaccounted for?' She was being sarcastic, but the look on Anderson's face made her stop. 'No?'

'The Scanlon boy died,' said Anderson quietly, 'when he was six years old.'

'Nope,' said Mulholland. 'That was the youngest McSween boy – he was the one who died when he was six . . . or am I reading that wrong?' he added, aware that the other two were staring at him.

'Benjamin Scanlon born 1975, died 1981,' said Anderson.

'Andrew McSween, born 1974, died 1982,' replied Mulholland.

'So we are talking about two children who passed away?' asked Costello, nodding slowly.

They started going through the files quickly, looking for confirmation, Costello muttering about how much that bastard Warburton knew.

'I have a report here,' said Wyngate. 'Shall I read it? Yeah? OK, Benjamin Scanlon died at six years old – there's a file cross-reference number here, so it has been updated – somebody has been here before, in 2010.'

'Artie Kelly's review. Go on.'

'The boy fell and banged his head out on a routine walk with the rest of the family.'

Now it was Costello's turn to scribble something down, so hard the tip of her ballpoint nearly tore the paper.

Wyngate scanned the document, his nose inches from the contents. 'So the Scanlons, the McSweens and Eddie had gone for a swim, then for a walk up the hill at Invernock.' He raised a meaningful eyebrow. 'Is that near where Eddie lived?'

'Indeed. What were they doing?'

'Usual dog walk. Dougie taking photographs. Wee Ben was holding Veronica's hand on the hill path through the trees. He was pulling on her arm, and she let go. They were at the top of a slope. Ben fell, tumbled down through the ferns to the stream at the bottom. He tried to clamber back up, but fell again and must have hit his head. By the time they got to him, he was unconscious. He died later in hospital. There were large stones, hidden by the ferns, and he hit one, fractured his temporal bone. There's quite a long statement here from Veronica.' He shook his head, pulling out the odd word from the typewritten sheet. 'Listen to this: "Eddie would stay behind with us while the others went into the woods. Dougie always had his camera with him but it was a dull day. Brian had gone off with him to take some pictures. Boggle the beagle was running back and forward." One adult paired with one kid. How many kids look back and think that the perfect childhood maybe wasn't so perfect after all?'

'And Andrew McSween? What happened to him?' asked Costello.

'He went for a walk in the woods and disappeared into the mist,' Mulholland said. 'At a holiday caravan park up at Oban.'

'That rings a bell with me. He was never found, was he? Bloody hell. So how many kids did the Peacocks have in all? At the start, I mean.'

'Five. Only three reached adulthood – two girls and one boy survived.'

'Losing two children?' Anderson shook his head. 'That's beyond unlucky.'

'Colin, Arthur Kelly wasn't daft. If there was something to find, he would have found it. Maybe they were outdoorsy, careless parents. And it's all here – it's all in this room. It's not as if nobody has pulled this together. This has already been investigated.'

'He might not have been asking the right questions. The Savile case wasn't until a couple of years later. That might focus our minds a bit. And what has changed? It wasn't the death of Dukes. I was moved to this case before his body was found. It was the letter. Warburton knew damn well there was something here to find and made that letter his excuse to open this up.' Anderson looked troubled. 'OK, let's look into the lives of those two dead children. Schools, hospital records – whatever you can find.'

'Jesus. I think I have found something else,' said Wyngate loudly. 'Here's a police report from 1976. It's about Veronica

Scanlon, aged six. A report of a sexual assault at Black Bay, Invernock.' He flicked through. 'It's reported, but I can't find anything else.'

'So it's been misfiled,' said Costello. 'Or did somebody want it misfiled? Wyngate, you try to track down info about that from any other sources.'

Anderson was frowning. 'That's starting to ring a bell with me. The beach, Black Bay. Do a Google search on that. It's famous for something else.'

'Well, you are probably old enough to remember it,' said Costello.

'I was two at the time,' he snapped back. 'Shall we listen to the tape now? That's where Warburton was pointing us?'

Wyngate opened a small padded bag and tipped out three plastic cases, each containing a cassette tape.

Five minutes later, they were sitting round the tape player, three of them drinking coffee, Costello sipping her tea.

The voices of two dead men filled the room, with the gentle rhythmic squeak of the wheels of the recorder, the sound of a sip from a cup, the tick of a clock.

There was the usual preamble, but no caution, just the names of who was present: Arthur Kelly and Edward Dukes. The attitude of the two voices suggested that the preceding conversation had been good-natured and now they were moving on to a more serious topic.

'Mr Dukes, I'm afraid we need to discuss a delicate matter.'

'You don't need to tell me; I can guess. They're coming after me again.'

'Who?'

'I wish I knew. There's somebody out there who likes to spread the word that I have an unhealthy interest in children – boys in particular, I believe. It's nonsense, of course, but rumour is a troubling and malevolent shadow.'

'Do you know who is spreading it?'

'I wish I did. But I'm getting too old for it, Arthur. I'm now faced with my mortality. I was diagnosed with prostate cancer last month, a wee reminder that I'm not getting any younger and I'd like my remaining time on this planet to have a bit of peace and quiet, and not be chased from my home every few years.' His voice dropped. 'I'm too old for it, way too old.'

'Eddie, I appreciate that, but we don't know how that person keeps tracking you down. Or who they are. You must have some idea. After the second arson attack, you have been subject to the best secrecy that we have, yet they still find you.'

'It's been five years since I moved here. It didn't take them long, did it?'

'You moved out of Clover Street of your own volition, Eddie.'

'Hardly. Somebody dropped a flaming rag through my letterbox. It was the dog barking that woke me up; otherwise, I could have been toast. Well, the flame went out before it hit the mat, but that's of little comfort. It meant they'd be better prepared next time, and I wasn't going to hang around for that. That same nutter's still trying to kill me.'

'He wasn't wrong, was he?' muttered Costello. 'This was ten years ago?'

'It was.'

'Well, it took them longer to find him this time. Something must have happened,' said Anderson, nodding for the tape to be restarted.

'We'll do all we can to help.' There was a pause, a shuffling, an investigator's tool for changing the subject.

'Were you ever married, Mr Dukes?'

'Never seen the point.'

'I've been married nearly thirty years and the point of it still escapes me,' joked Artie.

'Better off with the dog. She's always pleased to see me when I walk in the door.'

'You never wanted to marry Birdie?'

Anderson looked at Costello. The interview had taken a turn.

'No, I never wanted to do that, but what has that got to do with anything?'

'You've served your time. In the eyes of the law, you've paid your debt to society. Even then, I'd understand if one of Birdie's relatives thought that you didn't have the right to walk the streets a free man.'

'She doesn't have any relatives,' said Dukes.

'These are allegations of paedophilia, guaranteed to inflame the neighbours, denying you a quiet life. Who do you think fits that bill? Frankie? Douglas? One of the children? What's going on?'

'Bloody hell, that's close to home!' muttered Anderson, leaning forward.

'As far as I'm aware, nobody knows where I am, or who I am . . .'

'OK. Do you think there's something in your past that could be misconstrued? With all these historic sex abuse crimes, has somebody heard the wrong story, got the wrong end of the stick?'

'How many times have I heard that? No, we were the freedom generation.' Dukes' voice softened as he remembered. 'Douglas, Frankie and me. We were the young, handsome boys around the town. We had any girl we wanted.'

'And did you?'

'Did I what?'

'Have any girl you wanted?'

'Aye. When I could be bothered. For me, it was more about the dancing, the music. The clothes to a point. Don't get me wrong, we never checked the birth certificates of the girls that hung around edges of the dance floor. The girls were never . . . interesting enough.'

'Until Birdie?'

'Aye, but she could dance. She was a bloke in a frock – one of the guys. That's what was so special.'

'I can understand that in your youth, but later – the four of you? Things move on. One woman, three men?'

'We grew older, of course. We grew up, life got serious. The whole dance-hall scene changed and it wasn't for us anymore. Frankie joined the police. I was promoted at work. Dougie just refused to grow up.'

'Birdie married Frankie?'

'I was best man, Dougie chief usher. Wonderful day.'

'You and Birdie—'

'Never.'

'So why did you kill her?'

There was a pause, with just the sound of the tape rolling. Then the noise of somebody moving in a seat, a slow exhalation. All four occupants of the rooms leaned in to hear what Dukes was going to say next. They were experienced enough to sense that something important was about to be said.

'I've been on the run for a long time – not from the crime that I was convicted of, but from the gossip that I can never quite close my door on. I'm now a very old man. I've lived a long life, and there comes a time when you need to tell the truth.'

There was the sound of the tape grinding in for a few seconds.

Artie Kelly's voice was measured. 'I should maybe warn you to be careful what you say, Mr Dukes. If you want to make it official, we can arrange to have a statement taken, get it signed and recorded. You may want some legal representation.'

'I think the truth might be a good thing now, just in case I'm at the end of my days. I'm not keen on meeting my maker having lived a life full of lies.'

'Do you want a minister, a priest or anything?'

'No. No, I don't.' A slight snort. 'Maybe that wouldn't be such a bad idea, but it will keep for later.'

'Do you want to confess?'

'I'd like to confess that I have never touched, inappropriately, a child in my life – not one, not ever.'

'You've said that all along. Do you want to tell us something new?'

'I didn't kill Birdie Summer.'

There followed a heated discussion between Anderson and Costello. Wyngate got up to put the kettle on again, while Mulholland waited for somebody to draw breath so he could point out they were actually agreeing with each other.

Warburton had tasked them with investigating Dukes' death. And had then pointed them at the tape – a recording he obviously knew the contents of.

'Toastie must believe that one event is related to the other,' said Mulholland.

'And the same person killed both? And the forty-two years in between?'

'Listen.' Costello laid out the plan for the next steps of the investigation in the light of the viewing of the films, while Wyngate changed tack in the light of Dukes' statement. They needed to go back to the victimology, find out everything there was in the life of Edward Dukes – which didn't seem to be very much. Had they been sidetracked by what they had found at the murder scene? Was it just a gory attack on an elderly man by person or persons unknown?

And the rest of the Peacocks? Where were Dougie and Frankie? Were they still alive? If they followed the train of thought that whoever killed Dukes had something to do with paedophile accusations, then they were looking for a vigilante or something that reflected back to the children who were around him as a younger man. As Mulholland had pointed out, the children were young in the films, and the films stopped after a certain date. Something had gone wrong. Costello felt she was looking down a time tunnel and could not see the other end.

Wyngate had a sheaf of larger printed pictures and started to pin them to the wall. 'So we have Marilyn Summer, more commonly known as Birdie, married to Detective Inspector Frankie Scanlon, who I can't find a death certificate for – or indeed any trace of him in the last twenty years. I'm still looking, but all normal lines of enquiry go nowhere. I'm waiting to hear back from the lawyer who oversees his police pension. Scanlon hung around with our deceased, Eddie Dukes, who has lived the last twenty years as James Pearcey, and their mate, Douglas McSween, who's also difficult to trace.'

'Are we seeing a pattern here?'

'McSween's a more common name, but I can find nobody in the right age bracket. There's a big file of newspaper clips in there. These guys danced – you know, all that "let me shake your tail feather" type of stuff. They were a real phenomenon back in the day. They got into all kinds of nightclubs – well, dance halls. If the Peacocks were there, then it was *the* place to be. They were the YouTube stars of the day – the influencers, if you like. And good God, could they dance! There's a clip of old film on YouTube showing them dancing out of the dance hall, on the street, then they dance on to the bus and off at the next stop. It was a publicity piece for the Palomino Club, but you can tell that folk know who they are. Look at this.' He put up an old photograph, still bearing the U-shape of a rusted paperclip in the upper right corner. It showed the three

young men, in their early twenties, dressed in tails and tap shoes
– two doing the splits and one caught mid-air, legs akimbo in
readiness for landing. 'This was fifteen years after the end of
the war. This generation had lost parents. They had all of their
lives in front of them and they danced as if it was their last day
on earth. Eddie tall, distinguished, clever. Dougie, the small
joker. Frankie, the mad, bad boy.'

'Who went on to become a cop,' sniffed Mulholland.

'He certainly did,' agreed Wyngate.

Costello asked, 'So what does that tell you about the selection
process back in the day? You had to fail the exam and be tall
enough. So, Birdie – what's her story? She was murdered when
she was – what? – in her mid-thirties, by our victim who admitted
it in 1978 but denied it in 2010?'

'Well, Birdie was the envy of all the girls on the Glasgow
dance-hall circuit; she was scandalous back then. She went out
with two of them.'

'Is that a euphemism of the time – "went out with"?'

'What do you think?' Wyngate placed a copy of an old
newspaper picture, the image clearly made up of dots and spots.
'Just look at her! Nobody would kick her out of bed.' It was
obviously Dukes in the picture. He had his arms around a dark-
haired girl with a Doris Day smile, a wide swing skirt, a white
sleeveless top. She had appeared later, older, in the holiday film
with the headscarf on. From the look of the photograph, Dukes
had just caught her after flinging her over his head. To the left
and to the right were the other two, Douglas and Frankie, arms
out, like a magician's assistant. They were all smiling, laughing
– good friends having fun.

He peered closer at Birdie's face – not a pretty face, but a very
attractive girl with black-lined, almond-shaped eyes and a full
rosebud mouth. It was a face of her time. She looked full of fun,
and she wasn't going to take herself too seriously. 'Time passed,
they had their day, they went separate ways. They grew up.'

'But you can't trace them. Have they pulled the same trick
as Dukes? Frankie was a cop – could have helped with the
muddying of the waters?' suggested Anderson.

'Somebody has – there's no record of their deaths. I'm trying
my best.'

'Dukes had a funeral suit out.' Anderson's hand floated out towards Costello.

'Charity shop?'

'Not in lockdown. MacMillan said something about going to a funeral. There was an order of service among his personal effects. What was the name? Strange name.' Costello closed her eyes. 'Fuck! The name was McSween, but not Douglas. I'll phone MacMillan. He's out of hospital.'

Anderson nodded, feeling that they were getting somewhere. 'The only person Dukes knew was MacMillan. He's much younger, way shorter than Dukes, and has a heart condition. Would he be capable of doing that to Dukes? I'd imagine the old guy could defend himself pretty well.'

Costello scrolled through her phone. 'OK, let's think this through. What's the only thing that has continued in lockdown? Funerals. Did somebody from his past hear something at this funeral? That would fit the timing of the letter and the murder – such a short time frame.'

'One of the kids?' Anderson thought for a minute. 'We need to be cognizant of time passing – that kid could now be in their fifties or sixties.'

'Like MacMillan. His wife – she grew up in Invernock. Keep going, Wyngate. Where are we on the car that was driving around Invernock? The nurse or the one that was looking for the way back to the motorway.'

'The nurse has been traced – she's with a practice in Greenock – but no word on the black car,' said Mulholland, 'and if it was one of the Peacock kids, there's only three left to choose from.'

'If you read through the case notes, and the two big reviews that have already taken place, you get a sense of conspiracy and smoking mirrors. There's a load of crap flying around, but it never leads to anything solid. The one definitive historical crime is the murder of Birdie, which Dukes was convicted of, served time for and now says he didn't do. We've no evidence of child abuse. We have a murder victim. Two maybe.'

Anderson, Mulholland and Costello sat back in their seats, looking at the wall, wondering what to do next.

'Warburton knew exactly where this was going to take us – that's why he gave us so much evidence. Sneaky bastard.'

'Do you think we could phone him and ask him what the hell we are supposed to be investigating? Save us a bit of time?' asked Mulholland.

'I don't think he wants to tell us anything. Fettercairn the journalist knows something about this. Warburton's not contaminating our minds with any Police Scotland, Strathclyde Police or City of Glasgow Police ideas.'

'So we are working to the agenda of the slightly right-wing press?'

'No surprise there. The Peacocks did lose two children, both accidental. Is that something?' asked Costello.

'Two boys.'

'One accidental death. The body of Andrew has never been found. Plus Veronica's alleged sexual assault. What about the other girl, Loretta?'

'Her mother, Catherine, divorced Dougie. He married his second wife, Penny, very quickly afterwards. Penny's the mother of the two boys.'

'So Catherine removed her daughter from the situation? The one child who appears to be unscathed.'

Anderson's interest was piqued now. 'OK, so that mum removed her daughter. The mother of the other girl was killed, maybe not by Dukes. If that's what Warburton wants us to look at, then that's what we should do. She's the connection: Birdie. Let's go back to Birdie. Who killed her? What do we think?'

'Well, she settled down by all accounts, married Frankie, had her kids, Ben and Veronica. She's a happy stay-at-home mum, getting out the fondue set, the Blue Nun and the hostess trolley for her dinner guests, so they could all come round and use the avocado toilet. I'm sure Veronica is the girl on pause in the film. She was a wee girl playing in the garden when her mum was stabbed by Dukes in her kitchen. It was reported that Dukes and Birdie had an argument, and he tumbled a chip pan full of fat right over her and then stabbed her in the stomach for good measure,' said Costello.

'So he wasn't messing around, then?' muttered Mulholland.

'Well, to be fair, she had been cooking the tea and the fat was in the pan warming up. He was holding a knife; he didn't deny any of it. They had a terrible argument. It was a plausible story – they had been such good friends for so long,' said Wyngate.

'Plausible? Shit!' muttered Costello.

'You heard what Dukes said: he didn't do it.'

'So why was he not shouting that from the roof? Why does he not say who did kill her?'

'He was protecting somebody then, and maybe protecting them now? He doesn't say anything after that, does he?' considered Anderson.

'Frankie? He'd have the pull to not have it investigated thoroughly.'

'So Eddie does jail time for his friend?'

'Do you think they were gay? Eddie and Frankie?' asked Anderson.

'Where did that come from?' asked Mulholland.

'Just a feeling? The dance thing? The Bible? The fact Dukes never married? I've not seen the list of girlfriends with Dukes, the way we see it with Dougie. It's just an idea. And the one person who really knows what happened in that house has never said anything about it. There must be a reason for that.'

Wyngate flicked through a file. 'And there was the fat in the face and the upper body. I'm sure you know how destruction of the face can be interpreted – wanting to destroy the identity of the victim, wanting to eradicate them from the face of the planet.'

'This was long before a criminologist came along to tell us why they did it,' Costello said sarcastically.

'Another theory? Frankie was involved in some kind of organized crime. A strike that close to home – take a razor or boiling water to her face – smacks of that kind of crime. The kids were close. "Touchable" as it says in the film.'

'And what? Dukes agreed to do the time?'

'So that Scanlon can stay a cop and steer investigations as he sees fit?'

'Except he didn't,' said Costello. 'He got out, left the force.'

Anderson's mind floated back to another face destroyed by acid and how the fate of that girl had coloured his own life so much. The threads of life may weave, but it takes an age for the picture to become clear. 'In her own house, that is brutal. It certainly sent out a message.'

'And added to that,' Wyngate said, 'if I am reading this right, Eddie served very little time. Less than four years. He was out by 1982.'

'You think a deal was made, and he confessed to a crime he didn't do and retracted it when he faced his own mortality.'

'Well, he's faced it now.'

Colin Anderson was trying to get baby Moses to go to sleep, and Moses wasn't having any of it. The little almond-shaped eyes stayed wide open, and the wee guy's mouth was set in a permanent grin that gave him the appearance of Winston Churchill in a good mood.

Anderson was determined to ignore him, continuing to read the story, trying different voices for the Tartan Witch and her friends. One voice was the version in English, another voice for the response in Scots. He found himself laughing at the word 'bahookie'. Moses joined in, giggling at a joke he didn't understand, but if it made Dad laugh, it must be funny.

Norma, tired from her day being spoiled with cuddles and cheese sandwiches at the forensic unit, was fast asleep at the end of the bed, occasionally sighing, frequently farting.

Anderson smiled at her, then started making faces at his adopted son, his blood grandson.

'One day the wind will change and your face will stay like that.' It was Brenda, standing at the door of Moses' bedroom. She eased herself into the small chair, her dressing gown tied tightly, dark shadows round her eyes.

'The girls have finished their first shift doing whatever they are doing. There's a WhatsApp video. They want you to look at it.' She looked nervous.

'Is it about Rodger the bloody conman?'

'I expect so. I'm so sorry for bringing him into our lives, Colin.'

'He fooled us all. I should've spotted something but I was busy, and he was clever.'

'Well, you'd better see what the girls want before you go to bed.'

'They are very keen, all of a sudden. Paige is very good at getting what she wants. I'll be through in a moment.'

He watched Brenda go back downstairs to the laptop. Moses' eyes floated from him to the door back to him.

Then Moses smiled at his dad and said, 'Bahookie.'

ELEVEN

Thursday 18th June

Email
To: DCI Colin Anderson
From: DS Tony Bannon
Hi Colin,

Thanks for the email. We had a review meeting of the entire case last night and everybody seems on board. O'Hare's PM initial report came back inconclusive; there are no injuries to Aasha's skin that couldn't have been caused by her time in the water. We're waiting on the toxicology.

We've trawled the interviews of the security staff and they agree with the course of events as Poole tells it. He certainly came back to the club. Cool and collected by some accounts, wound up and tense by others. The 'breath of fresh air' he went for may be a euphemism for scoring drugs, but we have no real evidence for that. There's nothing to suggest a cocaine rage. After talking to Costello, we re-walked the route last night. Poole would've had time to catch up with Aasha on the bridge and make his way back – a fast walk would do it. My young constable managed to avoid CCTV all the way. The camera sticks to the walkway, and all he did was go over the barrier and walk on the grass. How Poole would know that was a blind spot, I don't know, but there's no doubt he's bright. On the CCTV, on the way to the site at the river, we can see somebody in dark trousers and a white long-sleeve shirt walking towards the flats where Aasha's shoe was found. (Thank Costello for prodding the river authority on that. They confirmed that the tide would have taken her to where she was found, give or take a few hundred yards.) The CCTV footage is ten minutes too early for the timing to be sweet for Poole, but we're doing another run on that today to establish if we can get back quicker. We have some hope that he will crumble. O'Hare won't say whether Aasha had sustained any defensive injuries, but he's confident that there was no sexual assault.

I'll let you know how it pans out.

I see we are both in the papers. I'm dragging my feet with a racially motivated crime and you are dragging your feet with the investigation of historic child abuse.

In reality, from the gossip on social media, Poole was dead set on doing medicine. His dad was definitely set on him doing medicine and his grades were good enough, but the class numbers were full. The uni, according to him on Twitter, has to take so many fee-paying students to allow the course to go ahead, so he lost his place to some Asian students. He may believe that he lost his place to Aasha and this might be a sore point, even if it's not true. Like you, I get the feeling that Poole was fond of Aasha. I remain unconvinced of a racial motive.

I've heard that O'Hare is never deliberately obstructive. There will be a reason for what he is withholding. I'll keep you posted on what transpires today. I am going for the big interview with Poole – now that we have better timings, I'll throw that CCTV footage at him and see what he says.

Tony

Costello woke up very early, got showered and then phoned the hospital; there was no change in Vera's condition. She spent ten minutes watching the news on her laptop. The coverage on the BBC of Aasha's death had become respectful and distant, the lawyers sensing a court appearance soon. Then Toastie Warburton appeared, assuring the public that all complaints of harassment due to race or gender were taken seriously, but denying that a special task force had been set up to investigate a recent incident related to historic abuse. She watched him skilfully evade the question while getting the message out. There was something about his podgy, avuncular face that made you believe him.

How much of what they were doing now was simply to appease the media?

But it was interesting, this cold case, reading and reviewing. The answers were either there or they were not; there was nothing else to find, only facts to reinterpret.

She poured another cup of tea and opened the blue file, marked *CS 1* in the upper right corner, content to read while munching on her toast. The desiccated elastic band snapped in several places as she tried to pull the few sheets of foolscap from their cardboard cover. Something about it reminded her of a legal file, or papers from an old insurance document. She scanned over it, looking at the handwriting: royal-blue ink and a fountain pen, an educated hand with the lower-case G and Y forming a loop. Distinctive. She read it quickly at first, stuffing her face with toast, licking the butter from her fingertips, then wiping her hands down the front of her T-shirt as she became more and more engrossed.

It was an unofficial document, she was sure of that. It was uncorroborated evidence, a series of sequential reports that somebody had written, and despite it not being of any real value, it had got filed away with the rest. It was not documented, correctly noted or stamped, but it made compelling and uneasy reading. It was from somebody who did not want to be identified and the officer in charge had named 'CS 1'. There was a lot of talk of abusive and sexual activities, never specified but more than hinted at. 'They liked their boys young', 'the girls were safe', 'separated the kids up in the woods', 'explicit pictures.' 'What really happened to Ben? He was growing old.' Costello wondered where it was all going. The writer didn't sound like a victim – they sounded more of a powerless confidante of the victims, who were named. She recognized the names as those of the Peacock children as she had listed them on the whiteboard. Lori would be Loretta, Benji Benjamin, Andy, Ronnie would be Veronica, she presumed, and Brian was always Brian. Through the document, which was in six different parts, written as the witness kept recalling another story to tell – or were they imparting more information that they had just found out? – there were precise little ticks in red ink. These looked more recent than the handwritten pages. They were undated but had been in a box from the review in 2010. She read it through, trying to see it with the eyes of the detective at the time. Was this a record from a concerned person, listing incidents they had witnessed? Or that they suspected? They recorded it and sent the instalments to a detective. The tone of it sounded empathetic, intelligent with the occasionally formal phrasing 'consistent with'. They asked a lot of questions. 'Is that normal? I want you to know what is going on but I cannot tell you who I am.' It wasn't vindictive or threatening. The voice sounded close to the Peacocks, speaking about them coming home from a holiday in Arran or a weekend at Aviemore, and they were familiar with their ages, but talking vaguely as folk do. 'I think Ronnie must have been about ten or so at the time.' More interesting to Costello were the ticks that were speckled through the document, confirming a statement; others were marked by a question mark. Confirmed by other documentation or not? She tried to think how good this was as evidence, especially now on a cold case. Somebody had taken it seriously enough to cross-check the contents. And what had sparked CS 1 in the first place? It was a one-way conversation. Six letters, then they stopped. Because something had happened to the writer? Because they had achieved their purpose?

Or because it was too late.

Costello got up and wandered over to her big window, looking down at the river. How had this come about? The writer had been around the family. A friend, a friend of Birdie perhaps. The writer knew the three men well.

One of them lost his wife, his friend was doing time for her murder, the third one was a womanizer. She thought of Eddie and Dougie. Frankie was a police officer. Did the writer suspect a cover-up? Then something had happened to spark an investigation. She needed to get all this stuff in chronological order. Wyngate was already getting to grips with the massive timeline, but Mulholland was still struggling to locate these people.

Smoke and mirrors?

Investigative noise to drown out the real crime?

How many child abusers got away with their crimes because there was no evidence, no reliable witnesses? That was the nature of the beast. Somebody had gone through this blue folder carefully but had not tossed it in the bin. Had they put it in with the other evidence for a future investigation to come across? But who was it? Were they still around to be interviewed?

Somebody had murdered Eddie Dukes. Her original thought – that he was tortured while being forced to watch that film – was maybe still valid. Dukes might have only held on to the innocent films, the incriminating films destroyed when they went their separate ways. And what had caused that? The death of Birdie? Had she come close to finding out what they were doing?

That theory did not explain why the kids appeared to be so bloody happy. They'd get the psychologist to assess the behaviour of the children on the films later, and consider if that happiness was genuine.

Brenda was already reading the morning newspaper and eating toast by the time Anderson appeared at the breakfast table. Norma had very quickly developed the habit of hanging around under Moses' baby seat, catching any scraps the toddler dropped.

Anderson said good morning and opened his laptop, as Brenda switched the kettle on again. It had become the domestic life they had both slipped into: family time. Moses was sitting in his highchair, moving Rice Krispies around on the table, then sliding them off to Norma. The boy needed routine, and because of that the family was forced to follow. For Anderson, breakfast had never been a family affair. In the early days, it was a sink full of nappies, Brenda in a foul mood due to lack of sleep and at least one child screaming: Claire, then Peter, and, on a bad day, both of them. In those days, Anderson had grabbed toast and coffee, and got out of the door as fast as he could; sometimes he didn't hang around for the coffee. Nowadays, there was no nagging, none of those phrases that used to be hurled at him like a well-aimed machete. *Well, just make sure you do. I am left to do everything around here. You just disappear out that door. If that's your bloody attitude, don't bother coming back.*

Now he was older, the job could wait or he could send

Costello. They chatted about Moses. Brenda planned to spend
the day in the garden as the weather was going to be nice.

'Is there a parasol somewhere?'

'In the basement,' replied Anderson, and then offered to get
it out for her and bring it up the steps before he went to work.

She thanked him. They were behaving like adults: none of
the screaming matches of the last few years. And while much
of it was because of Moses, much more had been because of
Rodger or whatever his name was, and the way that man had
got under Brenda's skin. It took Costello to point out that Rodger
had hurt and embarrassed her. She had loved him, and not only
was his betrayal of her cruel and criminal, but it had also broken
her.

'Remind me before I go out. I think the base is still attached
– you'll never get it up those stairs.' A smile passed between
them.

He began to read the news. Aasha's photograph filled the
front page. 'Jesus, where are they getting all this race stuff
from? I warned Bannon the media would see it that way.'

'Was she Pakistani? Muslim?'

'No, her mother was Indian, her dad was Italian, and she was
born a Catholic in Romford.'

Peter arrived at the door in T-shirt and shorts, bed head and
yawning. 'If you think that's bad, Dad, you should see what's
going round social media. If they catch the cop in charge, they'll
lynch him.'

Anderson and Brenda exchanged a glance. Even wee Moses
stopped chewing on his cereal and rolled his blue eyes sideways,
regarding his big brother with a degree of awe, as if he had
never heard the teenager speak before. Norma broke the silence
by munching on some cereal.

He had, his dad had noticed, been getting up and out of his
bed; he was talking and reacting to the rest of the family, which
was not normal for Peter Anderson, aged fifteen and a half. A
weird civility had settled on the Anderson household in the
absence of Claire and Paige, the catalysts of drama.

'Nice of you to join us for breakfast,' said Anderson. 'That
doesn't happen often.'

'No point, when the Sad Sisters of the Apocalypse are here,

is there? But if you want me to go away, I don't have an issue with that.'

'No, stay and eat your toast,' said Anderson.

'I have stuff to do.'

'What kind of stuff?'

'Stuff. Just stuff. Any juice in the fridge?' Peter got up, not answering any of the questions in that teenager way of being too important.

'Girlfriend?' mouthed Brenda to her husband behind their son's skinny back.

Anderson smiled. 'Boyfriend, for all I know.' For a moment, they were back together, the way they were twenty years before. Her eyes fell back to the newspaper. 'Who is threatening to lynch him?'

'Everybody,' said Peter, opening and closing cupboard doors.

'Try the big white thing – that's the fridge,' said Anderson.

'I'm looking for the marmalade.'

'It's on the table. Can you be more specific than that? The lynching?'

'Well, all these folk on Facebook – those that like to be offended by bloody everything – they are now offended that the police are doing nothing. Black lives matter.'

'Are they saying that we are doing nothing because she's Asian?'

Peter stopped halfway through ramming the door closed. 'No, half of them are saying that. The other half are saying that the investigation is having more funds poured in because she is Asian.'

'Surely there's a voice of reason in the middle.'

'It's Facebook, Dad. There's no place for those with a voice of reason.'

Anderson took a deep breath. 'Peter, DS Bannon is just as committed to the job as I am. Have you ever heard me say, "Yes, I'll try harder because their skin is a different colour"? What pish are you reading up there?' He shook his head in dismay.

'Come on, Dad, I've heard you say that pretty blonde dead women get more attention than young men.'

'Peter, they get more attention from the media. They do not get more attention from the senior investigating officer and his team. Sometimes it's hard to get some publicity for a case when we do need help from the public, because all the press are interested in is reporting something stupid said on Love Island. And other cases do get a lot more attention because of human interest. They read tabloid fodder because that's what they are given to read. And that is a shitstorm that Tony Bannon is about to walk into – from the look of this, already has.'

Peter sat down beside them and started talking to Moses. The two-year-old was not yet verbal, but he could make himself understood perfectly well. The family had been told to force him to speak, so when he pointed at the orange juice and made a noise, he wasn't to get it.

Anderson zoned out from the happy noises and scrolled through the papers, which were full of the usual political squabbles, fighting over furlough, payments for the self-employed, half the country straining to get back to work as the other half had little interest in doing so. He was reading some of the comments on the BBC webpage when he felt Brenda tap his arm and slide the folded-over newspaper on top of his laptop. He saw the picture, an old one of Archie Walker, the Chief Fiscal who had pissed off Costello by bringing his new girlfriend to the barbecue, the one who may or may not have leaked something to Fettercairn. He read the by-line. Then the name. Clarissa Fettercairn had been on track to get a story in one of the dailies.

It was a whole article about nothing but the current climate of direct action, statues being torn down and rioting – a real kick to the hornet's nest. The subject may have changed, but the two witnesses missing were truth and fact. It was an opinion piece, and it was all about nothing – 'there had been allega-tions', 'sources close to' and 'it is understood that'. There had been a series of deaths of those who, it was alleged, were involved in a paedophile ring that had been working quietly behind the scenes for many years.

It ended with a cryptic line about a seaside village with a history of long-reported but ignored paedophile activity, with a former senior police officer at its core, which made Anderson turn back to his laptop.

The atmosphere was buoyant in the annexe. The briefing left the team with a sense of purpose: today was the day they would pull it all together.

Costello had received a cryptic voicemail from Valerie Abernethy, telling her to Google a paralegal called Mary Travers. Valerie was a lawyer – she'd have contacts who'd know a paralegal. She deleted the message, not wanting to join in the gossip surrounding Archie Walker's mysterious companion, but logging the name at the back of her mind for future reference. She was already back at her place by the window, going through files, methodically opening them and closing them, the pile to her right getting smaller as the one on the left grew. Wyngate had said little about his meeting at Complaints, probably because he had been told not to, so he was busily extending his timeline with a piece of wallpaper lining, just in case anybody asked. Above it was a typed sign, *Operation Pavo II*, and underneath, handwritten, was *Pavo cristatus: the Peacock* crossed out and *Peafowl* written over it, but the point was made. The police had been down this road before.

'Have you seen this?' asked Mulholland, limping in.

'Go away, I am busy,' answered Costello.

'You are not too busy to see this. Your old pal Archie has got himself in a bit of bother.'

'He's not my old pal. He's an arse,' said Costello, off the window ledge and beside her colleague in an instant.

'Oh, Costello, I thought you quite liked him.'

'I did like him, but then he became an arse, so I don't like him now.'

'He's in trouble for pillow talk with some young lady.'

'Mary Travers, the paralegal?'

'Have you seen her? She looks like you. But nicer.'

'No, he wouldn't do that. He's Mr Proper and spreadsheets and everything—' She looked at the picture he was holding. 'Oh my God, has he actually done that?'

'Try to keep the delight out of your voice,' warned Anderson, looking over her shoulder, recognizing the article. 'He knows the investigation is ongoing, but it's scaled down to a single small team as they are not given adequate resources despite a recent live complaint.'

'Who is that, then?'

'He's been set up, hasn't he?'

'By that blonde tart with the hard face? The Mary doll.'

Wyngate's fingers were flying over his keyboard. 'Hang on, I'm just Googling . . . Oh, listen to this . . . She lost her job at the fiscal's office in Edinburgh and she has a previous link with Fettercairn, on her website – the Forgotten Victims one. She identifies herself as a whistle-blower.'

Costello gave a snort of disgust. 'Well, I'm not putting Clarissa Fettercairn up on my board, even if she turns out to be the one who climbed into Dukes' attic and strangled him with her cashmere scarf.'

'She would have strangled him with a *silk* scarf actually, but get her name up there anyway,' said Anderson. 'She's an agitator in this. She runs that website ForgottenVictimsScot.com and it gets a fair amount of traction among those who have suffered abuse but never got satisfaction in the legal system, which is fair, given Weinstein, Harris, Savile and God knows how many others.'

'But that has nothing to do with this, has it?' Costello didn't move. 'I'm not validating the gutter press by writing speculation as fact.'

'Well, I can't write it up – I can't get up there,' said Mulholland. 'I have a hole in my leg.'

'I know. I can smell it from here.'

'I have parmesan on my pasta,' admitted Wyngate.

'Really, is that a euphemism as well?'

'Children, do you mind? Costello, I am your senior officer, so kindly write it up on the board,' said Anderson. 'Put a question mark after it if it makes you happy.'

'As you ask so nicely.' Costello slid off the desk. 'And seeing that peg leg here isn't capable. Fettercairn is a journalist. She's behind the Lyonns letter getting all over social media, forcing Toastie Warburton to stick his evil face on the TV, placing the mental health of the country in jeopardy with his big fat sweaty fizzog on the plasma widescreen,' said Costello, writing the name with such venom that the marker squeaked like a mouse having a go at the *Hallelujah Chorus*. 'What kind of journalist is she?'

'Apart from absolutely gorgeous, with great legs?' Mulholland pointed to her picture in the sidebar.

Costello turned from the board. 'Two? Does she have two

legs? A matching set? Imagine that. Vik, wouldn't you like that?'

'You're mocking the disabled.'

'No, I am mocking you. She's freelance . . . Is she a redhead?'

Anderson snapped. 'Fuck off, Costello. No, she's not. And stop right there and listen. We missed something. Gordon Ellis Whyte was born in Invernock and left there when he was twenty-one. I bet he was active in the seventies and eighties.'

'As in Gordon Whyte, child rapist and murderer?'

'He died in jail, did he not?'

'Yes, and although he was convicted for three child murders in England, he's suspected of the Donna Arden disappearance in Edinburgh. He did go back to Invernock to visit family in the twenty years before they caught him. Think about that. Mulholland, you are on this. Fettercairn wants to write a book about the cover-up that she thinks has happened over historic paedophile activity around Invernock. Does she know something that we don't? I think she suspects that we – they – missed a chance early on to put Whyte away, and they did nothing. That's why she knows there's a book in this. She might be right.' He waved a hand over the pile of boxes. 'And in among all this is that incident with Veronica Scanlon that we can't find. How do we move this on?'

'I'll have a look online for any reference. It might not be accurate, but it will give us an idea,' said Wyngate.

'Good thinking. I suspect that's what she thinks and that's what we have to prove one way or the other.'

'Is it true, though?'

'We can't prove a negative. And it doesn't work like that, does it? If we investigate and find nothing, she'll say, "Oh, you see, there is a cover-up and you four are part of it." If we investigate and find that there was a paedophile ring going on, if Ellis Whyte was part of it, she will say, "See, I told you so," and take all the credit. It's a lovely thing called a lose–lose situation. She's not going to leave us alone, is she?'

'Nope,' said Anderson, 'but we could stop being sidelined. We have the death of Eddie Dukes, we have that letter. We have Dukes being harassed for years by somebody who thinks he is

a paedophile, so we investigate that. If there's another reason
for his death, then that might be the end of it. We have the dog
being wagged by the tail here.' A thought popped into his head.
'Talking of the dogs, the torture to Norma was confirmed. That
may be why Dukes was so compliant. He loved that dog.'

'I don't think I'd love a dog enough to let somebody attack
my genitals with a knife,' muttered Mulholland.

'I doubt he knew what was coming. It does mean something,
though. The person who did this did not kill the dog, just hurt
her enough to scare Eddie. Bad enough, but it means something:
the killer hates men and loves dogs.'

'That's most of the women I know,' said Mulholland.

They looked at the board, the picture of the three young men.
The Peacocks. 'What secret bound them together for thirty
years?'

It was Costello who broke the silence. 'When is the PM?'

'O'Hare will let us know as soon as. Forensics?'

'Nothing through yet, but Mathilda says there's nothing much
to go on. All they have is a skin sample on the switch for the
loft ladder. She surmises they had bloodied their gloves and
slipped them off to flick the switch and walk away. There's no
DNA on the collar, and the beautiful shoeprint in the weeds
was MacMillan's after he remembered that he stood in the
flower bed to look in at the window. More interesting is that
the only laptop on the premises was used for banking and
playing Scrabble – no downloads of any kind.' Costello looked
down at her notes. 'The letter only had Lyonns' fingerprints.
The envelope was stuck very carefully, and Mathilda suspects
it was kept in a polythene sleeve before it was put through the
door of their house.'

'Really?'

'Something to do with static. So why do all that and put it
through the wrong door?'

'I'm not sure they did. Why were they so prepared?'

'What do you want to do now?' asked Costello, tilting her
head to one side. 'What would you say if I said we should have
a look at him? At Toastie?' She slid into her seat at the window,
looking from Anderson to Mulholland, her grey eyes perfectly
still.

Her companions both glared back.

'Are you serious?' asked Anderson.

'I'm perfectly serious. Look at his age and who might have been a senior officer when he was a junior officer. He might have seen something or been exposed to something. Maybe an incident that didn't make sense to him then and he was told to keep quiet about it.'

'Issues calling out a superior officer?' Mulholland shrugged. 'I've never been aware of that.'

'Yes, I've noticed that over the years,' said Anderson wryly. 'Maybe see if there's a Moby Dick in his past – the case that got away – before you put your career up the Swanee. He did talk about the pool at Invernock as if he knew it well.'

'Somebody else grew up there? Who was that?'

'Whyte?'

'Before that. MacMillan's wife?'

Costello nodded thoughtfully.

'So, technically, he could be a witness to the dark past of that wee village, and I suppose later I could bring him in and grill him deeply.' She smirked. 'I will grill the Toastie.' She swung round in her seat. 'Where are you with tracking these elusive people, Mulholland? You getting anywhere with them?' She looked at her colleague. 'Anybody close to Scanlon – he's the one we think is still alive.'

'Fill your boots,' Mulholland said, patting a thick pile of A4 paper. 'I was up all night doing that!'

TWELVE

'Nice wee house,' said Anderson, pulling into the driveway of Anne McLeod's cottage. She had been the easiest contact to trace, and the most accessible, living just four miles away, still at the same address and happy to talk. 'There was no reason for you to come with me. I think I could cope with this on my own. She used to work for Frankie Scanlon, but she has no real connection with Dukes at all.'

'She could be the writer of the blue file, CS 1? She went on the walks with the family sometimes.'

'Confidential Source One? She could be.' Anderson pulled the car to a stop in front of a dark-green front door with a highly polished brass letterbox. There was well-trimmed ivy round the doorframe, a clean black rubber mat sitting squarely at the front of the step. 'That's kind of my point. Nobody's close to Eddie Dukes. There're the three of them and then nothing. It's as if the Peacocks were an island and it exploded, leaving nothing behind except this woman. I want to get a feel for what she thought of her boss. She was Frankie's secretary, so what's she doing . . .' He stopped talking.

'She's opening her door – that's what she's doing.'

Anne McLeod, a small woman in her sixties, walked around with a bustling efficiency, dusters hanging out of the pockets of her canvas apron, and a black spaniel trotted after her, totally ignoring the strangers at the door. She was the sort of woman who would have a very neat greenhouse.

She gestured that they should follow her into a small cluttered kitchen that smelled of scones and good coffee, as Costello muttered that they were looking for somebody who liked dogs.

'So you are investigating these rumours as well?'

'Were you spoken to the first time – the review by Arthur Kelly?'

She nodded.

Costello leaned forward, patting the spaniel on its smooth domed head. 'I'd like, if possible, for you to give us some idea of Frankie Scanlon the man. I'd like to hear about him first-hand, as a human being.'

'Do you want to know if I thought he was involved in child abuse in any way? If you do, I can say no. He was a very good police officer, well liked and efficient.'

'You left your job shortly after he resigned?' Costello let her voice trail off, leaving an open-ended question. Anderson looked at her, wondering where the hell that came from.

Anne McLeod moved uncomfortably, taking a seat, resting the coffee pot down gently, constructing the answer in her head. 'I really liked working with Frankie. There's no way I was going to stay after he left.'

'Anne, did you have feelings that went beyond the normal for a detective of his rank and the woman who did the typing?'

Anne laughed a little. Two cups appeared and she lifted the coffee pot. Anderson gladly accepted with a nod. Costello declined and was offered tea, which she also declined.

Costello continued. 'I am very fond of Colin here, but I wouldn't walk away from my career if I didn't see his smiling face across the canteen in the morning.'

Anne pulled a face, still thinking about what she was going to say. 'I guess I was unhappy when he left, lost for a while. He protected me from the chauvinistic crap that a woman who worked for the Glasgow Police Force suffered in those days, and yes, I did miss that when he left.'

She stopped talking, and Anderson was left staring at the silence between them.

'But he was very much in love with Birdie. He was destroyed, absolutely destroyed, when she died.'

'Murdered,' corrected Costello.

This time Anne let the silence lie.

'He retired when Birdie was murdered?' queried Anderson.

'No, he retired when his son died – little Ben. He couldn't bring himself to work anymore, and he had Veronica to cope with. She was in a terrible state.'

'So he didn't retire when Birdie died?'

'No, later, when Ben died. He took months of compassionate leave when he lost his wife. He was distraught, as you'd expect.'

'You are obviously aware of the paedophile claims made by others about him.'

Anne sat back a little, crossed her legs, relaxed. 'And have you ever found out who was making these claims? I bet not. I bet there was hearsay and anonymous letters but never anybody – victim or parent, then or now – who has stepped forward and said, "It happened to me." There was never anything in it at the time, not now, not ever.'

'There was a folder, in a blue file . . .'

Anne looked up. 'Oh, you found that, did you? That is a weird document. It's almost accurate speculation.'

'Have you read it?'

'Yes, twice. And I discussed it with Artie Kelly when he was doing his review. It's written by somebody who pretends to know the family well. I suspected a friend of Birdie, or there was a friend of Eddie's – a woman who used to hang around him all the time, not seeing that he only had eyes for Birdie. She'd be long dead by now. I read about Eddie's death. Is there more going on there than the papers are saying?'

Anderson nodded.

'Was he murdered?'

'Yes.'

Anne closed her eyes, the palm of her hand to her chest. 'That's terrible. There was something about them, all of them – cursed almost.'

'Yes, I thought that. Why do you say the blue file was written by somebody who pretended to know the family well?'

She didn't hesitate. 'The names. The children were always called their full names. Frankie never called Veronica "Ronnie", never in a month of Sundays.'

'So what do you make of it?'

'Honestly? No idea. Muckraking? Somebody who had it in for Frank? But I have never heard anything, never experienced anything. The three men were close. They had this thing – they used to dance, Frankie and his two friends.'

'Eddie and Dougie. The Peacocks.'

'Yes,' she smiled, a fond memory. 'They grew up on the same street. Frank did national service out in Hong Kong, but they stayed close. I saw them dance much later, when they were past their peak, at some police functions. The three of them were very good, drunk but really skilful . . . dancing on the table, then balancing on the back of chairs. And again at the Palomino Club – they recreated the Nicholas Brothers that night. They were very close. But no, I never had any suspicions that there was anything going on with children. I refuse to believe that, but I could believe that they were gay – there was a very, very strong bond there. They delighted in each other's company, and it seemed that Birdie was a convenient decoration. That's what I think, looking back. I might be wrong, but there it is.'

Costello drew a finger across the kitchen table. 'So where are they coming from, all these rumours? Eddie had to be moved twice out of his house, and it looks like they finally caught up with him.'

She shook her head. 'He was a lovely man, a gentle man.'

'And Dougie?'

'The cheeky one, always up for a laugh. Frankie was a really decent human being. There's that thing my friend's granddaughter asked me about the *Top Gear* presenters. Who would you marry, who would you have an affair with and who would be your brother? As for the Peacocks, you'd have an affair with Dougie, marry Frankie, and Eddie would be the brother.'

'Which is what Birdie did?'

'I suppose she did.'

'What about after Eddie murdered Birdie? Did you ever think you and Frankie might . . .'

Anne smiled ruefully. 'I tried to be supportive. But he didn't want to know. He returned to work after he lost Birdie, but couldn't cope after he lost Ben. He nearly had a nervous breakdown, to be honest.'

'But his friend had killed his wife?'

'Yes, it sounds terrible, but it was a horrible accident and Frankie didn't blame Eddie. I did wonder – and I have no basis for saying this – if Birdie was suffering from some kind of mental illness. Frankie said that it was no longer Birdie looking after the kids – he was looking after all of them. He was less flexible at work. He was at the point of interviewing for nannies. The day she died was a very hot Saturday. I have always wondered if they got into a scuffle: she was trying to harm herself and Eddie tried to stop her. It's just something that has crossed my mind.'

'That would be sad, but why not say so? Why would Eddie confess?'

'No idea – to protect the children? There was no resentment, no animosity from Frankie. I thought I'd be the support for Frankie, but it was Dougie. I thought we were closer than we were, obviously. Then, when Ben died, Frankie left and didn't even say goodbye. He walked away. I never got a phone call or a Christmas card. He just wanted to be with his daughter. I can see that, but it did hurt. He was always . . . protecting her.'

'Do you know how Ben died?'

'He fell down a hill. Frankie said he always ran about without looking where he was going, the way kids do. Just running around mad, blind. Veronica tried to hold on to him, but he slipped through her fingers. I don't think she ever got over it; it all affected her mental health. Or was that because of the other thing? She was twelve or so at the time. Sorry, such a long time ago. Then Andy disappeared.'

'Or was that because of what other thing?' asked Anderson.

'Sorry?'

'You said, "Or was that because of the other thing?"'

'Oh, something had happened to Veronica as well. She nearly died in some sort of swimming incident.' Anne closed her eyes. 'She nearly drowned . . . or she saved another child from drowning. Like I say, it was a long time before I came on the scene, so I don't know. I know she was thrilled that her picture was in the paper. Her dad framed it for her.'

'Do you know where that was?'

Anne took a sip of her coffee and nodded. 'A beach, down the coast.'

'Invernock?'

'It could have been. Funny how it all turned out.'

'But you have done all right, got a lovely home. Did you ever marry?'

She shook her head.

'Was Frankie the love of your life?'

'I think so.'

'Can you recall what happened to Andy?'

She let out a long, slow breath. 'Recall it? I was there. It was just like every other time we were out together. The kids had all been playing in the woods – they were staying at a caravan park, and I'd nipped up for the day. It was a while before they noticed Andy was missing. I think Veronica panicked and sent Brian back to us at the caravan while she and Loretta went off to find him. They didn't. Nobody ever did. There was a huge enquiry – all the paperwork will be there. I can still see Frankie arguing that he should be allowed to assist on the enquiry, but he was a civilian by then obviously.'

'But you don't have a clear memory of the incident with Veronica at the coast?'

'No, but I know she became a very good swimmer after that. Frankie made sure it would not happen again.'

'They liked the water?'

'They did. Frankie was a swimmer and he liked to take the kids. Ben was an enchanting child with a huge mop of fair hair, a wee smiley face. You'll have seen the photographs. How could you recover from losing him?' Anne bit her lips, the forefinger of her left hand circling the top of her coffee cup. 'You know, after Frankie left, I went on the walk, the same walk, just to reconnect with them. I'd been there a few times, with Eddie's dog, my dog. It was a type of ground zero for me.'

'Were they all there when Ben died?'

'Yes. All the kids. The famous five. Have you seen pictures of Birdie?'

They nodded.

'Did you think she was stunning? Reminded me of Deborah Harry. Ben looked like her. Eddie said once that it hurt Frankie to look at Ben as he was so like his mum. I guess that can happen.'

'Was Ben the favourite?'

Anne thought, then shook her head. 'No. I think Veronica was the favourite.'

Costello looked out of the window to the azalea bush that was bouncing in the breeze, keeping away from Anderson's eye line. She heard raw jealousy in Anne's voice for a twelve-year-old girl and for her boss's wife who had eyes like Deborah Harry.

'In the end, nobody could match his daughter. They were on a little personal island. Nobody else was allowed on.'

Loretta Stirling, Douglas McSween's eldest child, had been tracked down to a small housing estate on the north side of Glasgow. After a progression through name changes, marriages, divorces, she was, indeed, her father's daughter.

The driveway was busy for such a small house. There was a buzz, incongruous in suburbia at noon on a Thursday. Anderson and Costello walked up the driveway, squeezing their way through the line of parked cars, one of them half up on the grass. They rang the doorbell, but their presence had already been noted by the gaggle of three women behind the front window. The door was opened by one of the group, her hair in curlers, wearing a silky housecoat. She smiled at them, looked down at their hands and then behind them, her smile drifting to confusion. She obviously didn't see what she expected to see.

It was Costello who spoke. 'We're looking for Loretta Stirling or McSween? Is she at this address?'

'Mum? Yes, but she's not been McSween for a long time.' The woman paused, then said, 'Hang on.' The door closed slightly and then opened again. 'Who did you say you were?'

Loretta was dressed similarly, with the addition of a neat head-scarf. She looked stressed, but not necessarily by their arrival; she seemed almost relieved at the interruption. Opening the door, she ushered them through the small hall into the kitchen. The door into the living room was closed tight, but it was evident that the noises of excitement from the other side had ceased. They stood in a very neat kitchen. Two bottles of champagne lay opened and empty, six used glasses stood neatly beside them, a few plates alongside. A box of unopened prosecco was on the floor, next to a dog food bowl and a small overnight bag. A celebration breakfast had just passed and they had interrupted Loretta stacking the dishwasher.

'What can I do for you again?' she asked, her voice weary now.

'I presume congratulations are in order. Are you the mother of the bride?' asked Costello, with enthusiasm, while alerting Anderson to what was really going on – judging by his face, he didn't have a clue. 'Nice housecoats. I like the script on the back.'

'It's what they do now. Part of the wedding nonsense that goes on, along with hen parties in Ibiza and chocolate fountains, the two-year-old daughter being a flower girl. But the fact remains, my eldest is getting married at three o'clock today in a wedding that's a third of what we paid for, so if we could make this quick.' She folded her arms, leaned against the sink and pursed her thin lips before speaking. 'If it helps any, I know my dad passed away recently, but I don't speak to my half-brother, so I didn't go to the funeral. There'd be a turnout of various wives – I didn't think I'd be welcome. Does that answer any of your questions?' She bent over to place the glasses carefully in the dishwasher, holding them tenderly by their stems. Then she gave the surface a wipe down, showing them the back of her dressing gown, with the legend *Mother of the Bride* in bright-red italic embroidery, before walking over to ensure the door was closed. Her daughter got there first, asking her if everything was OK, looking angry. The bride: it was her day and she was ready to defend it. She didn't look like a pushover; in fact, she looked every inch the female version of her maternal grandfather.

'Everything is fine. We just need your mum's help about something, and then we'll be on our way,' said Costello, with that slight grit in her voice that Anderson had tried to imitate without success. The door closed again.

'I'm afraid we have some bad news for you.'

Loretta's eyes flicked from one to the other.

'Eddie Dukes was found dead at his home.'

'Eddie? Uncle Eddie. Oh.' She turned round, back to leaning against the sink, her hand rising to her forehead. 'What happened to him?' she asked. 'Not natural, I presume, since you are here.'

'Can we ask where you were on Tuesday night through to Wednesday morning?'

She didn't need to think. 'There was a final dress fitting for the bride, with two witnesses, then I went to bed with my husband, but I was awake most of the night. My daughter was in the house as well. I don't think I've set eyes on Eddie since I was thirteen or so.'

'Did he or anybody else ever call you Lori?'

'No. Not ever.'

'We really want to know about the—'

'I suffered no abuse as a child, if that's what you are pussy-footing around. It didn't happen. I'm not in denial. It just didn't happen. After I spoke to Mr Kelly years ago, I think I figured out where this rumour had come from. There was a girl assaulted on Black Bay Beach when we were very wee. And then something happened to Veronica, but really we were too young to remember. But the abuse never happened to us. Anyway, my daughter gets married in a few hours and I have a lot to panic about.' Her attempt at good humour was a polite way to get them to leave.

'You've said why you didn't attend your father's funeral, but was there somebody specifically that you were keen to avoid, apart from your half-brother?'

'Mostly him. If you meet Brian, you'll understand. He's never forgiven me for Andy going missing, but in truth my mum taught me better. I didn't run off, and I did as I was told. I was very fond of my dad, but he was a rather free-range husband – the lovable rascal. He loved me and brought me up well. I'm honouring his name by getting a trophy at the dance school in the village named after him. He'd have liked that – he was all about the dance. He'd have liked that more than that peacock flower arrangement they put on the coffin – he'd think that was just a waste of money. I nearly cracked up when I saw that on Facebook.' She blinked slowly, as if she had said something that she regretted or a memory flashed past her mind. 'The funeral would have been . . . stressful. I want to concentrate on the happy stuff, you know. If there had been a week or two in between funeral and wedding, but well . . . he always chose his moments.' She looked sideways into the living room; the cops stood their ground, waiting. 'It was natural causes, wasn't it? With Dad?'

'Oh, yes, no question. It was the virus in the end.'

'Can you tell us, very quickly, what you think happened on the twenty-first of June 1978?'

Her answer was instant. 'Eddie Dukes stabbed Birdie.'

'I'm sure you were told the family version of it.'

She shrugged and the tension fell from her shoulders. 'That's what happened. My mum took me out of the equation before that, so I can't say anything.' She looked troubled for the first time. 'Later, we heard about Ben, and then Andy died as well . . . it was as if they were cursed.' She picked up her cloth again, wiping vigorously. 'It sounds odd, but they *were* cursed in some way – those three guys, you know. I remember my mum saying that they wouldn't get away with it, that life wasn't like that. They were lovely, talented, handsome intelligent men. We had the greatest holidays with them when we were young. The stories we heard growing up, the dancing – they were gifted

and there would be payback for that.' She nodded. 'I think my
mum was right. Eddie never found a wife, Frankie married the
perfect wife and Dad tried everybody else's wife. There were
rumours that Dad and Birdie stayed close, but I'm not sure –
they were both terrible flirts. The passing years didn't bring
them happiness. Is Frankie still alive?'

'We're having trouble tracking him down. You don't know
anything that might help?'

'No, I think he struggled after losing Ben, looking back. As
a kid, you hear bits here and there. He might have passed away.
Did he go abroad? I think Veronica ended up in care or something. Was there depression in the family? I can't recall. Sorry,
but we have to get on here.'

'Can you recall where she was?'

She thought for a moment. 'I think it was on the east coast,
because my mum said that was odd.'

'Odd?'

'Yes, too far to visit.' A shout came from the other room,
something the mum had to go and see to, but Loretta paused,
her hand up in the air as if she was catching a passing thought.
'St James, St Jude? Something like that.'

'Good luck. Have a lovely day and thank you for your time.
Sorry if we have put a damper on it.'

Loretta smiled. 'The bride has dealt with a dead grandpa and
a global pandemic. If you find Frankie, can you let me know?
I'd like him to know how I ended up – tell him about the girls,
the trophy.'

'We will.' Costello hesitated. 'You liked Frankie?'

'Yes, I did. Everybody did.'

'Would you say that Frankie never got over losing Birdie?'

'Don't get me wrong, that's a picture painted over the years.
My mum never liked Birdie. Back in those days, women didn't
like women like that – painted nails and short skirts after a
certain age. Birdie was always nice to me, but . . . well, she
was a bit of a flirt. I guess she just made other women jealous.
There was talk: "No wonder she was killed by her husband's
best friend; there must have been something going on between
the two of them."'

'Was there?'

'I was nine years old. I don't know. But I'd suspect my dad before Eddie.'

They went to the front door. The three bridesmaids watched them from the window.

'Loretta, do you recall the cine films that were made of you?'

Her face lit up. 'Oh God, yes, I had forgotten.'

'We have them now. When the time comes, you can apply for a copy. We enjoyed the jumping competition. You were robbed.'

Her face lit up. 'I certainly was! Oh my God, that would be nice, thank you.'

By the time they climbed into Anderson's old BMW, Loretta was dabbing her eyes. 'She's watching, you know, from the hall window.'

'Mmm,' said Anderson thoughtfully. 'I doubt she'd want copies of those films if they brought back traumatic memories.'

'Suppose not. You didn't help out much.'

'Too many women in that house.'

'Just to be sure, Douglas McSween did die of natural causes, didn't he?'

'Covid. I checked twice. Like she said, they were cursed.'

'By what?'

'By whom, more like.'

THIRTEEN

Everything in Dennis MacMillan's house was pale green. His wife, Maria, had returned from Swindon to look after him, so she took them through the house. Dennis was reclined on a sunbed in the back garden, reading a book about faith in the twenty-first century, a straw hat on his head to cover a sterile dressing.

They made their introductions, chairs were gathered, and Maria went off to put the kettle on.

'You look better than the last time I saw you,' said Costello, slipping off her jacket.

'I feel much better. It's just when I get up to do something, I get a bit woozy.'

Costello sat down. 'We'd like to know more about the last time you spoke to Mr Pearcey.'

'That was two days before he passed away. I got his shopping, I let Norma out. He was a bit down, which was unusual for him.'

'Did he say why?'

'He had read in the paper that a friend of his had passed away. It upset him that he couldn't go to the funeral and pay his respects.' MacMillan nodded at this point, recognizing how troubled a man of Pearcey's age would be by this.

'Did he say whose funeral it was?'

'Yes, but I can't remember. Maria, can you check my jacket pocket? Is that order of service still there, or on the mantelpiece?'

'So that was the funeral you had been at?'

MacMillan nodded. 'I only went to get him an order of service. There was no chance of me getting in, but they had a waiting area outside, with a TV screen, so I stayed.'

'Whose funeral was it?'

Maria came trotting back and handed over the small white folder with its black border to Costello.

'Here we are. Lambert McSween – they called him Dougie.'

'The cheerful peacock,' Costello said.

'Yes, that's right, there was the most beautiful floral peacock on the coffin. I've never seen anything like that before.'

'I saw this at the hospital but didn't make the connection. I don't know how I missed it. If I had seen this . . .'

'The daft name,' interrupted Anderson. 'He's not called Lambert in any of the documentation.'

The picture on the back page was unremarkable: an old man sitting in his garden. Inside were the usual hymns, prayers and some music she noted with a smile – 'Petite Fleur' and 'Just Walking in the Rain'. The inside picture was a black-and-white photograph of three young men, the picture taken from the floor, the young men sliding, arms wide, all in neat shiny suits, slim ties, very clean shoes with pointy toes.

The Peacocks. Three men live to be eighty plus. Two of them

are dead within a fortnight. As the casual chatter went on between Anderson and the MacMillans, she wondered about the third one and how difficult he was to find. 'Did anybody refer back to their dancing days?'

'Oh, yes, the Peacocks. There were a few stories going round afterwards – you know, with the tea and coffee.'

'So you went to the purvey?'

'Yes, it was in some hotel, I don't know. Catherine knew where it was.'

'Who's Catherine?'

He shrugged. 'She drove me to the hotel from the crematorium.'

Costello tried not to look at Anderson. She asked calmly, 'Did anybody show any extra interest in Eddie Dukes, or Jimmy Pearcey as you would have known him?'

'Oh, Eddie, yes, a few stories about him – you know the way these things go.'

Anderson prompted. 'So the woman who drove you to the hotel?'

'Oh, it was fine, we both had masks and gel, gloves.'

'Did she drive you back to the train station?'

'No, she drove me home. She said it might be safer driving rather than come back on the train. It was rush hour by then.'

'Back to Invernock?'

'Yes, she lived up in Greenock, I think she said.'

'Did she ask where you lived? Did she say anything about Jimmy, or how far you had to walk?'

MacMillan thought for a moment. 'She asked about the hill.'

'The hill?'

'Yes. I said I had to walk up the hill, and she said it wasn't much of a hill. She lived right at the top at Greenock.'

Anderson looked up at the brae. 'It's a fair hike. I walked it. It had me puffing.'

'Catherine thought I meant the hill up to that bungalow there,' he gestured towards the Lyonns' house. 'But I meant that one up there. It might not look such a big hill, but you should try it when the wind is in your face.'

So she knew. 'Did you get her name?'

'Catherine.'

'But Catherine who? Did you get a surname?'
He shook his head.
'What did she look like?'
'Small, dark.'
'What time would this be?'
'Six, maybe. Half six, I think.'
'Mr MacMillan, please think carefully. Did you ever say that you were looking after James Pearcey?'
'No.' His face changed as he joined the dots. 'Well, somebody did say something and I said that Mr Pearcey could be related to one of the men in the picture, that there was a likeness. That gentleman there.' He pointed to Eddie in the photograph. 'Don't you think there is a likeness?'
Anderson took a deep breath quietly. 'Can you tell me more about Catherine?'

Colin Anderson had been drinking a cup of very good coffee after a dinner of fish and chips, enjoying it all the more because of the peace and quiet. He was now nibbling Doritos he had found in the cupboard, and making mental notes, wondering how a man as unobservant as Dennis MacMillan had ever got through life. Costello had made a point, though – a valid one from his own experience. MacMillan would have noticed the hair, the hat, the jacket, the accent, the glasses, the eyebrows. And these days they were all easily altered within five minutes or so.
He was still considering who Catherine might be when the call came through on the laptop: Claire and an almost unrecognizable Paige up in Tyndrum sitting at an outdoor café, drinking something that looked cool and pale – unlike both of them who looked very hot and red.
They both started waving like crazy when they came on the screen. He could see the top of Claire's head, the right half of Paige's, her head covered in a green bush hat.
They looked too happy, and he was glad to admit, in a pathetic little way, that he was very pleased to see that they looked happy to see him. Paige specifically was thrilled to be there, forgetting to be cool, enjoying herself. It was good to see. They were out on their own.

They were both leaning forward, adjusting something, but they could obviously see him. When he waved to them, they waved and smiled back. He could see Claire brush away a tear from her eye, and he could feel himself starting to well up. Christ, she was fifty miles away. It felt like half a world. He picked up Moses, placing him on his knee, so Claire could see her wee brother. There was more excited waving. Moses recognized her and started pointing.

Claire's mouth was moving, her eyes shifting to the side. She didn't appear to be talking to her dad or into the microphone. Paige disappeared away from the side of the screen, to be replaced by a notepad with the words *How r u?* written on it, in thick marker pen – Paige's childish handwriting, big balloon letters, not joined up. He repositioned with a thumbs-up, then gestured driving with his hands. The laptop was lifted to show Brenda's Focus parked beside a lodge, in one piece.

The laptop returned to the two laughing girls, then Claire nudged Paige, who giggled a wee bit more and turned her back to the screen, pulling down the strap of her top, showing the red border of her suntan against the pale china-white of her natural pallor. Claire put her forefinger against the burned skin and pulled it away, indicating that it was too hot to touch.

Colin wagged his finger, reprimanding them for not applying all that expensive, waterproof, high-factor sunscreen they had used all their Boots points on when the Malawi trip had still been possible.

There was another conversation off the side of the screen; another white bit of paper appeared at the bottom: *2morrow 8pm? Mum?*

Anderson gave them the thumbs-up, and the screen swung away to give a brief glimpse of a bar behind them, a group of youngsters all the same age as Claire and Paige, all drinking, a large collection of motorbikes against the majesty of Ben Lui. The screen went black and he was left looking at the work emails he had been working through before the chips were ready.

Anderson pulled out a blank sheet of white paper, an old trick of the boss's that helped clear a confused head in a complicated case: a blank page and a sharp pencil. With a rubber. The muddle in the middle, that nasty bit in the investigation where it becomes a fog too dense to see through. So much information comes in from different angles that the victim gets lost. Anderson had no sight of where this was going. Indeed, he had a sneaking suspicion that Costello might be right. The paedophile story looked as if it was dead in the water, but there was something else swimming around.

Dennis's Catherine was added to the mix; there was no doubt in his mind that she had clocked Dennis, and had clocked who James Pearcey actually was. But who was Catherine? Costello had been scathing of Dennis's description. Catherine wore a mask that she did not remove, she wore gloves, she had brown hair, thick eyebrows, small glasses, well spoken, Glasgow accent – slightly posh, he thought. The build could be either Anne or Loretta. Mulholland was checking their whereabouts.

He had read the reports of Loretta and Brian McSween, the half-sibling and sibling of Andy, the boy who had vanished, probably fallen in water as his body had never been recovered. The reports were in the review of Artie Kelly. They had both told their stories, full of anger that such accusations had been targeted at their father in the previous review. That was understandable, but it didn't mean that their dad, Dougie, wasn't involved; it just meant that he had kept it from his kids. Yet there was no real physical evidence. There hardly ever was in historic abuse cases, and in child abuse cases even less so. The accused were already fading and passing away. By necessity, there would have been a closed shop of those in the know, and anybody with the inclination to speak out would have done so then, not waited until now. Maybe Loretta, looking back with an adult's eye, had hit the nail on the head. There had been a dangerous sexual predator around Invernock, but it was nothing to do with them. Unless, Anderson thought, he was about to be subject to some death-bed confession. Or somebody taking the last chance to get revenge on a mortal enemy by blackening their name with unfounded speculation, the kind that can never be refuted. Love withers quickly, but hatred can hold its breath for a very long time.

Time would catch up with the accused. Maybe it had. The

best way to interview some of those involved – the accused, the witnesses and the victims – would be by utilizing the services of a medium.

He poured himself more coffee out the pot and picked up his iPad to see the file with the original crime scene photographs. Twenty-first of June 1978. The kitchen of a suburban detached house, a hot day. It was forty-two years ago. The colour on the photographs would have suffered from chemical deterioration, but these had been transferred to electronic copy, which in itself was a little odd. The case had been solved. Had Warburton, or somebody higher up in the chain of command at Police Scotland, expected it to boomerang back and drift round to the cold case squad?

Marilyn 'Birdie' Scanlon's murder was not unsolved. Eddie Dukes had served his time. Here was Birdie, lying on her lino, surrounded by a pool of her own blood, shoe prints in the crimson red. He opened up the image on the screen, pulling it around, looking at different parts of the room as if he were there in person, poking around a kitchen that could have been his gran's. He saw nothing other than what was obvious: the terrible fatal knife wound to her stomach, the burns to her face, her short black hair wet and curled around the burned flesh. Her right arm was folded over her stomach, her left was bent at the elbow, the back of her hand almost covering her face. It was a fitted kitchen, blue and white, a chopping board lying out, knife neatly across it. The cooker had an eye-level grill; a knife and two spoons sat to the left of the gas rings; one pan remained, had twisted out from over the rings. The other sat at the bottom of the facing wall, having spilled its contents over the cooker, the floor and the victim's face.

He swiped on through the later photographs. For some reason, they were of much poorer quality, mostly black and white, the odd version of the same photograph in both colour and monochrome.

Then he looked more closely.

It had been a hot day in a hot week. The summer of 1976 was one of the hottest on record, but 1978 wasn't so bad. In those days, the climate still afforded three months of summer, where the kids went outside playing until it got dark. Most of the witnesses who had been interviewed had mentioned the heatwave in their statements: stifling, oppressive. There was a hosepipe ban, and they had been nipping out to water the tomatoes when the neighbours weren't looking. It was so humid; a downpour was expected to clear the air, and the rain had started just as the soul of Birdie left her mortal remains. There was something about that that made Anderson shiver. Not that it had rained, but the fact that people had mentioned it and associated the rain with the death of this lovely young woman, as if she took the sun with her when she passed away.

Anderson glanced through the observation part of the post-mortem report. The usual stuff: *The body is that of a well-nourished female Caucasian* and so on. Anderson skim-read it as he had done with a hundred of these. This was the pathologist's turn to state the bloody obvious. Then a line caught Anderson's eye. The victim had recently been exposed to sunshine, probably while wearing a bikini.

Anderson read that again.

Birdie with the porcelain skin? Was Birdie the kind of woman who would sunbathe in a bikini in the back garden? The weather was hot, so she might have sat out just one Saturday or Sunday. Sitting in the garden with a bikini, a gin and tonic in hand – maybe a Babycham in those days.

It was odd, though. He expanded the picture on the screen, looking at the tan line low on her anterior abdominal wall, another band of white across her chest and up round to the back of her neck as if she had been wearing a halter-neck bikini.

He scanned down, the image a little grainy, to another white band round her left wrist. She habitually wore a watch – a rare sight today.

Then he looked at the hands. Not delicate little hands he might have thought would belong to a woman like Birdie. It was there in her nickname, in those delicate features, her Deborah Harry eyes, that little rosebud mouth. He looked again and then looked at his own left hand, his wedding band. It had been on and off a few times in his married life, and although he avoided the sun – with his fair hair and light-blue eyes, he had always thought he was a strong contender for skin cancer – he could still clearly see a band of lighter skin under the gold.

Birdie was happily married; she'd never take that band off. It meant a lot more in 1978 than it did now. He was sure he'd read that there was a wedding ring in the personal effects removed from the body – he had recognized Scanlon's signature when he had collected it. He made a mental note to check it again.

Then he looked back at the crime scene pictures. It might have been the colour of the original photograph, but he was sure the deceased wasn't wearing nail varnish. Somebody – Loretta or Anne – had said she always wore nail varnish. Had they removed it at the post-mortem? Surely it was a shadow on the picture. Four shadows, one over each visible nail.

And what had Costello said about the attack on the face, the distribution of the injuries? Either a huge passion or a huge hatred? Or was it a lot simpler than that? Had somebody simply wanted to obfuscate the identity of the body.

How backward was it in 1978? They had bloods – groups if not DNA. They had matching fingerprints. They had a pathologist who was the best friend of the detective husband of the deceased, but even then . . . There were processes and protocols in place then, just as now.

It didn't make sense.

The idea formulating in his mind was too bizarre to contemplate. But that did not mean it was wrong, so he followed his train of thought, walking through to the kitchen, his coffee in one hand, the iPad in the other, Norma trotting behind him.

He realized that Helena's designer kitchen in black-and-white marble was the same layout as Birdie's had been. Birdie's was smaller, of course, without the island, but the triangle of the door to outside, the door to the hall and the cooker had similar positions and similar proportions. He stood up the iPad so he could look at it, as he put a pot on the stove, an Aga in his case, and stood sideways on to the back door, mirroring the photographs. In Birdie's case, that had been a very short distance. They were both three-doored kitchens. Costello had been right: you didn't suddenly boil a pan in order to throw it over somebody. What had it said in the report? Veronica, who was eight at the time, had said that her mum was upset. Her main evidence for this was that they had been sent out to play when a visitor was coming and they had made cake.

Had she sent the kids outside for a reason? A lover? Was there a confrontation? Dukes showed up, they argued? Birdie ended up getting her face full of boiling fat and a stab wound in the stomach, the wound being fatal as the blade had moved upwards into the chest cavity. Eddie Dukes was tall, Birdie was small. He would have needed to bend down, lowering himself to get the tip of the blade to travel in an upward direction. Why did he just not stick it in her chest the way any normal killer would? This didn't fit. Eddie Dukes, by all accounts, had been a good bloke, faithful to his friends. Birdie might have turned to him in times of trouble. She had called Eddie on the phone on the day she died – the day *somebody* died, Anderson corrected himself – asking him to come over. At that time, they lived only a few streets apart. There was a report, from a neighbour, who said she heard Birdie in the garden telling Veronica to go outside and play, and not come back into the house until she was told. It had been a very warm day, and Veronica remembered the back door of the house being closed, whereas her mum always left it open to keep an eye on the children. Veronica's statement had backed up what Eddie had said. She had wanted to go back into the house to see her mother, sensing her mother's distress about something. Just a wee kid worried about her mum.

He looked at the crime scene photo again, then his own kitchen – the cooker, the utensils in a rack on the right. In the photographs, they were on the left of the cooker. He swiped back and back, to the picture of them dancing. She wore her watch on her right wrist. Was Birdie Scanlon left-handed?

Anderson took another sip of coffee, screwing his eyes closed. The blank sheet of paper was still staring at him, waiting for his inspiration.

It smelled of a cover-up. But the only person who could have engineered the cover-up was Birdie's husband, Frankie Scanlon, and he was nowhere near the crime scene at the time. So that didn't make any sense either. Or did it?

He reached for the sheet of paper. He had two avenues of investigation now. If this dead body was not Birdie, then where was she? And who was this young woman, the unmarried sun-worshipper lying on the slab?

And was Frankie Scanlon of the City of Glasgow Police complicit in that cover-up?

That would explain why everybody was so hard to track down.

Eddie was the bright academic one. Did that make him the problem solver? For a murder so brutal, he had served very little time. Most of it in a soft environment where he had taught other inmates, encouraged them to read, aided their literacy. Birdie and Eddie trusted each other implicitly. They were close friends, like brother and sister. She would have reached out to Eddie.

That's why Eddie Dukes denied killing Birdie Summer. He hadn't.

By eleven o'clock, the scenario was driving Anderson mad. He lifted his mobile and spoke. There was silence down the phone. Costello was very quiet. He could almost hear the machinations of her brain. He realized that he had spouted out all his suspicions in a single minute, but she had not laughed. She had not dismissed it.

'OK,' she said. 'Why did nobody notice?'

'I think it was a slam-dunk that the body was Birdie. Can you recall who did the original PM?'

'It was Williams, Doctor Williams – do you know him?'

'Was he a bit of a drinker? What's the phrase – not so good in the afternoon? A bit unreliable? Retire early on health grounds? That's normally a bit of a giveaway.'

'Why are you doing this?'

'Doing what?'

'We are not investigating the death of Birdie. We are investigating the murder of Eddie Dukes and its links to an accusation of historical child abuse, but you are talking as if the murder of Birdie Summer wasn't what it appeared to be.'

'Are you saying that I am derailed from my professional duty? If I am right, there's somebody in a hole in the ground and nobody has noticed.'

'No, I am just interested in your motives. Is it because he

died before he could put it right? He had plenty of time to do so, and he didn't. Or is it because he died a sad and lonely old goat?'

'Better to be mourned as a murderer than suspected as a paedophile. And we need to prod a bit harder into this. There is a real victim here, who's not Birdie. Dukes spoke about her in the present tense on the tape, years after he pleaded guilty to killing her.

'Habit? Or because he knew Birdie was still alive?'

There was a long silence. 'I am going to call Warburton right now. He did say I was to call anytime day or night.'

FOURTEEN

Friday 19th June

Email
To: DCI Colin Anderson
From: DS Tony Bannon
Hi Colin,
We had a few developments in the case after looking at the dashcam from a taxi driver who circled the area twice in the time frame we are looking at. Neither of these developments is particularly positive. It turns out that the guy on the bridge walking after Aasha is not Anthony Poole; same clothes, very close in height and appearance, but we noted that Costello had reported that she had followed a man with a Boxer dog when she found the shoe at the river. Sure enough, further along in the tape is the dog, and the man we thought was Anthony is the dog's owner. He lives in the Kingston Quay flats. He's out with his dog most nights and he said that he may have seen Aasha walking in front of him. Even though it was past one in the morning, there was still a little light around, but she disappeared. We are thinking she disappeared from sight as she walked into the gardens at the first block of

flats. He walked on to his own block, number three. We have him on the security footage at the flats, I interviewed him myself and I'm sure he's innocent of any association with Aasha. He went home that night same as any other, and he's actually talking on his mobile during the time we think the attack happened, but he did mention that the woman was 'unsteady on her feet'. He didn't see Poole.

I presume that he wasn't interviewed at the time as we had no idea where she went into the river.

The second, more telling thing is that Poole has made himself unavailable for interview, which made me feel uneasy. We are having trouble contacting him. He seems to have done a runner.

Tony

Colin Anderson read the email, picked up his mobile and scrolled through the contacts until he found Bannon's number, left over from the Sideman case. He had found Bannon to be a good listener then; he didn't think he had changed much.

'Do you think his parents know where he is?' he asked. The noise at the other end suggested Bannon was driving.

'Well, that's the big question, isn't it? I am not sure about the dad, but the mum? I'd say not. She looks worried. There was a big blow-up on social media yesterday, over something that Anthony posted years ago, which might be why he's lying low. It's vicious.'

'Was that the comment about Asians buying themselves places at Scottish universities?'

'A variation on that theme, yes. Then a comment on a Twitter thread was repeated out of context, and the next thing is the university is calling Anthony in for a chat. He was well pissed-off when he came home from that, had a bit of an argument with his dad, went out in his car and did not come back. That's what the dad says, but he might be covering for him.'

'Do you think he's a flight risk?'

'Running would be the only real evidence against him. If he's actually done a bolter, then that's not going to look good for him at all.'

'It's an incredibly stupid thing to do.'

'Do you think the dad could have bought him a ticket just to get out of the country? They have family abroad.'

'That would be short-sighted in that we are one email away from knowing exactly where he is, and him not being allowed to get off the plane at the other end. What's your next move?'

'Issue a warrant for his arrest? Might just stick to "keen for him to come forward" to help with the old enquiries for now. Keep it sweet. I think that's right. I thought his dad was a strong character; maybe Anthony has just jumped. A sympathetic approach might just bring him back on his own recognizance.'

'What about Aasha's parents?'

'As you would expect, the mother is distraught, but the father is about to start asking questions of the investigation. Anyway, I will keep you posted with any updates. I just hope this doesn't end my career in CID before it's started.'

In the annexe, they chatted about the case over a breakfast of Greggs omelette rolls with extra bacon, coffee for Wyngate and Anderson, tea for Costello, as Vik sipped water and complained he had a sore stomach. But he had no cough and no temperature, so they sat him in the corner of the room and kept out of his way. They settled as Anderson sat at the front, facing them, his legs crossed, cup balanced on his knee. He explained that they were now looking for a woman about five feet four, totally average in every way, who drove a small black car. Mulholland's response was to slap himself on the forehead, but Wyngate wrote *The Driver?* up on the board and underlined it for good measure, before Costello added the names *Loretta*, *Veronica* and *Anne*, who were all the right height. That was all they had. And the fact that Catherine was the name of Loretta's mum, Dougie's now-deceased first wife, which might mean something or nothing.

Anderson then explained his theory. It was only a theory, but if he was right, it put a very different face on the murder of Eddie Dukes.

Wyngate nodded in enthusiasm, and Mulholland stared out of the window as if the words *Wild Goose Chase* were written in the sky. Costello threw her screwed-up roll wrapping in the bin from the other side of the room. 'Like I said, I'd be interested in knowing if Toastie was involved in this at any time. There's something he's not telling us.' She twisted her head round, making sure that the door was closed and that they would know before Warburton made another unscheduled appearance.

'He has given the green light for a budget for this,' said Anderson. 'Do you think this case has been with him all his professional life?'

'And he was waiting for a talented team of investigators to solve it?'

'But found us instead?'

'Can't find anything in the electronic store, but if he was a junior officer, it might not be under his name.' Wyngate shrugged. He had done his best.

'I have an appointment later with the second pathologist who did the PM on the person who may or may not be Marilyn "Birdie" Summer. That will be an interesting conversation,' said Anderson.

'What will they be willing to tell you? "Sorry, I cut up the wrong person." And if Birdie is not dead, then where is she and who was buried?'

Anderson had expected a confused silence where they could contemplate the difficulties with his theory, but Wyngate spoke straight away.

'The babysitter.'

'Pardon?'

'The babysitter.'

'What babysitter?'

Wyngate got up and adjusted the belt of his trousers before tucking his shirt in and walking over to the wall and the long stretch of paper. He pointed to the date of the murder: *21st June 1978*. 'Here, on the morning of the murder. Birdie was interviewing a babysitter. It's in the notes. The kids had baked the woman a cake – you can see the remains of it sitting on the sideboard in the crime scene photos. The plates were in the sink and there were glasses in the kitchen.'

'Anne McLeod said that Birdie was getting help as she was struggling a bit with the children,' Costello said, recalling the conversation.

'Do you have a name?'

'Not that I have come across yet, but I am still looking. She was there that morning but had left by the time the murder happened, so she wasn't of interest, I guess.'

'Who said that she had left?' asked Costello.

'Somebody . . . Leave it with me,' said Wyngate, his hand spiralling over a large stack of beige folders.

'So can you concentrate your efforts and confirm that she got home safely?' asked Costello, writing it up on the board.

'After forty-two years?'

'The investigation wouldn't have looked for her, would they? But her family would have looked, surely?'

'I'm trawling through MisPer right now,' asked Mulholland with little enthusiasm.

'It might explain the destruction of her face. The natural conclusion is that maybe somebody was trying to conceal the identity of the deceased.'

'And who was involved with this cover-up. Her husband? Her kids? The pathologist?' said Anderson.

'It's your bloody theory,' retorted Costello.

Mulholland spoke, his head held in his hands as if he was suffering from a really bad hangover. 'Before you all get carried away, it was 1978. The police weren't exactly in the dark ages.'

'But I'm on the trail of Veronica – well, I have found her ex-husband. Surely she's the one to talk to. How old was she when her mother was murdered? When she thought her mother was murdered?'

'Nine? Ten? Something like that?'

'She was eight. I don't think I'd want that discussion with somebody over the phone, Costello. We are talking about the death of her mother.'

Costello pulled a face. 'Are we, though?'

FIFTEEN

The old pathologist was a small man, very well dressed, a shock of grey hair above bright blue eyes that still twinkled as he sat at the window table of the tearoom overlooking the river. In the garden beyond, a couple of magpies were squabbling over something. Vernon Cameron had a reputation for being immovable in the witness stand, not usually a helpful thing in a pathologist, where everything was an opinion in a range from remote possibility to high probability. Beware of anything that seems very certain, especially experts.

'What do you want to see me about?' He rolled his eyes. 'If it's about another bloody case where the magic fairy of DNA has come floating out of the clouds waving a wand, then, to be perfectly honest, I am beyond caring. The past is another country and I don't want to go back there. I left all that behind.'

'I am old enough to be caught up in that myself,' smiled Anderson. 'I usually just tell myself that I did the best I could with the evidence that I found. We only gather the information; fifteen people decide on matters of guilt or innocence. If we all had the benefit of hindsight, then the world would be a better place.'

Cameron softened a little, leaned over on the table, moving his cup of Earl Grey over to one side. 'What do you want to know?' His eyes opened wide, keen. Anderson knew the type. He bet the pathologist had never actually stopped working. Bored with the bridge, the golf and the morning coffee at the garden centre, he was keen to have his expert opinion sought once more.

'Birdie Scanlon.'

Cameron's face twitched a little; he certainly knew the name. 'Marilyn Scanlon – Marilyn Summers as she was?'

'Summer,' corrected Anderson.

'That was a very sad case. Edward Dukes went down for that. Two wee kids left without a mother. No winners there.'

He smiled. 'But that was years ago. He'd have served his time and got out by now.' A cloud seemed to pass over his face. 'Was he that fatality in Invernock?'

'He was indeed. How did you know? It's been kept very quiet.'

'Because you are sitting here talking to me? And that was a suspicious death. It didn't say the name, but the age would be right. I know there was a connection with Invernock.'

'Do you recall much about the case? About Birdie? The victim?' Anderson asked, not too pointedly, he hoped.

'She was married to Frankie Scanlon.' Again, he gave that slight sniff. 'Tragic all round, that family.'

'Why do you say that?'

'You'll have read up on it, so I'm sure you are well aware. What do you want to know in particular?' asked Cameron, sounding now as if he was on a professional roll.

'Were you aware at the time of any rumours that something wasn't quite right? Or anything that you felt did not fit?'

The eyes turned a slightly steely colour of blue. 'I was the second pathologist, there to corroborate. Shields was the senior. He died on a golf course in Spain.'

'Three years ago? Yes, I know.'

'You have been doing your homework.'

'I am a detective,' said Anderson in a manner that he hoped was disarming rather than sarcastic.

'And quite a senior one at that. So why are you sniffing round this case now? Forty years later?'

'I always pay attention to what my younger detectives say. What they see with their keen little eyes. We are taught to be tolerant of them. It wasn't like that in your day – it was more speak when you were spoken to. I bet you would never dream of questioning your superiors. I was wondering if you recalled anything about that case that you might want to revise now with hindsight. I'm giving you the chance now to ask that question. My DI does that all the time; she's bloody annoying, but seldom wrong.'

The blue eyes remained cold and unimpressed.

'When she questions something, she tends to have a valid point. Just wondering if you recalled any concerns you wanted to raise about Birdie.'

Cameron was quiet for a while, staring at Anderson, blue eyes searching for a clue. Anderson could see him doing this in the witness box, before a piece of incriminating evidence was planted in his hands by opposing counsel.

'It was a very sad case. She was a beautiful woman – more than a bit of a celebrity in her day if I remember correctly. In the early sixties? There was nothing official, but there was talk that the other chap . . . well, she was' – he paused – 'still close to him while she was married to Frankie Scanlon. That's the oldest motive in the world, isn't it?'

Anderson nodded. 'Except that the affair would have been with Dukes, wouldn't it? He was the one that killed her. The rumour was about McSween.'

Cameron took a while to respond. 'But it was Dukes who was in the house when she was murdered. Rumours, nothing more. Scanlon was a fair but formidable character. He and the senior pathologist, Shields, knew each other well – same lodge, same golf club. That was important in those days.'

'Doctor Cameron, can you recall the findings at the PM?'

'I'm sure it's not beyond the bounds of a detective of your standing to find the report and read it.'

'I want your opinion. Here's a copy.'

As Anderson handed the folder over, a light bulb seemed to go on behind Cameron's eyes. A recognition that he was being given a chance to right a wrong. The old pathologist reached forward and took the file with fingers that still looked as if they were washed forty times a day, and given the virus of the recent few months, they probably were.

He placed the file on the table in front of him, holding it down against the light breeze. 'Let me try to recall it first. Dukes stabbed her.' His right hand moved towards his lower left abdomen, indicating exactly where the knife had gone. His recall was good so far. 'Then he spilled boiling water – was it water? No, it was chip fat. I have a vague memory of somebody saying how odd the scene smelled – like a chip shop. There had been fat warming on the cooker, correct?'

Anderson nodded.

Cameron was encouraged, and his eyes closed slightly, reaching into the recesses of his memory to retrieve more detail.

'There had been some discussion that the secondary damage had been accidental. The pan had been on the cooker, knocked over in the struggle. The kitchen was a relatively small space. There'll be a drawing of the layout in the file. Dukes was a tall man. Birdie was short, very slim.'

Anderson caught on to that comment. 'She was short, Dukes was tall. It was a kitchen knife and it was moving sharply upwards?'

'Yes, nothing odd about that. People don't stand to attention when they stab each other, DCI Anderson.'

'Were there any other signs of a struggle on the body?'

'I don't recall the body being covered in bruises. Nothing like that . . . or maybe . . .' He shook his head. 'Sorry.'

'There were some bruises of different ages – they were explained by boisterous play with her small son.'

He nodded. 'In that case, I think we may have needed some supporting evidence. Are you putting a different interpretation on that now? Do you think our opinion might have been swayed because her husband was a senior police officer?' He nodded his head from side to side as if he was considering it. Then shook it. 'No, the injuries in domestic violence have a certain pattern; this was different. And nowadays, the destruction of the face – oh, you would have a whole queue of experts coming out to chat about the significance of that.' He sighed. 'A handle sticking out in a small kitchen. There were public information films on the TV about that at the time – "Turn the Handles Inwards", and a small child crying in pain after being scalded. Did we get it wrong, DCI Anderson?'

'I don't know, to tell you the truth. But you did what you could do. There was a kitchen, a knife, a pan of hot fat, and two people there. Do you remember why Dukes was there at all?'

'Well, we thought that she had called Dukes on the phone because her husband was away . . . But why had she called him? No, I don't know. I was thinking, with the daughter and the son being so young, they wanted to keep Mum's memory clean for them. But do you think they were having an affair?'

'Personally, I doubt it. But Dukes admitted the murder. He came quietly.'

'He was devastated.' Then he corrected himself. 'Or so the gossip in the queue in the canteen said at the time.'

'It was a hot summer day, the kids were outside, and there was a big case about to break . . . Her husband was away?'

Cameron shrugged.

'It was the day of that bank robbery in Barrhead,' prompted Anderson.

'Yes.' A memory came to light. 'I remember there was one almighty downpour. The scene-of-crime guys who went out to Barrhead got soaked, and much of the external evidence was lost. There were a lot of bank jobs in those days, but the cases that came under my knife were mostly violent deaths, killed by somebody they knew and trusted.'

'Do you have any doubts about the case at all?'

He shook his head. 'The daughter had come back in, saw him standing over the body. She gave her testimony, you know, wee Veronica. I think she was such a brave wee girl. I think it changed her.'

'I think it damaged her.'

'You may be right. My granddaughter is that age – gives you some perspective on the situation, how so very young they are.' He shook his head. 'Nowadays, there's counselling and all sorts. In those days, I think her granny probably sat her down and had a nice wee chat. And the boy – there was a boy. I forget his name?'

'Ben. He was six when he died.' Anderson wondered, looking over his shoulder, watching the magpies. 'Nothing odd about the actual post-mortem itself?'

'Like what? What are you getting at?' Cameron said with a sideways flick of the head.

'Did the injuries match the knife?'

'Yes.'

'The incisive edge, the angle of the wound? All that squared?' He kept his eyes drifting out of the window, thinking again.

'I don't know what you are getting at. Is this case going to be reopened?'

'Not in that sense. Only because of the connection to Dukes' death. I'm just looking for anything that doesn't fit, anything at all.'

He nodded slightly, not sure of himself now.

Anderson said, 'Anything else you can remember about the PM?'

'Everything will be in the report. There was nothing tangible and no big points to argue. It didn't go to court so the results were not challenged in that sense.'

'Do you ever remove nail varnish for a post-mortem?'

'We can do, but that's not done by us. It would be noted when the body came in. There's a whole forensic treasure trove under the fingernails.'

'Was there in this case?'

'No, it would be in the file if there was. We didn't have the expertise in those days that the boys have available now.'

'Any doubts you had about the identification of the body?'

'We all knew who she was.' He caught Anderson's reaction. 'Are you questioning her identification?' He slapped himself on the forehead. 'You are going to say the three magic letters again, aren't you? Bloody DNA?'

'My team can find records of tissue samples being taken, but not the samples.'

'They'd mostly be destroyed long ago, but interesting all the same. They normally retain some, so yes, I'd say that was unusual.'

Anderson was treating himself to a coffee and a fudge doughnut in his car. He needed to think. Cameron could shine no light on it, but there was something in his manner that said he wasn't outraged by the suggestion. He had decided to scan a copy of the post-mortem report over to Professor O'Hare. He had Dukes' post-mortem scheduled for later that day, so they could chat then. He had reread it himself, unable to find a mention of the body having nail varnish removed by a technician.

The dead body was a right-handed, sun-worshipping watch wearer with hazel eyes and natural nails. Birdie was left-handed, pale and brown-eyed with habitual bright red nail polish. It wasn't much.

They were on the trail of Veronica who had been so traumatized as a child that she had suffered from mental health issues most of her life, whereas Anne McLeod was sharp, with a lifetime to brood. The jury was out on Loretta. Warburton was very keen for them to proceed: 'The reputation of Police Scotland will be well served by financial and human resource investment in this team and a positive outcome.' Or something like that. Why did he give them all that background material? Because he knew something. Maybe Costello was right. Maybe they should be talking to him.

Was Frankie Scanlon in on the switch of identity of his wife? Was it his idea? Surely he must have known.

Eight women between fifteen and forty years of age had been reported missing in the loose time frame of June 1978. Wyngate was pedantic but he would get there. The records would have been handwritten then typed up, card-indexed and cross-referenced. It was like dancing on breaking ice.

Was it worth pursuing? If he was right, there had been a family waiting for a young woman to return. But was this the most cost-effective way to get to the answer? How long had passed since then? Forty-two years? Anderson would allow Wyngate a day on it, then get the focus back to the driver. They could solve the case if Dennis MacMillan had been more observant and less trusting. They'd put pictures of Anne and Loretta in front of him, see if that sparked any memories. They'd add Veronica once they got a picture of her older than eight. Maybe put a mask on the picture, see if there was any recognition of the eyes, the shape of the face.

It was all a matter of priority.

He opened his iPad. Wyngate's report was typical: succinct. Eight files, with edited highlights. Had nobody thought to look? It was accepted that it was Birdie in the house and it was Birdie on the slab. It was as simple as that. Nobody thought they should be looking for anybody else. The deceased must have resembled Birdie in some way, the babysitter the Scanlons were looking for.

Wyngate had found something very telling: the Scanlons lived in a cul-de-sac, a small square off a road. Wyngate had surmised that in 1978 a single woman looking for a job as a babysitter would not have had a car, so she would have been walking to the bus stop. Witness statements reported a neighbour who lived on the corner, a house with gnomes in the garden, seeing a woman walking down Loch Road as if she was going for the bus. She was in a rush because it was raining. The original investigation presumed that was the babysitter leaving. Nobody came forward to say their relative was missing after going for an interview at that address. Had the Scanlons interviewed her beforehand, and this was a 'come round and meet the kids' type of interview? Frankie claimed that he didn't know her name, nor did the children.

Anderson sipped his coffee, thinking it through. In the house, Birdie and the kids were joined by the babysitter. Babysitter was seen leaving by the neighbour, Eddie Dukes appears, has the fight with Birdie, kills her. Eddie admits it. So why should they look for the babysitter? Cut and dried. The dead person was Birdie . . . her husband said so, he identified the body on the slab . . . The body with an unrecognizable face, Anderson recalled, reading slowly the description of the babysitter given by the neighbour with the gnomes: dark hair, slim, young, wearing big sunglasses. It had been a hot day. She had a knee-length waistcoat with a long-handled Dorothy bag over her shoulder, bare legs and a short dark skirt. Anderson had a vision of a very old Coca-Cola advert.

Anderson scrolled to the old crime scene photographs. A woman goes into a house and puts her handbag down. There are introductions, a short interview, a quick hello to the kids, then send them outside and 'come into the kitchen for a coffee'. Then brutally stab her, maybe change into a skirt that looks like hers, pick up the babysitter's stuff and walk out. The dead person is identified as Birdie, but in reality the woman who walks away is Birdie. Anderson shrugged; that wasn't right. They had eaten the cake. The kids had spoken to her. They'd had lemonade in the garden. Why did Frankie say the children never met her? And where did Birdie go with only a small bag? The police at the time would have timed it and dismissed it, but was any of that fixed in a timeline by a disinterested party? There was no date-stamped CCTV in those days.

Plus, the kids knew which woman was their mother and who was the babysitter. They wouldn't lie – they were eight and three or something. But there was something in that chain of events that was not right.

Birdie might have been ambidextrous. She could have bought a bikini and spent the summer sunbathing as her husband was so busy at work. Mrs Corner House with the gnomes knew Birdie. She would have known if it was her.

A cold thought entered his head. What if they were looking at this the wrong way round? Did the Scanlons go out looking for somebody that could be Birdie in build and colour? The face doesn't matter; they can chuck boiling water or something. Scanlon was a cop, so everyone will take his word for it. They'd put the victim's prints up as Birdie's, maybe those from the glass of lemonade. They baited the woman with the offer of a babysitting job, which made sense given their troubles with Veronica and Ben. They select someone whom nobody will really miss. The phrase 'dead ringer' sprang to mind. Cruel beyond belief. And how does that conversation go? Frankie said to Eddie, 'Please pop round, stab a woman to death, and pretend that it's Birdie, then serve time in jail. Meanwhile, I'll be away, free as a bird. Thanks, matey.' What is the point of that? And where's Birdie?

Could it have been done without Frankie knowing? Was he so distraught that he just said it was Birdie on the slab without really looking? Eddie served minimal time and Birdie got away. From what? A violent marriage?'

Eddie allowed her to get away, did the jail time for her because he loved her? So why did they not get together afterwards. Did they intend to walk into the sunset, but something happened? It didn't pan out for them? Did Birdie need to get away from Scanlon, so she plots all this and runs? He was a ranking police officer – maybe he had too much hold over her. Eddie was her knight in shining armour. There was no recorded history of Frankie being violent.

It was all speculation. He swiped back to Wyngate's list, looking for a young woman with no family or close friends. Nobody who would miss them.

There were four names. Ages thirty-two to twenty-four. The description didn't fit for the fourth one – she was quite a heavy girl – but it was difficult to choose between the other three.

Then he remembered the PM report said that the woman had borne a child, before June 1978. Single mothers weren't totally

acceptable in society back then. It was something that would
have been gossiped about. Was that why she was away from
her family? Frankie's friend did the post-mortem; nothing wrong
with that. The story as it was told fitted the findings in examination, except maybe a slight difference in eye colour which they
noted but ignored – the wrong box was ticked, nothing more
than that.

It was a whole different country; a different kind of traveller
used those roads.

He swiped back to the photograph of Birdie's face, that
picture of her dancing with the Peacocks, three men who were
very close until she died.

Or until Ben and Andrew died, to be more accurate.

It was about the children.

And that was not the same thing.

He looked out at the sky. Dark clouds were rolling in; it was
going to thunder. The socially distanced queue outside Greggs
started to scatter for their cars, hurrying. Hurrying because they
were getting wet. Somebody dashed into the shop to get shelter,
keeping close to the wall. The pavement was so hot that it was
almost steaming. He closed his eyes, thinking of the neighbour
with the gnomes. She'd said the babysitter was hurrying because
it was raining. The same terrible summer downpour that had
wrecked the evidence at the scene of the Barrhead bank job.
And that, he realized with a shiver, left a lot of time unaccounted
for.

And why was the girl wearing sunglasses when it was raining?

Professor O'Hare was in the morgue muttering to Dr Gibson
about a second wave of the virus and that somebody sensible
should be in charge now.

'I'd bring every single politician of every party down to that
makeshift morgue and ask them how they would feel if it was
their granny. That would sober them up a bit. I'm going to write
up Aasha Ariti and call Anderson tomorrow with the prelim
results.'

'That case belongs to DI Tony Bannon now, I think. Colin
Anderson is on the murder at Invernock.'

'Not both of them?'

'Nope, check the paperwork. And I think they are here, both of them,' she added lamely.

'We will do the tox results on the girl first. If that goes well, we can then report on Dukes. The place is staying open because of the backlog, so we can work as long as we like.'

The body of Aasha Ariti was remarkably unmarked. He looked everywhere but could find no signs of violence apart from one bad bruise on the back of her head and some other bruising on her shoulder blades. There was some grazing around her right shoulder, and her lungs were heavy with river water. She had drowned in the Clyde. There was no sign of any sexual activity beforehand. There were stretch marks in her dark skin that showed she had lost weight.

O'Hare saw movement behind the glass of the viewing gallery and switched the intercom on.

'Thank you for coming along. I think you both need to see this and have a chat about what is going on here, so we really understand it.'

'Aasha Ariti?' said Tony Bannon, looking very uncomfortable. 'I am actually the SIO.'

'He is,' added Anderson. 'There's no reason for me to be here.'

O'Hare ignored him. The grey-haired pathologist slipped on a pair of steel-rimmed glasses. His voice was grave when he spoke. 'You are a human being, Anderson. You are a father of a daughter a similar age to Aasha here, and I believe that Claire is at the same university.'

'Indeed,' said Anderson, folding his arms and trying to ignore the sight of the young lady lying in front of him. 'I think Tony and I are both struggling with the fact that there's no cause of death as yet.'

'We have a very clear suspect, but the clock is ticking. We can't charge him with her murder until we know that it is murder,' said Bannon. 'The main suspect cannot be located at present, so we need something to move the situation on.'

'Good, I'm glad you have held off from charging anybody with murder.'

The two detectives exchanged a glance. Bannon bit his lip, sensing something coming his way.

'The media pressure has been intense.'

'We don't let the media run our investigation or my office. Although no doubt Trial by Facebook is coming. This year I have seen two suicides where social media was strongly implicated. DI Bannon, as you are the SIO, as far as Aasha here is concerned, can you talk me through what happened to her that night?'

So Bannon, a little non-plussed, talked him through Aasha going to the nightclub, his voice tinny and echoey on the hard walls of the morgue below.

'Did the notes say something about having to go back to the house to get her red dress? Why was that?'

'Why was what?'

'Why did she go back to the house for a dress? How recent is this photograph of her?'

'One of the last pictures taken of her. I called her mother for it. She was actually wearing her cousin's dress – that's why she went home to her aunt's house if that's what you are getting at.'

'Why did you need such a recent photograph? Any reason?'

'Yes, in the older pictures on the electronic file she's much heavier. Her face looks quite different, so it wasn't such a good likeness.'

'And they were not taken such a long time ago,' said O'Hare with a tinge of regret. 'There're many signs that she has been on a recent diet – you can see that she has stretch marks and areas of loose skin. I presume her cousin's the same size that Aasha is now.'

'Do you think she's been on a mad diet?' asked Bannon. 'I'm thinking of the way she stepped back on the stairs. Was she showing off her dress to Anthony or was she showing off her new figure, so much so that he didn't actually recognize her at first?'

'She has lost weight, but please go back and speak to the parents, the aunt, the sister, the cousin. What diet was she on? I suspect it might be a meal replacement three- or four-hundred-calorie job. She had thought that she was pregnant, so that fits as these diets can stop menstruation. Her GP does ask her about the noticeable weight loss and she says it's due to a healthier lifestyle. She was lying. And her GP knew she was lying.' He lifted back the sheet and opened a path of jet-black hair to reveal her scalp, showing patches of thinning. 'And there were no medications prescribed, so what was causing all this? She wasn't stupid; she'd know the sign of any illness. Other consequences are heart arrhythmia and brain haemorrhage and, maybe more importantly for us, hyponatraemia – low blood sodium. I read in your report, Colin, that she was only drinking water when she was out.'

'Yes, we could rule out her being drunk straight away.'

'Did anybody say she was drunk?'

'Poole describes her as slightly drunk as they left the nightclub. The man on the bridge said she was walking unsteadily.'

'She said she was feeling unwell.'

'So she goes out for fresh air, then she has a period of confusion where Anthony thought she was drunk, and then more confusion, which is why she wandered off.'

'And somewhere down at the river, she leaned against the railing, no doubt aware that something was very wrong. She goes into the gardens at the flats, maybe trying to get to somebody's front door, then she slipped into unconsciousness and fell in the water. Her blood findings support that, but I've sent more away for further tests.' O'Hare continued, 'If she was losing weight at six or seven pounds a week, then she would have developed issues, and with my back-of-a-fag-packet calculations I think she was on that trajectory. I think that's what happened to Aasha. Anthony could be totally honest in what he says. Her family will be devastated, but I really don't understand why she would do this to herself.'

'For the wedding. There was a family wedding.'

'God, she was a medical student – surely of all people she would have understood, so maybe you two should do something about it.'

'Like what?'

'Who knows, but get it stopped. If an intelligent young woman can end up in a river because of something that's sold over the counter then . . . then somebody needs to do something about it. I'm fed up with people being pressurized into harmful behaviours. It's a toxic world out there. And me? Well, I'm busy enough with illegal substances, never mind legal ones.'

Up in the gallery, Anderson turned towards Bannon who had covered his face with both hands. He gave him a consolatory pat on the back. 'It's the right outcome, and we weren't to know any of that.'

'The shit is going to hit the fan.'

'And how much worse would it be if you had arrested him? Situations like this are how media liaison earn their wages, so don't stress about it too much.'

O'Hare's voice was wafting out again. 'So this gentleman' – he held up a picture of Dukes – 'was a bit more straightforward in terms of cause of death. The motive for these injuries is outwith my clinical knowledge.' He brandished a file. 'Here's a list of the injuries as incurred by Edward James Dukes at the hand of somebody who was determined to torture him for some reason.'

'Definitely torture?'

'Oh, I would say so. This went on for a very long period of time. It's a recognized pattern – with a twist in this case. The actual cause of death, I think, is straightforward strangulation. The wrist injuries were to extract information – painful but by no means fatal. The injuries to his testicles were post-mortem, something to be thankful for. I presume those were a message for you. Was he a rapist or a sex offender? Something like that?'

'Are you sure about the torture?'

'There are very fine bruises in a line around the dorsal aspect of the wrist, none on the palmer aspect. His hands were fixed tightly, palms down. And then there are the very bloodied puncture marks on the dorsal wrists where the nails had been hammered in, one on each side. So the fine lines were made by your common and not very imaginative cable ties, which were then removed. So I think the wrists would have been firmly held in place by the cable ties round the wooden arms of the chair. So why the nails? Unlike the testicular injuries, these were pre-mortem, carried out to cause pain – perhaps to gain information? The testicle insults were just for our benefit. The actual strangling would have brought about a rather merciful death.'

'I'm pretty sure he could have done without it,' said Anderson. 'So he was tortured. The dog was tortured. Would it have taken a lot of strength?'

'I don't think so. He must have been compliant at some stage. I was a little confused by how exactly it happened. He was in a loft?'

Anderson explained.

'OK, so he may or not have been a paedophile. That would explain why there was such destruction to his genitals. By somebody who didn't have the nerve to do it while he was alive?'

'Or was that the conclusion they want us to jump to because it fits the narrative? He could have been killed for some information that he was unwilling or maybe unable to give. His bank card details maybe. "Tell me now and I'll strangle you. Don't tell me and I'll keep hurting you until you do and strangle you anyway."'

'Did he have any secrets?'

'At the moment, too many to mention. This gentleman—'

'Give me ten minutes and I'll meet you in the office. I've left that other report in there.'

Bannon and Anderson sat and argued the toss about Anthony Poole back and forward. Could they have played it differently? Probably not. Was there going to be a shitstorm? Definitely. Bannon walked to the window for a signal and phoned it in, passing it up the line.

O'Hare bustled in, followed by a cloud of Hibiscrub. He sat down, ignoring Bannon, and opened the file, running a very clean fingernail along the text. 'Was Dukes convicted of the culpable homicide of this young lady in 1978? Too long ago for me to recall.'

'Yes. What did you think?'

'It all made sense to me. But one thing did strike me. Did you notice the knife?'

'What about it?'

'It was a normal kitchen knife.' He turned towards Anderson

and held a pencil to his chest. 'Even if this was incredibly sharp, it would still need a fair amount of pressure to puncture the abdominal wall, upwards and inwards. It stops when it hits a structure too hard to penetrate, but the hand will keep going; it always does on these knives. That's why daggers and fighting knives have the crossbar. The killer would have had a cut on their hand. Exactly here' – he indicated the web of skin between his thumb and forefinger – 'exactly where you have that nasty blister. So there would have been a mix of blood at the scene and, even after all these years, the killer of Birdie will have a scar – I'd bet my last Jaffa Cake on it. Dukes did not.'

Costello's Fiat returned to the car park. Anderson watched from the window of the incident room, waiting for her to get out, but she stayed in it for five minutes or so before she eventually emerged. She didn't appear to have been talking on her phone – just sitting very still. He knew she was seething. He could feel it from here. Anderson presumed that when she did decide to join them, she'd have moved into rant mode. He noted the way she closed the car door very gently, then leaned against it to shut it with a vicious bump of her hip. Her anger would be controlled until she had an audience and then she'd have fury writ large on her face.

Right on cue, the door banged open, and she marched over to the kettle, switching it on with some violence.

Both Wyngate and Mulholland became very interested in their laptop screens.

'What's up?' asked Anderson.

'I'll bloody tell you what's up. That bloody Joanna Craig. That cow has accused me of taking ten grand from her mother's flat. Me? Ten grand from wee Vera?'

'What?' Mulholland and Wyngate both looked up.

'Yes, ten fucking grand – and do you know who is backing her up in this shite?' Her bony finger pointed from her outstretched arm; she was looking at Anderson but her finger pointed to Wyngate. 'His bloody friends, bloody Knobby and Plod.'

Anderson glanced at Wyngate who explained. 'PCs Howie and Follet. They were on the door outside Mrs Craig's flat after she was found with that head injury.'

'Well, seemingly – seemingly, the old dear has all this money there, and it's not there now. And I–I . . .' She nearly exploded. 'I am supposed to have gone in there and taken it between the time of Vera being taken to the hospital and Knobby and Plod turning up. I ask you!'

'Why are they saying that?'

'They think I knew it was there and I just lifted it. I was keen to get into the property and very keen to find out where the will was!'

'Why do they think that?'

'Yes. Why do they think that, Wyngate?' She turned on her younger colleague, her grey eyes blazing.

'Because I might have told them that. Mathieson asked me at the meeting. You did say that, Costello. You asked me where my mum kept all her important stuff – insurance papers, wills, etcetera.'

'That wasn't what I meant. I was looking for Joanna's details.'

'Well. I know that, but all I said was . . . Then I said that you had checked all her valuables—'

'To make sure they were still there,' hissed Costello.

'It was only after I said it that—'

'I'd be quiet if I were you, Wyngate.' Anderson's voice was calm. 'Was there any money in the flat?'

'How should I know? But it seems that somebody said to Joanna that I knew about it, and if it was missing, then I must have taken it. They say I knew about the money because I was doing the shopping, and now Mrs Allan has claimed that I wanted her out of the way in the ambulance, and Knobby says that I tried to pull rank to control the situation.'

'But they have no proof.'

'They don't need any, do they? I knew there was something wrong when I set eyes on her. Cow.'

'Well, go and speak to Vera.'

'She's unconscious.'

They all looked at each other.

'She might not pull through. And Joanna – Joanna knows about Harry . . . She said that to Mathieson: "I know who her brother was." And she's going to the newspapers – probably to Clarissa Fettercairn and Mary Travers because she'll really get a sympathetic ear there, won't she, when she casts doubt on my professional integrity? I think it is officially going to Complaints.'

'Mathieson wouldn't touch that with a bargepole.'

'She already has,' said Wyngate.

'Look, this Joanna woman has an agenda. Let's get after her and find out who she is?' suggested Mulholland.

'Let's not bother,' said Anderson calmly.

'What the fuck is this – Let's Hate Costello Week?'

Mulholland opened his mouth, but Anderson cut in, 'They aren't suspending you, are they?'

'No, not yet. Not until there's some evidence Joanna can produce. Vera habitually takes two hundred pounds a week out of her Cashline account, all from the hole in the wall. She takes it out as soon as her late husband's pension goes in, to keep her balance down so that she gets some kind of allowance. Mrs Allan knows about that, so Joanna presumes that I must know too.'

'What are you have supposed to have done with the cash?'

'Stuffed it up my arse, I guess.'

'Why are upstairs taking it seriously at all?'

'Because Knobby and Plod have gone on record as saying that I was very keen to get back into the flat.'

'So you were, but we went in together.'

'Yeah, that's the other thing: they think that you are my accomplice.'

Wyngate winced.

'No, look, be logical. You didn't do it, so there can be no evidence that you did. She thought her mum had money and the money is no longer there – if it ever was there,' reasoned Anderson.

'So what we need is for Vera to wake up and say what she did with the money. If she never wakes up, then this will stick to me and my reputation like a black shadow.' Costello waved her hand at the timeline on the wall. 'That is what all this is about – it's noise. One unsubstantiated rumour after another. There is always somebody who will believe it. You can never, ever close a door on that. This has been going on for forty years and we are still talking about it. So I am told to keep a low profile and have a cup of tea.' She paused, then screamed, 'Oh, for fuck's sake!'

'What's up now?'
'Who ate all the Hobnobs?'

The assault when it came was brisk but not brutal. Anderson had been making his way to the small car park behind the annexe, down a narrow path, thinking about the headache he had from staring at a computer for six hours. He didn't hear the footsteps rush behind him. The first thing he knew was a blow in the back that pushed his face into the wall. That was the first pain: the thin skin over his cheek against the hard porous brick. His first thought was that somebody had stumbled into him; he expected a call of 'Oh God, I'm sorry' or 'Are you OK?' Then maybe a flick of his jacket as a swift hand relieved him of his wallet. But the pressure on his back increased, squeezing the breath from him; it felt like a shoulder into his spine compressing him. He waited for the knife at his neck, but all he heard was somebody breathing hard – nervous even.

'What do you want?' asked Anderson, with the little air he had left in his lungs. He was speaking into the brick; he didn't know if he was even making sense.

'Stop it, just stop it.'

'Stop what?' hissed Anderson, genuinely confused.

'You are ruining the name of a great man. You must stop it. Do you hear me? Stop it. I've fucking had enough of it.' Anderson was pulled away from the wall and then rammed back into it. The pain in his cheekbone was intense. 'Fucking enough.' The voice sounded upset, almost tearful.

'I'm a police officer,' he said.

'Yes, I know. And that makes it even worse. You should be better than that – better.' There was another jolt, a slam into the brick again.

'Is this about Dougie McSween?' asked Anderson, guessing on the only male child left alive.

'Oh, Jesus.' The voice behind him started to break up, and the pressure released a little.

Anderson struggled to keep his voice calm. 'I'm going to step back, OK? Whatever this is, we need to talk about it. We need to talk – otherwise, I cannot help you.'

The pressure on his back released further. Anderson took a

few deep breaths before he stepped away from the wall, suspecting that this was not a violent perpetrator; this was somebody who had got themselves into a mess.

Anderson had had a long, hard day. They had been making progress, only to be sideswiped by Costello. He wanted to get home and see Moses. He was tired of thinking. He took one slow step back and then turned quickly, raised his right fist and rammed it deep into the face of his attacker. Once the knuckles connected with the cheekbone of his assailant, the latter went down like a sack of potatoes, squealing like a pig.

Anderson was trying to calm down, so he didn't help the guy up, but just let him lie on the ground until he decided to stand up, dust himself down and introduce himself properly.

The man slowly pushed himself to his feet, his hands walking up the front of his thighs as he tried to straighten up. Anderson stood well back just in case, but his assailant started to sob.

It took ten minutes for him to stop crying. He went from deep sobbing to being breathless, his ribs heaving as he fought to get air into his over-stressed lungs. He looked exhausted as he slid back down to the pavement.

Anderson felt the need to do something, some activity. *Use up the adrenaline, use up the adrenaline*, he could hear his old counsellor say. He needed to exercise his old bones to keep the demons away. If he did his Tai Chi for half an hour every morning as he had been advised, he might be able to cope with situations like this a little better. The PTSD he had been suffering for a couple of years after the fire that nearly killed him, nearly killed them all, had faded with good treatment to an uncomfortable memory he could access when he wanted to. It didn't pop up unwanted at the scent of a burning flame, the crackling of wood on fire, or a news clip of the bush fires in Australia. The panic had slowly backed off like a defeated dog; it simply disappeared into the distance. He had never thought he'd be one to suffer from mental health issues – he had always thought of himself as level-headed. The ability to recover and rationalize: bad things happened, and all you could do was minimize the risk. Anderson knew he had been lucky that the treatment had worked for him. He had so much to get better for, to go home for. He had his children, he had Moses, his career. He might even have a wife. He had a lot of stability and security. He had no idea where he might have ended up if he had been living back in that bedsit, staring at the four walls, with only his TV and fear for company.

He looked down at the man, now curled in a ball at his feet, wondering what had driven him to this.

'You OK, mate?' Anderson prodded him with the toe of his shoe. 'Do you want a hand up?'

The sound of Anderson's voice brought the other man to his senses. The heaving chest stilled, the gasping was curtailed and his sobbing quietened. He slowly got back up to his hands and knees, before wiping his nose with the sleeve of his jacket, and then, very unsteadily, tried to get to his feet, as if his lower back would snap if he moved too quickly. He swayed, his arm stretched out, wavering for balance.

Anderson offered him a steadying hand. The younger man, if he was younger, looked up at him, his face bloodied where Anderson's fist had caught his cheek. Snot and tears poured down his face, the tracks of tears light against the grimy grey of his skin.

'I'm sorry,' he muttered, wiping the back of his hand over his nose, making a smear of green and red.

'Yes, you will be,' said Anderson pleasantly. 'Do you want me to arrest you now or should we go for a cup of tea somewhere and talk about it? My car's round the corner.'

They sat in Anderson's messy BMW which still smelled slightly of dead dog. They both had coffee, both had settled for a muffin.

'Why are you raking up all these lies about my father?' His eyes were full of pain, a tortured soul.

Anderson wondered about his mental health. 'Your father?'

'Douglas McSween.'

'One of the Peacocks. I was talking to your sister on Thursday.'

'My half-sister,' he snapped. 'She didn't come to the funeral. And my father was not a paedophile. Why are you investigating him as if he was? The constant besmirching of his name. This has followed him around for years and none of it is true. It made his life unbearable. I saw the newspaper today. You folk never think, do you?'

'To tell you the truth, we are not investigating the Peacocks for any activity involving young children. We're trying to figure out who is spreading these rumours. We're on the same side here.'

'Uncle Frankie was a cop. You should know that he wasn't into any of that stuff.'

'Well, being a serving police officer does not automatically exclude you from wanting to break the law, but that's not what we are looking into.'

'Really? Doesn't look like it from where I'm sitting.'

'Who is doing it? Who has it in for those three guys? It follows them around, this gossip. Some malicious person just goes around spreading lies.'

'You can't slander or libel the dead, can you? They are really going to ramp it up now, aren't they? I've been reading the papers, I know what they are saying.'

'I've read that, but is it because your dad passed away so recently? Is that why this is so raw?'

'Suppose so.'

'OK, so let me ask you a few questions. Can you remember the day your wee brother disappeared?'

'You see, there you go again. It always goes back to that . . .'

And with that, Anderson was left looking at an empty seat and hearing ringing in his ears from the door slamming.

SIXTEEN

Saturday 20th June

Email
To: DCI Colin Anderson
From: DS Tony Bannon
Hi,
   Well, it's got out to the media that we are not seeking any third party in the death of Aasha Ariti. The rumour

is that her death was alcohol-related, so the parents will make a statement after they have spoken to O'Hare. He has offered to talk to them later today and try to explain better than I obviously did.

It turns out there was a complaint about Poole made by another student at the university, re his attitude towards some Chinese students. We are still looking for Poole, but so far all leads are coming up blank. Interestingly, when we told his mum and dad O'Hare's findings from the post-mortem, they could still shed no light on where he was, although we could see the relief was overwhelming.

Oh, and, Diane, my old boss at Complaints and Investigations, has just called me to sound me out about DI Costello. Seems there has been an allegation made against her. Totally unfounded as far as I could see, but if a complaint has been made, they have to investigate. You might want to warn her.

Regards,

Tony

'Before you ask, I ended up having a coffee with Douglas McSween's eldest son, after he rammed my face into a wall.'

'Really? That looks sore.'

'You should see the state of him.' Anderson sat down. 'He threw his coffee all over the inside of my car. He's a little volatile.'

Costello looked at his face. 'Bloody hell.'

'Yip. No wonder his sister doesn't talk to him. I think that his father's death has really affected him, or one of his other childhood traumas,' he added. 'He's more upset by the death of Dukes, and I didn't tell him the manner of it. It would seem he hates the idea of his idyllic childhood being tainted. He freaked when I asked him about the day his brother died.'

'And it *was* an idyllic childhood. The child psychologist watched the films and said there's no stress on those kids at all. Some are more confident than others, but the relationship with the adults is normal. Are you charging him with assault?'

'We have enough paperwork to do.' He clapped his hands in enthusiasm, getting them up to speed with the changes in the Ariti case.

'Seriously? She died because she felt she needed to be thin?' Costello's voice was steely cold.

'Not got time for a feminist rant now, Costello. That's the way of the world.'

'So good enough to argue that she was "of colour" but not because she was damaged by a thousand images of the perfect woman being thrown at her every day?'

Anderson held his hands up in submission. 'It's not your job, it's not mine. This is our job here and, thanks to Mulholland and Wyngate, we have a full day of interviews ahead.'

'Is there any trace of Frankie?' asked Wyngate, keen to move the situation on.

'He doesn't drive, he doesn't have a car or a credit card, he doesn't vote, he has a NI number but it has no current address, and his passport has lapsed. He went to Spain in 1987, then nothing. Nobody knows where he is. As far as I see, there's no death certificate. He has faded away,' said Mulholland.

'Well, I've been looking at the disappearance of Andrew McSween. Did his brother say anything about it?'

'It wasn't a viable topic of conversation.' Anderson slapped his ear gently: the tinnitus was still there.

'One common factor when both boys met their demise, presuming that Andrew is dead, is that it was an occasion when everybody was there – you know, an extended Peacock picnic. So Anne McLeod was there, both times.'

'It happened up in the woods behind a campsite at Oban. Anne had driven up for the day. Andrew's body was never found. It's suspected that he drowned – there's a lot of lochans up there. They searched for a whole week and found nothing.'

'Any trace on Veronica?'

'Still looking for her husband, then I'm going back all the way with her – going back to the hospital she was in and her designated care worker. Of them all, she's the one who has been most affected by . . . by whatever it was they were subjected to.'

The four of them sat round, Costello with her fingers still on the keyboard, the other three with their heads turned, all looking at the wall.

'There is a problem with this family. They lose their children or . . . well, you need to look at the bigger picture to see the pattern here, don't you? Too much coincidence, and then you add into the mix the fact that Dad was a senior detective and the rumours that follow these Peacocks round,' considered Anderson.

'There's the driver of a small dark car following them around. Do we like Loretta, Veronica, Anne or another we don't know about yet?'

'Anne drives a navy Corsa. Loretta has a red Audi, but there's also a black Sandero registered at that address. I'm trying to get a trace on their movements, but I suspect you will have to re-interview them. And, by the way' – he consulted a bit of paper – 'Loretta was off work the day of the funeral. She had a meeting at the Blair Hotel about the wedding arrangements but left at two p.m. No alibi after that. I'd have to approach the family to take it further, see when she got home. Do you want me to do that now?'

'Keep it on the list. I'm keen to find Scanlon.'

Costello pulled a face. 'Despite what may or may not have been going on with abuse, those kids lost two of their pals. That was trauma enough. They are victims of that. It seems to diminish them in some way to call them survivors, a bit "boo sucks" to those that did not survive. I mean, Veronica was placed in a protective environment – her dad paid to keep her safe. They don't all have that privilege.'

'Don't repeat that outside this room or I will lose your manpower . . .'

'Woman power.'

'. . . to a course on political correctness.' Anderson rubbed his face. 'Brian, who does suffer from mental health issues, said that he was not abused, but there's something about the way he acts that doesn't sit right with me. He did say that when he went to his father's funeral, neither Frankie nor Eddie was there – hardly anybody was from those days.'

'And McSween definitely died of natural causes?'

'It doesn't matter how often you ask the question: he died of the virus after complications.'

Anderson heard Wyngate click away at his keyboard. 'Do we think that Scanlon is still alive? Something gives me the impression that Toastie thinks so, but I can't be sure. Surely the fact he's so difficult to find is evidence in itself. He's still in receipt of his police pension; that takes me to a legal firm who are not happy to chat, but I suspect they are dealing with his affairs. Or his estate.'

'And Veronica is also nowhere to be found. She walked out of that school, disappeared, got married, then disappeared again. What do we think about that? I'm phoning the old matron's assistant later as it's too far to drive.'

'And then there were none. The last one left standing is the killer. Or is there a forgotten victim out there, somebody that has no other connection with that family. There could be any number of victims – survivors who have been waiting, biding their time until the right moment came along for them to make their move. Revenge, as they say, is a dish best served cold.'

'Well, I'm blagging my way into the hospital first. I'll be back as soon as. I can't sit here with those accusations hanging over me.'

Costello had gone home to shower. The heat of the annexe made her uncomfortable and she thought it wise to be completely clean to visit Vera. Unlocking her door, she heard the dull voice of Joanna Craig, obviously on her mobile, walking around inside, crossing the hall behind the front door from bedroom to kitchen and then back again.

She didn't mean to listen, but just by taking a few steps towards her neighbour's front door, bending down so her outline was not seen at the glass panel, she could hear her own flat being described. No doubt Vera's was being discussed: three bedrooms, views over the river . . . The voice faded and returned as Joanna walked backwards and forwards, through the hall, walking from room to room. It was obvious to Costello that she was getting a valuation.

Costello judged that Joanna couldn't be in two places at once, so she had a quick shower and headed off to the hospital, where she paid a fiver for a cup of tea and a biscuit in the coffee shop in the large atrium. By the time she walked to the lift, the tea was burning through the cardboard holder round the cup and scalding the skin of her hand. In the lift, she was so tightly packed between other visitors that she couldn't shift her handbag to change hands. By the time she got out of the lift and found the room, the tea was cold.

She learned from the nurse at the station that Mrs Craig had regained consciousness. Closed to visitors, but not closed to the police on an active case, which Costello neither confirmed nor denied. She was here, so she flashed her warrant card.

Mrs Craig looked delighted and then worried to see her. She pulled herself up on the bed, the dressing across her head making her look like Blackbeard's cleaner.

Costello dragged a chair and placed it in the corner of the room.

They chatted, all the usual stuff at first. Then, at the first lull in conversation, Vera Craig said, 'I'm so sorry.'

'What about?' She waited for the old lady to broach the subject.

Vera's old fingers pulled up the thin duvet, as if she hoped to disappear behind it.

Costello sensed her tension. 'What is it, Vera?' she asked pleasantly, thinking that her daughter had said something the little old lady was not comfortable with. Costello was nothing but a friendly face popping in, and although Mrs Craig could sense Costello on the landing at all hours of day and night, opening the door with a request to pick up this or get that, it was never onerous. If she had been attacked, the issue was with the residents buzzing people in without knowing who they were. That was a lecture for the community police to give; they were all responsible for each other's safety.

Then, looking at the tiny wrinkled face, the wadding round the head wound, the thin-lipped mouth moved. 'I'm so sorry, it's just that the young man with the terrible ears, he has gone to so much trouble, and all along it was me. It was only me being a daft old woman and I didn't know that all this was going on. He came to see me. He was so sweet and earnest. I didn't have the heart to tell him that there was nobody else there. I fell. I'm sorry.'

'You fell?'

'Twice. I got up and tried to clean up the blood, but I don't know what happened after that. I really can't remember.'

'Well, I will call DC Wyngate. I know he'll be very relieved. Vera, did you have money in the flat?'

'Yes, I did keep some.'

'OK. Can I ask how much?'

'About ten thousand pounds. I thought it was safe, with you being a police officer, but Joanna was saying . . .'

The door opened behind her. Joanna came in, saw Costello and snapped, 'Excuse me.'

Vera recoiled immediately.

'Are you OK, Mum? Don't speak to her. She stole your money. I saw her car drive away when I was on the phone.'

Vera's eyes fluttered to Costello, their message clear. Then Joanna looked in her mother's face, her thumb on her mother's chin, turning her face so their eyes met.

'I was just paying her a visit, being neighbourly,' said Costello.

'And you're forbidden to do that.'

'Oh, nobody told me.'

'Well, this is harassment. We've made a complaint.'

Costello turned to Vera, almost pinned to the bed. 'Mrs Craig, I'd better go now. I'm glad you are feeling better. I didn't take any money from your flat, and I know you know that.'

Mrs Craig looked shocked. It seemed as if she was not aware of it either. 'My money?'

'Yes, she took your money – the ten thousand pounds,' said Joanna.

'Difficult to do when I didn't know about it. So we'll see, Joanna. We'll see.' And Costello closed the door behind her.

'Just to warn you that Costello is sitting in her car again, so she's in a mood,' said Anderson as Mulholland limped out to the toilet and Wyngate looked intently at his laptop.

Five minutes later, Costello stomped into the room. 'What a cow, that Joanna. Wee Vera is just lying there, terrified of her daughter. And I've no proof that I didn't take the money. I don't have proof of any of it.'

'They have no proof that you did. It's a load of crap.'

'So what am I to do? This woman has me over a barrel. She could ruin my career.'

'And mine.' Wyngate's face was as miserable as Costello had ever seen it, his features concertinaed and collapsed into the lower half, as if it would take a lot of effort to ever smile again. And in that moment, it looked unlikely.

Costello leaned back and swung her boots on to the tabletop, clasping her hands over the gap in her open jacket, her fingers interlocking like an interested psychiatrist.

Anderson was calm. 'Well, the first thing is to congratulate yourself that you did the right thing, and you had clearance to do everything that you did from above, so you were in a chain of events that you had no real control over. Were you there as a neighbour or a police officer? It was the former. Then you can write a complaint about Knobby and Plod for not doing their jobs properly and putting the wind up everybody. They presumed what had happened because you were an eyewitness, reported it to be so. An over-tired, half-asleep witness who had an emotional interest in the case.'

'I think the bitch daughter is thinking about putting that flat on the market.'

'But her mum isn't dead. Yet. Or is she going to take Vera to live with her?'

'There's something not right about this entire situation. Vera is under pressure from her daughter, and she's scared. I've seen enough abuse victims to recognize it.'

'I was frightened of Joanna when she spoke to me,' admitted Wyngate. 'And I am used to dealing with scary women.'

'On a daily basis,' muttered Anderson, glancing at Costello from behind a computer screen.

'So maybe she's just taking advantage of the shortcuts Plod and Knobby took. Would you do that, Colin? Accept blindly the thoughts of somebody half-asleep. I was a witness, but they should have done their job properly – got witness statements, door to door, flat to flat, investigated who used the lifts – but they jumped the gun and drew a very wrong conclusion. There'll be an enquiry into how all this went wrong, and you and I are going to find ourselves dragged into it. Yes, Wyngate, you took their word for it, but they gave you a biased version of events because it suited them.'

'You didn't report on it, Costello.'

'I offered to, they said not to bother. So I didn't,' she said. 'They might have spoken the truth, but they were lazy, I believe. They repeated what I said – I was there, remember, lying on my sofa, with my front door open and my hall door open. I could hear what they were doing. They were talking about football and having a wee rest on the stairs, waiting for somebody more senior to turn up. When you did, their respect went out of the window and they abused you, mocked you – all that Big Ears and Noddy stuff. There's no room in modern policing for that. They should have passed on the information they had gathered in a professional and concise manner.'

'But they didn't.'

'Exactly. Was Vera Craig pushed or did she fall?'

'She said herself that she fell; I doubt she was coerced into that. But there's something about all this that just does not fit.'

'Joanna was on to Diane Mathieson at Complaints. Bannon told me.'

'Well, that's me sunk.'

'I wouldn't be so sure. I think Mathieson had her fingers burned in the Sideman case; she will go carefully now.'

'Carefully as in hippo in an outrage.' Costello looked round. 'I suppose that Joanna will inherit everything that Mrs Craig has.'

'Don't even think about it. We can't do an investigation into the financial status of her daughter just for you to prove a point.'

Costello looked at the wall, her eyes scanning over the names. 'That's a point, actually. Inheritance. Who gets Dukes' house? There must be a will, a lawyer, a something somewhere.'

'I know the answer to that,' said Anderson through his laptop screen. 'Ingram Selwood, a company in the middle of Glasgow.'

'Hang on, hang on,' said Wyngate. 'I'm sure . . .' He flicked furiously through sheets of paper on his spiral pad. A smile lit up his face. 'That's the same legal firm that looks after Frank Scanlon. That's where his police pension goes.'

'This is getting interesting. Could we do a backwards trace on the houses that Eddie Dukes has owned? He's been in this one for ten years. Hill houses along that coast are not cheap.'

The three of them considered that for a very long moment, interrupted by Costello thinking out loud. 'Could that be the pay-off for going to jail for the murder of somebody who was not Birdie? Was Frankie supporting him? Bought him his first house to get him on the property ladder when he came out of jail?'

'He'd get Birdie's life insurance.'

'Bloody hell, is this going to be something as basic as an insurance scam?'

'How are you fixed with your workload, Wyngate?'

'I am pretty full. Tracing cars, Veronica and Frank – nobody is easy to find in this case. But Brian found you . . . I was thinking that if we dangled a carrot, they might find us.'

'Was that what Eddie was tortured for? The whereabouts of Frankie? Veronica, even?'

'There are a lot of people hiding. How is Mulholland doing with the missing woman – the list from 1978?'

'Where is he, anyway?'

Anderson pulled a face, 'He went to the loo. Is he making a phone call?' He walked round a stack of folders to the door and opened it, listening down the corridor. Then he went out. Costello and Wyngate heard his footsteps quicken, breaking into a run as he shouted, 'Costello, call an ambulance.'

It took the ambulance ten minutes to arrive. Wyngate was dispatched to inform Vik's mother and make sure she got to the hospital to see her son. Vik had looked terrible – white, sweating – and he was in some respiratory distress by the time he was covered in a blanket on the stretcher. The paramedic had cut the leg of Mulholland's designer suit to relieve the pressure at the operation site, now swollen, green fluid seeping through the dressing. As one paramedic cut through the second dressing and padded it, he looked at his companion and said, 'Well, at least it's not coronavirus.'

Anderson said he'd stay in the office as Costello already had an interview booked in, and she was glad of the fresh air and the time to think as she walked down Hyndland Road to meet at an outdoor café. Lynda Armstrong, one of Veronica's named carers at St John's, had been easy to track as she had a social media presence. She was living in Glasgow and had agreed to meet in one of the coffee houses that was now open. She was

a tall, thin woman, lecturing at the university, and from the look
of her, Costello would guess it was politics or feminist studies.
There was something about the number of scarves she wore
round her neck that sounded her alarm bells. Costello was
feeling rattled after Mulholland's collapse, so she was glad for
a seat, a cup of tea and fresh air.

'Yes, I recall Veronica Scanlon – funny kid, damaged goods.'
Lynda sipped a latte with caramel syrup which Costello had
paid for. 'God, she was fragile – like deep down. I was only a
few years older than her, so within the boundaries of care I
guess we became friends.'

'Did you talk a lot?'

'Not at first, and she didn't speak to anybody else either, but
we did in time. I was part of her journey, the process she was
going through. She was still finding her way through the
emotional fog, if you will.'

'I won't, thank you,' muttered Costello. 'What was her
emotional state like?'

'She was both lovely and awful in equal measure. Still, you
think there but for the grace of God go I. If I'd been through
what she had . . . I mean, to conceptualize what she had
witnessed was so utterly traumatic.'

'The death of her mother.'

She placed a ringed hand, palm up to Costello's face. 'The
murder of her mother. Can you imagine that?'

'Oh, yes, I used to fantasize about killing my mother. She
was that kind of mother.'

Lynda's face was frozen in sincerity. 'Well, Veronica was
very close to her mother, and years later for her brother to slip
from her grasp as she was trying to hold on to him, actually
trying to help him cling to life. Then he's gone. That burned
deep in her mind. If she had held on until her daddy got there,
she could have saved him. She always felt that her dad blamed
her. Can you imagine that degree of survival guilt? Maybe all
along, she should have blamed her dad.'

Costello lifted her hand to the scar on her hairline, a present
from her brother when he tried to murder her. Her dad had
saved her. She felt brief empathy for the troubled Veronica.

'Did she talk about Andrew?'

'Lost in the mist? Yes, Veronica was dipping her toe into a friendship with the other girl. They were out for a walk, talking to each other, acting more like babysitters than two young girls who wanted to talk about David Essex and the Bay City Rollers. You see, Ms Costello, there was no room for them to grow up, to express themselves. They were, collectively, "the children". There was no expression of self, so she self-harmed a lot. We really struggled to get her medication right. She was a non-person at times.'

'In what way?'

'Just that she wasn't there. She was absent. You could talk to her for days and not know anything about her, other than losing her mum and her brother. Her dad's friends . . .'

'Eddie and Dougie?'

'Well, I can't say much, but when there is a victim presenting in that fashion, there does tend to be an abuser in the background. And if you snapped that girl in two, she'd have the word "victim" drilled right through to her core. Now, of course, we're much more enlightened, and I think she started to present with an extreme form of borderline personality disorder. She struggled with her identity – she really had no concept of who she was and where she belonged in the world, you know. She struggled to find her feet.'

'Don't we all?'

'Yes, but there was the huge, extremely swift change in her perceptual concepts, the degree of her self-mutilation.'

'When? At the time her mother was murdered?' asked Costello.

'No, later in our care, when her dad abandoned her.'

Costello noted the use of the word abandoned and asked, 'Ever any sign of her mutilating others?'

Lynda ignored her.

'Obviously, I don't know much about it, but don't sufferers of BPD tend to indulge in risky behaviour patterns – drug abuse, promiscuity, gambling? Veronica has no criminal record, no bad debt – nothing shows that pattern. Or am I way off here?' Costello asked, fishing.

'Even back then, she had poor control over her antagonistic behaviour and was very confrontational when threatened with abandonment.'

'Understandable, when her father abandoned her,' agreed Costello.

'I'd really like to see Veronica if you know where she is. I'd be interested to see how she has managed over the years, how she has coped with her paranoia, her emotional detachment and—'

Costello interrupted. 'Would you expect her to hold a grudge?'

'Oh, yes – for months, even years. Some delude themselves that avenging that grudge can redress their emotional imbalance, put them back on the right track, so to speak.'

'And does it?'

'Of course not.'

'And now we're looking at the Peacocks, if you're familiar . . .' nudged Costello.

'Oh, yes, I've done a fair bit of reading about them. There's a section about them in the cultural history museum in Glasgow. I was looking at the methods of access these men had, looking at the Peacocks through those eyes.'

'Access?'

'To children. They kept it within the family – those three men considered themselves family.'

Costello waited to see if any direct evidence was going to come her way.

'Something happened to her father. I can't recall what, but Veronica tried to escape. Dawn Flanders, another resident, went with her . . .' Lynda shook her head, aware of saying too much.

'Escape?'

'Well, Dawn was a right tough nut and they decided to make a run for it. They were fourteen, and they realized they could get over the far wall. According to Veronica, she was already crying and wanting to come back when they got to the wall, but she said Dawn pulled out a knife and forced her to help her over. And over the two of them went. They could have been away, but Veronica refused. There was a fight, the knife got pulled, they both got hurt. Veronica was stabbed through the hand and into the leg. Dawn got stabbed in the leg. That, unfortunately, turned out to be fatal. They were found lying in the grass, at the bottom of the wall. They must have been lying for half an hour or so, both unconscious. Veronica survived. Dawn passed away, and there was a whole kick-up about it, as you can imagine.'

'There would have been a fatal incident enquiry.'

'Oh, there was. I recall being terrified of the fiscal, all that machismo oppression. Who was where and when, how did they make their way from one part of the building to another? They asked us over and over again. How did they escape? Like it was Colditz.'

'You do make it sound like a prison.'

'Well, it was an educational institution, but it was a prison in reality, of course. In those days, men believed in institutional violence and repression. Veronica was a victim. She had huge issues.'

'You only have Veronica's version of events on the night of the escape, is that correct?'

'Well, yes. Dawn died of blood loss.'

'One knife?'

'Yes, look, Veronica was a victim. She was always . . . well, I really have to say that I'm no longer comfortable talking about this. She had big issues with her mental health. It's nothing trivial we're talking about, and she has a right to her confidentiality, no matter where she is.'

'Legally, that confidentiality goes out of the window when there's a life at risk, especially if the life at risk is hers. It's not like we're going to blast it all over the place, but the person in charge needs to know what we are up against, so we can try to ensure the safety of others as well as her.'

'Well, you need to get a warrant or court order as you won't hear it from me, no matter what she has done. This is not a police state.'

'No, it's not. If it was, I wouldn't have bothered buying you a coffee.'

When Costello got back to the incident room, Anderson was sitting at his desk, scrolling.

'Have you heard how Vik is?'

'They're pumping antibiotics into him. He's in a bad way. They have asked Wyngate and his mother to stay there.'

'I think that's a good idea. Mulholland's an only child – his mum might need some support.'

They both slumped into their seats, suddenly tired, the wind taken out of their sails. Anderson stared at the mess, files strewn everywhere, coffee cups, Mulholland's jacket still on the back of his chair.

'How did you get on with Veronica's care person?'

'She was a pain in the arse. But she told me one interesting thing. There was another violent incident in Veronica's youth, where she was stabbed by another girl. It sounded fifty-fifty, but the other one died.'

'Really? That sounds familiar. What kind of place was St John's in reality? Was she there to be helped or was she there because Frankie wanted her out of the way?'

'It'll be interesting to see what the old matron's assistant has to say about Veronica,' said Costello. 'She sounds such a trau-matized wee girl. It was a small, selective, expensive place. She was there for five years. Frankie didn't even take her home for the summer holidays. She stayed there all year. Was she under some kind of care order or was there just nothing to go home for, nobody to go home to? Poor kid. And Colin, you're a dad – would you not want Claire at home, especially if something had happened to Brenda and Peter? If Claire was thirteen, would you not want to take care of her and make sure that she was safe from all the evils of the world? That wee lassie had already suffered so much loss.'

'I think I would, but then I'm not Frankie, and Claire is not Veronica.'

'You're not so different – both dads are cops who know the nasty side of life, and both kids have suffered loss at a young age.'

'Or was Veronica incarcerated there so that nobody believed what she said? The bigger difference is society. Nowadays, you'd be expected to have her at home – but in those days? I don't know what society would make of a man like that living alone with a young daughter with mental health issues.'

'He sells the family home, understandable when you think that his wife, or so he claimed, had bled to death in that kitchen. Too many memories for him – so yes, he'd have sold it.'

'Or if he needed the money to send Veronica to this place, or to pay off Eddie? She was in a locked school, basically. How much did they listen to what she said? She saw a woman die, believed it was her mother, Colin. Her wee brother slipped out of her fingers and that resulted in his death. Her wee friend wandered off into the mist at Oban and was never found.'

Anderson closed his eyes, leaned back in the seat and then stared at the ceiling.

'Why don't we go back to first principles and look at the money. Frankie would have been on a good salary. Birdie was insured. Would the insurance pay more if she had been the victim of violent crime?'

'Frankie gets the insurance money and the money from the sale of the house. He moves to a smaller place, pays for Veronica's care, in inverted commas, and then he pays Eddie Dukes when he comes out of jail, four years for culpable homicide. Served less than three.'

'And much of that in a soft prison.'

'Somebody said that Veronica was in the paper, that she had the article framed. She was a swimmer – she used to swim in the Firth in the summer on a daily basis. There's one incident that I think Wyngate found where she swims out and raises the alarm for an older woman who got into difficulty. She wasn't strong enough to bring her to shore, but she held the woman up and screamed until two men swam out to the rescue. She was about, what, six then? A wee celebrity.'

'Six? That's really young?' Anderson shook his head in disbelief.

'And then later that year there's an allegation of a sexual assault – same beach, Black Bay down at Invernock. That was before the marina was as big as it is now. After that incident, most people went to the open-air swimming pool.'

'Wyngate did come across this obscure website. It links the Scanlon family with paedophile accusations but not in the way we might think. Veronica, down at the beach at Invernock, the tenth of July 1976. There was a mighty hoo-ha about her being touched inappropriately by a stranger, a man she later identified as a Daniel Fishbourne – she looked at him, pointed him out.'

'Did we not think that it might have been Ellis Whyte, the

child killer? You said he was born there, may have been honing his skills on the locals before he left?'

'That's all with hindsight. The police arrested Fishbourne there and then, but dropped all charges later due to lack of evidence.'

'Fishbourne denied it to the day he died. Nobody else was ever suspected. Kelly's review in 2010 said that Ellis was on the east coast that weekend, and that's why the rumour followed Fishbourne around. It ruined his career. Frankie hated him and was warned off to let the police do their jobs. The care team in charge of the six-year-old reported that they were convinced she was telling the truth.'

Anderson swung round in his seat.

'That's interesting . . . Not sure where it fits in here, though.'

Costello's phone rang so she lifted it up and pulled a face at Anderson, then turned to look out the window.

He couldn't help but hear what she said.

'Hello, Diane. Yes, I know. Complaints . . . No, I didn't know that she had money in the house . . . I don't know why Joanna said that Vera had told me because she didn't . . . and no, I wasn't looking for her will . . . I was looking for Joanna's phone number . . . Wyngate knows that . . . No. I didn't expect to get anything in her will. Where is all this coming from? . . . Yes, I did her shopping . . . I was being neighbourly . . . Yes, I was keen to look round the property . . . I was looking for Joanna's phone number . . . and yes, I did have a set of keys . . . Pardon?' Costello turned to Anderson, her face was white. 'In that case, I think I need to consult the Federation, but yes, I can make that. This is a complete load of shite.' She swiped her phone off and started swearing again. 'What a fucking joke.'

'Was that Diane Mathieson from Complaints by any chance?'

'The Gruppenführer herself. She was warning me. Joanna Craig is tying us all up in knots. Mathieson suspects Ms Craig might be making a career out of this.'

SEVENTEEN

Sunday 21st June

Costello was already on the phone when Anderson walked into the incident room. From the look of the half-eaten cake and the empty cups, she and Wyngate had been there for some time, although the meeting had been called for nine a.m. to give them an extra hour. Wyngate had checked up on Mulholland; his condition had deteriorated a little during the night.

'Aasha's mother,' mouthed Wyngate, shrugging to indicate that he had no idea about the reason for the call.

Seeing Anderson, Costello said, 'Do you mind if I put you on speakerphone, Mrs Ariti? My colleague has just come in – the man who was with me when we found your daughter.'

She nodded and pressed the icon.

'So that's all it was, then – she was starving herself?' The voice from the phone floated out, forceful and wanting answers.

'It's tragic, but not as uncommon as you might think.'

The noise of sobbing filled the room. 'We brought her up to be stronger than that. She was such a bright, kind-hearted young woman. She died because her boyfriend finished with her and went out with some skinny malinky instead? He put a picture of her up on Instagram – the same one, again and again. It wasn't a good picture, and she thought it made her look fat. It really got to her. She was losing weight for the wedding. They haven't even finished making her dress.' She started to cry. 'Are you sure . . . are you really sure that's what it was – the diet?'

'There are still test results to come back, Mrs Ariti, but the pathologist is sure.'

'He was very kind when he spoke to me.'

There was a long pause. Costello looked at Anderson for help, but he shook his head.

'We do see it a lot. Nobody knows the stresses their children are under nowadays. They go off into the big world and they appear to be coping, but deep down, nobody knows.'

'I guess you are right.' Her voice broke. 'Did she look OK – you know, when you found her?'

Costello shrugged at Anderson again. What was she supposed to say to that? When Costello saw her, Aasha had been in the water for over twenty-four hours.

'She looked at peace, Mrs Ariti.'

'This is where Elizabeth Shand was last seen on the sixteenth of June 1978 – it was a Friday night.' Wyngate looked up at the flat, the dirty windows, the boarded-up doors, the knee-high grass with the obligatory mattress lying upright against the wall. 'If she ran away from this, I can't blame her,' he said. As they stood on the pavement, a nosy rat stuck his head out and had a sniff at them. It retreated, dismissing them as neither dangerous nor edible.

'I can't see Birdie Scanlon trusting anybody who came from this background to look after her children. Especially with her husband being a cop.'

'Maybe that didn't matter. It might be more of a sacrifice they were after. Somebody troubled.' Wyngate looked round. 'Do you mind them?'

'Who? Wife-beating bastards like Muir?'

'No, rats. The girls have a couple of them – nice wee things. You can teach them to do tricks, they know their names, they come when they are called and can understand simple commands.'

'Good God. Any more of that and they will be recruiting them for Police Scotland. Shall we?' She indicated the front door. 'I think we should take a deep breath before we go in.'

'How do you want to play it?'

'Keep it nice. We have no real reason to be here.'

'Apart from the fact that he has a rap sheet as long as my arm for violence to women. And then Lizzie disappeared. She's the right age, right build to be the babysitter, and she had given birth.'

They walked up to the large main door, which was hanging

off its hinges, so they slid past it, clambered over an old pram parked across the close and made their way up the stairs to the flat, middle floor, right. Only the right side of the tenement was inhabited; the left side had been condemned, due to the bulging of the end wall.

'Is this safe?' asked Wyngate looking at the big crack in the step as they went up the stinking stairway.

'Safer than the piece of shite we are about to interview.'

Wyngate knocked on the door, and they both pulled out their warrant cards, ready; they did not expect to gain entry. Sandy Muir could smell a cop at a hundred paces.

The door opened a little way, and a small triangular face appeared behind it. It was difficult to know if it was male or female – pinched, thin, pale, anything from fifteen to thirty, or younger or older.

'Hi, I am DI Costello, this is DC Wyngate. Can we have a wee word?'

The door closed slightly but not entirely. 'Sandy? Police!'

A smoke-rasped voice fired out of the living room. 'Aye, ah thought ah could smell shite.'

'It's about a missing person report Mr Muir made in 1978.'

'Youse took yer bloody time.'

'Cold case,' smiled Costello politely. 'Can we come in and have a wee word with you, Mr Muir? You filed the report.'

The face went quickly to the side, and the door jerked open. An old man stood behind it, old enough to be the girl's father or grandfather. So he had another abusive relationship, picking on the younger and weaker, as he got older and frailer.

'Mr Muir, you don't know me, but we'd like to talk to you about the 1978 missing person report on Lizzie Shand.'

'Aye. Whit o' it?' His lips were lined with white foam. He hadn't washed that morning. The flat smelled, he smelled. Costello couldn't believe she was going to say the next words that came out of her mouth.

'Do you mind if we came in?'

'Aboot Lizzie?'

'Yes, Elizabeth Shand,' she repeated.

He nodded at his young companion and then the door opened

fully, and they walked to the front of the flat and the big room that faced the street.

'This one o' yon cauld cases we see on the tele?'

'Yes, Mr Muir, it is. We do periodic reviews of all the cold cases – you know, missing women, all that kind of thing.'

He sat down on the leather chair in front of a massive TV that was halfway up the wall. There was a cigarette packet on the burned arm of the chair, three dirty cups and a bottle of Thunderbird on the floor beside it, but apart from the smell, the flat was quite clean. All they needed to do was open the window. Costello was yearning for the smell of urine that had scented the stairwell. This was stale body sweat, old smoke and, she suspected, recent sex.

He didn't ask them to sit down, for which Costello was grateful.

'So something's come up, aboot Lizzie? She was up the duff, you know. Ah'd like tae know whit happened to ma wean.'

'You last saw Lizzie on the sixteenth of June 1978?'

'That soonds aboot right. Ah'd be lying if ah said ah remembered, but if that's whit ah said at the time, then that'll be right.' He smiled. He had one tooth, reminding Costello of the reruns of *Steptoe and Son*.

She could see a ghost of the easy charm that he used to trap vulnerable women – it was pleasant and comfortable, secure. He still had crinkly brown eyes that looked so benign they could belong to a puppy. He once put a hot iron through his girlfriend's skull. Costello could see him squeezing his pregnant girlfriend round the neck, keeping the pressure on with his fingers until she was dead.

'Do you recall the last time you saw her?' She had read the report, memorized it word for word.

'Aye, well. Ah think we wur in the pub and we came back tae the flat. We wur in Maryhill at the time. We wur having quite a wee sesh, me and Lizzie, and Tam from doon the street.'

'Thomas Whitehill?'

'She's no as stupid as she looks,' said Muir to Wyngate.

'Don't answer that, Wyngate,' said Costello with humour, not wanting to antagonize Muir. If he clamped up, they would get nothing. If he felt relaxed and superior, he might slip up and make a mistake.

'Aye, he wur here wi' his bird, noe name but she'd big tits, wee skinny arse. Lizzie wur pissed, she wanted mair vodka and hud a hairy fit. She fucked aff. Ah went oot after her, and the last ah sees o' her wis her walking up the street to the cemetery. It wis safe tae dae that then, safer than it's noo.'

'Well, that's underfunding for you,' said Costello mildly. 'And that was the last you saw of her?'

'Aye.'

'Did she have any family?'

'A ma she didnae speak tae. Ah spoke tae her a few times to see if Lizzie wis there, but she hadnae heard a dicky.'

'You believed her?'

'Ah did not. And ah suspected that she knew wur the baby wis, so ah pressed her, but she said nothin'.'

'Lizzie was living here at that time?'

'Gibson Street, ah think. Women's hostel, but she kept gettin' booted oot on her arse. Ah think she's dead.'

'Should we be looking for a body?'

'It's a dangerous city oot there.'

'I thought you said it was safe?'

'Safer, still perverts oot there walkin' the streets, tae clever fur youse tae catch, eh? Hidin' in plain sight – some o' them cops even. So excuse me, but ah huv better things tae dae wi ma time than breathe the same air as youse guys.'

He ushered them towards the door. A thin bony hand clamped on her shoulder, squeezing the bone.

'And if she turns up, ah wanna know where ma wean is. It'll be forty-three noo, needs to know who the da is, ah have that right. So if youse find her, get her telt.'

Even now the threat was there.

'If anything comes to light, Mr Muir, we shall do all that the law allows us to do.'

'You're a piece of shite.'

Costello and Wyngate walked towards the door. The shadow of the girl was still standing in the corner. She had not moved at all.

Wyngate was going out of the door; his hand was on the Yale lock, twisted the catch and opened it. He was out into the close when a hand shot out and closed the door, trapping Costello inside the flat. She turned and stared Muir right in his face. His breath stank, and she could see hatred flame in his eyes.

'You are a bit auld in the tooth but still tae young tae remember the perverts that used tae be on the streets in those days, in the City of Glasgow. The cops were up tae their shite like everybody else, and if ah'm thinking aboot whit happened to Lizzie, ah'd be looking a wee bitty closer tae home than here. In fact, if ah wis you, ah wouldn't bother coming out ma own fuckin' office.'

'If that is a vague accusation, do you have somebody in mind?' she asked sweetly.

'Me? Ah never says a fuckin' word. Now goodbye, sweetheart. On yer way. See how far yer investigation gets afore it's pulled from you like a deid rat oot a sewer.'

There was a knock at the door. 'Are you OK in there, Costello?'

'Yes, just coming. The smell in here is getting to me.'

Muir smiled at her as she opened the door.

As she passed, he leaned forward. 'Nae smoke withoot a flame hen.'

Without moving her head, she whispered back. 'And always fight fire with fire, Mr Muir.'

'Sorry, Wyngate, but I need to go home and spend an hour under the shower. You might want to as well. God knows what we might've picked up in there. I've a nice invitation to turn up at Partick Central and be interviewed about Vera Craig tomorrow. So after my shower, I'm going to the hospital to see how Vik is doing. And if I float past Vera's room and pop in to say hello, then so be it.'

Wyngate executed a quick three-point turn, desperate to get away before his tyres were stolen. 'You'll just get yourself into more trouble.'

'How could I be in more trouble? Vera needs to know what is going on.'

'I still don't think . . .'

'Well, you don't really get paid to think, do you? Tell Anderson that he's doing the other visit on his own. I'm sure he'll manage. Then we'll regroup tonight, or are you sloping off home?'

'I'll think about it,' said Wyngate. And he thought about explaining to his wife that he'd be working late, again.

Costello slipped the key into the lock of Vera Craig's flat, feeling like a thief. Joanna's hire car was not in the car park, so she presumed she had some time. She had her phone ready and she was going to photograph everything she could find that might give her a lead on Joanna Craig and her machinations.

When she arrived at the hospital, she had found herself on a list of banned people. There was only one person that Mrs Craig was now allowed to see, and the staff had instructions that if Costello persisted, they were to call security.

She asked who was the one allowed to visit, presuming it was Joanna.

The nurse didn't say anything, but rolled her eyes and said with precise emphasis, '*Some* members of the family are allowed.'

'The daughter, then? Shit!'

'Nope, she's banned as well. You can tell that we're upset by that.' The nurse smiled sweetly.

'OK, that's OK.' Costello was thinking hard.

'A middle-aged man with a bow tie. He brought her flowers. They spoke for quite a while. I thought it was her son.' She reached behind the computer screen. 'But she left this for you. You're the police officer, aren't you? Said you were to get it if you popped in, but said we were to remind you to be careful. Is there something going on?'

In the car, Costello had opened the envelope, found a key and took that as a sign.

It might have been Complaints and Investigations who had banned her, but she didn't see them banning Vera's daughter. And they didn't tend to walk around in bow ties.

At the flat, she walked down the hall, just as she had on the day when she had found Vera, but the place smelled of curry and strong perfume. There was a damp towel lying on the hall carpet. The place was a tip. The Viking longship was missing, as was its glass case. The silver spoons were gone from the wall. She saw them lying on the dining-room table, next to a laptop.

Mrs Craig's beautiful flat was a mess. The bed was a heap of duvet. The china doll was lying in the corner, its lace skirts up in the air, its creepy face smashed in. There was a faint scar on the wall, telling the story of where the doll had been thrown.

The kitchen was full of stacked takeaway dishes, and the smell of rotten leftovers floated from the bin. She peered into the toilet. It hadn't been flushed and there was a small mountain of dirty clothes on the floor.

Was Joanna really the daughter of wee super-clean Mrs Craig who loved her bleach and her Pledge?

She found a paper pad on top of a copy of *Miller's Antiques Handbook and Price Guide* on the dining-room table, beside a spoon that had been lifted from its cradle in the rack. There were two phone numbers scribbled down and some items of jewellery listed. She Googled the phone numbers on her own phone. The local number was McTear's Auctioneers' valuation line. The other was a London number, Christie's. Well, that was the boat and the spoons going up for auction. A few rings lay out on the table – older styles but probably full of quality gems. She picked up one of the rings, reading the inscription *Vera and Davy*, and a date: *23/10/1968*. Her wedding day? Sitting down, she knocked the pad with her elbow, revealing a mobile phone lying on the table where Joanna's right hand would have been. A woman like Joanna wouldn't go out without her phone – who did that these days? Was this a second phone?

It was locked, of course, but she held it up to the window on its side, looking at the pattern of fingerprints. People always slid their fingers the same way and never varied it. She bet Joanna cleaned her phone as often as she flushed the toilet.

She walked over to the window and on her fifth try the phone unlocked, and she scrolled and read. And read. Photographing the phone screen with her own phone. Suddenly, it all started to make sense. Why Vera Craig would not want DI Costello to ever meet Joanna Craig or Joanna Russell or Joanna McPherson. What a bitch!

She was still at the window, two phones in her hands – her own and what she now knew to be a burner. Then she heard a car come into the car park three floors below: Joanna's hire car zooming in at forty miles an hour. Costello watched as she got out, wondering if she'd been at the hospital and now felt the net closing. Joanna did look rather harassed, opening the boot and taking out a large empty holdall. A quick glance round the car park, then something made her look up.

And she stopped in her tracks.

Costello slowly held up her phone. Then the burner. She held them against the glass so Joanna could see.

Their eyes met for a moment, and Costello thought, *Well, come on, hen, if you think you're hard enough.*

EIGHTEEN

At the top of Mulholland's action list was a name, Mrs Jackie Mulroony, and a note that she might be worth a chat, plus an address. She was listed as the next of kin of a missing person, Maureen Laverty, a cousin who had walked out of the house and disappeared. Mulholland obviously thought it was a good fit. Anderson indicated and pulled the BMW up outside the neat bungalow in Rutherglen, a clean dark-red Corsa on the recently powerwashed monoblocked driveway, a fat yellow Labrador lying on the step, enjoying the early-afternoon sun. Anderson wasn't one for making tenuous connections himself, but he trusted Mulholland's instinct as a detective and a researcher. He couldn't bring himself to think of that healthy young man lying now in his hospital bed. They were talking of putting him in an induced coma. Anderson shuddered: that was a step too close to drifting into the endless night.

But his DS had been on to something, and as too much in this case had already been taken at face value, Anderson had clearly stated to his sergeant that he wanted no prior knowledge of what he had gleaned from his internet and background checks. So here he was, ignorant of the connection his DS had made.

There was a dog and a small dark car, whatever that was worth.

Anderson saw the pale-blue curtain in the front room being pulled to the side and let go. Mrs Mulroony was waiting for him. From the brief notes he had, she had not seen her cousin Maureen for forty-two years. He didn't see the point of keeping her waiting any longer.

Minutes later, he was seated in a padded carver chair round the dining table. A pile of photographs waited for his attention; the top one showed three teenagers piled up on a patterned blue velvet sofa, the wallpaper behind it equally hideously patterned in the geometric combinations of the 1970s. Also on the table was a family photograph album, a large pot of tea and a plate of Marks and Spencer's chocolate biscuits.

Mrs Jacqueline Mulroony, who asked to be called Jackie, was a youthful-looking sixty-plus redhead, dressed in a Lycra tracksuit and stocking feet. She explained, apologizing for her dress, that she had just been out with the dog, the Labrador called Chester, who was now locked in the kitchen, noisily sniffing under the door for a biscuit.

Jackie sat down opposite him, her fingers curled round a Dunoon china mug with a stag on it. She smiled at him nervously, as if she was about to be interviewed for a position she had no chance of getting. Anderson tried to stop his eyes floating to the montage of family pictures in the large photo frame on the wall behind her head. He thought he could track two of the three teenagers through the years, to their weddings, the christening of their own kids and, in one case, a Christmas with a grandchild, but the life of the dark-haired teenager with the bunches, wearing the red dungarees, stopped on the blue velvet sofa.

'I know you have spoken to DS Mulholland.'

Jackie nodded, her eyes narrowing in slight suspicion. 'Do you think you have found Maureen?'

'It's a theory we're working through, and there're things about your cousin that fit.' He took a sip of his tea, aware that Jackie was now looking more confused than anything.

'So what's this all about, then?'

'I won't lie to you. Maureen was your cousin and . . .'

'Past tense? Is she dead?'

'She hasn't been seen for over forty-two years. She was twenty-one or so . . .'

'When I last saw her, yes. My mother and her mother were

sisters, and Aunt Chrissie, her mum, saw her after that . . . but Chrissie's been dead for ten years or more, and my mother died not long after, so the story of Maureen, Mo, had kind of stopped.'

'She didn't go to her mum's funeral?'

'Or her dad's.' Jackie shrugged, took another sip.

'So the story of Maureen? What is it?'

'I don't know if any of it was true.' Another shrug.

'It doesn't matter. Anything you can tell us can be checked and verified, but at the moment we only have a missing person's report to go by. That was by a flatmate who said Maureen hadn't come home when expected, but the flatmate was away for a week, so we have no idea when Maureen actually did go missing. In the report, the flatmate said that Maureen had a boyfriend who could be a bit nasty. She was last seen in June 1978 in a café in the West End of Glasgow.'

'As far as the family knew, she got herself into trouble when she was seventeen or so.'

'Is that a euphemism?' Anderson asked. 'Given your age at the time and the fact it was the seventies?'

'To be really honest, I don't know, but I can't imagine anything else would splinter the family like that. My Uncle Drew was a bit old-fashioned.' She reached out and opened the photo album. A clean fingernail flicked through, then pointed to an overweight man in a good suit, standing with his arms round a slightly younger and darker version of Jackie, the picture obviously taken at a happy family occasion. 'That's him and Auntie Chrissie – their wedding anniversary, I think. They thought the world of Maureen – Mo. My mum got a bit fed up hearing how bloody wonderful she was. She was an only child. And then she was hanging around with an unsuitable man, then she was gone. In trouble . . .'

'My mum always used to say "expecting" in a very quiet voice.'

'She had her bottom button undone; seemingly, that was a sign of being pregnant.' Jackie laughed, and the tension broke.

'I've never heard of that one.'

'I didn't know if she was pregnant. Mum never said, but Mo was never around after that, not in our house. As I said, Auntie Chrissie saw her a few times. I remember Mum talking about

it, but there was a sense that she was trouble and, well, Mum
didn't want my brother or me to be affected by it, in case we
were led astray.'

Anderson nodded. 'Yes, I can understand that. Is that Mo?
In the dungarees?'

'The mighty Mo – yes, that's her. Must have been fourteen
or fifteen then.'

Anderson looked at the photograph, slightly faded, and the
same colours separating with age as on the pictures of the scene
where Birdie lost her life, or, much more likely, where Mo had
lost her life. She looked so young, so alive in the photo. It was
just as well she had no idea what lay ahead. His mind suddenly
flashed back to Mulholland. He needed to concentrate. 'Did she
look like that later? The hair colour, her build? When you last
saw her, can you remember? She's very slim there, dark hair
– was it always long? Was she still slim the last time you saw
her? Her eyes in this are a lovely shade of brown.' He turned
the photograph around and slid it across the table to her.

Jackie considered that for a moment, studying the picture.
'That's me in the middle, my brother on the bottom; God, we
must have been suffocating him. We all had brown eyes. Mo's
were a lighter brown, but we wanted lilac eyes like Liz Taylor,
so no luck there.'

Anderson let the silence lie.

'I think I remember Mum saying something like "the state
of Mo now". Auntie Chrissie had said she was dressing like a
bag lady, so skinny, and she had lovely dark hair and cut most
of it off. Mum said if I ever did that, she'd kill me.'

And DCI Colin Anderson muttered inwardly, 'Oh, shit.'

'You've found her, haven't you?'

'She's never kept the best of health, mentally or physically, so
behave. It took a lot of persuasion to let us visit.' Anderson
warned Costello who appeared to be in a weirdly buoyant mood.
He had already given Veronica Riley his mobile number, and
after they knocked on the door, his phone rang. He answered
it, then turned to the key box at the side of the door and spun
each of the dials until it opened. He lifted out the key, slid it
into the lock, opening the door a few inches before he returned

the key. All the time he was responding to the instructions coming down the phone with a 'Yes' or a 'Yes, I've done that'. Costello noted that above the key box were four bore holes from a recently removed name plate.

Her ex-husband had said that Veronica didn't keep so well these days and that she found life a struggle, adding that the stress of her childhood had always cast a shadow over her adult life, sometimes pushing her over the edge of paranoia.

Costello knew that James Riley had attended A and E once for injuries that may have been the result of spousal abuse. There were no charges pressed and there was a note that his wife's medication had been 'stepped down' at the time, an action that her mental health specialist considered ill-advised.

James had left her two years later and remarried – in fact, his present wife had been doing some shopping for Veronica during lockdown. On the phone, he had talked of her with empathy rather than hatred, while describing Frankie Scanlon as a monumental pain in the bum. Then he confessed that he had never met him, as the daughter and father were 'not close'.

Not close. Far away from being daddy's little girl.

As the door opened fully, Anderson shouted hello, switched his phone off and slid it into his pocket, then pulled out and used his hand gel, following the quiet voice that called, 'I'm in here.'

The living room had been converted into a bedroom, the curtains still closed. A bed with an air ripple mattress. They knew Veronica was fifty years old, but she could have been Loretta's mother. She had the face of Birdie, but the cheekbones that created the beauty in one were just shelves for hammocks of sagging skin in the other. Her right shoulder sat awkwardly on the pillow, the fist pulled under the blanket, a couple of tubes running to a white machine at the side of the bed. There was a commode to the side, and the smell suggested it needed emptying. Two walking sticks hung over the side barrier of the bed.

Veronica saw them looking and apologized. 'I'm due the nurse; I thought that might be her when I heard your footsteps.' Veronica Riley held out the skeleton of her left hand, and the skin at the back showed bruising and a nasty puncture wound as if a cannula had been removed. Anderson reluctantly took the bony fingers as Costello just nodded and introduced herself from the corner of the room, leaving Anderson the obvious visitor's chair. The whole room looked as if it belonged to somebody in their eighties and frail. Not like Eddie Dukes. Maybe Veronica's face was catching up with her surroundings.

'No doubt you are here about Eddie. I hope you don't want me to say that I'm sorry. He should never have got out. I know it was judged that he had served his time and paid his debt to society and all that crap, but she was my mother.'

'I'm sure you heard your dad say on many occasion that the sentence rarely fits the crime. I can't imagine how awful it was to lose your mum like that.'

'Why are you here?' Her face flushed with colour, and she reached round for the mask of her nebulizer.

Once she settled, Anderson took a deep breath. 'We are pursuing a strange line of enquiry. That maybe your mother was not killed by Eddie Dukes in 1978.'

'Yes, she was. I know, I was there.' She closed her eyes. 'I can still see it when I close my eyes.'

'What can you see?' he asked gently.

'Eddie standing, the knife in his hand. There had been shouting from the kitchen while I was outside in the garden. My parents never argued, my mum never raised her voice, so I ran into the kitchen.' She sighed. 'He was standing over her, with the knife. I think he was crying.'

'You witnessed something awful when you were very young. Does anything strike you as odd, now, looking back? You have had forty years to look at the situation.'

'I've been told not to. I have to put that memory in a box. The past is the past.'

'Veronica, can I ask you a very strange question? Have you ever had any reason to believe that your mother had survived that attack somehow? Christmas presents? Odd things happening on your birthday?'

'No. She's not alive.' The retort was that of a child, simple without emotion. It wasn't true. End of.

'Veronica?'

'No. Do you not think that's what I dreamed of, that she'd

come back for me? She never did.' Veronica considered this for a moment, closing her eyes dramatically, tilting her head to one side, suddenly looking every inch like her mother's daughter. 'No, somebody has you fooled,' she said again, as if after observing the crime scene in her mind's eye, she found nothing to challenge the evidence behind the facts as she knew them. 'I saw her body. I saw the blood. I think I went up to her. Eddie stopped me. Ben was behind me, screaming the place down.' She looked deeply into nowhere. 'I saw with my own eyes what Eddie Dukes did. I don't remember opening the door. I may have manufactured a memory of me standing there, still hanging on to the door and trying to figure out what was going on in our kitchen, as if I was frozen in time. My memory is that I stood absolutely still, with my mouth open, seeing what I was seeing but not believing it. In reality, I'm sure I barged in, shouting hello to my mum the same way I always did. I had no idea what was behind that door. Under the pulley, my mum was lying in the floor. I thought she had fallen. There was a man: Uncle Eddie. He was standing over her, trying to help her up. He was pulling at her arm, making her head jerk about. He had a knife.

'I can really only see, in the eye of my memory, her face covered by her dark hair. It stuck to her features like a mask. I don't know if that's real or not. So much of it could be a construct of my childish brain. I've been through so much bloody therapy that I'm not sure what's real or not. That look of horror and guilt on Uncle Eddie's face when he saw me. And the smell. I do remember the smell.'

'Can you tell us what happened to Ben, your brother?'

The sudden change of tack caught her off guard: the look of alarm, just a little confusion. A quick flick through the memory banks, as if looking for a lie that has been told and retold so often that it had started to grow into truth.

'I'm sure you know. We were out for a walk and he fell. I think I've told myself that it all went wrong when Ben died, but it really all changed when Ben was born – lovely, bubbly little Benjamin Scanlon. I was so excited when I went into the back bedroom to see him when he was born. I was six and had been told, vaguely, that I was about to have a wee brother or

a wee sister. He was born at home. I'd to go to the neighbour's,
Mrs Standing from across the road. She did all her own baking,
so the scones were good. Then my dad arrived, Mrs Standing
gave him a hug and they whispered something. Mr
Standing appeared and shook my dad's hand, slipped a cigar
into his top pocket.

'I was watching this from my seat in the kitchen, looking
through the gap in the door to the front hall, watching. They
chatted for a while; they forgot I was there. I lost something at
that moment. I don't think they handled it well. I mean, I loved
my wee brother and he was my shadow. I couldn't go anywhere
without him following me. As soon as he could walk, he was
always there, right behind me. Then Mum wasn't Mum anymore.
Dad was never there. The skies got darker, the summer shorter.
A long, long winter fell on our little house. Mum faded away
at that time, as if the nourishment she had in her body could
cope with me, but the additional strain of Ben drained her. It
tipped her over the edge. Dad was out working all day, most
of the night – making the world a better place, he said. Mum
died, we lost Ben, and Dad was so scared of losing me that he
never took his eyes off me . . . Which is interesting, because
after Mum died, I never quite looked at him in the same way.'

'What do you mean by that?'

'He stayed friends with Eddie. I mean, how could he do that?
I don't recall much about it – I don't think you notice the
subtleties of life when you're that young – but I do recall people
coming and going when Ben died. It was a usual walk, up
the hill. The dog was running around; I was keeping an eye on
Boggle, the beagle – I liked him. Ben wasn't going fast enough.
He was moaning and pulling on my arm. It was sore. I felt
Ben's hand slip from mine, then he was gone. He had slipped
off the path. I saw his face. He looked up at me, surprised that
his little boots were no longer on terra firma. He couldn't get
a grip on the slippery ferns and down he went, ever so slowly.
His arms reached out to me, grabbing at the fresh air, and then
he slipped away. Both his arms up over his head, kicking at the
sky, his green anorak, toggles flying through the air. I found it
funny. He was rolling down the hill, covered in ferns. I saw his
face. That is a picture that haunts me. Somewhere, as he fell,

he hit his head. Can you pass me that cup of water?' She reached out with her hand to take it, left-handed like her mother.

'Do you still speak to your dad?'

'Nope.'

'Can I ask why?'

'He left me at the home. It was awful there. If he had loved me at all, he would have come and taken me away, but he was too busy.'

'Busy?'

'Busy. I suspect it was his old secretary. Mum suspected something going on there, I think. He went abroad.' She sipped her water, the thought of that abandonment taking time to settle.

'Was it bad at the home?'

'It's taken me most of my life to get over what happened in there. I know now the trouble I could get them into, a lot of trouble, but at the time I was terrified. I'd lie in my bed, the blanket over my eyes, trying not to breathe while the matron did her rounds. I'd hear doors open and close. I stayed still. There was a lot of what I now know was abuse. But I am over that now. It was so bad. I had a plan to escape, to get away from the men.' Veronica's eyes lit up, then she closed them. 'I never did get away.'

'Dawn?'

Veronica gave a little snort. 'I often wonder what would have happened if we had made it.'

'Nothing.'

'I know that now, but I still like to dream of that life I might have had. We had it all planned. We sneaked downstairs, keeping to the side where the wooden steps didn't make a noise. At one point, the warden came round the corner, and I had to blend into the wooden panelling. He went right past me. Then I ran for it. I picked up my plastic bag and ran for it, jumping over the gravel, getting on to the grass and skirting round to the trees away from the bright lights of the house. From there, I just waited for one of the catering staff to go through the gates. We slipped out while the gates were open, right alongside his car, just as he was looking the other way to get out on to the road. It was dark. There was a park at the far side of the road and

that was where I was headed that night.' She paused, making
sure they were both caught up with the story.

Anderson avoided looking at Costello, knowing that this story
was at odds with Lynda Armstrong's version.

'They came quickly. This time they had dogs with them –
just the four of them. I ran for the rough ground. They didn't
see me. I was quick and it was dark. I rolled and hid, lying low
on a crack in the earth. As soon as they let the dogs go, they
found me within minutes. They walked me back – these men
who held all kinds of power over me, they weren't ready to
relinquish it any time soon.

'Back at the house, I was checked over and locked back up,
not in my own room where my books and posters were, but in
another room where there were chains on the side of the bed.
They'd come and inject me, the men, and then I would fall
asleep, a deep black sleep. And every time they did that, I'd
dream the same dreams of running and being free. I'd dream
of my dad, of us being together, in spite of the waking nightmare that he had brought me to that place and left me here. I'd
dream that the men came – they'd put their sweaty hands all
over me, their eyes inches from mine. I could feel their breath
on my face, and sometimes I thought I could hear their words,
but they were muttering; they had long and quiet discussions
at the other side of the room.

'That was on a good night. On a bad night, it would be so
much worse and I could be left bleeding and bruised. I could
feel the control they had over me, but I could never accept it.
Then when I got back to my room, I'd lie and look through the
upper part of the window to the blue sky outside. In those days,
the sky was always blue and I knew that one day, my blue-sky
day, I would get out and I would never come back. Then I did
get out and I never went back.'

The story went on for over an hour, Anderson becoming more
distressed than Veronica by the end of it. The nurse did not
appear, so Costello made Veronica a cup of tea and a sandwich,
while Anderson continued with a gentler interview, trying to
get her to open up about her life from the time she left the
school to the time she married Riley. But all her answers showed
that she saw that woman as a different person. Veronica Scanlon,

the girl in the film, seemed to have disappeared the day she left St John's.

Anderson drove the BMW round the corner and pulled into a petrol station, parking at the side and cutting the engine.

'You OK?' asked Costello.

'You could listen to that and remain untouched by it? How can you do that?'

Costello shrugged. 'It matters that we catch those responsible. We can't do anything for her. That's in the past. And I'm not sure that I believe all of it.'

'That's terrible.'

'In fact, I'm sure I believe very little of it. I'm sure she believes it. But time has passed. You looked at her like a dad looking at a kid. Not sure that's the best way to investigate a crime like this.'

'You are a hard-nosed bitch at times.'

'You notice that her right hand never came out from under the duvet. Her table was at the right side. She's right-handed. She never took that right hand out, even to eat the sandwich. She's a fake.'

'She's mentally ill.'

'She had the smarts not to show us her right hand. Just think what that means for a moment.'

NINETEEN

Monday 22nd June

Three people sat outside the room of the Chief Procurator Fiscal's office, waiting to be called in. Colin Anderson was slightly concerned about what he was going to hear in the meeting and how his wife might take it. Brenda was texting their son to make sure that Moses was OK, despite the fact they had left home less than twenty minutes before.

Costello knew why they were there but said nothing. She

had spent two hours at Archie's house the previous night and told him a few home truths, fuelled by his treatment of her at the barbecue. For the first twenty minutes, she didn't think he got more than two words in, and she had enjoyed it. She was sure that the minute she left, he had picked up the phone for some very long conversations about Joanna Craig, the legal firewall around Edward Dukes' finances and the truth about Birdie Scanlon.

Now, she wanted this meeting to be over. It was a distraction to the case. She wanted to apply for permission to see Veronica's medical records.

A change in the murmurings of voices inside the office caught her attention, but Costello couldn't hear any exact words. Two male voices, maybe three, talking seriously, but there was no sense of any dissent. They were still preparing and she bet somebody in that room had worked an all-nighter – probably Archie.

So she waited, and watched, enjoying the rare opportunity to examine her boss and his wife, as mismatched as ever they were; as opposites, they didn't even complement each other. They aggravated each other. This golden period in their relationship was happening because it played to Anderson's knight-in-shining-armour complex, with Moses, and the way Rodger the conman had broken Brenda. As soon as she was back on her feet emotionally, and Moses had grown a little, the tension would start again.

She had gone round to the house on the terrace the previous night to advise them of the meeting without telling them what it was really about, and it struck Costello that there had been no changes made to Helena McAlpine's house since the Andersons had moved in. Nothing. It was still a house of cream carpets, money and taste, not like their old house down near the hospital, where there had been kids, Lego and dirty washing everywhere. She knew they used one of the two lounges, and the kids had their bedrooms, but the posh room was never lived in – it was a shrine to Helena and Alan McAlpine. The Andersons lived in the kitchen.

The door of the office opened, and they were surprised to see a short dapper man, well-cut suit and a bow tie. Lee

Galbraith, the forensic accounting specialist from the Met, welcomed them in.

Archie Walker was sitting behind his desk. He got up and welcomed them all very warmly; it was very nice to see them again, and maybe, when this was over, they could get together with Valerie for something to eat. He didn't mention Costello's visit to the house the night before and she noticed the lack of any representative from Operation Felix apart from Galbraith. That could be a good thing or a bad thing.

They made their introductions. The Andersons had met Galbraith before, and Brenda was already close to tears just recalling that meeting. Archie was pouring out coffee, automatically giving Costello a black tea instead. So he remembered that.

'Nice to meet you, DI Costello,' said Galbraith, sitting down, opening his briefcase, keen to get to business. 'Did it not strike you as odd that you have been Mrs Craig's neighbour for all these years and she had never mentioned to you that she had a daughter?'

'Not really. We spoke about the weather and potatoes. And families can drift apart.'

'Well, we have always believed that wherever Rodger – real name Simon Russell – goes, working on his long con, somebody has been before, smoothing the way for him – an associate really.'

'I think I'm beginning to see . . .' said Anderson slowly.

'I think that might be his wife, Joanna Russell.' He held out a wedding photograph. They were young, but recognizable: Joanna Craig and the man they knew as Rodger. 'Joanna Craig, as she was.'

'That's a huge coincidence,' said Brenda, the photograph wavering in her hand, the betrayal working its way deeper.

'I think the point he's making, Brenda, is that it wasn't a coincidence,' said her husband softly.

'Operation Felix has always wondered how he knew so much about his victims. No wonder he fitted so well into your family; he had researched everything about you. The dossier on her laptop about your family runs to sixty pages,' Galbraith explained. 'I suspect they started working on their mother's

neighbour. Costello, single woman, big flat, good job and with
a presumption of inherited wealth as both parents deceased and
her being' – he paused – 'for our purposes, an only child. Then
they fell across the connection to Anderson and Helena
McAlpine, a much better financial proposition. And there had
been marital strife? They'd see that as an opportunity, a lever
to get in. So you see how the phone call from Joanna to Mrs
Craig would go, and that was all they needed. Rodger – Simon
– arrives in your life, a fully fledged version of what you need
him to be. In other cases, Joanna has posed as a carer, a neighbour, a friend who meets them walking the dog, always passing
information back to Simon for the big role he is about to play.
But now that he's in custody, he's saying nothing about her. He
said that he and his wife had separated many years ago. But
we have the phone, the communication between them, texts and
mobile calls going back over the years. So he is with us. She,
it would seem, has gone.'

'Was she planning to sell the flat?' asked Costello.

'Of course.'

'What was Vera supposed to do?'

'She didn't care. These people are professional. Their scam-
ming goes beyond what a normal person can conceive of. It's
their job. The lawyer would be presented with a document
passing the house to her daughter to sell, or a fake power of
attorney, a fake medical report recommending that Mrs Craig
is no longer fit to make these decisions. Fake passports,
fake ID.'

'And leave her with no place to live?'

'You'd be surprised how often it happens. What we are more
interested in now is that she's done a runner. We have been
going through Vera Craig's flat and have found the ten grand,
bagged up in a side compartment of a suitcase, ready to go. She
has gone a fair way in realizing her mother's assets into cash.
Simon is still in custody in London. This might break him – it
smashes his "I was only being nice and they misunderstood"
version of events.'

'He seemed so kind. He was kind and so . . . and I am obviously very gullible.' Brenda's voice was shrill.

'No, you're not. He's very skilled at what he does. They pick their mark and they will spend months, years, making sure that it works. They researched you for over eighteen months. You were a project to them. Colin being called away and then being caught by the weather in Glen Riske might appear coincidental, but ask yourself whether Colin would have gone if Rodger hadn't been in the house to help Brenda. They don't only manipulate the people; they manipulate the entire situation.'

'The intelligence he had about you on his computer is impressive. He echoed your interest in everything, so he slotted into your life exactly.'

It was Costello who broke the soundtrack of Brenda quietly weeping. Her husband put his hand over hers, and she didn't pull hers away. 'Did you visit Mrs Craig at the hospital yesterday?'

'I may have. I needed some background.'

'Background or evidence? Did you give her that key to give to me, knowing I'd go into the flat?'

'I work with people like Rodger all the time and some of it rubs off. He's not the only one to manipulate a situation. I know my mark, DI Costello.'

'I entered a crime scene unlawfully.'

'No, you entered it as a concerned neighbour.'

'Tell Diane Mathieson at Complaints that.'

'I already have.'

'That was sneaky.'

'And you are predictable.'

As she drove from the meeting at the fiscal's office back to the annexe at Partickhill, Costello received a phone call. She was needed at Partickhill Station, but the caller would not tell her why, apart from the fact that there was somebody there who wanted to speak to her. She ended the call, thinking about Frankie Scanlon. If he was around, he would know by now that they were looking for him. He had been a good copper in his day. He'd know that he was on their list of persons of interest.

She was shown into the long corridor with the family room at the end, and she nipped into the toilet to wash her hands, looking at her pale face in the mirror, her hair like a collapsing haystack. She assessed her thoughts and the best way to play this. He knew about interview techniques. Better to let him talk, be careful to give nothing away.

The family-room door was open, and an elderly woman in a light-blue anorak and a younger man in jeans with a hiker's rucksack were sipping some tea the constable on the desk had made them. Costello noticed the good biscuits, so that meant that these two were here for the benefit of the police. What it was about, though, she had no idea. If these two were Scanlons, they might be a wife and son, but not the man himself.

They had asked for her. They had not given any names but said they had information that was important to an ongoing case. They both looked very nervous.

Costello introduced herself and slid into the seat opposite them. 'Well, I hope we are looking after you OK. Was the coffee good?'

'We've come quite a long way.'

'From where?'

'From Lochgoilhead. We got the bus down this morning.'

'Oh,' said Costello. 'Well, thank you for coming such a distance.' She looked at the man and the woman. Mother and son, she guessed. The woman in her seventies. That put her in the age range of the Peacocks.

The door opened, and the same PC came back in, smirking and talking about the weather, very relaxed and casual as he put more coffee and tea in front of them.

'So what can we do for you?'

'I think it's more a question of what my mother can do for you, but before we do that, we need some assurances.'

Costello smiled at the old woman who looked half terrified.

'If we don't get those assurances, then we will leave without uttering a further word.' He was a small man; he wasn't used to making such statements and it did not ring true.

'I didn't do anything wrong,' said the mother, shaking her head slightly. 'I didn't.'

Costello recognized the Glaswegian behind her cultured Highland lilt, but the son sounded as if he had been born up there.

'I'm sure you haven't, but there's obviously something on your mind. Why don't you tell me what it is?'

She began to cry, gentle tears running down her face, making Costello feel like a right bitch.

'Mum, we're saying nothing unless we have assurances.'

'If you have committed no criminal act, then there's nothing to worry about.'

'What about wasting police time?'

'Yes, that's taken very seriously, I won't deny that.'

'OK.' The son took a deep breath. 'Over forty years ago . . .' He faltered.

Costello felt her spine tingle. 'I'm sure that anything you say can only be of assistance to us. What assurances do you want? If you killed somebody, then you need a lawyer present. If you only wasted police time, then please speak freely.'

The son asked his mother, 'Do you want me to . . .'

The older woman nodded and picked up her coffee cup, holding it in both hands as if the room was cold and it was her only source of warmth.

'My mother is Elizabeth McGillivery.' He spelled out the surname. 'Her husband was a fisherman from Lochgoilhead. They met when Mum was working as a barmaid up there.'

'Yes, her husband, but not your dad?' asked Costello gently, looking at the son, imagining him forty years on – a life of no fresh air and poor diet, strip away a healthy outdoor life and all the years, and she could colour in the rest.

'Yes.'

'Are you Lizzie Shand?' asked Costello quietly, leaning forward, trying to superimpose the wizened face in front of her on that old black-and-white poster.

The woman nodded.

'She prefers to be called Betty,' said her son. 'Now. She's called Betty now.'

Costello looked at the man – a younger, finer-featured version of his father. 'We're still looking for you, Betty.'

'She's very concerned, and so am I, that our whereabouts don't become known to my father.'

'Sandy Muir? He'll hear nothing from me. We visited him yesterday. How did you know we were there, so quickly?'

'That's not important. Do you have any legal obligation to tell him that you know where I am?'

'You are over eighteen. We don't need to do anything.'

'We know that he's still alive. Please don't tell him that you have found us.'

'We won't, I assure you. I wouldn't want him near my family. I'm sorry, I don't think I got your name.'

'John. John McGillivery,' he said, ready to challenge any correction. 'I've been worried that you might have to tell him.'

'You're a responsible adult. You can do what you like,' said Costello. 'But tell me about yourself, Betty. What happened to you? You were reported missing in 1978 by Muir? How did you get away from him? Did you plan it?'

'Yes.' She took a deep breath. She was ashamed of the story she was about to tell, of the woman that she used to be. An unmarried young woman who gave her baby away and then changed her mind.

'If you are about to tell me the story I think you are, then you have my admiration, Betty. I have read Muir's file. I know about your early life. I know it all.'

'You can be completely open,' said John, just as Betty's faded eyes swept up to meet Costello's. Her son didn't know all of it, she was sure of that.

'I'm glad that we can close the file on you, Betty, and that you're alive. And can you tell us what happened, just for the record. You're last seen out with Muir, Big Tam and a redhead of no name.'

'Sheila? Big Sheila McClymont. I haven't thought of her in years.' She sighed. 'That was the night I had planned to go, once they all got drunk. Wee John was staying with friends of my mum in Lochgoilhead; I was always going back to get him.' Her son reached out and touched her hand. 'But I knew Sandy'd never leave me alone if he knew, so that's why I did what I did. By that time, Sandy wasn't letting me out of his sight. There was one particular night I was lucky to survive. He was never going to let me leave. So I disappeared. First I went away to have the baby, lay some foundation, then I came back, so that I could leave for good.'

'He still drinks at the Glen Finnan,' said Costello. 'Is that how you knew?'

She nodded. 'The same family runs the pub. Word got round

that you were looking for me. The barman's dad knew where to call. They knew vaguely where I had gone, so I got a visit from the minister this morning.'

John's fingers tightened round his mother's hand. She was shaking at the memory.

'I bet Sandy had a young girl in tow, terrified, too frightened to speak.'

'He did. It should be easier now to get away, but she has to realize she needs to get away. It's so difficult for the victims to understand that they can break free. When you live with a controlling partner, that's an incredibly difficult decision to make, and you made it.'

'Yes. Well, no. It was made for me. I wanted to be with my son. If I'd come back with the boy, I knew he'd beat me again, he'd beat the baby. I had no choice. I went away to stay in a room with people who didn't know me. They trusted me, had faith in me, although I had no faith. Not then. I met John McGillivery, and he stayed, even though he knew about young John.'

'He was the only father I have ever needed.'

'I was so scared that he would find me.'

'Well, you're still in the system as a missing person. Did you ever think of coming home?'

She thought before answering, a pause before she said, 'Have you ever lived with a man like Sandy Muir? There was a police officer at one time – he took an interest and was asking questions about me. He tried to help.'

'Really? What was his name?'

She shook her head. 'I'd know it if I heard it.'

'Scanlon?'

'Scanlon. Fred? Frank? He offered me a job as a nanny to his children.'

'Were you allowed to take John to that job?'

She shook her head. 'No, he didn't know about John, so I couldn't take that offer, but I would have been too worried. It was in Glasgow, too close.'

'Really?' said Costello thinking back to how Lizzie Shand had appeared on their poster – the short dark hair, the slight build. Built like a bird. It would look bad if she took her pen out now and started taking notes, so she got up to leave.

John stood up, following her to the door, then hesitated. 'Is he as bad as my mum makes out – my dad?'

'He's much worse. You stay clear of him. The past is behind you for a reason, so keep it that way. Take care of your mum.'

TWENTY

Vik Mulholland had aged twenty years since Colin Anderson last set eyes on his long-term DS on the stretcher. They were all getting older, but he still thought of Vik as a young man. All time was relative. Mulholland must have been approaching forty, whereas Costello was towing it, as the joke went.

But right now, looking at Vik lying in his hospital bed, he thought he was in the wrong room, looking at the wrong bed. This aged grey-haired man lying in front of him, his face wizened and dry, an IV antibiotic drip taped on to his elbow. He looked close to death.

Why did he even bother coming into work? Why did he not say how bad he was feeling? The thoughts had kept Anderson awake that night, and eventually he had gone downstairs and made himself a cup of tea, Norma joining him but staying on the cushions at the far end of the sofa. He must have woken Brenda, who appeared, asking if the phone had gone, if somebody had called about Vik. Was there any news? There wasn't, but they got chatting, away from buzz and kids and dishwashers and conmen. Why had Vik come into work with full-blown sepsis brewing in his blood?

Brenda had thought for a minute and said, 'Because you three are all he has. He may appear to have it all, but he lives alone – his girlfriend is hundreds of miles away. He has a mother. And that's it. He's burned out his friends, and you, Costello and Gordon make him feel wanted, important. You are his family. How many times has he not gone for promotion because he'd rather stay with you lot. I'd go and see him tomorrow, Colin. It's sepsis. He's in a coma. You need to go now.' She didn't need to add *while you have the chance* . . .

So here he was, watching his young colleague covered in tubes and lines. A masked woman, in a gown, was sitting by the side of his bed. Vik's infamous Russian mother. Anderson stopped by the window of the room, his hand on the door, watching the scene in front of him. He had seen Vik's mum once, and guessed that she was not British by birth. She had worn her russet velvet scarf with elegant style, her hair dyed to the correct shade of auburn, piled high on top of her head like a neat bird's nest, stuck through with a couple of sticks. But now she was anonymous; she was a faceless statue, totally still. Anderson moved closer to the window and saw that her hands were placed on the blue bedcover, her knuckled fingers bending and gathering the fabric up in folds. Her eyes were closed, and the front of the paper mask was drifting in and out slightly as the woman talked. Anderson had no doubt that she was praying.

He slipped in the door. She looked up and nodded slightly but said nothing. She dropped her head again, continuing with her prayers. There was gentle music from a phone on a docking station, some light classical music, a lot of tinkling piano melody. He gently placed his hand on the old woman's shoulder, and left it there so that she didn't get a fright. She lifted a hand and briefly placed it on his, giving his fingers a little squeeze.

He walked round the bed, pulled up another chair and sat down, trying not to think of a time he had sat in the old hospital watching his daughter fight an infection. She had got over that. He prayed his colleague, his friend, would get over this.

Vik's mum raised herself from her bedside chair elegantly, then lifted the bed sheet around her son's neck, the closest thing she could get to tucking him in, still being a mum no matter how old the child.

He sat for a few minutes, looking at Vik breathing, thinking how much time they were wasting on this case. He heard the door open behind him, and Elvie McCulloch walked in. Anderson resisted the urge to hug her. She had been Vik's girlfriend for a long time but kept her distance, her work as a doctor taking her away. The marks on her face and her build

were the results of a medical condition she had suffered all
her life, and while she looked well, there was no doubting her
distress – it showed deep in her eyes but her face gave nothing
away. This was the woman, after all the blonde bimbos
Mulholland had clubbed with, he had fallen in love with; the
woman who insisted on taking jobs at the other end of
the country from him. Anderson couldn't work that out, but he
couldn't work out his own home life either. She said something
to Vik's mother in Russian. Why wouldn't she pick up Russian?
She was incredibly bright, out on a spectrum of her own.

With no emotion at all, she said to him, 'Costello is waiting
downstairs. They have found Frank Scanlon. The fiscal got a
court order for the lawyer to release his whereabouts.' And with
that, she switched back to Russian, dismissing him.

Like he said, on a spectrum somewhere.

He met Costello at the end of the corridor. She had been
pacing.

'How is he?'

'No change. Elvie said you have found Frankie.'

'We know exactly where he is. Wyngate and I have come
up with an idea. We need to get a coffee because we have a
plan and need you to sign off on it. And you won't like it.
The first part's easy, but we needed all sorts of permission for
the second bit. Operation Catherine. And you really are not
going to like it.'

'Whatever it is, don't bank on getting those permissions,'
Anderson cautioned.

'Already got them.'

'How so?'

'Traded information.'

Wyngate had traced every mention of the funeral of Lambert
Douglas McSween, starting off at the funeral directors and
following every lead on the winding trail of social media. Eddie's
killer was out there somewhere, and the supposition was that
they had been drawn out by the mention of Dougie's funeral
after years of lying dormant. So now he posted that Francis
Scanlon, formerly of Glasgow City Police, was having a get-
together for his eightieth birthday. The various parties for

friends, family and old colleagues had been cancelled because of the virus, so now they were having one big do at the golf club at the end of the month. He added a carefully worded request that anybody who wished to attend should phone Lorraine at the Abbey View Retirement Home and a number that was diverted to a mobile that sat on a desk in the incident room.

Wyngate had taken great care with the wording. Whoever she was, the driver of the dark car had picked up the information about McSween's funeral and, he hoped, would pick this up as well. Wyngate suspected that the driver, 'Catherine', was a social media 'friend' of Loretta, close enough to monitor but anonymous. There had been widespread chat on Facebook about Douglas's death being so close to the wedding of his granddaughter. They suspected Catherine would take the bait, but she would not turn up at the non-existent function. She'd approach Frankie in some other, more subtle way so she and he would be alone. The home knew not to let anybody in. Frankie Scanlon would be away in hospital if anybody casual called wanting to see him, and due to the virus there was no visiting without an appointment.

So far the phone had rung a lot, mostly via the announcement in the Police Federation magazine, old colleagues interested in a free booze-up. A few were looking for the wrong Frankie Scanlon. The real Scanlon had been hiding in Spain for thirty years.

Wyngate had been put in charge of Operation Catherine, sanctioned by both Warburton and Walker. He'd rarely been operational without Mulholland at his side, winding him up. The incident room was different without him – his OCD, his expensive aftershave, the constant sniping between him and Costello.

Wyngate sat in the room, the rain running down the window, and watched the clickbait announcement as it bounced around various social media sites.

The door burst open and Costello marched in, full of enthusiasm. Something had broken. 'Sorry if I'm late, the guys at Felix wanted to interview me again. But guess what? Just guess!'

'I'm too tired.'

'Mathilda has a match – that DNA sample on the light switch. Somebody came down the stairs, pulled their gloves off and flicked the switch to lift the stairs back up to the loft without thinking about it.'

'So who is it?'

'As yet we don't know, but – and this is the good bit – there's a close family relative currently working for . . . wait for it . . . Police Scotland. I'm on the track of his mother. A DS Jamie Dougan, works out of Stewart Street. His father was Adam Dougan, who also worked in CID, back in the day.'

'How far back in the day?'

'Far enough back that his dad married a woman . . .'

'A lot of men do,' agreed Wyngate.

'And that woman is Jamie's mother.' Costello was standing at the wall, examining the family chart as if it held all the answers.

'Am I missing something here?'

'The maternal DNA is shared, so Jamie's mum is also the mother of a daughter who left the imprint. The sample is female; it might be Veronica. It might be another female child. I was thinking that if Birdie here was having an affair with another police officer . . .'

'Not an unusual course of events,' agreed Wyngate.

'Or if the Peacocks were all sleeping with Birdie – all OK and wonderfully free love. But if she got pregnant . . .'

'It might explain why she got out of the situation so drastically.' Costello spread her hands, as if she had performed magic.

'It might explain the extent of the cover-up.'

'I spoke to Jamie briefly on the phone—'

The door opened and Anderson walked in, his face grave. 'They've found Anthony Poole.'

'Does he know that he's off the hook?'

'No.'

They walked quickly, not speaking as they strode through the old tenements into the warren of service lanes and garages, footpaths and outbuildings. Anderson leading, weaving his way through the narrow paths and alleys. The tenements, often six or seven storeys high, blocked out most of the sound, much of the light. Insects buzzed around them as they walked through the long grass of a disused side alley. The red sandstone walls on either side were covered with ivy and moss, and the grass underneath was now flattened by occasional tyre tracks that became more established as the alley joined another, which then opened out on to the main thoroughfare of the back courts.

Costello spotted Tony Bannon, at the side, standing in a stone archway between the two tenement blocks.

His face was to the wall, arms above his head, crossed against the bricks, his forehead on his forearms. A man alone. A man defeated.

Costello walked on, leaving Anderson to do what he thought was best.

She knew what she was walking into as soon as they turned the corner. A makeshift tent was leaning against an old, disused garage, keeping the scene free from the hundred prying eyes that could be looking from their high vantage points. Scene-of-crime officers were getting ready to move the body. Costello showed her badge and asked if she could have a look.

Anthony Poole was hanging, his body moving in an unseen draught. He had thrown a rope over a wooden beam in the garage. Then he had put stones in his pockets, climbed on top of a wheelie bin, tying a knot, making a noose.

Then stepped off the bin.

She looked round. Anderson had his arm around his distraught colleague.

She turned away.

TWENTY-ONE

Tuesday 23rd June

'They've knocked St John's into flats, you know.'
    'Have they?' answered Anderson, not really listening, his mind still turning over the suicide of Anthony Poole.
'Half a million, they are going for. Anyway, got hold of Elsie

Graham, the former under-matron of St John's or some fancy
job title like that. She couldn't tell me much.'

'Good job that you didn't drive all the way up there, then.'

'She's a bit old-school, if you pardon the pun. Refers to it
as a school for disturbed children. She said that Veronica
Scanlon was obviously struggling with what she saw when her
mother was murdered. Then what happened to her wee brother
– all the usual stuff you would expect. Their residents came
from all over, but were mostly those that had families who still
cared what happened to them and wanted to put their hands in
their pockets to provide better social care for the kids.'

'That sounds laudable.'

'But the interesting bit . . .'

'I'm glad there is an interesting bit,' said Anderson.

'. . . is when I asked her what she thought Veronica Scanlon
might be up to? Want to guess what her answer was?'

'Surprise me.'

'She said, "Why, what's she done now?"'

'Thank you for coming all this way, Miss Fettercairn.'

The journalist's eyes flickered from DCI Anderson to the
small hard-faced blonde beside him. Then back again. There
was a sign of a slight tension – not in the journalist's face but
in the way her back stiffened a little and her hands flattened
on to the top of the table, the way she folded her arms tighter
than was absolutely necessary. Her lips, similarly, were jammed
close.

'I'm sure you recall that I am Colin Anderson, DCI here at
Partickhill covering both Major Case and Murder Squads.' He
paused to let that sink in. Without looking up, he opened the
beige file that lay on the table in front of him, thick with dog-
eared papers that had been well read and thumbed. 'And my
colleague here is DI Costello, also of the MIT and Major Case
Squad. We work very closely together on many cases, which I
am sure you know, as you are a respectable journalist and very
thorough.' He let that drift round the room for a moment. 'And
I'm sure you know about our very high clear-up rate.'

Clarissa Fettercairn nodded. 'Oh, congratulations on doing
the job that you are paid to do. You can sit there all you like

and bring out as many files as you want. I'm not going to reveal the source of my information.'

Costello made a point of jotting that down in her notepad, exaggerating her hand movement as if joined-up writing was something new to her. Anderson turned his head slightly to watch. Once her hand stopped moving, she laid her biro down on the table and Anderson turned back to Fettercairn. And smiled.

The journalist sat back, looking from one to the other, obviously realizing that something was up.

'So, Ms Fettercairn. Just to put you in the picture. We're well aware of the identity of the source of your so-called intelligence and I'd like to point out that you haven't put in print anything that's not already in the public domain.'

'It's in the public interest.'

'Shite,' said Anderson politely.

The journalist opened her mouth, but Anderson cut in.

'What you did do was put a lot of information in print about the Procurator Fiscal that was purely personal and is of no use to, or interest to, the public at large.'

'That's a matter of opinion.'

'A matter of opinion that will be discussed between the Crown Office and Procurator Fiscal Service, the newspaper and your editor. And then maybe back to us, the police.' Anderson looked at Costello. 'What about you, Costello? Do you fancy her chances?'

'Well, let me think about that for a moment.' Costello looked at the ceiling for a millisecond. 'Nope.'

Fettercairn opened her mouth and smiled, pointing a slowly uncurling finger in Costello's direction until a beautifully beige Shellac fingernail was pointing directly at her face. 'Oh, you are *that* Costello.'

'I am a Costello, but whether I am *that* one remains to be seen.'

'So, who is Daniel Fishbourne, Miss Fettercairn?' snapped Anderson. 'And before you ask, we do mean *that* Daniel Fishbourne.'

She froze immediately, her head tilted to the side slightly as she considered denying it.

Anderson leaned back in his chair. 'You see, we are also very good at our jobs. We see here a conflict of interest or a lack of disclosure at best. As you know, we are looking into a case of historic child abuse, something that you yourself have expressed great interest in. So you will have no problem, I am sure' – he paused – 'telling us anything that you know about Daniel Fishbourne. Date of birth, 1927. Place of birth, Gourock. He moved to Invernock later, about five years later to be precise.'

'Does the name ring any bells? We have come across him in another parallel investigation,' added Costello.

'Frankie Scanlon threw him down the stairs,' she snapped.

'Which is not good, we agree about that, but you obviously do know him – otherwise, you wouldn't know that, would you?'

'I don't know him as such. He died many years ago.'

'He was named in a child abuse enquiry.'

'He was innocent.'

'He was pointed out and identified by the victim.'

'She was mistaken.'

'She pointed out and identified him twice.'

'Yes, I know.'

'She was six years old at the time.'

'She was mistaken.'

'She identified him twice. What are the chances of two paedophiles being active on the same beach within a couple of weeks?'

'Veronica . . .'

'So you know it was Veronica?'

'She was mistaken.'

'Was she? It couldn't have been Gordon Ellis Whyte; he was given an alibi that he was in Cellardyke on the east coast that weekend, which is why the accusation stuck to Fishbourne. Those false alibis were given to Whyte by his wife. Whyte was a truck driver – the same thing happened with the Yorkshire Ripper, I believe. It wasn't a police cover-up. It was good police work and simple geography. They had no idea who Whyte would grow into. The police are not seers. They did not "miss" anything.'

'He was hounded out of town. He couldn't stay here.'

'Here?' asked Anderson.

'He couldn't stay in Gourock,' Fettercairn said quietly.

'Invernock. It was because the victim was the daughter of a cop and they brought everything they could against . . .'

'Your grandpa? Your uncle? Did he commit suicide in the end? It's an unusual name, and we have a report of a suicide in that name,' said Anderson gently.

'Such an unusual name. You must have lived most of your life with that, I reckon. Must have been hard,' added Costello sympathetically.

'My granddad committed suicide because of what that wee girl said.'

'No, she was mistaken. Your grandfather committed suicide because the gossip-mongers jumped the gun, people who gossip and spread news without checking the facts. Rumours were all over the place in those days, just as they are now all over social media, talking shite. Who is Mary Travers?'

'What does she have to do—'

'We know exactly who she is. Can you put her back on her lead and muzzle her? She may be well intentioned but she's way off beam. We will take criminal proceedings against her if we feel—'

'That's not our job, Colin, that's the fiscal's job,' offered Costello casually.

'Oh, you are right there. Can't imagine they'd have an issue with the way she's been bad-mouthing them, telling you what shit to print. She's the short blonde paralegal who thought this was going to get her somewhere, and well it might, but on the wrong side of the law. Mary Travers is a bit keen, a bit too keen to ruin people's reputations because she doesn't think the job is being done properly or quickly enough. That's either naïve, misunderstanding process or thick. Anybody who repeats or has repeated what she says as fact could be in trouble.'

'That's unfair.'

'Unfair? I can introduce you to a woman whose son has just hanged himself because of the muck that's raked up on social media. That is disgusting and dangerous, and, frankly, it's beneath you.'

'DCI Anderson?' asked Costello in mock politeness. 'These people spreading gossip without checking facts – you are not referring to journalists, are you?'

'No, Costello, I am not,' he answered with a similar attitude. 'I would have thought that, of all people, a journalist would be the one who would stand up for truth, maybe even justice, if that is not too much of a stretch for the Twitter-fed, laptop, latte-with-caramel-sauce generation. Somebody with sense could look at the bigger picture, as there is a very good book here, but you won't write it because the facts don't fit what is going on in your head.'

Costello nudged her boss. 'Wouldn't bother her. She doesn't check her facts – that's the whole bloody problem.'

'True,' agreed Anderson. 'Like I say, we know where all this is coming from, but we do like to catch every link in the chain so we know where the real blame lies.' He turned to face Fettercairn. 'If you want to talk now, you can.'

'Is this because of her?' Fettercairn flicked her manicured thumb at Costello.

'Is it?' asked Anderson.

'What have I got to do with it?' asked Costello with wide-eyed innocence. 'Me? You are talking as if I was the' – she paused, recalling the quote – '"brief fling with an unnamed senior detective who was rumoured to have a close relationship with the fiscal, at the time when his wife was very ill"?'

Fettercairn coloured.

'I mean, anybody would think we were investigating a murder in a care home or something.'

'And what were you doing?' asked Anderson.

'Investigating a murder in a care home.' Costello stood up and pushed her chair back, then lifted the file and pulled out a black-and-white photograph, a chiaroscuro of flesh, skin and muscle; only a recognizable eye referenced it as human. 'There you go, Clarissa. That's the victim of the psycho we caught. He took out a scalpel and removed her face. He sat her in front of a mirror so she could see, and feel, every single cut. You think about that for a minute, then you might want to look in the mirror yourself. Or you might want to write her story – that's a tale worth telling. Her name was Sandra.'

'You could donate all profits to those disfigured by crime,' suggested Anderson.

Fettercairn closed her eyes.

'She's owed a wee bit more respect than you closing your eyes.' Then Costello walked out of the room with the parting shot, 'Oh and, by the way, she didn't die. She's still alive, with no face.'

Anderson pointed at Costello. 'She did that out of badness. Needless to say, you picked the wrong one.' He got to his feet and walked to the door, opening it for Fettercairn. 'Off you go. We are busy.'

The journalist stood up, gathering up her handbag, her scarf and her dignity. 'You have not heard the end of this.'

'Oh, I guarantee it. Mind how you go, now.'

'Has anybody heard how Vik is doing? I called last night, but nobody was up for telling me anything.' Wyngate slipped his jacket from his shoulders. He looked over at Anderson who was sitting at his own desk, rubbing his nose where Brenda's Poundland reading glasses had been annoying him. 'Do you think he is going to be OK?' The DC regarded his boss with a pleading look in his eyes, the way he used to when he was a rookie on the job and got everything wrong.

'He's been moved to critical care or whatever they call it now. Septicaemia is a very dangerous thing, so it's touch and go, but as they said at the hospital, he is relatively young and healthy, so he should pull through. He has none of that co-morbidity stuff that O'Hare likes to talk about.'

'What's that?' asked Wyngate.

'When somebody has more than one thing wrong at a time,' muttered Costello, not looking up from the file she was scrolling through. 'Like stealing Hobnobs and voting Tory. You'll get away with one, but not both.'

'I have apologized unreservedly for exerting my taste in nibbles,' said Wyngate, pulling a packet of chocolate Hobnobs from his jacket pocket. 'And don't accuse me of voting Tory.'

'Stop it, you two. Elvie sends her regards and will let us know when it's safe to go and visit Vik. In the meantime, all we can do is pray or whatever makes you feel comfortable in a situation that you can do nothing about. So' – he stood up – 'are we ready to move on a situation that we *can* do something about?'

'I'm ready,' said Costello.

'Yes,' said Anderson, 'so you are.' He looked her up and down, in her blue uniform. 'That's not a good colour for you.'

TWENTY-TWO

Frank Scanlon was looking at a photograph – the Peacocks, Birdie and the kids all piled on to a rock. He closed his eyes, resting them from the sun that blazed in the window of his living room. Who took the picture? Everybody was there. It must have been Dougie's wife or girlfriend of the moment. That picture was the only thing he had from those days. He had been glad to leave everything else behind.

But now they had found him – he was sure of it. He was neither so old nor so senile that he didn't recognize subtle changes in the home: the way the staff looked at him, a slight deference in the way they dealt with him. In some ways, he quite enjoyed it. It was almost like being Frankie Boy again.

But if they had tracked him down, they had done it for a reason. Somebody out there had joined the dots from Dougie to Eddie, and that trail of poisoned breadcrumbs was leading right to his door.

Well, he'd live to see how that played out.

Funny how being old, deaf and a bit wobbly on the feet always led people into thinking that stupidity went along with it. Being grey in the hair didn't mean you were soft in the head. It didn't affect the way you wanted to live your life or the way you wanted to die, although maybe it did focus the mind a little. Douglas had gone. One of the funerals in his life that he really wanted to go to. He thought about Eddie. Steady Eddie, the best friend a man could have. They'd stood on that rock, the Peacocks and the next generation, watching the tide going out. They had taken a bet on who would be the last one to die. Well, they knew the answer to that one now.

Eddie used to say the outgoing tide was strong, sweeping up the shite and the detritus with it, leaving a clean shore behind.

That was what he needed to do, and with every turn of the tide he was getting weaker. Slowly, wave by wave, it was all moving beyond him. He looked at the wheelchair and padded his way back over to it, sat down and waited, enjoying the sun on his back.

He ignored the cleaner when she came in. She was new, Scottish, but didn't talk a constant stream of crap the way the other two did. He had positioned his chair in the corner, so he had a good light to look at the newspaper. It was slightly behind and to the side of the easy chair where he sat at night, under the light from the lamp. He watched the cleaner while pondering the answer to the crossword clue. This one was hopeless. So was the guy who had helped him in the shower that morning. How difficult can it be to help somebody take a shower without getting soap in their eyes? It was the little things that got to Frankie, like not being able to scratch when he was itchy, but this morning was the first time his hands had not been doing exactly as they were told. Tomorrow they might be a little better, the day after they might be a little worse, but by the end of the month they would definitely be worse. Wave by wave; you don't really notice if the tide is coming in or going out, but give it time. Just give it time.

The narrow plastic tube that used to be attached to the nebulizer was in his pocket. He had picked it up out of the bin the minute he read that Lambert Douglas McSween had died. They had agreed to put an unusual name in the death notice, so that the other two would know. Lambert Edward James Dukes would be next. He grasped the tube hard in both his left hand and his right hand, pulling it tight but keeping his hands low, covered by the blanket. It would be enough.

They had been saying something about his birthday, then said that a lady from the Police Federation was coming to see him to present him with something. Which he thought was a bit odd as he hadn't really served all that long – his career had been short but meteoric. He didn't believe that the Federation lady was coming out to discuss anything with him; he suspected they were coming out to get a story for the magazine.

He suspected many things.

He waited.

The cleaner was in the wet room now. He heard the toilet flush and the shower run. The smell of lavender bleach wafted out to him, stinking the place out.

Then there was a knock at the door.

The cleaner said that she'd get it, and she lifted her bucket, straightening her hat. She opened the door, said hello and was gone, leaving the other woman to walk in and stand in the middle of the carpet as if she owned the place. She took her time removing the mask from her face.

'Hello, Dad.'

She walked around the room, ignoring her father, looking out of the window and making little noises of approval about the gardens below. Then she sat down on the easy chair in front of the wheelchair and complained that her feet were sore and that her new shoes were giving her a blister. As she bent forward in the chair, he lifted his hands off his lap, feeling the effort and the strain in his old muscles. As she sat back, having eased her shoes off, sighing as the discomfort ebbed away, Frankie didn't hesitate. He lifted his hands and slipped the tube over her dark hair, over her face, then leaned back into his wheelchair and he held on tight.

That's all he had to do. Hold tight and don't let go.

He just needed to stay there.

She struggled, of course, trying to get her fingers under the tube that was compressing her neck, but couldn't quite manage, so she pushed her head back into the cushioning of the chair. Frankie pulled the tube tighter. For a bad moment, she pushed her feet down, straightening her legs, and the whole chair toppled backwards, threatening to crash into him and the wheelchair. But that was fine as long as he didn't let go. She made a few noises, grunting, but no wheezing, no shouting for help.

Eventually, she stopped struggling and the gurgling noise fell to a snorting, the whimpering fell to silence. He still held on, until he could no longer keep the pressure on the tube, then he let it go. It lay in his lap, flattened and distorted by his fingers. He was tired now. His arm ached with exhaustion, his strength wilting.

But he was relieved it was over. He could go to his grave

with a clear conscience, not worrying about what she was getting up to, what damage she was doing.

He felt something akin to happiness.

He looked at the top of her head, her dark hair glinting with chestnut in the sun.

He should really have done that years ago.

Frankie Scanlon was lying on his back, staring at the ceiling. His jumper was neatly pulled down over his waist, his trousers. He had one slipper on, its neighbour halfway across the carpet. The sock revealed a neat herringbone pattern. A table on wheels had been neatly parked, a small walking stick hooked over the handrail. On it was a magnifying glass and a folded-up copy of yesterday's newspaper; from the curl of the corners, it had been well read and scribbled on. Frankie's face and the backs of his hands were a deep brown, the tan of somebody who had habitually lived in a hot climate.

In the living room, on the chair with her head tilted back, was Veronica Riley. She too was staring at the ceiling. While her father's eyes were calm and contemplative, hers were red and teary, worn out by fighting for her life with the father who loved her. The plastic tube hadn't been that tight round her neck; she had fainted. When Costello and Anderson had entered the room and pulled her chair upright, she had come round almost instantly and had been sitting in the chair quietly ever since. Her eyes were watchful, feral. Her hands were clasped on her lap, her mask rhythmically billowing and sinking with each breath.

The old woman on the air mattress bed was gone. Someone else inhabited Veronica Scanlon now. She was watching her father through the doorway, wondering, hoping that the struggle had killed him.

Anderson checked the old man lying on the bed as he took a deep breath, exhaling through pale lips. He opened his eyes, flicked glimpses of cold blue under the eyelids, then he looked around the room, before settling his gaze lazily on the tall blond man at the end of the bed.

'Mr Anderson, I presume.'

'Hello, Frankie.'

'Will you get her out of here, please?'

'They are on their way, but she's not going anywhere yet. Are you comfortable, Mr Scanlon?'

'As comfortable as I can be.' He coughed, reached out a liver-backed hand and pointed towards the box of tissues. 'Easier in my mind now that it's all over.'

'Are you OK to talk now? We will need a statement.'

They had themselves almost witnessed the murder of Veronica by her father. He had not denied it or given a reason. He looked relieved, replete even; tired, but not distressed.

'You led her to me, didn't you?' Scanlon asked.

'Yes, you were the bait she couldn't resist.'

'The cleaner?'

'Our DI.'

'She uses too much bleach.' Frankie looked at the red marks on his hands. They were sore. 'Tell me that Eddie didn't tell her where I was.'

'He didn't, no matter how much she tortured him. It was the lawyer who told us. We had to draw Veronica out. We think that she's a double child killer.'

If Anderson wanted a reaction, he was disappointed. Frankie remained unmoved by the memory of his son being dropped down a steep slope, a very steep slope, and another small boy being led away through the woods.

'What did she do to him?'

'To Andrew? His body was never found.'

'To Eddie.' Frankie was impatient. 'What did she do to Eddie?'

'That conversation will keep for another day.'

'She killed him, didn't she?' He closed his eyes, and a tear ran slowly down his cheek. 'He was such a good friend to me, poor Eddie. Bloody hell. What did she do to him?'

Costello came in, breaking the silence that forced its way into the conversation. 'What did he do to her?'

He looked up. 'What?' He shook his head. 'He never did anything to her, he never did anything to anybody – he wasn't that type. He taught her to ride a bike, taught her to swim. That's all. You need to look at Veronica and see what follows in her path. We tried the best we could, but, oh God, I think we got this so wrong.'

Anderson asked, 'Frankie, who was killed in your house on the twenty-first of June 1978? Who was it? And don't lie. Please, no more lies.'

A look of respect crossed Frankie's face, then he nodded slightly, acknowledging that they probably already knew the truth. 'You have to understand that we're not bad people. We did the best thing at the time. Veronica has never been right in the head – well, not after the day at Black Bay Beach, not after that.'

'What happened that day? On the twenty-first? In your house,' Anderson persisted.

'I can't even remember her name, the girl who died. But it wasn't Birdie. I've no idea where she is or even if she is still alive. But she wasn't killed that day.'

'And who was holding the knife, Frankie? I doubt it was Eddie. Was it Birdie?'

'No, why would it be Birdie? She was just talking to the girl.' He was incredulous. 'It was Veronica. She killed the girl.'

They had let Frankie rest and have something to eat, while they had got hold of the lawyer so he couldn't say that he had no representation, but Anderson knew he was going through the motions. Frankie wanted to talk. He had probably wanted to talk for more than forty years.

'It was a mistake from the start. We should have kept dancing. Eddie, he just loved kids – not in the way you think. He just liked them. He should have got married, he should have lived my life, and he'd have made a better job of it. He taught all the kids to swim. I never had the patience and Dougie always got sidetracked chatting up some bird.

'When Veronica was six, two things happened. She got into the newspaper and she loved that. She was so young, but a good swimmer, you know. The story was she saved a woman from drowning – total rubbish, but she did swim out and the woman was in trouble. A man on the shore was watching Veronica, thinking that a young kid was out of her depth, and he caught sight of the woman. That man and then Eddie swam out and brought them both back, and it made for a nice wee

story – pictures, all of that – but Veronica would not let it go.
Then later, a few weeks later, a young girl called Melanie
Fletcher was assaulted. Badly. That was on the twenty-seventh
of June 1976. Two weeks after that, the tenth of July – the next
time we were at the beach actually – Veronica was swimming
in the sea, and then she came back to shore. Something happened
when she was behind the rocks – she was screaming, crying,
covered in blood. It looked like she had been assaulted sexually.
Or so she indicated.'

'She was six years old?' clarified Anderson.

Scanlon nodded, casually. 'Like I say, she was a good
swimmer.'

'And the assault – you didn't witness it? Or you didn't believe
her?'

'At the time, I believed her. We thought it was the same guy
who had hurt the Fletcher girl. Veronica pointed to the man who
did it. Well, I am not sure if she pointed to anybody. A traumatized
six-year-old pointed to a man who was standing in swimming
trunks, wet hair clamped against his head. That was Fishbourne,
the nearest man. I got him arrested on the basis that my daughter
had pointed at him. And we fancied him for the Fletcher incident
two weeks previously.' He closed his eyes, just an old man recalling
a memory that he wanted to forget. 'There was a Morris Traveller
in the car park; it appeared in a few photographs taken that day.
Twenty years later, they found out that Gordon Ellis Whyte drove
a Traveller at that time. But we arrested Fishbourne. And we
pinned the previous assault on him as well. He was local,
frequented the beach. It was neat. Then the hospital exam was
inconclusive. All Veronica's injuries were left-sided, as they would
be self-inflicted by a right-handed person. The forensics that we
had at that time couldn't make head or tail of the injuries.'

'So you didn't believe her?' asked Costello gently.

'We thought that something had happened, but not what she
had described. She needed help. She was displaying all kinds of
behaviour that wasn't normal. She picked out Fishbourne because
she knew him. Later, much later – remember, I've had a whole
lifetime of thinking where and when all this went wrong – I
wondered if she had seen the attack on Melanie Fletcher two
weeks before. Had she witnessed that? Whyte did assault Fletcher,

we know that now. We might have known it then if his bloody wife hadn't given him an alibi. We're on the beach that day and maybe Veronica "borrowed" Fletcher's incident, painting herself in as a victim. It got her back in the newspapers.'

Costello let that pass, unable to accept it. 'And Gordon Ellis Whyte slipped away to kill twice before he was caught.'

Scanlon was unaffected. 'We spent so long looking at Daniel Fishbourne that Ellis Whyte vanished from under our noses. We had a suspect and the real perp was off in the wind.'

'And Daniel Fishbourne fell down the stairs while in your custody?'

Frankie shook his head slowly. 'I might have been a bastard, but I wasn't stupid. He did fall down the stairs, he did exactly that. I didn't throw him. I was actually apologizing while taking him downstairs to release him out the back door, too many press at the front. I was explaining to him that my daughter had come up with this story. He shook his head while putting his jacket on. He had one arm in a sleeve, he had the other arm behind his back and he lost his balance and tumbled down the stairs – no way of stopping himself.'

'And you expect us to believe that?'

'I really don't care a fairy fuck if you believe it or not – that's what happened. But it cemented the idea that he was the one who had attacked Veronica and that I was right to do what some thought I did. I was acting like any angry father would. It was a lot of nonsense, but society does have an unfortunate mob instinct, don't you find?'

'So what about Ben?' asked Costello.

Frankie gave her an admiring smile. 'Bloody women, eh? Yeah, Veronica really went off the rails when Ben arrived. We hadn't intended to have another child as Veronica was such a handful. We thought we could protect her from the world. And protect the world from her.' He shook his head again. 'Big fucking mistake.' He looked at the palms of his hands, blaming them for not holding on to his daughter tightly enough to kill her.

'Mr Scanlon. Do you think your daughter killed your son?'

'I don't know. I really don't know. If we did know, everybody's life might have turned out for the better. And I have had to live with that.'

'Just to be clear, what happened on that day in 1978?'

He closed his eyes and sighed, either tired or bored. Costello suspected the latter. 'The kids were out playing. Look, we didn't want her to be labelled as an adult for something that she did as a kid. And that was a mistake.'

'But she was, what, eight at the time? She was just a kid, so, of course, you thought you were protecting her?'

'You have a daughter, Mr Anderson? I can tell.'

The DCI nodded. 'Yes, I have. There's no handbook, no crystal ball that tells you what they're going to grow into. I'm sure you and Birdie did what you thought was right.'

Costello bit her tongue, thinking of Maureen, the young woman caught up in this web. Lizzie, the one who got away.

Scanlon spoke, a version of events he had learned off by heart. 'The kids were out playing in the back garden. It was a very hot day. Birdie had been struggling with both Veronica and Ben, so she thought it might be better to get a nanny to help. She spoke to a few folk over the months and this name had come up – some desperate girl. Birdie made the decision, and the girl needed a job. I wasn't convinced. They met in the Willow Tearoom, and they liked each other. I think the girl came from Bridgeton like Birdie. They had both danced at the Barrowlands – there was a connection. As far as I could see, we were gaining a teenager as well as Veronica and Ben, but Birdie was keen and the girl came round to the house that day to meet the children. I have no idea what happened after that, but I presume they were in the kitchen talking. Birdie had invited the girl to stay for tea.'

She was always 'the girl', Costello noted, never called by her name, as that would make her a human being. And that might be a bit too much.

'Veronica came in and heard what they were saying. Birdie was at the cooker, explaining to Veronica who the girl was, and Veronica just wasn't having it. She picked up a knife, there was a scuffle and the girl was stabbed – fatally, as it turned out. The pathologist picked up that a tall man like Eddie would struggle to stab a short woman at that angle. I didn't tell him that I thought a child could have done it easily. He was confused. I saw the whole thing fall through at that moment, but he put it down to "one of those freakish things". He signed it off. He believed it was an accident. I knew differently. It was Veronica.

'Then Birdie phoned Eddie – he lived round the corner at the time. She was incoherent. He knew it was something terrible and presumed something had happened to one of the kids.'

'Why did she not call you?'

'I was too far away to do anything – I was in Barrhead. The girl died in Birdie's arms.'

'Her name was Maureen,' said Costello, unable to resist it any longer.

Scanlon continued as if he hadn't heard. 'Barrhead was a big job. I was busy. There were no mobile phones in those days.

'Looking back, I think they wanted to keep me out of it. Birdie would have wanted to do that. It was the last time I saw her. Eddie took the blame, and Birdie walked out of my life and didn't come back.'

'Why?'

'Because she wasn't safe round that girl. I was off work for a while, we moved house, Eddie went to jail. I made sure he was OK. He offered to do it – he was the one who realized that Birdie and the girl were similar. He was the one who "accidentally" knocked the chip pan over so the boiling fat would destroy her features. Birdie just walked away.'

'Where did she go? To Eddie's?'

'To Douglas. Then a flat, a new life.'

'She married another policeman.'

'Did she? Have you found her?'

'She has a son who is a police officer. Familial DNA was left at the Dukes crime scene.'

'Things you can do these days! Is she OK?'

'Appears to be.'

'I'm glad.'

Costello sighed. 'Did you ever think that Veronica was a minor and that she might have got help if she had been criminally charged? She'd have been put in care, good care?'

'In those days? There was no such thing. Today, it would all have been very different. Veronica was a devil; we did the best we could. I put her in St John's and she got treatment there.

It was the best choice for her. Much better than if she had been incarcerated.'

Costello frowned. 'Do you think she was abused there?'

'No, she was treated there. She tried to escape. She was so violent they had to strap her down sometimes. I got so upset visiting her that I just stopped going and left them to it.'

'What about Lizzie Shand? Was that you trying to find a babysitter?'

'Lizzie?' Frankie shook his head. 'Sorry, no idea.'

'So it was nothing to do with this case?'

'I've no idea who you are talking about.'

'What happened after Veronica left St John's? Did she come home?' asked Anderson, trying to fill the gaps in the timeline.

'No, she never came home. If she did, I didn't know. I went to Spain. I wanted to get as many miles between us as possible. I was scared.'

'Are you OK?' Anderson asked Costello.

His colleague was on the stairs outside, sitting hunched in the shade, her head in her hands. Costello looked thin and pale, worn out.

'I'm fine.'

'The way you walked out of there, I thought you must have felt faint or something.'

'No, not that. I felt that could have been my dad talking. He talked about his daughter the way I imagine my dad talked about Harry, taking him away from the rest of the family for our own good.'

'Oh,' said Anderson, realizing that the parallels of the two cases had gone right over his head. He had been in his own little bubble, with Moses, Brenda, Norma. He had forgotten, not appreciated, just how raw this case could be for Costello, whose family history reflected the case of Veronica Scanlon.

'I think I need a wee bit more than "Oh".'

'Two men had two psycho children and they each did their best to protect their children from themselves, but the people involved were not the same. Harry was not Veronica. You were not Ben. And your dad made better choices than Frankie Scanlon.' Then he realized what was going through Costello's mind. 'Do you think Harry would have killed you if you had been kept together as children?'

Costello shivered. 'No, I don't think that would have happened to me. Harry was very different from Veronica. But she did do it, didn't she?'

'Her dad says she did. Wyngate is looking back over the facts of the case. Veronica wasn't considered a subject for investigation. She was only eight or so. Who would think that? And your dad took your brother away from you to keep a closer eye on him, to keep you and your mum safe. Birdie did a runner and left her daughter in her husband's care, left them at risk. That was what killed Ben. Birdie should have called the police when Veronica attacked Maureen, or maybe an ambulance. But she didn't. She saw it as a way for her to get out of it and she phoned Eddie. That was taking her chance – she didn't give a shit what that would do to Maureen's parents.'

'She couldn't have thought for a minute that she'd get away with it, running from her own child, terrified of her own daughter.'

Anderson shrugged. 'No matter what she was guilty of, she kept it to herself. Your dad didn't do that. I think he carried out his responsibility to the best of his abilities.'

'Getting away from the alcoholic mess that Mum was? You don't think that helped him make up his mind?'

'He didn't take you and leave Harry at the mercy of your mother, did he? And your mum, she might have disappeared into the bottom of a bottle, but I'm not sure I could have done much better if I was left in that situation. There but for the grace of God and all that. And Harry did try to kill you. It was your dad who stopped him.' He realized then that Costello was crying silently, tears sliding down her cheeks. Her hand was high on her head, fingers seeking and probing the scar her brother had given her one cold night beside a frozen pond in Glasgow. Her brother had crept up behind her. She felt him push her head on to the frozen surface, banging her face against it, and as she lay there, bleeding, she saw her dad's face pass under the ice below her.

'What is it that's annoying you? You have lived with that situation for years now. Frankie might have pushed a few of

your buttons, awakened a few memories in you, but you
processed all this stuff years ago. You'll be fine.'

'Yes, I will,' she said, but she didn't sound as if she meant
it. 'It brought it back, just something he said in there. I could
see my dad's face moving in front of mine. He looked so dead
– the white of his face. The lips were deep, deep red and his
hair was wafting around his head with the flow of the water. I
think I closed my eyes at that point. I don't recall seeing the
rest of him float past; it was just his face . . . that's all I recall,
just his face. I was bleeding. I didn't even know it was real or
not.'

'Oh, it was real, all right. I remember it: the ice and fog so
thick we couldn't see a thing. The pond. The dark, dark water.
I can see why that image is seared on to your brain, but you
got through that. I think that might have driven me mad if I
didn't have Brenda and the family. You do OK on your own,
you know, Costello. Your upbringing would have brought out
the worst in most people, but I think it brought out the best in
you. There's nobody else I'd rather have as my wingman.'

'Wing person,' she retorted.

'What's she saying?' asked Costello. Veronica had been in the
interview room for two hours. There was a lawyer with her and
an advocate from a mental health service.

'You don't have to be here, you can go home,' said Anderson.

'What's she saying?' she repeated.

'She's still talking about being a victim, how her family was
broken, how hideous it was, how she never got any help. How
she cried her eyes out when her dad went to work, how she
tried not to stress out her dad. She even told us how she pressed
her tearful face to the window, wanting to know when her
mother was coming back.'

'I wouldn't like to pick the bones out of what is genuine and
what is not.' Costello thought for a moment. 'She was very on
the ball when she killed Dukes – that showed extreme intelligence and forethought.'

'She did believe that her mother was being replaced by
another woman. Maybe Birdie did need help. I can imagine
Veronica wasn't a walk in the park as a kid. Birdie crying for

weeks, Frankie thinking he was doing the right thing, but all Veronica could see was that her mother was being replaced.

'Then she starts on the cake. Veronica didn't get one for her birthday but the babysitter got one. Her mum was too busy. The cake, the lemonade, the glass for the fingerprints. That telltale scar is very apparent now she's forgetting to conceal it.

'In the interview, Veronica then switches tack and blames it on Ben, how he was larking around when he fell, but everybody blamed her. Then it changes to "so many times my parents should have protected me, yet they let me down".

'The one thing that does ring true is the way her face lights up when she talks about when she rescued the woman from drowning, and then she was in the papers.'

'But she didn't rescue her.'

'I know, but she thinks she did; it fits her narrative. She loves talking about that. That adulation, that attention seems to have stuck – she wanted to be the hero. "That's when I realized I could be somebody and that one person could make a difference."'

'Leave them to it, eh?'

Costello shook her head. 'There's one more place to go. Somebody I want to talk to.'

The door was opened by a tall man, with curly black hair and the deepest brown eyes Costello had ever seen. He looked straight through them, without smiling, and raised an eyebrow, before pointing to a sign that said *No Cold Callers*.

'We are here to see Mrs Dougan, Mrs Alison Dougan.'

The man nodded, not in agreement, more that he had understood. He then furrowed the skin round his eyes; there was a familiar angle to the cheekbones, the set of the eyes.

Anderson and Costello both reached into their pockets for their warrant cards and showed them discreetly, keeping their hands low. Most people at that point have a look round to see if any of the neighbours' curtains were twitching.

This man didn't.

'Where are you from? Partickhill? Why do you want to see my mother?'

'It's a personal matter.'

'You are a rather senior detective, DCI Anderson.'

'Yes, I am. Can we have a word with your mum – might be better in private?'

There was a slow nod, and then he closed the door in their face.

'Is that a no?'

Anderson looked through the glass panel, into the hall. 'He's not gone far, in fact, and he's coming back.'

They both stood up again as the front door reopened, fixing a smile on their faces.

'Hi,' said Costello.

'Do come in,' the man said, standing to one side, letting them enter the pink-carpeted hall. 'First door on the right.'

Costello looked at the woman sitting in a chair by the window. Somebody had just turned off the TV. She couldn't help but look directly at her, noticing the odd hold of her left hand, the awkward position of the slipper on her foot, her heel stuck on the carpet. It looked as if she had suffered a stroke or maybe had some kind of medical condition.

Alison Dougan stayed sitting, a small dog curled into her side. The glossy magazine she had been reading was folded beside her, her shopping list ready to go.

'Please don't get up, Mrs Dougan.'

'What can I do for you? If you want to talk to Adam, he's not here. He's at the bowling.'

'It's you we need to talk to. Maybe in private.'

She might have been eighty years old, but her eyes flicked from Costello to her son, who was standing at the doorway, caught between the desire to protect his mother and the fact he was professionally outranked and these two members of a murder squad were here for a reason, and that reason may have nothing to do with him.

'That's if you are happy to talk to us, on your own.'

The way it was said, she got the message. She might have tried to brazen it out, but now she glanced a little tearfully at the doorway of the room. Just for a moment, Costello saw the young woman she used to be.

She said, 'Maybe put the kettle on, Jamie.'

The younger man relaxed and slid away towards what Anderson presumed was the kitchen.

'Do you want a cup of tea? I usually have something around this time.' She was very cultured, her voice rather posh, well dressed, neat as a pin.

'No, we are OK, but please go ahead if you want something.'

'We know we are disturbing you and your family, but we don't do it without good reason.'

She looked straight through Costello, a million emotions passing behind those eyes that were still incredibly deep brown, then she tilted her nose in the air, preparing herself for what was coming.

'So what can I do for you?'

'We have traced a family that is still looking for Maureen Laverty. I think you know where she is. She's buried under a stone that bears your real name, Mrs Marilyn Scanlon. Birdie.'

For a moment, there was no reaction at all. Anderson thought she was going to deny it. Then she took a deep breath, followed by a long sigh. 'Maureen. Maureen. I met her twice, maybe three times. That was all.'

'And why did you meet her?'

'She wanted a job with us and we thought that she'd be good, appropriate. I needed help with the children. We couldn't pay much, but she needed a place to stay more than she needed a wage, and she was willing to live in. She was very keen to be part of my family. I don't know what had happened that made her want to leave home so abruptly. I invited her round to see the children. Veronica and I had made her a cake.' Her story stopped there. She dropped her head a little, a few tears, real or fake – Costello could not quite tell.

And was past caring.

'Frankie had recognized there was something going on with her at home. There's only a few conclusions that we can come to about that, none of them pleasant.'

'She just got pregnant, unmarried, had to go away, have that baby and then return. Did you know that?'

Birdie shook her head. It was unconvincing.

'So she came to you as a victim, and ended up a victim.'

'I suppose so.'

'What happened that day?'

'Eddie's dead, isn't he?'

Anderson's voice was hard. 'He was murdered. But his death changes nothing. We know what happened.'

The dark-brown eyes flashed for a moment. She let out another long sigh.

'Have you applied that same logic to the death of Ben, to the disappearance of Andrew?' Her voice was almost offended.

'Do you want to come down to the station and make a full statement?' asked Anderson, fed up with her.

'The neighbours will love that,' said Costello. 'And Jamie will know exactly what it means.'

She didn't budge.

'Did you ever keep in touch with the police or the investigation in any way after you walked down that road?' asked Anderson.

The old lady shook her head.

'Not even to see if anybody was looking into what happened that day?'

She shook her head again, but her eyes were slowly looking round the room, coming to rest on the shopping list with its very distinctive handwriting, the loops of the lower-case Gs.

'Can we be left alone, my son and I?' said Birdie, her pale cold hands crossing in her lap.

'I'm afraid not.'

The room was quiet. There was the ticking of a clock somewhere in the hall. A car drove past outside, stopped. Somebody got out, a car door closed and the car drove away. There was the ching of the gate opening. Birdie's eyes drifted outside, swimming with tears – one of the few signs of emotion she had shown. Costello wondered what, or who, had brought it to the fore.

The door opened, and Jamie came in.

'Mum? Are you OK? What's going on?' He turned to the detectives. 'Why are you here?'

'We were talking about an incident in which a boy called Ben died.'

A look passed between mother and son.

'Do you want to tell us something about the way Ben died?' asked Costello gently, knowing that this woman had witnessed her daughter's violence first-hand. She would have heard about her son's death and surely questioned the manner of it.

'No, I'd like to ask you if you could maybe just leave us alone for a couple of minutes.'

'I think your son needs to hear it. And I know that you did what you thought was right. Nobody can blame you for that,' said Anderson gently.

Costello thought that there were many people who could blame her.

'I was married before, you see, Jamie. Your dad knows, but we never told you. And there was a situation, and I made a split-second decision that would last a lifetime. One minute, just one minute. That was all we had.'

'Mum, did you have to do something to get away from your first husband? Why? Did he treat you badly?'

The words that came out of the wrinkled rosebud lips were rapid and powerful. 'My husband treated me like a princess. I had to walk away from him, my lovely Frankie, because of that dreadful girl.'

Jamie looked at Anderson, his face confused.

'I've always regretted that. Every moment of my life.'

Costello tapped Anderson discreetly on the arm and nodded at the door of the living room. There stood her husband, Adam Dougan. He had heard every word.

TWENTY-THREE

Wednesday 24th June

Costello knocked on Toastie Warburton's door. She had said that she wanted a word. He had acquiesced.

Now, there was silence for a moment; she could imagine the desk being cleared, monitor screen being put into hibernation, him holding on to the hesitation.

'Come in.'

She took a deep breath and opened the door.

'Yes?' the Detective Chief Superintendent Crime Division asked, failing to hide the hostility from his voice.

Costello stood inside the door, holding the file she had in both hands.

'What's that you have there?' he asked, nodding.

'Can this be off the record, sir?'

'I doubt it.'

She placed the file in front of him, sliding it over the clean desktop. She didn't sit down; she remained standing, arranging her limbs and features into an empathetic posture.

Detective Chief Superintendent Crime Division didn't open the file but glanced at the date and case number, no doubt recognizing the initials and the handwriting scrawled on the outer cover, still musty and clinging on to its fine film of dirt, even though Costello had wiped it clean many times.

'My, my, you have been thorough.' He pushed his chair back from the desk and crossed his legs. 'I should have put a couple of more incompetent officers on this case. There's enough of them around.'

'I'll take that as a compliment, sir. That's all the paperwork that applies directly to this situation.'

He raised his head at the phrase 'this situation'.

'DCI Colin Anderson knows and the Chief Fiscal has read the file. They're the only other people who know the contents. You went to Invernock Primary School. I bet you played on that beach. The dates fit that you would have been there when Ellis Whyte was around, learning how to groom children.'

'You are correct.'

'It was later in his paedophile career that he decided he preferred girls to boys. Before that, he would assault anything. You'd be the right age – a wee boy, playing on the beach. There's a statement in there that I think you may not want others to read. You have a distinctive name.'

Warburton stared at her for a long minute. 'My mother didn't realize what was going on. It was only when the later assaults by Ellis Whyte became public that my parents paid attention to what I had said, and while they had reported it, maybe it was not taken as seriously as it should have been.'

'Ellis Whyte could have been stopped many times, but he

never was. So the fiscal knows that you have the file. Clarissa Fettercairn has her story and it's her story to tell. I was just aware that you may not want your story to be part of that.'

He nodded slowly.

'Although times have changed and victims do speak out, that must be their choice. I had my past shoved in my face recently. It's not nice.'

He nodded again. 'Thank you for your discretion.'

She turned to leave. 'It's nothing nowadays, you know – nothing at all.'

'It was everything to me.' He smiled weakly. 'Everything.'

'Times are different now.'

'Maybe they are. People are not.'

DCI Colin Anderson and DI Costello got out of the Beamer and by tacit consent began to walk round the cemetery. The case was closed. The air seemed fresher, and they had both had a good night's sleep. They were back in the Procurator Fiscal's good books – the entrapment of Veronica had been deemed a success. There was a whole panel of experts queuing up to decide exactly what disorder she had. It was a topic they returned to time after time: what was going on in her mind. They had even sat and watched the films again with hindsight. None of these children had been subject to any abuse from an adult. The real threat had been from someone much closer to their own age.

Watching those films, the kids engaged with Dougie and Eddie more; they were more involved, more fun. Frankie was either with the guys or having a cigarette on his own. There was no real interaction with his own kids, easy to see now they knew what they were looking at. Frankie talked a good game at being a dad.

The lasting relationship, the great friendship, was between the three blokes, the Peacocks. Dark-haired Veronica, a skinny wee thing with eyes so black they seemed bottomless, ran around, twice shouting for her mum's attention, then for her dad's, getting neither. She climbed a rock on the beach. It was a big rock and she couldn't get down. It was Eddie who gave her the round of applause, then came to her rescue. He was the one looking out for her.

'I was happier thinking that Frankie and Birdie were lovely people and Veronica was born with some kind of personality disorder, but I'm not so sure. No matter what she may or may not have been born with, they didn't do much to help.'

'They were both very self-absorbed people.'

'That's putting it mildly. How could her mum do that? Run away from her – that lassie needed help and treatment.'

'And locking up.'

'Well, she will be now.'

'Why did she do it?'

'Finding her dad became her obsession. He had rejected her, more than once. She'd worked out for herself what was going on when her dad stopped coming to visit her at school. But was she ever subjected to abuse? Who knows. I believe that Frankie was on the lookout for a vulnerable girl who was built like Birdie, I'm sure of it. He was after Lizzie. Then Birdie found Maureen. He was lying when he said that the kids never met the babysitter.'

'They weren't to know that Veronica was going to stab her, were they?'

'Did she?' Costello sulked.

'She did. She has the scar. Veronica killed both Ben and Andrew. They were her rivals as far as she saw.'

'There's too much pre-organization. It was planned.'

'That doesn't make sense.'

'I know, but it feels right. That's the issue, but it's not reality. It's the way Veronica sees reality.'

'What time did you tell Jackie?'

'Half past. We have a bit of time yet.'

'Have you recovered?'

'Och, yes. I don't know who I feel more sorry for: Frank for having Veronica as a daughter or Veronica for having Frank as a father.'

'They both had Birdie. Maybe it's hereditary – you could ask Lynda whatsit. Her with the degree in scarves.'

'Or I could pull my eyes out with a fork.'

'And there's Betty McGillivery, giving it all up for her son. Well, getting away from Sandy Muir was a no-brainer, but not easy to do in those days.'

'Not easy to do in any day.'

'How's wee Norma?'

'Still not decided whether to keep her or not.'

'Yes, you have. You're keeping her. You don't talk about your dad much.'

'There's not much to say.'

'Well, serial killer or good at sandcastles? What end of the spectrum was he?'

'More the sandcastles. We used to build lorries in the sand. He died when I was eighteen. And that was that. He taught me good values.'

'Yes, he did. My mum taught me to never have kids in case the wee bastards turned out like me.'

'Good thinking.'

'And Dukes? Serial killer or sandcastles?'

'Sandcastles, I think. I suspect he genuinely loved kids. He didn't do what he did for Frankie or Birdie; he did it for Veronica to give her a chance. And look how she repaid him.'

'We should have let her loose on Frank. He deserved it. Eddie didn't tell her where he was, though. How strong that bond was, eh? All that dancing.' Costello thought for a moment. 'Do you think it went wrong because they stopped dancing? They had that wee bit of celebrity, then lost it.'

'Maybe they spent their lives trying to recapture that magic. Here's Jackie coming. I'm no good with crying women.'

'You are, actually – one of your few talents.'

'Oh God, she has another two women with her.'

'Her daughters, Anderson. They are here to see where their cousin is buried – they have a decorated slate with her name on it. They want to put it on the grave until it all gets sorted. Just make the introductions and leave them to it. They don't need us. Why did you bring me along, anyway?'

'They wanted to meet you, to say thank you.'

'Aye, well, it's not often that happens in this job. The daughter has been in touch – the one that Maureen had, I mean. She's been trying to trace her birth mother for years, kept updating her contact details. She's a granny herself now, so that family has gained a whole new load of relatives.'

'That's not going to end well.'

'Oh, I don't know. Moses didn't do so bad, did he?'

Her phone went. 'Excuse me.' She took the call, falling behind Anderson as he walked up slowly to meet the three women, on their way to the grave marked *Marilyn Scanlon* but holding the remains of Maureen Laverty.

Costello had a short conversation and then ended the call and jogged to catch up with Anderson.

'Wee Vera passed away during the night.'

'Bloody hell. I am so sorry.'

Anderson stood with her for a moment. She was still looking at her phone.

'The brain bleed was just the start of something. They had told Joanna, but she never told me. If I had known, I'd have gone to see her. I feel like shit now.' She swore quietly. 'Be bloody ironic if Joanna inherits the flat after getting ready to sell it out from under her. Where is the justice in that?'

'Who said there was any justice in any of it?' Anderson sighed, watching the three women walking slowly up the hill, their arms linked, and allowed himself a wry smile.